STARGÅTE
SG•1•ATLÅNTIS ™

STARGÅTE
SG•1•ATLÅNTIS

POINTS OF
ORIGIN

Volume Two of The Travelers' Tales

STARGATE SG-1 and STARGATE ATLANTIS... Stargate SG-1... © 1997-2019
... ... MGM ... All Rights Reserved.

SALLY MALCOLM (EDITOR)

FANDEMONIUM BOOKS

An original publication of Fandemonium Ltd, produced under license from MGM Consumer Products.

Fandemonium Books, PO Box 795A, Surbiton, Surrey KT5 8YB, United Kingdom

Visit our website: www.stargatenovels.com

STARGÅTE
SG•1•ATLÅNTIS™

ISBN: 978-1-905586-72-1 Printed in the USA

CONTENTS

Editor's Foreword

Last year we published our first collection of short stories, *STARGATE: Far Horizons*. It was so well received by Stargate fans that we decided to publish another volume this year.

STARGATE: Points of Origin looks at beginnings of all sorts — from General Hammond's first encounter with SG-1 back in 1969 to Dr. Janet Fraiser's decision to join the USAF, from Ronon Dex's first days as a soldier on Sateda to Sam Carter's first days in command of Atlantis.

And, as you'd expect from our dedicated authors, the stories range from exciting, to creepy, to humorous but all capture that sense of adventure and esprit de corps that we so love about STARGATE SG-1 and STARGATE ATLANTIS.

Thank you for reading — and I hope you'll enjoy stepping through the gate with us again for ten brand new adventures…

Sally Malcolm
Commissioning Editor
November 2015

STARGATE SG-1
Precognition
Jo Graham

Cheyenne Mountain, July 10, 1997

The project was called Stairway to Heaven but it was a gate that went nowhere. George Hammond looked out the conference room window at the shape shrouded in drop cloths, dimly lit by a few hanging lights. The main power wasn't on. There wasn't any reason for it to be.

He put the briefing binders down on the scratched conference table and sat down thoughtfully in a rump-sprung chair. The whole installation was a little run down, a little out of date, just like him. He was less than a year from retirement, and this was the ideal job to conclude his career, winding down a project that had seemed like a good idea but had gone nowhere. It was a nice, quiet coda to thirty years of service, an end not with trumpets but with teeny, tiny violins.

General George Hammond snorted. He was feeling sorry for himself, and that was unworthy. He'd had a good run. He'd done a hell of a lot of interesting and useful things in his career, even if none of them had been historic. Thinking you're going to make history is a young man's dream. In real life, if you're lucky you do more good than harm and leave the place in better shape than you found it. He'd done some damn useful things, and that was more than you could say about this place.

He flipped open the blue binder again. A piece of alien technology discovered by an archaeological dig in Egypt that created a stable wormhole to another world. Impossible, unlikely, amazing, extraordinary — and ultimately a dead end. There was a house he'd visited once with his wife, on vacation sometime in the seventies, a folly of some kind, built with stairs that led up to ceilings and doors that opened onto walls. No reason for it. Just the kind of thing an owner with too much money thought was clever. The Stargate was the same thing, General West had told him when he handed over the metaphorical keys. It was a door that opened on a wall, stairs that led to the ceiling. A door that opened on a world rendered uninhabitable by a nuclear explosion, a gate to a destroyed gate. George was welcome to it.

He put the binder carefully on the table and went down the metal stairs to the control room, then around and out to the floor of the room that held the Stargate, the chamber that had once been a missile silo twenty-eight years earlier.

The drop cloths that shrouded the ring moved faintly in the breeze from the air conditioning, swaying slightly as though they concealed something other than the wall behind it. But of course there wasn't anything. It was just a concrete wall. And still he had to see.

"Take that thing off," he said, and the Airman ran to pull on the ropes that held the drop cloths.

They cascaded to the floor with a susurrating sound. It gleamed in the scant fluorescents, dark and quiet with the sheen of alien metal. A ring. A gate. A door with no key. George stood and looked at it for a long time.

Then he went in his office and sat down at the battered general issue desk. There was the promised pile of folders on his desk, and a copy of his orders. Clean up. Get everything in order. Make sure the thing is really useless. Arrange for its study just in case there's anything more to be read in its carvings. Pack it up and put it away.

George read through the memo three times.

Make sure the thing is really useless.

He called the lieutenant in, a boy who clearly wished he were somewhere much more exciting than underground in Colorado. "What's this pile of personnel folders for?"

"General West said there were some routine transfers, sir.

He's taking Major Wright with him, so there needs to be a new research team head. Also Sgt. Devry is about to finish his enlistment and has declined to reenlist, so he needs to be replaced too. That's a couple of possible replacements for Devry, and someone who used to be with the research team who's asking to come back."

George snorted. "Doesn't he know we're shutting down?"

The lieutenant shook his head. "Captain Carter is pretty persistent, sir."

George spread the folders out. "That's all then, son."

A replacement for a sergeant. An ambitious young man who would need to be told he was barking up the wrong tree. A dead end, a door to the heavens draped in drop cloths, a promise unfulfilled.

George flipped the first folder open and froze.

Twenty five years and more had passed since he'd seen that face, but he had not forgotten it. The same wide blue eyes and pointed chin, the same cropped hair that should have been unattractive but wasn't, the same determined look straight at the camera without the slightest hint of a smile. Captain Samantha Carter.

Cheyenne Mountain, August 3-4, 1969

"Foreign agents in the base?" Lieutenant George Hammond shook his head in disbelief. "How did they get in?"

"We don't know that, sir," the sergeant said, unlocking the door of the storage room. "The major just said that you were supposed to catalog all of their equipment and do it fast because he's sending them out in the morning."

"Ok," George glanced at the things spread out on one of the long folding tables — jackets and boots, patches and packs, four very lethal looking automatic weapons of a variety unfamiliar to him. "Who are these people?"

"The scuttlebutt is that the leader says he's an American named Luke Skywalker." The sergeant flipped over a very ordinary looking dog tag with silencers on it. "His tags say different."

George picked them up. "O'Neill, Jonathan J. 799-36-6412 AF." He looked up. "What the hell?"

"He's a spy," the sergeant said. "He's pretending to be American."

"Why would a spy wear tags with one fake name and then give another fake name?" George asked. "Doesn't that make it clear one of them is fake?"

The sergeant shrugged. "They're Commies. They don't think like that."

"They didn't launch Sputnik by being stupid," George said. Something was weird here. Something didn't fit. He looked down the table, picking out pieces. Uniforms, certainly. But if they were trying to look like American uniforms they weren't, not quite. The color was off, the style of the patches. And that was something that anybody would know. You could buy a jacket in any surplus store. There was nothing secret about it. There was no reason that anyone with half a brain wouldn't get the color right. Any spy who wanted one could just buy the right jacket. If you'd already infiltrated the United States, you could go downtown to Buddy's Army and Navy rather than sneaking around in something that wouldn't convince anyone that it was modern General Issue for two seconds. And that thing — a flat panel with a tiny screen and nine number buttons, straps to hold it onto your arm like a watch — what was that supposed to be?

And then he saw it, a bulbous pistol with an elaborate grip, surprisingly light in his hand when he lifted it, with no lever or handle for the chamber, just a tiny round port like you'd plug in a telephone or something. "A ray gun?" He turned it around in his hands, keeping it pointed well away from himself and the sergeant.

"The major wants all this stowed for transport, sir."

Some sleek, cool metal he'd never seen before... "What is it?"

"My orders are to forget I ever saw it, sir, so I'm afraid I don't know what you're talking about," the sergeant replied unhelpfully.

George nodded. "Thank you, Sergeant." He lay the ray gun down with the other things as the door closed behind the sergeant, letting his hands stray over the equipment. Pistols — those were obvious in their use, though once again not the right ones, not the .38 M41 that the Air Force used. He picked one up, examining it. This was a 9mm Beretta. Why would you carry the wrong handguns when you could buy a used .38 Special anywhere? Something wasn't right. Something didn't fit.

There was a cardboard box full of tactical vests and he picked one up. A small yellow piece of paper fell out, an ordinary piece of lined paper torn neatly from a legal pad. Written on the outside was one word, "George." He unfolded it and for a moment he froze, disbelieving. "Help them," it said. "August 10th 9:15 am, August 11th, 6:03 pm." In his own handwriting.

For a moment he toyed with the idea that he had misread it. But no. That was what it said. Then perhaps he had written it himself. Perhaps he'd written it just a few moments ago for some unknown reason. But why? But why would he do that and how would he forget it? He wasn't so lightly convinced of his own insanity as that.

Which meant the note was real. Impossible as that was, it was real. And the only people he could get any answers from were the spies.

"Help them." His instructions to himself were unequivocal.

Arranging to blow a tire on the truck they were being transported in wasn't as hard as it ought to be. First he volunteered to be in charge of the three-man detachment. Easy. Nobody particularly wanted to go — it was boring. Second, since he was going, it was easy to stand around by the front of the truck waiting for people. When nobody was looking, it took thirty seconds to bend over and drive a nail into a front tire, and two more seconds to pull it out and plug the hole with a wad of chewing gum. That was a patch that wouldn't last long — just enough to get out on the road away from the base. Third, it was easy to tell the driver to pull over when the tire blew, easy to tell the two Airmen to take care of the tire while he got in the back and guarded the prisoners. After all, that was what he was supposed to be doing.

George climbed in the back of the truck, drawing his pistol. The handcuffed prisoners sat two to each side, the black man and the woman to his left, the young man and the older man, the one who was either O'Neill or Skywalker, to his right. He pulled the door shut behind him.

"Flat tire?" the older man asked mildly, a tone that might have been sarcasm or just curiosity.

"I'm the one who arranged it," George said. "But before I can even think about doing what's asked of me in the note, I need to know who you are and who gave it to you."

The older man looked blank, like he had no idea what George was talking about. It was the woman whose wide blue eyes fixed at a point on his shirt front. "Oh my God," she said. She swallowed. "My name is Samantha Carter," she said. "And you gave me the note, sir."

"What?" the older man said, still looking completely confused.

She looked at him in turn, and it didn't escape George that she addressed him as sir as well. "Sir, before we left, General Hammond gave me a note and told me to keep it in my vest pocket until I got to the other side."

"It's addressed to me," George said to her. "In my handwriting."

"What's it say?" the older man asked.

"Help them," George said. "And seeing as helping you will undoubtedly lead to a court martial, I'd like to know why I would do that."

"Because it's your idea," Samantha Carter said brightly. She'd been taken aback a moment only, and now she was the first one to have a grip on the situation, whatever the hell it was.

The older man wasn't far behind. "Albeit one you won't have for thirty years," he said.

"What?"

"I know this is hard to understand," Carter said, "but that's roughly how far back in time we've traveled."

And that was a bullshit answer if he'd ever heard one. Just because he read writers like Heinlein and Bradbury didn't mean he thought that time travel was real. Sure, it was a wonderful idea to play with. Sure, there were lots of amazing things that happened in science fiction, but they didn't happen in real life. Real space exploration was about boosters and physics, and it was happening in Florida, a long way from Colorado where he'd wound up in a completely boring posting that wouldn't lead anywhere. He'd joined up to go to the moon, inspired by Kennedy's call to go into space, and it was dawning on him that he was no closer than he'd been as a space crazy high school student. This had to be some kind of joke, some practical joke that people who knew him were playing — let's see what George will do when he thinks he's got some for-real time travelers! It'll be hilarious! Only not.

"I'm sorry," he said, and turned to go. "I can't help you."

"Wait, wait," the younger man said. "We can prove it."

Everybody looked at him.

"What's the date?" the older man asked.

"August 4," George said. "1969."

"'69," the older man said, turning to his right. "What happened in '69?"

"The moon landing," the younger man said. "That was just a couple of weeks ago, right?"

Of all the stupid… "The entire world knows that."

"Not too many people know you watched it from your father's bedside in his hospital room just two days after his first heart attack," the older man said quietly.

George swallowed, his eyes never leaving the man's face. He hadn't told anybody about that. Not any of his friends in Colorado, not even his girlfriend long distance to Atlanta. He hadn't even told his mother. She'd gone home to get some rest. His dad was supposed to be resting. "Turn on the set, Georgie," he'd begged. "I gotta see this. I've got to know if it works." They all had to know if it worked. Was this going to be a triumph, or a terrible disaster? Would this end in a crackle and Walter Cronkite solemnly taking his glasses off and asking people to remember these brave men? He'd watched from the bedside chair, his hands knotted in his lap for the last few seconds. When Armstrong had said, "Tranquility Base here. The Eagle has landed," he'd been unable to stop grinning, tried not to glance at his father and see the tears creeping from the corners of his eyes. His father would never forgive him for seeing him crying. And so he'd kept his eyes glued to the screen instead, his heart in his throat.

No, George had told nobody about that. Maybe someday he would. Maybe someday he'd tell a friend.

"How did you know?" he asked.

"Because we know you," the man said. "Will know you. For some reason, thirty years ago you decided we were going to need help. Otherwise you wouldn't be standing there with that note. Are you going to listen to yourself? Or not?"

George looked from one to the other. Carter was waiting, her mouth slightly open as though she wanted to say something but wasn't sure if she should. Spies. An elaborate practical joke. Some kind of test of command potential. All of those were possible. But why would spies have the equipment wrong? That wasn't the kind of mistake Soviet agents would make. However, it was the kind of thing that would happen naturally in the future. The shade of fatigues would change. The make of the standard issue ordnance would change. But it would be a stupid mistake for spies to make, and spies weren't stupid except in movies.

A practical joke? A test of command potential? But how did they get the note? How did they get a note in his handwriting that he was sure he hadn't written?

Hadn't written yet. As Sherlock Holmes said, when you have eliminated the impossible, whatever remains, however improbable, must be true. He had not written that note in the past. So he must have written it in the future.

George holstered his pistol. Instead he got the handcuff keys out. "There are two other men including the driver."

"Thank you," the older man said as he unlocked them, a heartfelt thanks that bore out that this was not a joke or a test.

He bent to unlock Carter's cuffs, and she winced. There was a long stapled cut on her right hand. He turned it into the light. "I'm sorry, miss," he said. "Did I hurt you?"

"It's captain," she said, and then smiled as she glanced at his insignia. "And it's alright — Lieutenant." She looked like that pleased her for some reason. "May I see the note?"

He sat down next to her to get it out of his breast pocket.

The older man leaned forward. "Look, we don't want to hurt anyone, but we are going to have to knock those guys out somehow."

George pulled out the ray gun. "Will this do?"

He'd done what the note said. He'd helped them. And for his pains they'd stunned him with the ray gun and left him lying in the middle of the road with his men. Which, as the one who was probably O'Neill and not Skywalker had said, probably saved him from court martial. He'd been reprimanded, of course. He'd stood like a stone with his ears burning while he heard some things about "complete incompetence" and "tomfool kids who fall for the oldest tricks in the book". He'd kept his eyes forward and done his best to sound like the kind of dumb jarhead who couldn't possibly have imagined that the prisoners might escape. In the end they'd bought it. After all, which was more likely? That he had a message from the future or that he was wet behind the ears and gullible?

Unless they got caught. He'd waited. He'd thought. They'd get caught, surely, in those first days, those first months. Any day they'd be recaptured and there would be more questions. Months turned into a year and nothing happened. Not another word. Wherever Carter and the other people from the future had gone, they'd disappeared entirely from his world. Carter. O'Neill. And the others whose names he didn't know. He'd probably never know what happened to them.

Thirteen months later he woke up in the middle of the night in flight school, a realization on the tip of his tongue. Of course he'd know. He'd see them again to hand them the note. In twenty-nine years he'd be a general just as she'd said, and there would be time travel. He was living inside a story more marvelous than anything Bradbury or Heinlein had ever written and it was true. He was the protagonist, the one man in the world who knew what the future held. He was either crazy or uniquely blessed, and it was probably the latter. George Hammond had a date with the future.

Above North Vietnam, November 2, 1971

"Shelby one-two, I've got five bogeys at seven o'clock. About four miles out." Belzebub's voice crackled in his headset. "Hey, you hear me, Lone Star?"

"Roger," Lone Star, aka George Hammond, replied. "I see them. You got an egress plan?" Five bogeys were a lot of Russian MiG fighters, and there were only two of them, even without one salient fact. "I've got one Sidewinder. That's one." All his other missiles had been fired over the target. It had been a long ground support mission, and the rest of his ordnance had been expended.

Belzebub didn't sound more hurried than usual. "Turn to 035. That'll bring us out on top of Paper Doll." Paper Doll was the USS Santa Fe, lying twelve miles off the coast of North Vietnam. The Santa Fe had surface to air missiles aplenty and could cover them. The MiGs would be crazy to follow into that kind of fire.

"Roger that." Now if they were lucky, the MiGs would have already used up their missiles too... He turned his Phantom, the plane quick and responsive in his hands. It was a sweet fighter, no doubt about that, but somehow the Pentagon, in their infinite wisdom, had decided to arm them with missiles only. They had no cannon, no guns. Once the missiles were fired, the Phantoms were unarmed. But then they weren't supposed to need them. Strategic doctrine coming down from the highest levels said that the war could be won without dogfights, without the air to air one on one combat that was now as antique as the biplanes that had first fought it. This was the age of the machine. It was the age of clean war, won from above by bombers who never saw the targets they hit. There would never again be a need for solitary heroics.

Bullshit.

Belzebub twisted, putting his Phantom into a near-vertical climb as one of the MiGs fired an air to air missile.

George's headset shrieked with the warning tone for missile launch. "Got one on you."

"Roger, dropping chaff." Belzebub's voice was only a little fast, his radar signature blurring as he released the strips of blowing tinfoil that were supposed to confuse the missile.

"I'm on this guy. Tally ho." George dropped instead, pulling away from Belzebub and the falling chaff, the missile chasing it. The MiG wouldn't quite resolve in his sights, bobbing and weaving as he tried to get a lock on it. Together pursuer and pursued streaked over the green hills. "Down on deck," George said, dropping through 1,500 feet.

"Get me a lock," his gunner said. "Half a second."

"Roger that," George said. "I'm on him, Frank." A tone alerted, and in the split second the lock held Frank fired their last Sidewinder.

The MiG was fast, but the Sidewinder accelerated at better

than twice the speed of sound, faster than the MiG's climb. It caught it at the junction of wing and body, a bright flare of explosion rendered perfectly silent by distance. George doubled back, turning over the emerald forests and beginning to rise. "Belzebub, I am returning to our exit corridor." A few minutes and they'd be over the ocean, the Santa Fe waiting offshore. Just a few minutes…

Belzebub was just ahead, free of pursuit and heading toward the sea.

A shrilling two tone alarm broke in. On the comm, Belzebub swore. "Shelby one-two, I have a SAM launch." Somewhere down in those green hills was a man with a surface to air missile launcher, and Belzebub had just flown right over his head.

"I see it." And he did, launching almost on Belzebub's tail, the missile's path clear on his screens.

"Taking evasive." Belzebub pulled up sharply, almost standing his Phantom on its tail, racing for the skies. The missile matched his turn.

"Right behind you." George followed, feeling the g-forces in the pit of his stomach as his plane matched Belzebub's move.

"Releasing chaff," Belzebub said.

On the screen the missile didn't veer. The alarm tone didn't change. "You have no joy, Belzebub. Repeat, you have no joy." George leveled out and then followed Belzebub into a roll so that the ground twisted beneath, jungle giving way to a flash of white beach. And then they were over the ocean climbing toward the thin scrim of cloud above. Mach 2, Mach 2.1, and still the missile stuck. It was closing. It had a slight edge, and it was gaining on Belzebub fast.

Every movement seemed to take forever, as though the world had shifted into slow motion. Any second now it was going to hit. Belzebub's life was measured in heartbeats. He had a wife and baby at home, people who needed him. And his life wasn't charmed.

Like mine is. Certainty surged through George, the sudden, startling clarity of belief. He was going to be a general. He was going to live thirty years. And he wouldn't die today, and neither would Belzebub, not if he made the universe choose.

"Turn to 240," George said. "Now!"

It would be a stupid, foolish move for Belzebub normally, bringing him closer to the SAM, not further away, but he trusted George. He did it.

"Frank, drop our chaff!" George pulled up, passing over the turning missile with scant meters to spare, their chaff falling almost on top of it, a wave of light aluminum foil meant to confuse the guidance systems and convince them to acquire a fake target.

It did. It thought it had made contact, and it blew.

For a moment the world went light and then dark. His eyes couldn't keep up with the sudden, searing light. Light and dark, light and dark, light and dark... George felt his head hit the canopy, his ears ringing.

Light. Dark. Light. Dark. He tried to fight his way back to consciousness. Someone was yelling something. Someone was yelling.

"Damn it George! You foolhardy SOB!" It was Belzebub — Jake. He was yelling in the comm. He was ok.

Light. Dark. He opened his eyes, feeling his eyelids like lead. They were in a flat spin plunging toward the sea. Every alarm was sounding, every light red. Shrapnel had ripped through flight surfaces, engines and fuel lines.

"Frank?" His gunner. What about Frank? "Frank?"

He could hear Belzebub on the comm. "Paper Doll, I have a chute. Repeat, I have one chute. George! George, do you hear me?"

One chute. That meant Frank had punched out. It was just him, unconscious for seconds in his shredded plane, the ocean coming up with alarming speed.

"George! Do you hear me?"

He could move his hand. He could move it. The release lever

was right there. He closed his fingers around it.

The force of the ejection knocked every other thought from his mind, 7 g's right there, the thrusters beneath his seat blowing him clear of the falling plane. He could only close his eyes and grit his teeth, up and then tumbling wildly for a moment. And then the sudden catch. His parachute had opened.

George looked up. It spread red and white against the sky. The wind dragged all other sound away.

Below, the sea was deep blue, almost unreal looking. The sea. It was better to bail out over the ocean than over land. Less chance of capture by the Viet Cong. And there was the Santa Fe. It couldn't be that far away. Surely it wasn't.

Now the waves had crests, slight touches of foam at their tops. A few hundred feet. Blue. So very blue. His feet skimmed, the drag pulling him down, and then he plunged in belly first, the parachute collapsing around him. He got a mouth full of seawater. Hold your breath. Release the chute. Befuddled, weighted down by the cloth, weighted down by waterlogged boots and flight suit, he was sinking. Sinking. Pulling him down....

He was not going to die today. The young woman's face swam before his eyes in the back of the truck. "General Hammond gave me a note and told me to keep it in my vest pocket." Samantha Carter. "General Hammond gave me a note." "General Hammond." He couldn't die. He had a date with the future.

And then he was bobbing up, the light on the surface of the sea above like a windowpane. He broke through it, gasping in the air. His life vest had inflated. No, he'd inflated it. He'd done it in what might have been literally his last breath.

But no. Here was one breath, and here another. He got his helmet off, cracked visor and all, and laid his head back on the breast of the ocean. Breathe. Breathe. The life vest held him up.

Above, something silver turned against the distant haze of cloud, against the blue, blue sky. It left a vapor trail.

His radio. His beacon.

"…Paper Doll, I have a chute in the water but no movement. Coming around for another pass…" It was Belzebub's voice, stressed and far too fast, though he always talked fast by George's lights. "Lone Star. Lone Star. Shelby one-two. Do you copy?"

The plane was turning, preparing to sweep over just to his right at a thousand feet. George lifted an arm and waved. He didn't know if the motion could be seen. His beacon. He should turn it on. It shrieked on the radio frequency.

"Paper Doll, I have a beacon!" Belzebub sounded triumphant. The plane's jet wash sent a shiver across the waves around George. "He's waving! George, can you hear me? Do you copy?"

Transmit. Yes. "Roger that," George said. His voice sounded shaky even to him. "I think I hit my head pretty hard. But I'm with you."

"Paper Doll is coming your way. ETA is about… seven minutes." Belzebub was coming around for another pass, a long turn radius out of his sight. "Can you hang on?"

"I've got to, don't I?" George said. "Unless you're planning to beam me up."

"I don't think I can do that," Belzebub replied. "I left my starship at home."

"Then I'm hanging on." George made himself relax. No point in wasting his strength fighting the waves. The ship — the Santa Fe — would be here soon.

"I'm going to be right here, buddy," Belzebub said. "You keep talking to me. You said you've got a head injury. So you stay with me and keep talking. Paper Doll is on the way." The other Phantom swept over again.

"What about Frank?"

"He's about two miles on from you," Belzebub said. "He's in a life raft and he's not injured. He's good to hang on while Paper Doll gets you first."

"You sure?" It all seemed strangely unreal. A head injury. Right.

"He's sure," Belzebub said. "I've got him in sight on every pass and I've got him on the radio too. Frank's fine. We're going to get you first. So just keep talking to me."

"I'm talking," George said. It would be so easy to go to sleep. But that was a bad idea.

"You're crazy, you know that? That's the craziest maneuver I ever saw."

"It worked."

"You took the hit instead of me." Belzebub's voice almost choked.

"You've got a wife and a little girl." He could just lie back on the waves. The Santa Fe would be here soon. Just stay conscious. "You've got to get home to them."

"You're getting home too, buddy. You hear me?"

"I hear you, Jake." Waves cresting. Washing almost over him. Ride them up and down. Stay conscious.

"You think you can't die or something?"

George laughed. It sounded weird even to him, but then everybody would put it down to a head injury. "I know I can't die. I'm going to be a general."

"You sure are." Belzebub's voice was calm. "You just hang in there. Paper Doll's launching a boat. They'll be there in two minutes. And I'm right here. Talk to me."

"Do you believe in time travel?"

"No. And I don't believe in UFOs either. Or little gray men from Outer Space."

And there was something orange, the boat coming toward him, a sailor with a line in the prow.

"You should," George said. "I'm going to be a general." And darkness took him.

It was a long convalescence stateside. While George was in the hospital two amazing things happened. He was awarded the Distinguished Flying Cross for saving the lives of Captain Jacob Carter and his gunner, and he met Mary Anne.

Mary Anne was a physical therapist, and the moment he saw

her he was smitten. Red hair and freckles, a no-nonsense manner that belied her years — he would have asked her out but he was too shy. Besides, if he did she'd say no and he'd be assigned to another physical therapist and he'd never see her again. So he didn't, not until the last day.

Mary Anne looked at him sideways, mascaraed eyelashes too dark for her hair, and gave him a knowing smile. "I thought you'd never ask," she said.

They were married on June 4, 1972. Jennifer was born in August of '73 and Emily in May of '76, but by then they were in Germany. Emily was born at Rhine-Main, and she had a Steiff giraffe the size of a small pony that Jacob Carter sent with a note full of good wishes. He had a little boy now to go with his daughter, and he was at Edwards AFB in California. Jacob was headed for the top.

George wasn't. He never did get back into tactical aircraft. That was a fast track, and once you stepped off it you'd never get back on. Every up and coming kid was dreaming of being a fighter jock. You only got one shot at it. He'd been sidelined by a head injury and it was more than a year before he was cleared to fly again. By then it was a moot point.

He made a fine Executive Officer. He was steady, organized, and good with people. He was adept at handling the intra-personal aspects of a squadron, with keeping everything running smoothly on the flight line and everywhere else. He was a competent guy, a stable guy. He wasn't drinking and running around and showboating. You could trust George Hammond.

But he was no tactical genius. He wrote no notable books, formulated no key doctrine. And he was old fashioned, a little out of step with the modern Air Force. His notions of solitary heroics and small teams didn't fit in the post-Vietnam military, where everything was about making technology smarter and humans less engaged. Leading thinkers expounded that the future of the Air Force was in unmanned satellites and orbital gun platforms — you wouldn't even need pilots, just controllers on the ground who made decisions by committee that were carried out by computers. George was out of touch. A good guy, but not one who had what it took.

Of course Jake got derailed too. His wife died suddenly in an accident while he was at Tyndall AFB in Florida, and he stepped back from the flight line voluntarily. A single father couldn't take those kinds of risks. George sent flowers but didn't go to the funeral. He was in South Korea then, a liaison post that you could take your family with you. The girls loved Korea.

The first time he was passed over for his star he wasn't surprised. He knew how it worked. He knew that was for men (or women, now) who had distinguished themselves. He hadn't. He was solid. He had no blemishes on his record, not except a mistake that had let some prisoners escape years ago, the carelessness of a young lieutenant, but being solid wasn't enough. Sometimes he thought about them. Sometimes he wondered. Did he remember what had really happened? Or was it, like Mary Anne thought, something he'd dreamed up floating in that lifejacket waiting for the Santa Fe to pick him up?

"You'd had a head injury and the brain does funny things under pressure," she'd said. "Sometimes you come up with reasons to stay alive. You come up with reasons to survive. Maybe you imagined that you had met a time traveler who told you that you were going to live thirty years more. It's a good strategy. You can't die because you have a destiny."

"It worked," George had said.

"It did," she replied, and put her arms around him. "And I'm glad it did, because if you'd died I would never have met you. You told yourself a story to stay alive."

And maybe that was it. Maybe that was what had happened. He'd imagined a science fiction story like the ones he read and cast himself as the hero. He'd persuaded himself that he couldn't die because he had a destiny.

George was in Alaska while war swept across the Gulf, pushing papers while Instant Thunder roared. Tactical commands went to other people, and by now he wasn't surprised. That was a game for go-getters and the politically well connected, for the grown-up wonderkids who'd embraced strategic bombing, or for commanders in Powell's cautious mode. He was neither. He was beginning to seem as antique as the Phantoms on display at various aviation museums, living history.

He got his star in '91, the same year Mary Anne was diagnosed with cancer. She never quite saw it. Congress confirmed right after she died. Some might say it took the heart out of him, but it didn't. He was just as meticulous as before. He was just as steady. George Hammond didn't make mistakes. You could count on him. His superiors always did. Calculated risks, careful planning, always keeping his people out of trouble — that was George Hammond.

Jennifer got married in '95, when he was in California closing down an air base that was being sold as a commercial property. It wasn't needed anymore. It was surplus. The runway was too short for modern jets and it wasn't worth it to update it. Sometimes you just had to let things go. You just had to recognize that the world had moved on.

The girls were gone, off having lives of their own. Emily was getting her doctorate. Jennifer had a daughter of her own, his first grandbaby. He'd retire in a few years, thirty years and more in the blue suit, since he'd answered Kennedy's call to space, dreaming of adventure and saving the world. If time travel wasn't real, he'd made his peace with it. It had served its purpose.

And he had served his. A good career, a decent career. He'd done more good than harm, and that's all you can ever expect. He'd take his thirty years and be proud, even if he'd never gotten to the virgin moon.

Cheyenne Mountain, July 10, 1997

General George Hammond stared down at the folder in his hands, sitting at the battered general issue desk in his office in a closing facility. Captain Samantha Carter looked up at him on glossy paper, her face as solemn as it had been mobile in his memory. He remembered it well. It was a face he had remembered for a long time, the face of one of the spies he'd helped escape.

Her latest letter was clipped in the front of the file. He skimmed all her carefully worded arguments. She should come back to the program. She had a doctorate in astrophysics. She was eager to research the Stargate, even if the program was being shut down. Could she at least have a few months? She was sure there was some application that might be attempted.

Captain Samantha Carter. It had been twenty-eight years since he'd seen her, since she'd told him her name. At least it had been twenty-eight years for him. For her it hadn't happened yet.

The world twisted, a Moebius strip of paradoxes that made everything make sense. There are lots of Carters in the world, and Samantha was a popular name in the sixties, but she was Jake's little girl, the one he hadn't seen since she was a toddler. That Samantha Carter. He'd released her because she had a note from him and she'd told him he'd be a general. He'd saved her father's life because of that certainty. Now she'd followed her father into the Air Force and was certain she could make the Stargate work.

Of course she could. She had. If she hadn't, neither of them would be here. She would make it work, and she would use it to go back in time.

George's hand shook as he picked up the telephone. He dialed the number and greeted the aide politely, went through the commander of Nellis AFB, waited patiently while someone fetched Captain Carter from whatever lab they'd stuck her in. George had waited a long time. He could wait ten minutes for someone to come to the phone.

"This is Captain Carter." It was the same voice he remembered, noise in the background, as though she'd taken the phone in a busy hangar.

"Captain, this is General Hammond. I've been put in charge of the Stairway to Heaven. I've got your letter here and I have a question. Do you think there's any way to use this for temporal displacement?"

He heard her breath, and the suppressed excitement in her tone, though she tried to keep it steady. "That might be possible, sir. We don't really know. General West was interested only in spatial displacement. We didn't delve very deeply into other applications at all."

"But you do think temporal displacement is a possibility?" he asked.

"I think it's a possibility, sir." He could hear her swallow. "We don't really know enough about the device to be certain about all its applications. It's possible that further experiments…"

"Good," George cut her off. "Then you'll work on that as soon as you get back here, Captain." He hung up before she could thank him over and over, closed the folder and went down to the echoing chamber below.

The Stargate waited, shrouded in its drop cloths, a silent, empty ring. Empty, yes, but it was not a dead end. It wasn't a door that led nowhere. He looked up at the gray beams above, the dim lights and pitted concrete, his heart swelling as though to music only he could hear. One day soon it would flare to life. One day soon they'd step through into something unimaginable. It was all real, and anything was possible.

George Hammond had a date with the future.

STARGATE ATLANTIS
Cotermino(us)

Peter J Evans

"Hello? Can you tell me your name?"

He blinked, momentarily confused. The words seemed to come out of nowhere, strange and frightening, emerging from a hazy darkness to startle him awake. He turned, trying to find their source, but the world was off its moorings, tipping and spinning about him. He had to grab the edge of the gurney with both hands to avoid falling off.

Something was wrapped around his arm, rubbery and entirely artificial. He stared down at it.

"Hey! I need to you to focus."

"I'm fine." He shook himself. "Just tired, is all. Been a long day."

The world was already solidifying, sharpening into angular panels of ochre and dull silver. He could see chrome, hovering rectangles of blue-white light, a bulky crimson figure with a glass face.

It was Keller, completely encased in a hazmat suit, peering through her visor with an expression that was half grief-stricken, half resigned. Why did she look so sad?

"Please tell me your name," she whispered.

"John Sheppard, same as every other time you've asked." Her gloved hand was still around his arm. He pulled himself free, as gently as he could. "Do you want my rank and service number too?"

Keller sighed. "No, that's all right." She straightened up, the suit's rubberized fabric creaking almost comically. "Sorry, didn't mean to snap at you. I just thought, maybe this time..."

"This time?"

"Never mind. But try to stay with me, okay? You keep drifting."

"Heard every word, doc." He was lying, of course. His attention had been on the observation deck, high above him, and on the two figures standing there.

They were gone now, and the deck was empty and silent. He nodded upwards, at the space they had occupied. "Who was that?"

"Who was who?"

"Up there. A man and a woman, they were watching us." He hadn't been able to see their faces, but there was an unsettling familiarity to them. Just before Keller had spoken to him, Sheppard had seen the man raise his right hand, a faltering, awkward gesture that could have been anything from a greeting to a signal for silence.

Probably medical staff, he decided. After all, he had been under observation since his return from the city.

He got up. It was very late, and the isolation room was in half-darkness, the paneled walls almost lost to shadow. The only light came from Keller's visor and the banks of flatscreen monitors set up around the bed. It was a cold, disorientating place, too tall and wide, full of unnecessary angles. Little wonder he had suffered a moment of dizziness.

"Look, doc, there's nothing wrong with me. Not that a good night's sleep won't fix."

"I'll be the judge of that." She folded her arms awkwardly. "You've been through a lot. We don't know anything about where you've been, or what happened while you were there. I can't just —"

"Am I sick?"

Her expression darkened. "No," she breathed.

"And I'm not injured. I'm just too tired to think straight."

"I hope so. Let me do a few more tests to make sure."

"Fine," he grumbled. "Can I at least grab a coffee first?"

The sky above him was clear blue and painfully bright. Towards the horizon, thready clouds glittered pinkly against the climbing sun. There was a wind blowing in off the sea, sharp and cool, and he could hear the whisper and slap of waves far below.

He cupped a hand to his brow, squinting at the sunrise. "Morning?"

"Morning."

He turned, saw Sam Carter walking across the pier towards him. He raised his coffee mug. "I was just wondering where the night went."

"Doctor Keller said you were exhausted. Do you remember going to bed?"

"I don't even remember getting up."

"Glad to see you're on your feet again, anyway." She stopped alongside him, stood gazing out over the sea. "Was it like this?"

"The city?" He shook his head. "No, nothing like this at all. It was…"

He paused. The details were hazy. Trying to pin them down was like holding droplets of mercury; the more he tried to grasp them, the quicker they slipped between his fingers. Not for the first time, he found himself chasing memories through the corridors of his mind, but the effort was exhausting, physically painful. Within seconds a dull ache had begun to beat behind his eyes. "Darker. A lot more enclosed, but somehow bigger. I don't remember seeing the sky there at all."

Carter frowned at him. "Are you okay?"

"Just a headache."

"You know, if your arm's still giving you trouble, there's no shame in going back to Keller."

"My arm?" He lifted his left hand, turned it experimentally. "There's nothing wrong with my arm. You're sure you don't mean Teyla?"

"I thought your initial report mentioned an injury." She looked unsure. "I must have remembered it wrong."

He grinned at her, ruefully, over the mug's steaming rim. "Yeah, well. Given how messed up I was when I came back, my initial report is subject to change without notice." Sheppard could see that the answer didn't satisfy her. She was worried about him, about everyone who had ventured into the alien city, and with good reason. Whatever had happened there, it had affected him in more ways than he could comfortably name.

"Listen, just give me a few hours. Some gym time, a gallon or two of this…" He downed the last of the mug's contents. "I'll have it all clear inside eight hours."

Carter gazed at him strangely for a few moments, then nodded. "Very well. But I'm going to need a solid report by then at the latest. The IOA have gotten wind of what happened, and they're asking questions about that city I can't begin to answer." She folded her arms. "Right now, we can't even agree on why you were there in the first place."

There was a howling in the city, faint but unceasing, like the raging of a distant storm. Sheppard had been hearing it ever since he'd arrived. For hours now it had been his perpetual soundtrack. It had counterpointed his every action, punctuated every word he said. He was already convinced that, should he somehow find his way out of the city's confines, the howling would simply follow him. Its endless lament had crept into the dark cavern of his skull, and he would never be free of it.

More maddening than the sound itself, though, was Sheppard's complete inability to determine its source. It certainly wasn't due to an actual wind, at least not one close enough to feel. The city's air remained utterly motionless, flat and unmoving. As lifeless, he would find himself thinking in unguarded moments, as the miasma lurking within a closed coffin.

He scowled, pushed the thought away. The city was unnerving enough, without adding mental images of premature burial. He took a lungful of the dead air, just to prove to himself that he could. "Anything?"

Ronon Dex shook his head. "Looks clear."

Teyla Emmagan padded past Sheppard, moving silently

across the chamber, brushing its black walls with her finger-tips. She peered cautiously down each of the channel openings as she them passed by. "I am sure I saw something move," she whispered.

"Bring it on," Dex muttered. "Haven't spotted so much as a bug since we got here."

For a moment, Sheppard found himself almost agreeing with the Satedan. He and his companions had been negotiating the city's labyrinths for longer than he liked to recall, and in all that time he had not seen one single hint of life.

Sheppard had been in dead places before — tombs, long-abandoned spacecraft, the aftermath of battle — but none of them had the utter, endless sterility of the vast structure surrounding him. Even corpses, he knew from bitter experience, drew flies.

There were no flies in the city. There were no plants, no moving water, no mechanisms or enemies. No doors or windows, curves or color. Just an insane, unspeakable sprawl of channels and their connecting chambers.

Every channel he had encountered had been identical; a narrow, empty space between two vast walls of black stone, so tall that their upper limits — if they even had limits — were lost to darkness. The channels were perfectly straight, their walls smooth, vertical, unbroken by the slightest flaw or feature. Each ended in a small polyhedral chamber, which connected to more channels and so-on, in endless, unceasing progression.

The number of channels accessible from each chamber varied, but only in multiples of three.

With utter darkness above him, and no movement of the air, Sheppard had no way of knowing whether he stood beneath a distant ceiling or a starless sky. His only light came from below, spilling out of hair-fine spaces between the walls and the seamless floor, a nauseating grey glow that made him feel as though the city was upside-down, flipped over to leave him clinging to the ceiling.

He was the insect here, he realized. "Come on. Let's keep going."

"John, I know what I saw." Teyla moved closer to him, her face ghostly in the pale, inverted light. "We are not alone."

"Okay," he said, trying to sound more hopeful than he felt. "Maybe it knows the layout."

Dex nodded. "I say we go after it. Make it tell us how to get out."

Teyla seemed unsure. "What if it's dangerous?"

"Never stopped us before." He turned, began to stalk away down a channel, his shoulders brushing the walls as he went.

Sheppard sighed, then set off after him, making sure Teyla was close behind. He had long since given up on navigating the city's pathways by any logical means. He had tried marking the walls, but nothing he carried would scratch them or stick to them. Besides, he had the distinct impression that the structure of the place was shifting around him. Even if he did manage to retrace his steps, he had no proof that the path behind him would be the same going back as it had been moving forwards.

Right now, all he could do was keep the three of them together. If they separated, lost sight of each other for a moment, they would all die. He knew that as certainly as he knew the beat of his heart.

"So," he muttered, somewhat despairingly. "Are we having —

— fun yet?"

Dex grinned wolfishly, whirling the quarterstaff over in his hand. "Oh, this part's always fun."

Sheppard saw the Satedan break left, and had about half a second to decide whether it was a feint or not. He went with his instincts, ducked back and to the right, and felt the tip of Dex's staff hum past his shoulder.

He grinned, bouncing on his toes. "Gotta be faster than that."

"Okay," said Dex, and jabbed the staff's blunt tip into Sheppard's gut.

He hadn't even seen blow coming. It took the breath from him; distantly, he felt the gym whirling, quickly at first but then more slowly, as though he were tumbling through some thickening fluid. The lights faded as he went down, the walls darkening into featureless shadow.

Had Dex really hit him that hard? He felt as though he were dying.

The crash mat slammed painfully upwards into the back of his head.

Sheppard cursed, saw his own quarterstaff go skittering away. He rolled frantically, half-expecting another blow, but Dex was must have been more forgiving than usual. Sheppard scrambled back to his feet, scooping up his fallen staff as he did so.

Dex was smirking. "Let me know when you want to quit."

"Just getting started." Sheppard dropped into a defensive stance and brought his staff up, two-handed. A couple of breaths had his head clear again, his vision pin-sharp. That's what he had needed, he thought grimly. A little adrenaline to clear away the alien city's last shadows.

He watched Dex circling him, padding to the right. There was something odd about the way the Satedan was moving, a hesitancy, almost too slight to notice but impossible to miss now that he knew it was there. Dex probably didn't realize it, but he was holding himself slightly askew, as if favoring his left side.

If it was a ruse, it was a convincing one. Sheppard launched himself forwards, aiming for the Satedan's right, but as the inevitable block came for him he twisted, rolled under it, whipped the staff up to land two solid blows on Dex's weak side.

Dex stepped back, jaw clamped down hard.

Sheppard straightened. "Okay, we're done."

"You got lucky."

"Damn straight I did. No way should I have been able to get one up on you like that." He nodded at Dex's left arm. "That still giving you trouble?"

"It's fine." The man rolled his head around on his neck, wincing a little. "Too long wandering around that damn maze, that's all."

"The city?" Sheppard headed towards a bench on the far side of the gym. His towel and water bottle were there, and he suddenly felt very thirsty. The headache he had developed on the pier still hadn't faded. "You want to know something weird? I keep calling that, but the more I think about it, I must have remembered it wrong. It really wasn't a city at all."

"What else do you want to call it?"

"Search me. All I know is, cities normally have buildings. Doors, at least." Sheppard dropped onto the bench, opened the bottle and took a couple of long swigs. "Do you remember seeing any doors?"

"No."

"It's driving me crazy." The headache was prodding at him again, as if in warning. "How did we get there? I don't even remember what planet we were on."

"I'm not sure what planet you're on right now."

"Ronon, this is important."

"Not to me. I honestly don't remember anything about it. And you know something?" Dex turned away. "That doesn't bother me at all."

With that, he was gone.

Sheppard turned the bottle over in his hand. Beads of condensation glittered on its surface, but the water inside it had been warm and flat, tasteless. It sat in his gut like lead, faint waves of nausea joining the drumbeat behind his eyes.

Disgusted, he went to set the bottle down, but it slipped from his fingers. He watched it tip, slap onto the mat, and roll mockingly under the bench.

He sighed, leaned down to fumble for it. As he did so a shadow crossed him. Someone else wanting to use the sparring area, he guessed. "Just give me a minute. I've got this."

There was no answer. Sheppard glanced up, opening his mouth to speak again, but he was alone. The gym was empty, its lights turned down, the far corners already too dark to make out.

The bottle was in his hand. He rose, grabbed his towel and headed for the exit. He didn't want to be among shadows any more.

The city changed almost without warning. In one heartbeat John Sheppard was trudging wearily along a channel no different any of the hundreds he had walked before, and in the next he was at the threshold of a space so vast, so open and vertiginous that it stopped him dead in his tracks.

After so much enclosure, the scale of it literally staggered him. He had to reach out to the channel wall for support, the hated black stone suddenly a welcome source of solidity. Behind him, Teyla had jolted to a halt, as stunned by the sight as he was.

Ronon was still a few paces behind. He hadn't seen it yet.

Sheppard had no words. All he could do was take his hands from the channel wall — somewhat reluctantly — and step out into the void.

The space, as far as he could gauge, was circular, a great dish or bowl, its faceted floor so far below him that he could barely make out the countless shapes and structures that formed it. Towards the center of it the floor rose again, curving seamlessly upwards to form the base of a tower that must have been thousands of feet high. He could not see its top; just as it had in the channels the light here came from below, from the ocean of polyhedra seething beneath his feet. Sheppard could not tell if he was standing above an open dish or within the confines of an immense, hollow torus.

Ahead of him, the gray-lit floor of the channel opened into a broad highway suspended in the air, three lanes wide or more, its edges knife-sharp, its far end stretching so far away from him that perspective narrowed it to a thread long before it reached the tower. There, other paths sprawled outwards, hundreds of them, maybe thousands, rendered hair-fine by distance, a flat dimensionless spider web miles across.

The sight was impossible, insane. In the channels he had been an insect. Here, he was a mote, a mere speck of dust. Too small to exist.

"Oh man," he whispered. "What have we walked into here?"

Ronon stopped at his side. "Okay, you got me. I'm impressed."

"Not the word I'd use."

Teyla was at the edge of the highway, peering over its razored edge without fear. "John," she called. "Look down."

"Thanks, I'll pass."

"The structures are moving."

Carefully, Sheppard crossed the surface to join her. As he neared her he slowed, checking his stance, placing his boots carefully. The P90 was slung against his chest, weighing him slightly forwards, and he had no idea if the flooring under him would remain stable as he neared its margin. He didn't want it to flex suddenly and pitch him off the side of the path. That would be too undignified an ending.

He stopped slightly further from the edge than Teyla — drawing a slightly amused look — and leaned out.

"Whoah." Vertigo swooped up through his spine. He had flown high in his time, high and fast, but there was something about standing untethered above a sheer half-mile drop that made his balance rebel.

"You see?" Teyla breathed, her voice thick with wonder.

Sheppard nodded slowly, resisting the urge to pull back from the sight. If the drop was dizzying, the complexities below him were worse; of the untold thousands of blocks and planes that formed the base of the cavern, not one was still. Every structure he saw, from the simplest cube to the most tangled mass of polyhedra was marching to its own rhythm, turning, rising to fall again, sliding over and under and through each other.

This was not a city, he realized. It was a machine, a device of unimaginable complexity, and in perpetual motion.

"Shame Rodney's not here to see this," he said.

"With us, or instead of us?"

Sheppard made a noncommittal noise. "Either or." He stepped back, and gestured towards the tower. "You think that's where we need to be?"

"I do not know." She glanced briefly back over the edge. "I hope we do not need to be down there."

"No kidding." Negotiating a path through those restless forms would be impossible, he was sure. None of them looked likely to stop and wait for a human to pass safely by. "So I reckon two, maybe three miles?"

"It is hard to judge, but yes. No further than four."

"Okay." He squared his shoulders. "If we set off now, we should be there by-"

There was an electric snarl, a whiplash of energy. Light blazed past him, scoring a track of pain across his retinas. He ducked back, whirled. "Ronon, what the hell?"

Dex was aiming his blaster back towards the channels. "We've got company."

Sheppard turned to follow his gaze. There was someone walking along the channel towards him, almost entirely obscured by shadow.

Teyla had been right. They were not alone. Sheppard brought the P90 up fast, centered it on the figure's skull. "Hold it right there."

Despite his words, the figure didn't pause. Its pace was measured, unafraid, approaching step by unhurried step until it emerged from between the channel walls, and into the cavern's meager light.

At that moment, Sheppard realized that warnings would be wasted on the new arrival.

He had been wrong about the figure being hidden by shadows. It *was* shadow, a walking, moving silhouette cast from smoky darkness. Its form was still definite — a slender humanoid somewhat smaller than himself — but the stuff of it was swirling, raging, edged on one side by twisting shreds of black-

ness guttering away as if blown by the constant, howling gale
Sheppard could hear but still not feel.

It was close now. Within the smoke, he could see tatters
of anatomy bob and swim, components of life disassociated,
untethered, set seething and roiling like a shoal of terrified
fish. Sheppard muttered a curse, braced for recoil and squeezed
the P90's trigger, stitching a line of holes across that terrible,
gaseous head.

The bullets did exactly what he had feared, whined clear
through the figure and away, not troubling it for a moment.
In response, the shape simply walked up to him, reached one
slim arm past the gun and brushed his hand.

Its touch was fire, ice, pure voltage. It ripped a howl from
him. Sheppard stumbled back, every nerve fizzing, his skin
spewing black wisps as if the shape's hazy state was infectious.
He tried to raise the gun again, more in a gesture of defiance
than any hope of defending himself, but his strength was gone,
ripped away by the inexplicable wash of alien sensation. All
he could do was drag himself further away.

The shape had stopped. It stood motionless, only the ragged shreds of its outline whipping in the unfelt wind. Its head
was tilted slightly, as if in confusion.

"John?" Teyla had darted close to him, past the creature,
keeping her gun centered on its torso as she advanced. "Are
you all right?"

"Don't…" The words lodged, crackling and dry, in his throat.
He tasted dust. "Don't let it touch you."

"Watch your back!" bellowed Dex.

Sheppard cursed, hauled his heavy body halfway around. A
few meters further up the suspended path, the air was growing dark.

A second creature was there, moving towards him, knitting
itself from threads of gluey smoke as it walked.

He turned back to Teyla. "Run," he hissed.

"Not without you."

"I'm done. Can't even-" He looked past her, eyes wide. "Ronon!"

The Satedan was wreathed in smoke.

A third shape had appeared behind him, coalescing in moments, and its streaming hands were wrapped around Dex's head. Sheppard saw the man convulse sickeningly, every muscle locked rigid, eyes screwed shut, mouth gaping in a rictus of horrific pain. His blaster fired, once, his finger jolting uncontrollably on the trigger, sending a lash of plasma into the floor.

Sheppard lurched towards him. He heard Teyla scream a warning, but before he could take another step the first shape was in his tracks.

Its hands were up, reaching for his eyes, and-

It is the hot season, and the warm, dry air is full of drifting spinetree seeds. Their perfume is intoxicating, the twisting tracks they carve through morning's mist have a beauty that is almost sensual. Father brushes them away with his hand as he rides towards me, expertly bringing his stiltbeast to a halt at the edge of the gel lake.

Mother has woven crysgems into my hair, a gift for the journey. I turn to show him, wheeling on the spot. The light of the upper sun flicks blue sparks from the gems into the corners of my vision, stars in daylight.

I feel the stiltbeast's cool breath on my skin. Father is smiling. He reaches down to me, and whispers my name.

"John."

The voice came from darkness. It was faint, but insistent; a crackling whisper in his right ear. All Sheppard could do was lie like a loose sack of grain and listen. His body was not his own.

"*Colonel Sheppard? John, can you hear me?*"

He blinked. The shadows were beginning to recede. Edges were resolving themselves around him, surfaces reappearing, combining into furniture, books, pictures, a paneled metal door. The familiar landscape of his quarters.

He tried to mumble a reply, but his tongue had glued itself firmly to the roof of his mouth. "Bhr…"

"*I'm sorry, say again?*"

"Right here, Colonel." Sheppard sat up, carefully, working his jaw loose, the bed creaking softly under him. He had meant to spend just a few minutes resting before getting to work on Carter's report, to ease the dryness in his throat, the thudding pressure behind his eyes. His body, though, must have had other ideas. He hadn't even managed to remove his headset before sleep took him.

Trying to rest had been a bad move, he thought sourly. Not only had he lost untold hours, but he felt worse than he had done back in the gym. The headache was grinding, now. The bones of his skull felt too small, too delicate to successfully contain what lay within.

"*Glad to hear it,*" Carter replied. "*You've been offline for quite a while. I was beginning to worry.*"

"You and me both." He glanced at his wristwatch, wondering if he had somehow slept clear through until the early hours, but the digits made no sense to him. The watch had somehow been set to timer mode, and was steadily counting down towards zero.

A little more than six hours gone. Less than two to go.

"*Are you all right?*"

"Yeah, I'm fine. Have the IOA been in touch again?"

"*More than once. I don't know what their interest is in that city, they're keeping me out of the loop for some reason. But John, they keep asking me how you ended up there.*"

"They're trying to find it."

"*Looks that way.*"

"Bad idea." Sheppard swung his feet carefully down onto the floor. "Really bad idea. Colonel, my memory of that place is like Swiss cheese, but I can tell you this; *nobody* is going back there. Ever."

"*I'm inclined to agree. And trust me, any report I make to them will have that front and center. But I need something, John.*"

"I'll do what I can."

"*Thank you. And in the meantime, get yourself back to the Infirmary. You sound awful.*"

The headset clicked silent. Sheppard let out a long breath, let his heavy head fall forwards. For a few seconds he tried to remember if the room had been dark when he had lain down, but fixing the moment in his memory sent a new spike of pain flaring up through the base of his skull.

The alien city still had its claws in him. It had put a mark on him that hadn't even started to fade. Yet another reason to make sure that the IOA never discovered how to find it. Sheppard reached over to the lamp he kept beside the bed, squinting as he readied himself for the inevitable stab of light, and then realized that someone was in the room with him.

He froze.

There had been no sound, no sense of motion. No physical indication that he was not alone. The feeling of being watched, though, was overpowering. There was someone very close, studying him with a frightening intensity.

He waited, every sense straining, listening for a breath, for the slight movement in the air that would tell him where the watcher stood.

For a dozen heartbeats, nothing. And then, at the far corner of his vision, a piece of the darkness shifted.

Sheppard launched himself forwards, off the bed, dropping and turning in one smooth motion. Pure reflex had taken over; without conscious intent he had his sidearm up and aimed, his other hand on the light switch, body tensed to leap up and back towards the door.

He hit the switch, finger tightening on the trigger.

There was no target.

Sheppard held his aim for a few moments, then rose slowly. Both hands were on the gun now, arms locked straight. His observer could only be hiding on the far side of the bed.

There was, of course, no-one there.

"This," Sheppard croaked, "is getting real old, real fast."

The gun muzzle was vibrating. He lowered the weapon slightly, took one hand off the grip just long enough to wave the door open, then stepped through backwards as it slid aside.

A shadow loomed to his left. He spun, brought the gun up one-handed and came within a hair's width of putting a bullet through Rodney McKay's forehead.

The man yelped, floundering sideways, shielding his head with a computer tablet. "Whatever I did, I'm sorry!"

"Rodney?" Sheppard lowered the gun shakily, making sure his finger was off the trigger. "What the hell are you doing out here?"

McKay peeked out from under the tablet. "Trying not to get shot in the face?"

"Were you in my room?"

"When?"

"Just now."

The scientist was putting his arms down, a look of wary indignation on his face. "What in God's name would I be doing in there?"

"I dunno." Sheppard holstered the gun, feeling spectacularly foolish. "Watching me sleep?"

McKay just stared at him.

"Okay, forget that part."

"I'll try. It won't be easy." McKay peered through the doorway. "Did you seriously think someone was in there?"

Sheppard waved the door closed. "Just my mind playing tricks," he muttered. "It's been getting pretty good at that lately. What are you doing out here, anyway?"

"Looking for you. I need to talk to you about something."

"Can it wait?"

McKay's eyebrows went up, as if the concept was entirely alien to him. "Wait? Why?"

"Because I'm tired and I feel lousy."

"Oh. Then no, it can't wait."

Sheppard sagged. "Fine. Just… Not here."

McKay appeared to ponder for a moment. "We'll go to the lab. It might be easier if I show you, anyway. I've got some stuff running you might want to see." He frowned. "As long as you promise not to point the gun at me again."

"I'm not promising anything. It's been that kind of a day."

The pressure in Sheppard's skull had receded somewhat by the time he reached McKay's lab. In its place, though, was a new concern; his left arm had begun to twinge intermittently, firing blunt jolts from shoulder to wrist whenever he moved his hand.

He had fallen asleep on it, no doubt. "I need a vacation."

McKay didn't pick up on the quote. "I won't argue," he replied, stopping in front of the lab door. "You look bad."

"Thanks."

"Actually, you look worse than bad." McKay was edging slightly away. "You're not contagious, are you?"

The door slid open onto near-darkness, studded with constellations of fluttering LEDs; the racks of servers lining one wall must have been engaged in furious activity. Sheppard went in, found the nearest chair and dropped into it. "Keller said I wasn't sick."

"And you believed her?" McKay strode past him, tapping keyboards as he went. In his wake, a succession of flatscreen monitors lit up from standby, panels of pale blue light suspended eerily in the gloom.

Sheppard looked around. "Where's Zelenka?"

"Who knows?" McKay had stopped at a nearby bench, its upper surface a small forest of cables and computer equipment. He tugged a keyboard out from under the mess and rattled off a rapid series of commands. "Asleep, probably. Are you going to have time to finish Sam's report?"

"You heard about that?"

"Mmm." A larger monitor had awoken under McKay's ministrations. There was some kind of graphic on it, a complex 3D structure rotating slowly within a mesh of hair-fine gridlines. "All clear within eight hours, wasn't that what she said?"

"No, that's what *I* said."

"Oh. I must have remembered it wrong."

Sheppard stiffened. "*What* did you say?"

"Look, just try to focus." McKay finished typing, stabbing at the *Enter* key with what Sheppard considered to be a wholly unnecessary flourish. "I really need you to think back."

"Not exactly my strong suit right now."

"John, this is important. Ronon won't talk about it, and I can't even find Teyla. Can you remember anything at all about leaving that city?"

"Well, at least you're not asking me how I got in."

"I don't *care* how you got in. I need to know if there was anything at all unusual about the gate you used to come back."

"Damn it, Rodney." Sheppard glared at him. "I've got the IOA breathing down my neck, Sam poking me about it every five minutes, and now you're on my case too?" He stood up, a little too fast. The motion sent a thorn of pain into his wrist bones. "Don't you understand? Remembering hurts! I'm doing everything I can *not* to remember!"

McKay looked grim. "You need to start."

"Why? Why is this even important?"

"Because," said McKay, "I'm pretty sure that when you gated back to Atlantis, there was something already in the wormhole with you."

There was a long silence. Finally Sheppard gathered his wits. "That, uh… That sounds kind of crazy."

"Zelenka said the same thing. Then he said *I* sounded kind of crazy. Which may be part of the reason he's not here. We, ah, kind of had words…" McKay shrugged. "You know what he's like."

"What *he's* like."

"Point is, I knew something was screwy with the gate after you three came back, you know... The way you did." McKay had the good grace to appear slightly apologetic when he said that. "So I checked the timestamps. Your transit time was one point eight seconds longer on the return trip."

Sheppard frowned, mulling that over. Theoretically, the time it took for an object to travel between Stargates had a fixed correlation to the distance between them. It often didn't feel that way to the object itself — the difference between subjective and objective time within the confines of a wormhole was still a matter of fierce debate — but to an outside observer, the time out should equal the time back precisely.

Unless something catastrophic happened between journeys. "Could an endpoint have moved?"

"Not unless it made a sixty light-year hyperspace jump without anyone noticing. And given that both of them are planets..." McKay shook his head. "I had a few other ideas. A hypersurface deformation in Minkowski spacetime, some kind of interplanar anomaly affecting energy density, maybe even a Klein flaw..."

John Sheppard was no slouch when it came to higher mathematics, although he usually chose to keep that fact to himself. But McKay was talking about realms of theoretical physics that would have made his skull ache even without the mystery hangover. "Rodney, you mentioned something earlier about focusing. Remember that?"

"What? Oh, sure. Anyhow, I went over the sensor logs, and it turns out the event horizon threw a howling fit for that extra one point eight seconds. Spewed out a whole storm of exotic particles and resonant frequencies just before you came through. I thought it was just noise until I started picking it apart."

Sheppard gestured at the desk. "Is that what all the spaghetti's for?"

"Yeah, I had to temporarily beef up the transient storage.

This is complex stuff."

"Not just noise then."

"Anything but. The particle emissions are pretty solid evidence of a hyperdimensional incursion." He went back to the desk, tapped out another command string. A new graphic appeared on the monitor, a flat disk, ripples and peaks crisscrossing its surface in a morass of intersecting waves and interference patterns. "I've run these simulations, oh, nineteen times? Same result each time. Something with too many dimensions became temporarily coterminous with the subspace bridge."

Sheppard went over to stare at the screen. The animated disc was fascinating, hypnotic, oddly beautiful. It looked like a pond in a hailstorm. "Too many dimensions... Sounds like it's not from around here."

"Definitely not local. And I can't imagine how anything from a parallel plane can intersect with ours by accident."

"Are you saying it *wanted* to be here?"

McKay shrugged. "Who knows? Maybe it's predatory. Maybe it was trying to study our dimension through the wormhole interstices and fell in — press your face against too many windows and I guess one of them's bound to open. Point is-"

"What's that?"

"Hm?" McKay glanced up, following Sheppard's gaze. "I told you, a simulation."

Sheppard was moving slowly around the desk, his eyes fixed on the large monitor behind. The graphic on it was still turning slowly within its cage of gridlines. "I've seen that."

"Huh? How could you possibly... Hey, have you been in here?"

The graphic had been edge-on to Sheppard when he had first looked at it, but now his simulated viewpoint was angled enough for him to see its true form: a flattened torus, surrounded by a labyrinth of fine threads, a complex disc of channels and chambers.

The number of channels connecting to each chamber varied, but only multiples of three. "I was there. Rodney, that's a map of the damn city." He turned back to McKay, aghast. "Where did you get that?"

"Extrapolated backwards from the particle burst." McKay was looking intently at him, obviously concerned but, at the same time, strangely observant. "John, trust me. That's not what you think it is."

"I know what it is, damn it. I was there. We were all there. Ask Teyla, get Ronon in here…" He trailed off. McKay had touched a control on his desk, and the torus was falling away from him.

The gridlines thinned to a haze as the graphic's scale decreased exponentially. In moments the torus was joined by two neighbors, themselves webbed together by their own network of channels. And just as swiftly, three had become nine, and then dozens, then too many to count, a galaxy of whirling points arcing down and away in an awful, vertiginous swoop.

Until, finally, there were no individual channels and toroids anymore. Just a single, ghostly structure rotating in front of him, lumpy and convoluted, strange and complex and utterly alien.

But for all its strangeness, John Sheppard knew exactly what he was looking at.

Atlantis, as though understanding Sheppard's need for solitude, chose not to trouble him with company as he left the lab. He walked its corridors alone, and in silence.

The implications of McKay's theory were unthinkable. He simply could not imagine some predatory entity lurking in the wormhole's throat like a spider in a tunnel; it flew in the face of everything he knew about gate travel. Even McKay's assurances that he was massively oversimplifying the concept didn't make it any more palatable. Whether an alien mind had been inside the subspace bridge or dimensionally coterminous with it made little difference. The idea still made his mind rebel.

It was just possible, he supposed, that he, Teyla and Ronon — or the stream of energy they had been converted into by the Stargate — had collided with a wormhole anomaly on their way back from the city. He certainly *felt* as though he'd collided with something recently, although a Mack truck fitted his mental image more accurately. Such an event might explain both the extended transit time and the adverse effects he and his companions had suffered on their return.

But to consider the anomaly as having conscious intent was a horror too far, despite what glittered in the darkness of McKay's lab.

The extrapolation graphic filled every monitor. Sheppard raised his fingertips to the largest screen, brushing the warm glass as if trying to reach past it, to feel the structures rotating beyond.

It was alive, there was no mistaking that. He was no longer looking at geometry, but biology: nine interwoven lobes of labyrinthine tissue, three branching cords twisted one around the other in unsettling, yet graceful symmetry. "Is this what it looks like? What its brain looks like?"

"God no. That's just a CGI metaphor. It's what a hyperdimensional brain would look like if it was compressed into four-dimensional spacetime." *McKay's face was lit by the graphic, shifting planes of blue ghosting his skin.* "In reality, it would look like-"

"A city," *Sheppard breathed.*

No, if anyone was oversimplifying, he decided, it was McKay. The city and the anomaly could not be the same. The particles emitted from the event horizon prior to Sheppard's return must have come from the city itself, or been reflected by it, confusing the data.

Sheppard couldn't recall how long he had been in the alien construct, but it had been a lot longer than one point eight seconds.

He stopped where he was. "Sorry Rodney, this isn't Fantastic Voyage. No Raquel Welch for you."

He had spoken aloud. There was no-one to hear him. The part of Atlantis he had wandered into was utterly deserted, shadowed and silent. Not even the wall lamps seemed to be working.

Sheppard glanced around, puzzled. Had he really been so lost in thought?

There was light ahead of him, a pale slab in the gloom; a junction, he guessed, the corridor in which he stood meeting one that was at least partially lit. He started towards it, eager to be out of the darkness, and as he moved he saw a figure step out from around the far corner.

Suddenly, John Sheppard was very glad not to be alone here. Atlantis was a massive structure, and the total number of humans inhabiting it almost vanishingly small. Still, to go for so long without seeing anyone had unsettled him.

"Hey," he called, raising a hand.

The figure didn't move, just stood watching him, silhouetted by the light. Sheppard found his pace slowing.

"Who's there?"

There was no reply, no reaction. Just a faint fluttering around the figure's outline, as though it were made of smoke.

Sheppard stopped dead in his tracks. "You," he snarled.

Fury boiled in him, sharper and hotter that the pain in his skull and arm. He surged forwards. Before he knew it the pistol was leaping in his hand, the hard flat snapping of gunfire echoing from the walls as he put three shots through the figure's torso, one through its hazy head.

It darted away, leaving threads of itself to twist in the air.

He broke into a run. The knowledge that gunfire had no effect on the creature meant nothing to him. He didn't care how it had tracked him down, found its way to Atlantis to torment him a second time. He didn't care that it was probably going to kill him. He just wanted to get his hands on it, to rip the gaseous stuff of it apart. One final payment for all the woe it had caused.

Sheppard hurled himself around the corner, half expecting to find the shape's inky hands reaching for his eyes again, but it was already at the next junction. It was taunting him, playing with him. Staying just out of reach until he was exhausted, before turning back to wreak ruin on him.

He was long past caring. He sent another couple of bullets up the corridor to herald his approach, and kept running.

Again, as he drew close the figure breezed away, to the left this time. Sheppard scrambled to the place it had been, barely keeping his balance as he ducked around the wall, then sprinted towards the next junction.

There wasn't one. Just black sky, and the stark, merciless light of a million stars.

Sheppard stumbled out into fresh air. The corridor had terminated abruptly, a low archway meeting what looked like an open gallery. He was on one of the piers. His solitary walk from McKay's lab had taken him much further than he had thought.

He reached the gallery rail and stopped there, panting. It was very dark, the lapping sea around him black and unseen, but to his left the great towers of Atlantis glowed from within, spearing the air like glittering shards of crystal. There was a breeze, cool and soft, and he could smell the tang of salt and ozone.

The creature had vanished. Presumably it had tired of the game. Sheppard slapped the rail angrily. "Damn it!"

"John?"

He whirled. Teyla Emmagan was emerging from the arch.

Sheppard sagged back against the rail. "Oh man, am I pleased to see you."

"And I, you." She smiled. "You look-"

"Bad, I know. People keep telling me." He glanced quickly left and right, but there was no sign of the creature. "Those things are here. One of them was just ahead of me."

"I know." She nodded. "It's all right, John. You can put the gun away."

"Where have you been? I haven't seen you, not since..." He had been about to say *since we got back*, but before the words could reach his lips he realized they were meaningless. He had no actual memory of returning to Atlantis. Nothing, if he was honest with himself, before waking in the isolation room.

"I am sorry," Teyla replied. "I needed to be alone, to try and make sense of what has happened."

"Hope you've had better luck than me." There was a movement at the far end of the gallery. Sheppard turned to see Ronon Dex striding towards him. "The gang's all here, huh?"

"Good to see you too." The Satedan joined him at the rail. "Nice night," he muttered. "Pity, really."

"Why do you say that?"

"Because it's not going to last."

As he spoke, the air beside him grew dark.

Sheppard cursed, leapt back. Three of the shadow creatures were forming around him; one slight and slender, the others larger, inky silhouettes coalescing from the sharp night air. He brought the gun up, but before he could fire Teyla's hand was on his forearm.

"John, no," she whispered. "They are no different to us."

The figures weren't moving. For the moment, they seemed content to stand where they were, watchful and still, their essence flying from them in perpetual ribbons. Sheppard kept the gun up, but took his finger off the trigger. "What are they?"

"Travelers," she told him. "Like us, perhaps. But they can no longer remember themselves."

"We still can," said Ronon. "Not sure for how long, though."

He held up his hand. The tips of his fingers streamed like black smoke.

Beyond him, the sea was changing.

Sheppard walked past Dex, to the rail. He could see threads of light under the black water, shifting and sliding over each other as they rose to the surface. And in the far distance, the horizon was boiling upwards, silent and slow, curling upwards in every direction.

Far above him, the stars were going out.

He sighed. "We never left, did we?"

Ronon chuckled. "We were never there."

"This isn't us. This is a dream of us." Teyla was standing next to him, watching the world grow facets and channels.

"So who's dreaming us? Rodney's wormhole entity?"

"That was not Rodney." The horizon was gone, now, curling up over their heads, and the sea was a seething mass of polyhedra. "The entity cannot comprehend us. It is too big, too different."

Sheppard nodded. Suddenly, the holes in his memory made sense. There were things he could not remember clearly because they had never happened. "It's been trying to talk to us, though. The whole time. Using our own memories."

Teyla touched his hand. "All it has is what we brought with us."

"Talking to us, interrogating us…" Ronon shrugged. "It hasn't been making a lot of sense."

"Yeah," Sheppard sighed. "Yeah, it has."

"It had to be here," said Sheppard, gazing up at the rippling, mirrored disk at the heart of the Stargate. "It couldn't be anyplace else."

"*You're using some pretty relative terms,*" said McKay, his voice a sharp crackle in Sheppard's headset. "*Try to stop thinking about physical locations.*"

"Try to shut up," growled Dex. He was glaring at the three shadow creatures. They were standing at the base of the Stargate, in postures that spoke of wonder, or possibly terror. "So do we know what it wants, yet?"

"I think so," said Sheppard. "I got asked the same question so many times I stopped hearing it."

"How we got here?"

"*Ah, you're not actually-*"

"Shut up."

"The way in is the way out," Teyla said quietly. "The entity is as trapped as we are."

"And the way in is the one thing we've all been doing our best not to remember." Sheppard's left arm was streaming smoke, now; not black, but crimson. Another mystery he lacked the energy to solve. "I'm guessing it wasn't fun."

"That is what it needs from us. From all of us." Teyla stepped towards the shadows. "They resisted remembering for so long that they lost everything."

"Or maybe their memories weren't enough." The event horizon was in turmoil, its metal surface leaping and boiling. "I've seen its brain, kind of. Maybe it needed more than three people's memories to find the way."

"So what do we do now?" Dex had his arms folded defensively. "Draw it a map?"

Teyla shook her head. "I think this is enough."

The walls were darkening, the metal panels flattening out, threads of gray light weaving across them in fractal branches like mercury injected into a vein. Sheppard could see the spaces between the branches twisting, turning over, growing more sides than they could possibly sustain.

The sight made his eyes ache. "Should have known that wasn't really McKay," he said to Teyla. "He'd have yelled at me for getting fingerprints on his screen."

"We must have remembered him wrong." She smiled sadly. "Perhaps he will be more like Rodney next time."

He stared at her. "Wait, next time? What do you mean, next time?"

There was no answer. She was already beyond speech.

The room was unfolding, its surfaces sliding over and through each other in impossible patterns. The air was dislocating into razored shards. Sheppard looked wildly around, trying to fight down a rising panic, but the motion set his vision spilling wildly. For a sickening instant he was seeing through the wrong eyes, watching himself tessellate.

Then he was seeing through all their eyes at once.

Then sight was gone, and there was only the pressure in his head, folding the very stuff of him over and over into a singularity, an infinitesimal point of unimaginable pain and terror, flung headlong into the rushing, dimensionless dark…

It was late, and the infirmary was very quiet.

Atlantis was enjoying a period of relative calm. Off-world missions had been suspended while the Stargate's systems were being tested, and as a result the number of medical emergencies had dropped to zero. For days now there had been no fevers to soothe, no burns to salve or wounds to close. Only the isolation room remained active, and activity there was being kept to a minimum for the benefit of its only patient.

The trauma staff were on standby. The beds were empty, the blades and needles tidied away. The lights had been dimmed. The only sounds John Sheppard could hear were the whisper of the air system, the soft click and hum of sleeping machinery, and the hurried yammering of his own heart.

He had been standing at the door of the observation deck for almost a minute now. Had the infirmary been fully staffed, no doubt he would have been asked why, but he wasn't sure he could have given any kind of sensible answer.

And yet, passing his hand over the wall panel was far harder than it should have been.

The door whirred aside. Sheppard stepped through and began to make his way up the steps, carefully, his good hand on the rail. He was still unsteady on his feet, shivery and unbalanced, and he could not risk a fall.

The deck itself was in darkness. Sheppard peered around the corner, and saw a slim figure standing at the rail, forehead resting against the thick cold glass of the window.

"Colonel," he said quietly.

Carter straightened, turned. "Wow. You look really bad."

"Ah, thanks?"

She frowned. "I mean it, John. Shouldn't you be resting?"

He shook his head, regretting it instantly. His skull felt heavy, but oddly delicate, as though cast from wet plaster. "Trust me, rest is the last thing I need."

"If you say so." She nodded at his chest. "How's the arm?"

He followed her gaze, to the pressure sling binding his left arm tight to his body. And a memory, sudden and clear; the ravine edge giving way under him, boots sliding wildly on wet rock, an ill-advised grab at the dark space between two tilting boulders. The wet creaking snap of bone.

His gut lurched at the thought of it, and he looked up, away from the sling and back to the window. "On the mend. Is it time?"

"Yeah, almost." She checked her watch, and sighed. "Eight-hour cycle, more or less. Keller's still trying to find out why."

Sheppard stepped up to the rail. "How long is she lucid for?"

"It varies, depending on what she's asked, but never more than a few minutes. I guess there are specific triggers that put her back under, but we're still learning what they are."

"And this is cycle number…?"

"Nineteen."

"Damn."

Below him, lying still and silent under a silvery thermal blanket, was a young woman. She was pale, her face as white and immobile as paper, her exposed arms heavy with drip feeds and bio sensors and complex, twisting tattoos. Her hair was a strange color, bluish-blonde, and braided through with what looked like glass beads. In the darkness of the isolation room, among the shadows and the chrome and the flat blue glow of the monitors she looked ethereal, ghostly, impossibly delicate.

"Do you recognize her?" Carter asked him.

"Never seen her before, sorry."

"It was a long shot. Ronon and Teyla said the same thing." She folded her arms, tightly against herself. "I was hoping maybe she'd been on the planet with you. That if you saw her again…"

"Sam, there was *no-one* on the planet with us. The whole mission was a bust." Had the young woman's eyelids fluttered?

The isolation room was too dark, he couldn't be sure. "We wandered around in the rain for two hours looking for that weapons cache, then I fell down a hole and we came home. If there was anyone living there, we sure didn't meet them."

"The three of you went into the gate together."

"Yeah."

"And six people came out."

Sheppard gripped the safety rail with his one good hand. Its solidity was a comfort. "So they tell me."

He couldn't remember returning to Atlantis after M3L-628. If he had ever formed memories of that time, they were lost to him, hidden away between walls of neural trauma. But he had read the reports, seen the security footage. He had watched himself slump bonelessly out of the event horizon, Teyla falling at his side, Ronon Dex taking two entirely unconscious steps before he, too, crumpled.

And a moment later, three more figures spilled out.

He hadn't been able to watch what happened next, not for long. Perhaps, had he been feeling stronger, not so disorientated and fragile, the sight wouldn't have affected him so badly. After all, he had witnessed horrors before, of a thousand different hues. But to see the newcomers wracked with convulsions, to hear their shrieks, watch them claw at their own eyes… It was too much. He had turned away from the screen, and not looked back.

Two of them, the older man and woman, had died there on the gate room floor. Only the girl down in the isolation room, sitting up now with her white face a mask of confusion and pain, had lived.

It was possible that the others had been her parents, but no-one could be sure.

"I've tried to remember what happened," he said quietly. "Believe me, I've tried. After I came to in the infirmary, that's pretty much all I did, but I got nothing except a blinding headache." He shrugged, lopsidedly. "There's a feeling, that's all…

Like I was somewhere else. For a long time."

"According to McKay, just over a second and a half." Below them, a figure was sitting down next to the girl, bulky in a crimson hazmat suit. Keller, reaching out to a put a gloved hand on the newcomer's arm. "He keeps talking about a detour, as if you were snatched out of the wormhole, or met something already in it…" Carter shook her head. "It doesn't make any sense to me. Probably doesn't to him, to be honest."

"If anyone knows," Sheppard muttered, "it's her. But she can't tell us a thing."

"She told us her name."

"She has?"

"Nineteen times. She told us she's called John Sheppard." Carter sighed. "I don't think any of her own memories survived. Anything she once was is buried under layers of you, Ronon, Teyla…"

Sheppard didn't speak. The girl was looking up at him, calmer now, and in response he raised his good hand in a pathetic half-wave. But even from this distance, in the dark, he could tell that she was already slipping away.

Maybe it was better, he thought despairingly, if none of them remembered. If McKay was right, he had been gone for less than two seconds, and it felt like he'd been tortured a month.

Had the newcomers already been there, suspended in McKay's detour?

And if so, for how long?

The thought pierced him. He dropped his hand, stepped back from the rail. On the far side of the glass, Keller was shaking the girl's arm, trying to get her attention.

"Hello? Can you tell me your name?"

STARGATE SG-1
A Woman's Army

Geonn Cannon

Being on time was five minutes late and, by her own rubric, Janet Fraiser was running twenty minutes behind schedule. She cursed the time-suck of changing elevators and the general slowness of the ride as she descended into the bowels of the base. She stepped through the doors as they opened and stopped in her office long enough to drop off her things and exchange her coat for a lab jacket. She found Lieutenant Evans and thanked her for filling in until she got there.

"It wasn't a problem," Evans responded. "Things weren't too busy down here."

Janet swept her gaze across the infirmary beds and only one that she could see was currently occupied. The unfortunate Sergeant Siler was getting his wrist wrapped in gauze. There was another bed hidden behind a closed curtain that probably held a patient, and she knew SG-4 was isolated in another area due to an unfortunate reaction to some local flora. "I'll believe it when we see it. What have we got?"

Evans handed over her clipboard so Janet could examine the overnight reports. "Well, you saw…" She nodded toward Siler.

"Yes," Janet said. "As long as he's stable, I don't need to know the details of his latest exploit."

"All right then. Just the headlines. A medical team was just dispatched to the gate room a few minutes before you arrived. SG-9 was scheduled to come back ten minutes ago, so I assume it's something to do with them. The members of SG-4 are responding well to the antibiotic you put them on. Hopefully we'll be able to drop the quarantine tomorrow if they continue to progress."

"Good work." She let the papers fall and handed the clipboard back. "Has anyone on SG-4 started showing ill effects from the rash?"

"Nothing."

"Fantastic. I'll check on them myself when I have a few minutes."

The medical team that responded to the gate activation returned with the two members of SG-9 propping their leader up between them. Janet caught the colonel's eye and they shared a silent exchange. Colonel Greene shrugged apologetically. The woman was a former college athlete and constantly overexerting herself on missions. If it wasn't a sprained wrist, it was a twisted ankle. She tried to be a superhero when it came to her team. Janet respected the intention but sooner or later she knew the colonel's attempted heroics would lead to a much greater injury. She moved on an intercept course to give Greene a proper scolding when a strident voice stopped her in her tracks.

"Doc! There you are."

Janet closed her eyes and dropped her head back at the thought of dealing with her most stubborn patient. She turned and stalked toward the man sprawled on one of her exam beds, one foot swinging over the edge of the mattress. He was at least laying down, which meant he probably wasn't going to make a run for it, but she stood between him and the exit just in case. She stuffed her hands into her pockets and glared at him like a gunslinger getting ready for a shootout.

"Colonel O'Neill." She spoke his name in an exasperated sigh.

"I come down here for a couple of aspirin, and your goons won't let me leave."

She kept her voice measured and calm. "I would apologize, but I'd have done the same thing if I'd been here. You are overdue for a checkup on that knee, and I don't want to rush one before your next mission. If you just wait patiently we can get this over and done with so you can ignore your checkups for another six months."

"You're holding me hostage."

"You want to see hostage?" Janet stepped forward. "Some of these beds have straps, you know."

He narrowed his eyes at her. "You wouldn't dare."

"Try me. You came down here for aspirin. That means your knee was hurting. I wouldn't let you out of this bed now if Anubis himself landed on top of the mountain."

Their standoff was interrupted by the arrival of Daniel Jackson. He stopped short next to Janet, looked between the two of them, and then took a step back. "Am I interrupting something?"

"Yes," Janet said without taking her eyes off Jack. "But go ahead. I needed to check on Colonel Greene anyway. If Colonel O'Neill gets out of that bed, sound the alarm."

He stopped her from walking away. "Oh. Actually I was looking for you."

Janet broke off her staring contest. "What's wrong?"

"Nothing. General Hammond wants you to sit in on a briefing with us."

Jack sat up. "Us? Us being SG-1, us?"

Janet aimed a finger at him. "You. Stay."

Jack pointed accusingly at Daniel. "He was *dead* six months ago. Why aren't you bugging him for one of these checkups?"

"Because he actually shows up when we call for him," Janet said. "We finally got you down here, and we are not letting you go unless the fate of the world is involved."

"She's right, Jack. Apparently Lieutenant Evans called General Hammond to let him know you were unavailable for the rest of the day. He said you could sit this one out."

Jack looked hurt. "The hell you say."

"It's a purely diplomatic mission," Daniel said.

Some of the fire went out of Jack's eyes. "So... my options are..."

"You can sit around the infirmary being bored, but get your

exams out of the way, or you can go be bored on an alien planet." Daniel shrugged. "If you want to go, I'm sure General Hammond would be happy to—"

"No," Jack interrupted. He sank back down onto the pillows. "No, you kids have fun."

Daniel said, "I thought you might feel that way. Jack, be good and when it's all over they'll give you a lollipop."

"They never have sour apple," Jack grumbled.

Janet asked Lieutenant Evans to continue filling in for her, and thanked her for calling General Hammond. Daniel was waiting for her in the corridor.

"Busy morning? Usually it takes at least an hour before you're that irritated with Jack."

She sighed. "I was late because Cassandra and I had an argument this morning. Actually it was more like the greatest hits of five other arguments we've been having lately."

Daniel smiled and stepped into the elevator with her. "Well, she's an incredibly bright teenager and you're just her mother. What do you know about life?"

Janet chuckled. "Exactly. We finally reached a stalemate, but I'm sure it's going to explode again once I get home."

"Like I said, she's a smart kid. Eventually she's going to figure out you were right all along. Just try not to rub it in her face when she apologizes."

"Thank you, Daniel." She looked at him. "You know, he wasn't exactly wrong about you. The only data we have on unascended beings is what little we were able to glean from Shifu. There could be lingering side effects we can't run tests for."

"At the risk of sounding like Jack, I feel fine. And unlike Jack, I would definitely come running to you if anything felt even the slightest bit off." They arrived at their destination and stepped out of the elevator. Daniel put a hand on her arm to keep her from continuing into the briefing room. "While we're on the subject, I wanted to thank you for everything you did for me last week, after the *Stromos* incident."

"I did what any doctor would have done."

"No," Daniel said. "You definitely went above and beyond the call of duty. I've only been back a month, and it's no secret that my memory is still spotty. It's better than it was at first, but there are blank spaces. Having a dozen other identities dumped into my head could have been a disaster. I don't want to think about what might have happened if you hadn't been there to keep everyone in line."

Janet shook her head. "I didn't do anything."

"You saw what happened to Pharrin. Every personality swarming at once, his own lost somewhere in the shuffle. It was a… it was a whirlpool with the jets turned on high. But you kept each of the personalities in my head focused. The lines never blurred. That's why I know the memories and the personality I was left with were wholly mine. I don't think I ever thanked you properly for that."

"Well… you're welcome, Daniel. But once you've downloaded one friend from the base computer, anything less is child's play."

They started walking toward the stairs. "And for saving my glasses while I was…" He gestured vaguely toward the ceiling and wiggled his fingers. "At the time I didn't remember what a hassle it was to replace them."

Janet smiled. "We had them in the infirmary after you, um." She didn't want to say 'died,' but every other word didn't seem big enough. "After. Then enough time passed that throwing them away seemed like giving up. We've all seen enough miracles here to know better than that."

General Hammond was seated at the head of the briefing table when they arrived. He was engaged in conversation with Sam, while Teal'c sat on the General's other side with his hands folded in front of him. Hammond ended his conversation with Sam and nodded to her. Janet took a seat and opened the folder that had been left for her.

"Glad you could join us, Doctor. I'll let Dr. Jackson explain why you're here."

Daniel cleared his throat and moved to stand next to the projection screen. "Three years ago, SG-1 visited a planet called Ialara. It's a fairly developed society on par with Earth in the late nineteenth century. The main continent was broken up into eight different districts called cantons. When we visited, the Stargate was controlled by Banu Canton. Their leadership was interested in establishing a relationship with Earth. Unfortunately, not long after that first visit, a civil war broke out. Their closest neighbor overtook Banu's capitol and captured the Stargate. The Banu government was able to get one last message through, warning us to stay away, before they sealed the gate and went into hiding. This morning, we received a new message. The Banu have recovered their territory and negotiated a ceasefire with their enemies."

Sam said, "I assume that means they're not asking us for arms."

"No," Daniel said. "While the Banu were able to recover control of their cities, their people suffered greatly during the time they were exiled. Their people are sick. Their doctors don't know why." He nodded at Janet's folder. "After they made contact with us, a MALP was sent through to make sure there was no airborne contagion."

"Dr. Fraiser, despite Dr. Jackson's assurances that this situation is safe, I won't order you to take this mission unless —"

Janet stopped him with a raised hand. She had been skimming the MALP readings while Daniel was talking and she could confirm whatever disease had struck these people wasn't airborne. "I can have a team ready in half an hour, sir."

Hammond nodded. "That's what I thought you would say. But I wanted you to know you had the option."

"Thank you, sir. But I don't believe there is an option here."

"SG-1 will accompany your team to the planet. You'll leave as soon as Dr. Fraiser's team is assembled. Major, I assume you can handle this one without Colonel O'Neill."

She smiled. "We'll try to make do, sir. Teal'c has been practicing his pop culture references to take up some of the slack."

Teal'c glanced at her and Sam had to fight back her laughter. Hammond dismissed them, and Janet began compiling the list of who she would take with her. Sam hurried to catch up with her as she walked to the elevator.

"Hey. Rough morning?"

"Is it that obvious?"

Sam wrinkled her nose. "Ah, not really. Cassandra sent me a text message. Apparently you two have been going at it pretty hard, huh?"

Janet rolled her eyes. "You could say that. Tell me again why I thought it was a great idea to be a single mother to a genius?"

Sam rubbed Janet's shoulder. "Because she needed someone and you have a big heart. And because you love her."

"Yeah, yeah, yeah," Janet said.

Sam laughed. "And because you know you're not really a single mother. You know she has her uncles. And I'm just a phone call away."

Janet smiled and squeezed Sam's hand. "I know. And I'll be eternally grateful to the four of you." The elevator arrived. "For now I need to put together my medical team and find someone to watch her while I'm off-world."

"Never a dull moment," Sam said.

"I'd kill for a dull moment."

"When we get back, I'll take you and Cassandra rock climbing. You'll be too tired to fight, and I can act as an arbitrator."

Janet sighed blissfully. "That sounds amazing. Thank you, Sam."

"Sure. I'll see you in an hour?"

"Should be plenty of time."

Sam nodded and headed for the stairs while Janet took the elevator back to the infirmary.

Janet sat on one of the benches in front of her open locker. She had changed into her desert BDUs, her cap sitting beside her on the bench on top of the heavy tac vest. She dialed Cassandra's number even though she knew it would be turned off and buried deep in the bottom of her book bag while she was in school, but she had made a promise that she would never go off-world without letting Cassandra know. She listened to the brief message and waited for the beep.

"Hi, Cassandra. It's Mom. A mission came up, and I have to go away for a little bit. I'm not sure how long I'll be gone. It shouldn't be too dangerous but SG-1 is going with me, so I'm sure I'll be just fine. I've already called Mrs. Bernthal from next door and she'll check in on you tonight." She looked down at her boots. "I'll see you soon, or I'll have General Hammond call you if we can't come back right away. Sam said she wants to take you rock climbing when we get back, so that should be fun. I love you, Cassandra. Be good."

She closed the phone and put it in her locker. Her medical team was busy gathering what they would need for work in the field. They were bringing everything necessary to diagnose and hopefully treat whatever was ailing the Ialaran people, but also antibiotics, bandages, gloves, and hydrocortisone to ensure their hospital was properly stocked.

Everyone else on the base thought the Stargate was the best ride in the universe. It certainly was thrilling. But she couldn't shake the twinge of anxiety she always felt before going through it. She understood the science well enough to know how dangerous it was, but the Ancients were certified geniuses and, in the seven years she'd examined SG teams, there hadn't been a single instance of physical deformities caused by wormhole travel. But knowing it was safe and preparing to walk through that big blue puddle to an alien planet were two different things.

There was no question, however, that the fear was worth it for the job she was doing. It was the job she was always meant to do. She remembered being young, fresh out of high school and thinking about her future. She was married young to a man she thought was the love of her life, but she'd made the mistake of choosing someone like her stoic, Army officer father and wound up with a controlling chauvinistic pig.

Her dream was to be a doctor. Unfortunately it was an expensive, almost unrealistic dream. She knew her parents would find some way to make it happen for her, but Janet came up with a better idea: the Air Force would pay for her medical school and she would get to practice real medicine. No paperwork or insurance or bureaucratic headaches that came from working in a hospital. She was fascinated by exotic diseases, and being a doctor in the military would let her travel all over the world to find and treat them.

Janet smiled and looked around the locker room. If only she had known the scope of what she was getting into, the mysteries that awaited her. She stood up and pulled on the rest of her gear. Her team was probably almost ready to go, and she didn't want to keep SG-1 waiting. She fitted the cap onto her head and took a deep breath before she stepped out into the corridor.

Sam, Daniel, and Teal'c were waiting at the base of the ramp when she arrived. Two of her nurses, Sarah and Wendy, were loading the last few medical kits onto the FRED. Sam noticed her arrival first and signaled the technician in the gate room. The sergeant acknowledged her and began the dialing procedure.

Sam approached Janet. "Did you call Cassandra?"

"I left her a message."

"I know it's tough for you going off-world without talking to her."

Janet nodded. "Yeah. But this is just a humanitarian mission. Reestablishing ties and providing medical care to the wounded. No cause for alarm."

Teal'c eyed them warily. "I believe if O'Neill were here, he would admonish you for tempting the fates in such a manner, Dr. Fraiser."

Sam said, "Well, it's a good thing he's not here."

The Stargate blossomed to Janet's left, and she turned to face it as the explosion settled into a shimmering pool of blue light. Seven years after the first time she watched it happen and it still seemed impossible to her. Sam and Teal'c led the way up the ramp, followed by Daniel guiding the FRED. Sarah and Wendy were on one side of the supply transport with Janet on the other. She watched as Sam was swallowed by the rippling event horizon. Sam, who was smart enough to know exactly what was being done to her on a molecular level, didn't even flinch as she went through.

Janet still closed her eyes. In her mind it was a bit like jumping over a wide puddle; just push off and let momentum carry you the rest of the way. The tip of her nose tingled before the sensation spread to the rest of her head. She felt as if something grabbed her and pulled her forward. Both of her feet were off the ground for a few seconds longer than she anticipated but then she felt hard stone under her boots. She put a hand against the FRED so she wouldn't stumble. The Stargate disengaged behind her, and she adjusted the brim of her cap as she examined her new surroundings.

The Stargate was standing in an open-air plaza constructed of brown stones. There were eight arched entryways, two in each wall, and all of them had been fortified with iron bars and sandbags. Through the palisades she could see the sky was darkened by a field of thick, cottony storm clouds. The air was cool and sweet with the smell of a recent rainfall, but Janet could feel the humidity rising.

Daniel was already introducing the team to their welcoming party. He turned and gestured to her. "And our Chief Medical Officer, Janet Fraiser. Janet, this is Amos Magasi, Taoiseach of the Banu Canton." The man was shorter than Daniel, with thinning red-blonde hair and a friendly smile. He and the rest of his party all wore variations of the same suit. His epaulets were larger, however, denoting his rank, and he offered his hand to her.

"Dr. Fraiser," he said. "I thank you for coming so quickly in our time of need."

"Of course. I hope we're able to help."

He glanced at Sam and Daniel. "I am afraid that you may not have the chance. Major Carter, I must confess that the stalemate we mentioned when we contacted you this morning is already beginning to crumble. The delegation we sent to negotiate a more lasting peace was attacked before they arrived at their destination. We're not sure if the truce was a ploy all along, or if the attack was carried out by a splinter group. Either way we cannot guarantee your safety during this visit."

Janet and Sam exchanged a look. Sam said, "We can call this off until the climate is a little calmer, but I'm leaving it up to you, Doctor. If you and your people are willing to stay, we'll stay."

"I appreciate the offer, but we're already here. These people need our help. I'd like to stay."

Sam nodded. "Then we'll stay. I'll contact General Hammond for a backup team just in case things get hairy. Mr. Magasi, if you'll show Dr. Fraiser where she and her team can set up…?"

"It would be our pleasure, and our great relief."

Sarah and Wendy unloaded the heavy medical kits from the FRED, taking only what they could carry for the time being. Teal'c lifted the kits without being asked, and Janet nodded her thanks to him. One of the Ialaran men remained behind with SG-1 while the others fell into position around Magasi. Janet realized they were a security detail and warily scanned the world beyond the arched doorways. The plaza was surrounded by rolling green hills that looked vibrant under the thick blanket of clouds. There were no signs of imminent danger, no echoes of cannon fire or pillars of smoke in the distance, but she was grateful she had Teal'c by her side.

They paused so one of the guards could unlock a door that presumably led into the building. Magasi turned back to look at her. "I will take this opportunity to again thank you for coming to our aid, Dr. Fraiser. I could say it a hundred times more and it would not be enough. We are extremely grateful your people allowed you to help us, given the current state of affairs."

"I'm a doctor," Janet said. "My people understand that I'll go where I'm needed."

"Dr. Fraiser is also a soldier," Teal'c added when it was clear Janet wouldn't do it herself. "She is more than able to defend herself if the situation arises."

She smiled and he inclined his head to her.

"A soldier and a physician? That is an interesting dichotomy, is it not?"

Janet said, "I suppose it can be. But I'm helping people who put their lives on the line every day. Being a soldier myself means I don't have to rely on them to worry about me if things go bad."

Magasi nodded and led them into the building. The corridor was narrow and completely dark due to the fact its windows had been boarded over. The guards produced handheld light sources to push back the shadows and the group was forced to move in a single-file line so they weren't bumping shoulder against shoulder.

"I truly do wish we had waited to contact your people. We assumed the Faratar Canton was well and truly beaten back. We underestimated their tenacity, it would seem."

"Your people must be in dire need of assistance," Teal'c said.

Magasi sighed and nodded. "Our physicians are flummoxed, and people seem to be getting worse every day."

"Hopefully we can find what's causing it," Janet said. "Our instruments indicated the air was free from contamination. Have there been any signs that it's become airborne?"

"No, we do not believe so. The ailing have had visitors who have shown no signs of contracting the illness. And our doctors are able to tend to the sick without succumbing themselves."

Janet said, "Okay, that's a good sign. We're still going to use level-three precautions until we know what we're dealing with."

They moved through a wide foyer, down a flight of stairs, and into a large room which had been converted into an infirmary. Janet did a quick scan and counted twenty beds, all but a few of which were filled with patients. Magasi paused at the foot of the stairs and pointed at an arched doorway on the opposite side of the room. "There is another room through there with just as many people."

"Are the patients coming from any specific part of the city?" Janet said.

Magasi said, "The city is surrounded by farmland. The majority of the ailing are from there."

Teal'c said, "Would your enemy not have passed through those farms upon their retreat?"

"You're thinking biological warfare?" Janet said. Magasi looked confused, so she explained. "There's a chance your enemy is using this disease as a weapon. They might have poisoned the livestock or the water supply so these people would get sick."

Teal'c said, "It would explain why they have begun attacking again, now that your people are vulnerable."

"Abominable," Magasi said. "I do not believe even the Faratar would do something so ghastly."

One of the guards said, "They wish to annex this land, subjugate the people. Why would they poison that which they wish to own?"

"Those in search of power have done far worse things in the heat of battle."

Janet held up her hands to stop the debate. "Okay! We don't need to know exactly how this illness began, right now we just need to know what it is. Sarah, Wendy, set up over there, please?" She scanned the patients and said, "Do they know who we are? Why we're here? I don't want to just start poking and prodding without a little bit of introduction."

Magasi nodded. "We informed them that specialists were coming. They might be a little trepidatious about having an alien treating them, but I am certain it will go away if you can help ease their pain."

"I'll do what I can." She put on a pair of gloves and moved to the nearest patient. He was lying on a bed high enough that she didn't have to crouch or bend over to converse with him. His trembling hands were folded on his chest, and he was sweating through his thin shirt despite the cool temperature of the room. She offered a reassuring smile. "Hello. I'm Dr. Janet Fraiser."

"And I am Whara." He looked past her to Magasi. "Taoiseach Magasi says you are from another planet."

"That's right. It's a place called Earth. From what I've seen of your world, they're very similar. We're just a little farther along when it comes to medicine and technology. I'd like to see if I can help you."

He smiled weakly. "That would be great, Dr. Fraiser."

"Call me Janet." Wendy brought over a small medical kit. "Let's start with your symptoms..."

She spoke to several of the patients and compared their initial symptoms with those Sarah and Wendy examined. Fever, headache, nausea, cough, and abdominal pain seemed to be universal, while some were also complaining of chest pain and shortness of breath. She had just finished with her last patient when Sam came down to tell her SG-2 and SG-3 had arrived. "They're setting up a perimeter," she said as she looked around the sickroom. "Just in case the other side tries to attack again. Daniel is trying to set up a high-level meeting to discuss a more solid truce."

"Colonel O'Neill is probably furious he's missing this now."

"Oh, I'll never hear the end of it. 'Carter,'" she said, affecting a deeper, gruff voice, "'Why is it when *you* do a boring diplomatic mission, you get to have all the fun?'"

Janet chuckled. "Poor guy."

Sam looked at the patients. "How are things going down here?"

"As well as can be expected, given the circumstances. I asked for a room with ventilation to the outside so I can run some tests. I'm rushing as carefully as I can because I know General Hammond will want us back as soon as possible. Hopefully we'll know more in a few hours."

"Hours as in home by dinner or…?"

"I can't be more specific, Sam. I'm sorry. Ideally I would say you have to wait two or three days for just one result, but I know we're working against the clock."

Sam said, "Okay. Let me know if you need anything from us."

Janet thanked her and went into the makeshift laboratory. Magasi had left hours ago, but his men were still lingering near the stairs. She couldn't tell if they were there to watch her team or if they were acting as security in the event of another attack. Whether they were guards or babysitters, she was glad Teal'c had elected to remain as well. There was a high window that looked out at ground level, and Teal'c was positioned on the steps so he could see out. He loomed large above the Ialaran officials, a silent warning that Janet and her medical team were protected.

As Janet began the tests, she thought about Magasi's skepticism of her 'dichotomy.' A doctor who also served in the military. Of course she wasn't a front-line soldier. She didn't carry a P-90 into war zones to shoot Jaffa, but she had the training to do just that if the need arose. She likened it to the fact that Daniel had also become proficient in using firearms due to the nature of their jobs.

Her ex-husband had been equally confused, but for different reasons. He, like her father, was an Army grunt. There was a time just after their marriage when he tried to convince her she didn't need to work at all. She was fresh out of high school and still trying to decide what to do about college, and he floated the idea of becoming a homemaker like her mother. "There's no shame in it," he said. "Lots of women are homemakers and they're happy."

She agreed with him on that point. Her mother was one of the most fulfilled women she knew. Marjorie Fraiser raised three children while her husband was deployed. She would knit and make alterations for the other families in the neighborhood. She taught Janet the importance of having a sense of humor and living a life that was her own and not beholden to anyone else. It was her mom who convinced her to think about the military.

Her father wanted her to join the Army, like him, but her heart was set on the Air Force. She knew the Army would make her into a soldier that could mend a broken bone whereas she preferred to be a doctor who happened to have a rank and followed regulations. She wanted to be part of something, not just another cog in the machine. The Air Force would provide that.

She waited until her mind was made up before she suggested the idea to her husband. The first time she brought it up, he laughed and kept reading his magazine. The second time, he only looked at her as if she'd started speaking another language. He didn't grace her with an actual response until the third time she said she wanted to join the Air Force.

"You outta your mind, honeybuns?" He didn't even bother taking his eyes off the game. "There's a reason why they call it 'this man's army'."

"I'm not joining the Army. I'm joining the Air Force. They've had women since World War II."

"I don't know, Janet. Why don't we think about it for a little while before we do anything drastic?"

So Janet thought about it. She thought about it as she studied for and took the qualifying test, which she passed with flying colors, and the physical fitness test. When she got her results, she placed them on the dinner table just after her husband had been served. He frowned at them where they lay, and then finally picked them up and ran his eyes over the words.

"What is this?"

"It's my future," she said as she began eating. "You can either be a part of it or not."

He stared at her and then dropped the papers. "I'm proud

of you, baby. Those are some good scores. But just because you
got in doesn't mean you have to go."

"I'm pretty sure that's how it works."

He put down his fork and rested his hands on either side
of his plate. "I'm not going to be married to some flygirl soldier, Janet."

"I'll be a doctor first, a soldier second, and I doubt I'll actually be flying anything. And if that's not a person you can be
married to… then that's your choice."

The divorce went through quicker than she would have
thought. She knew he was reacting from a position of pride, a
necessity to protect himself in the eyes of his macho friends.
She considered herself lucky that she'd only lost three years
to his special brand of shortsighted misogyny. Soon she was
too busy to waste much time thinking about him. The only
time he crossed her mind was when she knew he would've
been irritated. Late hours studying instead of taking care of
him, focusing on her work rather than fulfilling his every need.

Janet pushed thoughts of him away and forced her mind
back to the task at hand. She was running the serology by rote,
using whatever shortcuts she could think of that wouldn't
compromise the results. Outside the air was suddenly split by
a wail that rose in volume until it was impossible to ignore.
Her Scottish grandmother would have warned her it was the
banshee's cry, but Janet spent most of her childhood in Texas.
She knew a storm siren when she heard one, no matter what
planet she happened to be on.

She rose from her seat and left the lab to make sure her
instinct was correct. Teal'c had taken note of the siren as well.
He held his staff weapon with a tight grip, ready to use it at
a moment's notice, and was turned so he could see the window without moving his head. The Ialaran guards were gone,
but Janet tried not to read too much into their absence. Teal'c
looked over at her before she could announce her arrival.

"Is everything okay?"

Teal'c said, "The leader of the Ialaran guard assured me it was nothing more than a weather alert. Immediately thereafter he and his men left to see if their assistance was required."

"And that took all of their men?"

"So they claim," he said quietly.

She could see through the window that the sky had darkened dramatically in the time she'd been working. She wished she'd had the foresight to adjust her watch to local time; the change in light could be due to a storm moving in or simply the approach of night. Teal'c's radio came to life with Sam's voice. She was speaking in a hushed tone that amped up Janet's worry.

"Teal'c, come in."

"I am here," he said.

"How many Ialaran guards are with you?"

Teal'c said, "They departed at the sound of the sirens."

"That's what I was afraid of. I think they know something they're not telling us. They've doubled up on guards, and every point of entrance has been turned into a blockade. And Magasi has been acting squirrely since we dropped you off in the infirmary."

Teal'c looked at Janet, who said, "Squirrely, uh, it means he's been jumpy and tense."

"I see." He inclined his head toward the window and looked outside as he ran this through his mind. "Major Carter, do you require my assistance?"

"Not yet. I just wanted to make you aware of the situation."

Janet stepped closer so she could be heard over Teal'c's radio. "Sam, it's Janet. Do you think we're at risk?"

"Not from the Banu. But I think they've gotten word their enemies are about to make a move, and they're keeping that information from us for some reason."

Janet said, "Well, it's obvious. They don't want us to leave. They finally got a medical team here that can help their people, and now they think we're going to run."

Sam said, "I'm starting to think that might not be such a

bad idea. Banu Canton pushed back their enemies once before. If we went back to the SGC until things cooled off again…"

"I won't go," Janet said. Teal'c looked at her curiously, but she ignored him. "Major, we have no idea how long it would be before we came back. Every person in this room could be dead by then. If we don't find out what's causing people to get sick, it could spread. I'm staying here until I have some answers."

There was silence on the other end of the radio. Finally Sam came back. "Okay. I'll contact the SGC to let them know things are heating up here, and I'll push Magasi for more information."

Teal'c said, "I would like to remain here with Dr. Fraiser and her team."

"I was just about to suggest that. I'll let you know if we need you up here."

He dropped his hand from the radio. "You would truly remain even if the fighting were to reach this building?"

"Of course," Janet said.

"Then I shall not leave your side."

Janet smiled. "Thank you, Teal'c. I'm going to get back to my work."

He dipped his head in a bow.

Janet checked in with Wendy, who was helping to make the patients comfortable, and then returned to the lab. Sarah looked up from her own work. "Everything okay out there?" she said.

Janet took her seat. "Night, war, or a storm. Maybe all three."

"Well, General Hammond promised us 'interesting' when we signed up."

Janet laughed. "That he did."

The war resumed at six-thirty in the evening, by Janet's watch. She knew it was much later on Ialara but it was hard to gauge having spent most of her time holed up in the lab. At first she thought it was lightning cracking overhead, but she quickly realized it was artillery fire. Teal'c received an update over the radio and left his post at the stairs to explain to her what was happening. Apparently Faratar Canton had used the storm to cover their approach, attacking as the people of Banu Canton were taking cover. Sarah finally got up the courage to ask Teal'c if they were in danger.

"Major Carter does not believe so. Magasi has surrendered the pretense of normalcy and admitted they are under siege. I believe the combined forces of the Banu military and the teams sent by the SGC shall be sufficient to hold off any direct attacks."

Janet had joined them again. "I think they'd be even more sufficient if you're up there with them."

"I shall remain here to watch over you."

Janet sighed, "Teal'c, if they get this far, we'll already be in deep trouble. I'll feel a lot safer if you're topside keeping them at bay." He hesitated again, so she put her hand on his arm to guide him back to the stairs. "I'll be fine here with Sarah and Wendy to keep working on the illness. You're wasted down here. Tell Sam I ordered you to leave your post and go help."

"I do not believe you have the authority—"

"Teal'c."

He wisely reconsidered finishing the thought.

"We have radios to call for help and we have guns to hold off anyone that does get this far. Just go up there and make sure they don't get a chance."

"As you wish, Dr. Fraiser."

He turned and ascended the stairs two at a time, ducking through the doorway at the top and disappearing onto the ground level. Outside, Janet heard another volley of small-arms fire. It sounded even closer than it had before, but her anxiety was eased by the familiar clatter of a P90 in response. She looked away from the rain-streaked window and saw Wendy and Sarah were watching her. They were Air Force officers, just like her, and she knew they would have made the same decision if they were in charge.

"How are we doing?"

Sarah said, "We can have extremely preliminary results

from the serology in a few hours. We can look for specific things and eliminate what it isn't."

"A few patients required tranquilizers when the storm moved in," Wendy reported. "They're resting comfortably, and I'm monitoring them to make sure there are no adverse reactions."

"Keep up the good work, Wendy. Sarah, let's get back to it."

Well aware of how long she'd been on the planet, and knowing how she would react if a member of any team revealed they hadn't eaten, Janet searched the pockets of her vest until she found a protein bar. She tore it open and ate as she stared at the work table.

She wanted to be confident for Wendy and Sarah, and especially for SG-1, but there was a possibility she wouldn't find the answer. She'd operated under much stricter time limits than these, been forced to compromise proper procedure to beat a ticking clock, but there wasn't much that could compare to an army beating down the door. If the Faratan Canton took over again, there was a chance anyone she saved would just be taken prisoner or killed. But she couldn't think like that. She had to keep searching for the answer as long as she was able.

She had trained for moments like this. She had spent years studying how to isolate and treat exotic diseases in the most remote locations imaginable. Of course, at the time, her idea of a remote posting was Afghanistan or maybe Sudan. Alien worlds were an impossibility she never even once entertained. In her time at the SGC she'd seen truly remarkable, terrible things. She now faced diseases that had no corollary on Earth, or which affected alien physiology but couldn't cross over to the Tau'ri, or ancient viruses that had been wiped out for centuries only to thrive on some alien world. In all these cases it fell to her expertise to find out what was causing the ailment and not only how to cure it, but how to ensure the diseases didn't spread to Earth. It was a responsibility she didn't take lightly.

And she would never forget how fortunate she was to serve at the SGC. Seven years earlier she'd been working at the Air

Force Academy Hospital when she was ordered to report to Cheyenne Mountain. Their chief medical officer had been killed and she was the closest ranking physician available to fill in. She didn't know what to expect when she arrived at what she assumed was NORAD, but the stack of non-disclosure forms and the veritable wall of security made her incredibly anxious as she was led into the bowels of the mountain. Despite all the buildup, when she finally stepped out of the elevator she found herself in the same unremarkable concrete box she recognized from other postings. Between her own work and her father's career, it seemed half her life had been spent in corridors just like that one.

Standing at the intersection of the corridors was General George Hammond. Janet smiled when she thought about the first time she met him. Hammond looked like a big bear of a man but his face was kind and comforting. He chuckled slightly when he saw how wide-eyed she was. "It's a bit daunting, isn't it?"

"Yes, sir. I thought I was only filling in until a more permanent replacement could be found."

"That was the plan. And if you decide to leave after you see what I'm about to show you, no one would think any less of you."

"But I still had to sign a novel's worth of NDAs just to hear the pitch?"

"It's a hell of a pitch." He was leading Janet away from the airmen who had escorted her this far. "How much were you told?"

"The doctor I'm replacing was killed," she said, "and that this is an unexpectedly dangerous posting. I assume that was a reference to the fact this mountain a potential target for terrorists."

"In a manner of speaking." They had arrived in the briefing room. A blast door covered the window at the far side of the room. Hammond approached it and rested his hand on a button. "Once I press this button, your entire world is going to change."

Janet smiled. "I'm not a fan of hyperbole, sir."

"Nor am I."

He pressed the button and the blast door slowly lifted.

Janet stepped forward, the smile fading from her face as she approached the glass. She couldn't make sense of what she was seeing. Her mind tried to fill in the details so that she thought she was looking at the aft-end of a shuttle, but there was only a single engine. But after taking in the whole picture she realized there was nothing behind the massive ring. Even more curious was the ramp leading up to the circle.

"What is it?"

Hammond looked at his watch. "You finished your paperwork faster than I thought you would. In a few minutes you're going to see something truly remarkable. Dr. Fraiser... that is the Stargate."

She watched the technicians moving around in the room below as he explained. Giza. Abydos. Parasitic aliens in giant pyramid ships. When he was finished, Janet laughed.

"I assure you I'm serious."

"Oh, I know, sir. I know. But aliens? A portal to outer space? Soldiers going through and fighting aliens? What could you possibly need me for?"

The Stargate suddenly came to life and Janet took a step back. Hammond stepped closer to her and they watched as the technicians fled and armed soldiers took position with their weapons aimed at the empty center of the ring. Janet stared at that empty space but an initial flash of light made her close her eyes. When she opened them something else had filled the space. Something she didn't have the words for. It swirled out like a giant fist made of water before collapsing into a serene pool that bathed the room in soft blue light. Seconds later, a team walked through the wall of water.

"Where did they come from?" she whispered.

"A planet called P41-229. It's a mostly uninhabited planet approximately thirty-five hundred light years from Earth. That is SG-1. As for what we need you for, Doctor... we need you to keep them safe."

Janet breathed in and whistled slowly. "Sounds like a heck of a job. I assume I start now?"

Hammond smiled. "Let me show you to the infirmary."

Her first assignment at the SGC had been post-mission examinations for SG-1. Since then she'd examined the team countless times. Before, during, and after missions they would come to her — or be brought to her, as was often the case — and it would be up to her to find out what was wrong. Adult alien male stung by an unknown alien insect. Two adult human males and one adult human female suffering addiction-like effects due to an Ancient device worn as an armband. Unknown residue causing the team to have vivid memories of a person who never existed. And, of course, there was the time the entire team was replaced by robots. Their work was dangerous, but at least it was never boring.

Her reverie was broken when Daniel cleared his throat behind her. She realized how close she had been to dozing off as she turned in her chair to face him. He was standing in the doorway, his uniform rumpled and wet at the shoulders from being out in the rain.

"Hi," she said. "Sorry, I was off in my mind. I thought you were setting up negotiations with the other side."

"I was. I am. It's a work in progress, and at the moment they're refusing to talk. I was wondering if you had anything that could keep me from falling asleep. I want to be awake if the other side agrees to come back to the table."

"Sure. I have some caffeine pills here somewhere." She went to their supplies and retrieved the bottle. "Other than the stubborn negotiators, how do things look up there?"

He sighed heavily and swallowed the pills dry. "Two steps forward and one step back. The same as it always is." He looked through the door at the patients. "And down here?"

"Oh, you know. Identify and cure an alien disease in the space of a single evening. Kid stuff."

Daniel smiled. "You know, Jack does the same thing with Sam that she's doing with you. Points her at some piece of technology she's never even seen before and tells her to figure it out. Most of the time she has about five minutes to become an expert. He has faith that she'll succeed because he knows what she's capable of. Sam wouldn't be pushing you to solve this puzzle unless she really thought you could do it. With anyone else, we probably would have been back on Earth hours ago."

"Thank you, Daniel. And, you know, figuring out common ground between two alien cultures is no mean feat, either."

He smiled. "I wasn't fishing for the compliment, but it's appreciated. I better get back up there." He held out the bottle to her.

"Keep it. We don't have any coffee and we all have a long night ahead of us. Just use it in moderation."

He thanked her with a nod and went back up the stairs. Almost as soon as he was gone, Wendy called out to her. "Dr. Fraiser? Could you come here for a moment? Please?"

Janet retrieved the wadded-up wrapper of her protein bar and put it in her vest pocket. Wendy's voice had come from the second chamber, so she passed the beds of the sleeping patients and entered the darker room. They had three lighting sources set up to provide the most light, and Wendy was standing just behind one of them where the shadows were thickest. A man loomed behind her with a blade against her throat.

Janet stopped where she was and lifted her hands to show she wasn't carrying a weapon. The man wore a uniform that didn't resemble Magasi or his people, so she assumed he was from the other canton. Rain and sweat had left streaks in the mud on his face. He strengthened his grip on the handle of his knife and rested the blade against Wendy's throat. Wendy held her chin up and stared at Janet with frightened, unblinking eyes.

"Who else is here?"

"Just another nurse," Janet said. "She's unarmed. We're all unarmed. You don't need that knife."

"You were just talking to someone. I heard a man's voice."

"He left. He went back upstairs. We're alone."

He showed his teeth, either in a grimace or a smirk. "You're not Banu and those aren't Ostan Canton uniforms. Who are you? Where did you come from?"

"We came through that ring in the courtyard. It's called a Stargate." She smelled ozone and heard water dripping onto stone; she assumed the man had crawled in through some sub-basement or sewage line and the way was still open. She tried to hear if anyone else was following him, but the room seemed still. "We're doctors. Taoiseach Magasi asked us to come here to help with the outbreak."

"Outbreak." He looked at the patients and took a shuffling step back. He pulled Wendy with him, using her as a shield. "What... what happened to them?"

Janet lowered her hands a bit. "Oh... oh, God, you don't know? Magasi implied that the illness was the reason your people retreated."

He narrowed his eyes. "We know nothing of this illness."

"Oh. Oh, no." Janet met Wendy's eye. "Did he get the vaccine?"

"No, Dr. Fraiser." Her voice was strained but her eye contact with Janet was steady. "I didn't get a chance to warn him."

Janet said, "Sir, I am a doctor. I don't care about your war, I only care about treating my patients no matter who they might be. And I think you're about to become one of them. This disease is extremely contagious. Just being in this room and breathing the air means you're infected."

He blinked rapidly. "You're not wearing any masks."

"We've been inoculated. It was the first thing we did when we came to the planet. That's why Magasi had to call aliens to treat his people. Do you feel queasy? Like your stomach is unsettled? That's one of the first symptoms."

"There are others?"

"Shortness of breath, tremors, blurry vision... No one has to know you're here or that you received treatment. But if you start feeling those symptoms, I need to give you the inoculation as soon as possible." Outside thunder cracked, and Wendy hissed as the blade nicked her skin. Janet winced in sympathy. "Sir. Please. You said yourself that we're not part of this war. I don't know if Magasi's side is right and I don't care. We don't have weapons. We're physicians. We're only interested in treating the illness."

"You're lying." He squeezed his eyes shut and opened them wider, furrowing his brow. The man was obviously exhausted, but she knew her list of symptoms had worked their way into his brain. Now every twist of his stomach and every drop of sweat in his eye was a sign he was succumbing to the illness.

Janet hardened her voice. "Look, it's your choice. Either you put down that blade and let us help you, or you collapse and we try to keep you alive. I'm just afraid you'll take my nurse with you when you fall and then you'll be completely out of luck. Make your decision before the sickness makes it for you!"

He dropped the knife to his side and shoved Wendy away from him. Janet stepped forward to catch her before she hit the ground. "Are you okay?" she asked.

Wendy said, "It's just a little cut."

An arc of blue light shot past Janet, rising from a low angle near the ground. The soldier managed to take one step before the zat blast hit him. He tried to remain upright but succeeded only in moving the knife out to one side so he didn't fall onto it. Janet turned as Sarah closed the zat and pushed herself up off the floor. She had been crouching against the wall so the intruder wouldn't see her when she leaned out to take the shot. She was pale, and her hands were shaking as she put the weapon back on her thigh holster. It took her three tries to make it catch.

"I've never shot anyone before," she said.

"You still haven't. Not really." Janet reached out and patted her arm. "Contact —"

Sarah said, "I already radioed them. Teal'c is on his way."

"Good work. Both of you, excellent work. See if you can find something to tie him up."

As if he had been summoned, Teal'c burst through the doorway and descended down the stairs at a dead run.

"Slow down!" Janet said. "We've taken care of him."

Teal'c looked at the man, rising from an attack position to a more restful stance. He offered Janet one of his rare smiles. "It would seem you did not require my guardianship after all."

"Never mess with a doctor," Janet said, sweeping her hair out of her face. "We know the best ways to screw you up."

"How was he able to gain access?"

Wendy pointed across the room. "He crawled in through that. I think it's some kind of drainage pipe that leads outside."

"I will ensure that no one else takes advantage of it." He crouched and lifted the man as if he weighed nothing. "And I shall find a place to keep him securely."

"Thank you, Teal'c. Sarah, would you help Wendy with the cut on her neck?"

Sarah said, "Yes, doctor."

Janet inhaled slowly to steady her jangled nerves and then went back to the lab. She had a real enemy who needed to be vanquished, and she doubted it would be defeated as easily as the Faratar intruder had been.

Someone gently squeezed her shoulder and then rubbed her back. "Janet?"

She opened her eyes and sat up as she remembered where she was. Sam chuckled. "Easy. It's just me. You fell asleep."

Janet groaned and rubbed her eyes. The basement was considerably brighter than she remembered it being. The sounds of the storm had abated to leave the world silent and still.

"Q Fever," Janet said. "We figured it out this morning. It's a bacterial infection that can be spread by contact with farm animals. That's why the cases were coming from the outskirts of the city, the farms." She rubbed her face. "I need to start treatment."

"Your nurses are already administering antibiotics."

"Right." She remembered giving the order before she called

Sam on the radio to report their breakthrough. But first she'd put her head down to rest her eyes. How many hours had it been? "Sorry."

Sam leaned her hip against the table. "Hey, going by Earth's clock, you've been awake for about thirty-two hours. You were dealing with an alien outbreak and, according to Teal'c, you fought off an intruder at the same time. I think you earned a nap."

Janet sighed. "I suppose so. How about you?"

"When the storm passed, it was easier to see where the Faratan squadrons were set up. They were willing to face the Banu weaponry, but P90s and Teal'c's staff weapon have more range and firepower than they expected. We managed to run them off pretty quickly this morning. Magasi is worried that they might try again after we leave."

"You can tell Magasi he might have a bargaining chip. Q Fever has an incubation period of about forty days. If the Faratan people were living in this city and eating its animals, there's a good chance they're going to have an outbreak like this very soon. If they don't already. Magasi can offer the treatment as leverage to stop further attacks."

Sam said, "That would be a nice, peaceful solution to this whole mess. I'll run it by him."

"Let him know that I'm willing to train their physicians so they can administer the treatment themselves."

"I will." She straightened and started to leave, then came back. "You know... back on Earth, it's the day after we left."

Janet frowned at her, not understanding. "Yes?"

Sam smiled. "Happy anniversary."

Janet tensed slightly. She didn't mind Sam knowing, but she was still surprised. "How did you know?"

"You told me once a few years ago. I was over to play chess with Cassandra, and you mentioned it in passing. The anniversary of leaving your husband and starting on the path to the Air Force. Heck of a celebration, huh?"

"I can't think of a better way to spend it."

"Well, if you'll give me a chance to change your mind, I'll treat you to a girls' night when we get back to Earth."

Janet said, "That is a deal. We'll have one of the boys check in on Cassandra."

Sam chuckled. "I'll let you get back to it. General Hammond wanted an update, so I'll let him know that we shouldn't be here much longer."

Janet turned back to the work table. It was hard to believe how far she'd come since that one decision. The choice to let the Air Force pay for her college had been a means to an end. She never expected to love it so much. She never dreamed she would love it so much. And of course she couldn't have anticipated the opportunities granted by being assigned to the SGC. She was treating an alien on a regular basis. Her daughter, her gorgeous and brilliant pain in the butt daughter, was from another world, and Janet never would have known her without this job.

She got to travel to strange, faraway lands and usually still be home in time for dinner. She was practicing true frontier medicine in a way modern doctors could only dream of. The work was difficult, sometimes verging on the impossible, and it was extraordinarily dangerous on so many fronts. But she knew that she made the right decision all those years ago. She was exactly where she belonged, and there was nothing about her life that she would change even if she was given the opportunity.

The universe had given her a job, and she intended to do it as long as possible, no matter where it took her.

STARGATE ATLANTIS
Iron Horse

Amy Griswold

Specialist Ronon Dex put his feet up on the seat across from him, watching the Satedan countryside roll by outside the window of the troop train.

Ara elbowed his feet out of the way and leaned forward to look out the window herself. The troop train was crowded, but Ronon and his friends had found two rows of seats facing each other, and piled all their gear on the empty seat beside Ronon. "I can't believe we're finally getting out of that dump," she said.

"You say that like the training grounds aren't your favorite place in the world," Tyre said. He stretched out his own legs, propping his feet on the heaped-up packs. "Who doesn't love getting woken up an hour before dawn to run five miles?"

"I don't know," Ronon said. "Who doesn't?"

Ara kicked him in the knee in a friendly fashion. "You're such a good boy."

"We'll see how good he is once we hit the capital," Tyre said. "Myself, I'm looking forward to being in a town with some actual nightlife. Besides the rats trying to get into the mess hall garbage cans."

The train rattled across a narrow railroad bridge, shaking and swaying as they crossed the gap. They were passing through high hill country, the bare caps of the mountains jutting up like bleached bone from out of their skin of trees.

"It's probably going to be boring," Ronon said.

"Honor guard for the Travelers' first visit to Sateda in almost ten years," Tyre said, rolling the words around in his mouth. "That has a nice ring to it."

"Honor guard means we're going to stand around while important people talk," Ronon said.

"Don't be a sourpuss," Ara said. "We'll have all that off-duty time to spend in the capital. Come on, you grew up there. Don't tell me you don't know all the best dance halls."

"Or at least all the worst bars," Tyre said.

Ronon didn't particularly feel like pointing out that he'd been seventeen when he'd left the city to begin his years of military training, and that his mother would have dragged him out of a dance hall by his ear if he'd ever ventured inside. "Sure."

"See? We'll be in good hands," Ara said.

"If we keep out of Kell's way."

"That's the beauty of it," Tyre said. "He's the Task Master, so he's going to wind up entertaining the dignitaries."

"Or at least having a seat somewhere far down the table from the dignitaries," Ara said.

"I don't know, I get the impression he's in good with some people," Tyre said. "In any event, he'll be busy, and as long as we report for duty in the morning reasonably sober —"

"And don't get arrested," Ronon said.

"Then we've got the whole city for our playground."

The city had never seemed much like a playground to Ronon when he was younger, just the dull concrete and brick backdrop he trudged through on his way to and from school. He'd been happier out in the woods with his grandfather, learning to track and hunt on crisp mornings when his breath fogged the air. He had to admit it would be different, though, coming back to the city in a sharp uniform, and heading out for the evening into streets filled with bright lights and laughter and music.

"We probably shouldn't get arrested," Ara said.

"You worry too much," Tyre said. "We'll be fine. And there'll be all that sweet Traveler merchandise on sale, too."

"Marked up about five hundred percent from what it would sell for anywhere but Sateda," Ronon said.

"It will be by the time it gets into stores," Tyre said. "But we can get it directly from the source."

"We're not really going to get to talk to the Travelers," Ronon said, and tried not to wonder how much one of the Travelers' energy pistols would sell for. About a year's pay, he figured, even at the prices the Travelers charged at the trading fair on Belkan. By the time the stores in the Satedan capital marked them up, nobody below Kell's rank would be able to get their hands on one. He'd seen pictures, though, and couldn't help dreaming.

They were rattling their way downhill when the train began slowing. A chorus of complaints and catcalls arose throughout the train compartment.

"This isn't a local!" someone yelled.

"Maybe we ought to get out and push!"

"Hey, conductor, want to buy a map?"

Ronon frowned. "Think the train's broken down?"

"No," Ara said, pushing the smudged window down and leaning halfway out to see, her hands braced on the window frame. "The flag's out."

"Something on the line, maybe," Ronon said. But they were past the mountain cuts where loose rock slid down to block the tracks every spring, shaken free as the winter's ice melted. The tracks here ran through a wide river valley, the river itself lazy and tame where it spilled from the towering dam that overshadowed the valley.

The train shuddered to a stop, and then sat unmoving. As the delay dragged on, the complaints increased in both volume and profanity until the compartment door finally opened and Kell stepped through.

The noise cut off abruptly, and the troops scrambled to attention, Ronon finding the best compromise he could between standing straight and knocking his head against the low roof of the train compartment.

"We'll be getting off here," Kell said. He cut off the beginnings of a roar of protest with his expression alone. Some of the officers at the training camp had done a lot of shouting, but Kell had never needed to. He was the kind of man soldiers listened to, the kind of man they respected. The kind of man Ronon wanted to be himself, one day, although he hoped he wouldn't have thinning hair by the time he wore a commander's uniform.

"Yes, Task Master!" he said, which he hoped excused adding, "What's the holdup, Task Master?"

"A good question, and one that's going to get an answer, because that wasn't either a complaint or unprintable — yes, I heard you, Viren, so watch your mouth. This, ladies and gentlemen, is the town of Ironlode. This morning, an earthquake brought down a rockslide that destroyed several farms and a good part of the town as well. They've got missing people, wounded people, and no one to sort it out but a handful of nurses who happened to be on the last train through. We will be sorting it out for them." Kell looked around the compartment. "Any questions?"

"No, Task Master!" Ronon said, and pushed disappointment firmly aside. Being in the army was supposed to be about helping people, not about being admired in his uniform. Besides, if they sorted it out quickly enough, they might not miss the party entirely.

He clambered down from the train and out onto the platform. The town nestled in a valley between two high hills, one rising to the top of the dam, with a winding trail climbing up to the cataract of water that rushed from the dam face, and the other sheltering the town to the south. The southward hill was marred by the broad scar of a mudslide, and Ronon could see the tumbled houses and broken trees at the base of the hill.

It was bad, but not as bad as he'd been afraid it might be. The town still stood, and although he saw a few burnt-out roofs, any fires caused by tipped-over lanterns or cooking fires had clearly already been extinguished. The smoke that rose from chimneys was scented with the smell of cooking food.

Tyre followed his gaze to the burned houses, and then looked up at the dam. "I thought the point of the dam was to get electricity out here."

"Electricity still costs money," Ronon said. "My grandfather lived in a little town like this. He still chopped firewood and used kerosene lamps. Said it was a waste of money to use electricity for anything but listening to the radio."

Some of his earliest childhood memories were of hunting in the woods near his grandfather's cabin. Later, after his grandfather succumbed to the Second Childhood, he'd gone out to the cabin with his father, and finally alone. Now, with his army duties, it might be months or years before he got back. This place smelled the same, though, the sharp smell of evergreen trees and the earthy smell of clay.

Kell was organizing the troops into patrols, forming them up on the wooden train platform and sending them off in small groups. Ronon took a step toward him, and then stopped as a young woman hurried up the steps to the platform, stumbled on the last step, and nearly pitched off the wooden platform into the shrubs below.

He steadied her on her feet, and she gave him a tired and seemingly automatic smile before her eyes focused on his face. "Are you in charge here?"

He shook his head with an answering smile and nodded toward Kell, who was surrounded by men waiting for their assignments. Her face fell.

"I'm a nurse. I have patients who need to be evacuated to the city. There isn't even a real doctor here, just a chemist's shop…"

"That's what I figured," Ronon said. The honey-blond woman's dress was streaked with rusty blood and darker soot. "It's lucky you were here."

She shrugged one shoulder, dismissing the importance of luck, or maybe of her efforts. "I was on holiday with my friends. We're all hospital nurses, so of course we got off here when we heard what had happened."

"It's not 'of course'."

"It is for a nurse." She nodded toward a large building that Ronon guessed was the town hall, its doors wide open and people camped outside on the lawn. "We've got half a dozen patients who need to be in a hospital. If we have to wait until the train comes in the morning, we may lose one of them. Is the troop train going to wait for us to get them loaded on board?"

"Hey, Task Master!" Ronon called.

Kell's head came up, his immediate frown softening as he saw the nurse. He waved off the soldiers gathered around him and strode down the platform to Ronon. "What's the problem, specialist?"

"This is…" Ronon began, and then realized he didn't know the woman's name.

"Melena Omi," the nurse said.

"She's got wounded people who need to evacuate by train."

"We'll hold the train rather than sending it on without us," Kell said. "You three help get the wounded loaded."

"Thanks so much," Ara said under her breath as they followed Melena into the town hall.

"What are you, squeamish?"

She elbowed him in the ribs, not gently. "No, I just prefer to deal with people who are bleeding because I hurt them. Not because they were just in the wrong place at the wrong time. That doesn't seem fair."

"Most of what happens to people isn't fair," Tyre said.

Ronon wasn't sure he agreed, but as Melena led him to the side of a little girl who couldn't have been more than six years old, he thought Tyre might have a point. Below the tourniquet on her leg, the skin of her ankle was gray above the heavy club of her bandaged foot, and the bandages were soaked through with dark blood. A hospital might pull her through, but she'd probably lose the foot.

The town hall was a single room with heavy trestle tables

pushed up against the walls, probably the site of holiday dinners and town meetings. Now it was a makeshift infirmary for what seemed like half the town, every chair and much of the floor occupied by people who were bleeding or nursing broken limbs. The worst of them were laid out on the tables, like the girl in front of him.

"Let's get you onto the train," he said, and bent to hoist her. She was clutching a rag doll in the crook of her arm, and clung to it desperately tight as he lifted her off the ground. Someone had made makeshift stretchers, but he didn't need help to carry her, as small as she was. She huddled in an unhappy knot, her lips moving against the doll's hair as if mouthing words of empty comfort.

He carried her out to the platform and handed her up to two other soldiers who were waiting to load people aboard the train, hoping one of them knew more than he did about children. When he got back to the town hall, Tyre was struggling to settle a restless man on his stretcher so that he and Ara could lift it.

"Just be still," Melena said at the man's head. She shook her head worriedly. "I'm afraid there's some internal bleeding. We need to get you to a hospital."

"You have to get out," the man said. "Get the children out."

Ronon frowned at Tyre, unsure of what to say. There might still be survivors buried under the rubble, but after so many hours, it was increasingly unlikely that anyone else would be found alive.

"There are patrols out looking for survivors right now," Tyre said, lifting the head of the stretcher while Ara hoisted the other end. "I'm sure we'll find them."

"No!" the man shouted, grabbing Tyre's wrist and almost tumbling off the stretcher to the dirt below. Ronon steadied the stretcher, and Melena grasped the man's shoulder, pressing him back down against the canvas.

"Hold still," Ronon said.

"Get them all out. The iron horse is gone. The earthquake is coming. You can't stay here."

"You're exactly right," Melena said, shooting Tyre a sharp look when he opened his mouth. "You can't stay here, because of the earthquake. That's why we're taking you to the train."

The man sagged back against the canvas as if abruptly running out of energy to protest. "Out of here. Yes. The earthquake is coming. Get them out."

Tyre and Ara hauled him away, and Ronon looked questioningly at Melena.

"He's confused," she said. "Not a surprise."

"He's right," an old man sitting in a chair nearby said. One arm was splinted, and there were dark bruises down one side of his tan face, but he sat ramrod straight, gazing out the window not in the direction of the rockslide, but up toward the distant shadow of the dam. "There'll be another quake."

"Sometimes there are aftershocks," Ronon said. "But they're usually not as bad as the first earthquake."

The man shook his head, uncomforted. "This morning was just the beginning. They've taken the iron horse away, and we'll all be buried or drowned soon enough."

"Iron horse," Ronon said. He looked up questioningly at Melena, who shrugged as if to say that she didn't know what the man was talking about either.

"A charm," the man said. "A statue. Up in the shrine at the top of the falls. That's where it's been since before the Wraith last came — more than two hundred years, it's been there. Maybe a lot longer than that. We found the shrine in my grandfather's time, when this town was building up and people started logging up in the hills. But we showed the proper respect. We kept the iron horse safe. And in return it's protected us all this time. Kept the earth from moving."

Ara and Tyre came back in at that point, and Ronon waved them over but motioned for them to stay quiet. "How does it do that?"

"How should I know? I only know it keeps us safe. It kept us safe. Until those city folk came in to build that dam. We told them that the iron horse had to be kept in its place, and they promised they would. Even built a little nook to put it in, out on the dam. And they hired on some of us to do maintenance up at the dam, and put in this electricity. Electric lights and all that. But they were only thieves in the end."

"You think the earthquake is because someone moved a magical charm?" Melena asked. Her voice was kind, but she didn't sound like she believed it.

"I know they did. Kif, the one who's bleeding into his belly, he was up at the dam when the earthquake came. He saw himself that the iron horse was gone, right before the quake hit."

"Huh," Ronon said.

"And I'll tell you another thing. Those city folk up at the dam, they made a lot of fuss over that horse when they first came, saying it should be in the Museum. I expect they sent it off there, and now we're the ones who have to pay for it."

"We'll see if we can find out what's happened to it," Melena said. "But now you have to rest. You're not a young man."

"I'm not going to get any older," the man said, and set his mouth in a firm line that discouraged any more attempts at conversation.

Melena drew Ronon and his friends aside. "People grasp at any kind of explanation when bad things happen to them," she said. "I just hope this rumor isn't flying around making everyone worry that there's going to be another earthquake."

Ronon shrugged. "What if it's true?"

"Come on," Tyre said. "An iron horse in a shrine that prevents earthquakes?"

Ara shrugged. "I've heard of stranger things."

"There's no such thing as magic," Melena said firmly. "This is just an unfortunate superstition."

"I didn't say it was magic," Ronon said. "But Ara's right. The villagers believe this thing works —"

"Because they've never had an earthquake since the town was founded. Just like a lot of other places. It's a coincidence."

"And the fact that it was missing this morning?"

"A coincidence," Tyre said, although he sounded less confident.

"If it even happened," Melena said. "The townspeople believe that the charm protects them from earthquakes, they have an earthquake, and, big surprise, someone who's badly injured and confused remembers seeing that the charm was missing from the shrine. I'd be more surprised if no one claimed the charm was missing."

"I think we ought to tell Kell," Ronon said.

"And I think you're crazy," Tyre said. "If you want to convince our Task Master that you believe in every campfire story you hear—"

"Maybe we should go up on the dam and take a look," Ara said. "At least we can see whether the thing is still there or not."

The town hall door burst open at that moment, and a woman in coveralls stood in the doorway, her face grim. "You can't let anyone go up on the dam," she said. "You've got to evacuate the town. There's going to be another earthquake, and I don't think the dam is going to stand the strain."

Shocked voices rose in alarm.

"You're all going to be fine," Melena said. "Wait for the soldiers to help you board the train." Tyre and Ara picked up the nearest stretcher, moving with more urgency now, as Melena caught the newcomer by the arm and dragged her past the door into the town hall's kitchen. Ronon followed.

"I have injured patients here!" Melena rounded on the newcomer. "You can't come in here and frighten them like that."

"They ought to be frightened," the other woman said. A nameplate on her coverall pronounced her name to be Soro. Her heavy braids were straggling down out of a knot at the back of her neck, and her brown skin was streaked with blood, but she didn't seem badly hurt. "The iron horse that should be up at the dam is missing."

"It's just a superstition," Melena said.

"You sound awfully certain about something you know nothing about," Soro said, more wearily than angrily. "Are you a structural engineer? Or a seismologist?"

Bright spots of color stood out in Melena's cheeks. "No. Are you?"

"I'm an engineer. But our seismologists were the ones who examined the artifact that was found up at the dam site. The statue is local workmanship, probably five hundred years old. The device *inside* the statue was made by the Ancestors. It's meant to neutralize tectonic forces — do you know what that means?"

Melena was frankly blushing, now, but she kept her chin high. "Sort of."

"Big shelves of rock move underground," Soro said, sliding her hands against each other. "But they don't move smoothly. Sometimes they get stuck. The pressure builds up, and then…" She shoved her hands past each other and let her fingers fly open. "You get earthquakes. The ground shakes apart. The Ancient device has been stabilizing this area, preventing quakes. It's probably just transferring the stress down the fault to somewhere else, but that somewhere else isn't an inhabited area underneath a massive dam."

"That's why you left the statue on the dam," Ronon said.

"As close to the original shrine as possible. That and the fact that we don't actually like antagonizing the local residents when there's an easy way to prevent it. But in this case, we would have fought to keep the iron horse in place. It's the only reason we felt safe building the dam in an area that would otherwise be earthquake-prone."

"I'm assuming your people didn't send it off to the Museum, then."

"We would never do that," Soro said. "Is that what people are saying happened?"

"People are scared," Melena said.

"They probably should be. No, I don't know what happened to the device. Yesterday it was up in its usual place — there's a niche for it built into the external structure of the dam. It's open to the front of the dam — we wanted to replicate the conditions of the original shrine as much as possible, and that meant leaving it exposed to open air and the spray from the waterfall — but we usually access it through a maintenance tunnel. The first I knew that anything was wrong was when Kif came running down saying that the iron horse was missing. Then the earthquake started."

"How safe is the dam?" Melena asked quietly.

"It's intact. But another big earthquake . . . I can't make any promises. We need to evacuate the entire river valley. If the dam breaks, it's all going to flood."

"Evacuate how?" Ronon asked flatly. "The troop train won't fit half the people in Ironlode, and that's just one town. I doubt there's a truck in town. The next regular train doesn't come through until tomorrow morning. We can radio back to Redfell and see if they can run a special train, but that may not get here any sooner."

"Then get as many people as you can out now and as many as you can tomorrow morning," Soro said. "I can't tell you exactly when the next quake is coming. It could be tonight, or it could be two or three days from now. But not much longer. And when it comes, it's going to tear this valley apart."

"Go tell all of this to Task Master Kell," Ronon told her. "He can radio back and try to get another train through. Tell him to send more troops down here to help load the less seriously wounded patients onto the train."

"What are you going to do?" Melena asked.

"Find the iron horse and put it back."

He filled Tyre and Ara in on what they'd missed as the three of them hiked up the hill toward the dam. "I figure the most likely thing is the iron horse is still here in town," Ronon said.

"Why would you steal it and then stay in town?" Tyre asked.

"Why steal it at all?" Ara asked. "If you're a local, and you know that the horse protects against earthquakes, why would you move it?"

"Maybe to destroy the dam. There are some old-timers around here who liked it better before the dam went in."

"If the dam goes, it's going to take out everything downstream," Ronon said. "No one would have done that. No, I figure one of two things. Either somebody who isn't from Ironlode moved it for some stupid reason — maybe they were cleaning, maybe they wanted to take a picture of it, whatever — or somebody who wasn't from Ironlode stole it."

Ara shrugged. "How does knowing that help?"

The trail wound back and forth up the steep hillside. Beside them, the dam face dropped off like a concrete cliff, water cascading white and furious down to the river below.

"Because either way I figure they're still here," Ronon said. "Melena said no one left town on the first train. She and her friends got off, but no one got on. If somebody moved the horse by accident, they would have taken it into town or into the dam control room, unless they were hurt or trapped somewhere up here. Which they might be."

"And if someone from the city took it?" Ara asked.

"Then they're planning to make their way somewhere else on foot. There's no other way of getting out of here without being noticed. Even if you had a truck, somebody would have noticed the truck."

The trail ran out shortly before the top of the hill, turning off toward the waterfall and then ending abruptly. Someone had put up a metal railing to keep people from falling. Above where the path ended — probably where the shrine had once been, when this was a lazy series of waterfalls rather than the spillway of an artificial lake — a set of much newer paved stairs ran up to a railed catwalk that stretched across the face of the dam.

"How do we get inside?" Tyre said.

"I'm not sure we need to get inside," Ronon said. "Stop walking around." He crouched to get a better look at the tracks on the trail. Someone had come up here in dry shoes, walked out onto the catwalk, and then come back in wet shoes. And the prints of the shoes were interesting. "Either of you see anybody down there wearing rubber-soled shoes?"

"The nurses," Ara said. "And our unit."

"Anybody else?"

"No."

"Neither did I. They're all wearing leather-soled shoes. Probably made somewhere local." He followed the tracks back to the trail, and then away from it, toward the top of the hill. "These shoes have rubber soles, but I've never seen a pair that made tracks like this."

"Somebody bought new shoes in the city," Tyre said.

"Maybe. It wasn't one of the nurses, though."

"They didn't even get here until after the earthquake," Ara said.

"And they've got smaller feet." The tracks were easy to follow. The ground was wet; it had probably rained not long before the earthquake, setting the stage for the landslide. "He came up here and started walking along the edge of the lake."

"Maybe he lowered it into the lake," Tyre said. "He could come back for it later."

Ara rolled her eyes. "If it were that close to where it's supposed to be, there wouldn't have been an earthquake, would there?"

"How would I know?"

"He didn't put it in the lake," Ronon said. "He turned off here." The tracks were fainter, here, but still possible to follow, and still going in both directions. Not only had whoever he was tracking carried the iron horse up to the lake and then into the woods that surrounded it, he'd come from this direction, too. "What's up here besides the lake?"

"Not much," Tyre said. "There used to be some towns up along the river, but they flooded them when they put the dam in. And the train doesn't run this way. I don't think there's a town closer than a couple of days' walk."

The underbrush was getting heavy, and he found a patch where someone had hacked their way through it with a heavy knife. He sniffed at the cut branches. "Smells like machine oil."

"There's nothing back here," Ara said.

"Something's back here." The tracks on the ground were getting harder to read in the springy underbrush, but whoever had come this way had blundered through the woods, and hacked at branches every time they got thick. Ronon pushed branches aside more carefully, and emerged into a small clearing between towering evergreen trees.

He drew his weapon, and after a moment's hesitation, Ara and Tyre did so as well. If someone was hiding up here, scared, Ronon didn't want to stumble on them unarmed. "Anybody here?"

If someone were up here hurt or lost, they would have called out. Unless they were unconscious. But the tracks were even and widely spaced, the steps of a man walking quickly, not staggering in pain and confusion. He kept his eyes on the tracks, trusting Ara and Tyre to cover him.

They led out into the middle of the clearing, and then abruptly ended. Beyond them, the grass was crushed under the weight of something heavy, with deeper indentations in regular shapes at both ends of a long rectangle. It looked like a vehicle had been parked there, if a vehicle could suddenly appear in the middle of a clearing without having been driven there. Only the shapes weren't wheels or treads, but something more like feet.

Ronon crouched to get a better look. The chemical stink was stronger, here, not just the smell of machine oil, but a sharper smell like kerosene. Some of the grass was brown, and when he touched it, it felt crisp under his fingers, scorched by the heat of whatever had rested here.

He rocked back on his heels, considering whether the explanation that sprang to mind was the only possible one. His grandfather had taught him that tracks told a story, but that the first story you told yourself about them was often just wishful thinking. He waited a minute for his grandfather's sake while Ara and Tyre circled the clearing impatiently, but his feeling of certainty didn't change.

"A spaceship landed here," he said.

Tyre and Ara descended on the spot, crushing some of the same grass in their eagerness. It didn't matter; he'd seen what he needed to see. He sketched out its shape on the grass for the benefit of the others.

"I thought the Travelers' spaceships were a lot bigger than that," Ara said. "Whole families live on them."

"They have little ships," Tyre said. "They use them to go from ship to ship. And sometimes to come down to planets. Didn't you ever listen to *Spaceman Kim*?"

It was a radio show that Ronon remembered mostly for its endless cliffhangers that had left the spacemen strangling in vacuum or fleeing from a dozen Wraith Darts. He'd wondered even as a child why the spacemen in the show didn't just use the Ring of the Ancestors to travel. Flying through space sounded dangerous.

"*Spaceman Kim* is made up to sell powdered tea," Ara said, as if talking to a small child.

"We know there are spaceships up there right now, right?" Ronon said, nodding toward the sky. "The Travelers. First time in ten years."

"You mean the people who are right now being presented to our leaders in the capital, minus one honor guard?" Tyre asked, sounding like the words tasted bad in his mouth.

They didn't taste very good in Ronon's, either. "We have to tell Kell about this. Somebody has to get the iron horse back from them before they leave."

"You mean before or after the council tells them how welcome they are to Sateda and what an honor it is for them to be here?"

"That's politics," Ronon said. "Who cares about politics? We've got to get this thing back before a bunch of people die."

"So let's go," Ara said, and they headed back to the trail at a dead run.

Kell listened soberly to Ronon's report when they reached him. "All right," he said. He frowned up at the dam for a moment, as if looking at it would give some hint at how long it would hold together. "We've loaded everyone who's willing to go aboard the train. The rest of the company is staying here to help the townspeople evacuate."

"Yes, Task Master," Ronon said, starting to turn away.

"Not you three. You get back on the train. I'll need you on hand to testify to what you found."

Ara and Tyre moved toward the train, but Ronon hung back. "We can't wait to tell anyone until the train gets to the capital," he said. "The Travelers may be gone by then."

"I'll radio ahead," Kell said. "You leave that to me."

Melena was climbing down from the train car as Ronon reached it, and he handed her down and then caught at her sleeve as she moved past him.

"You should get aboard," he said. "The train is about to leave."

"I've still got a lot of patients to deal with here," Melena said. "Cellese is already aboard to keep an eye on the serious cases. I'll evacuate with the townspeople."

Ronon was tempted to argue with her, but a glint in her eye suggested that wasn't likely to do much good. "Get to high ground as soon as you can," he said. "If there's another quake, anyone near the river is going to drown."

"The whistle's blowing," she pointed out, and Ronon shook his head in frustration and swung up to the train step. She turned her back as the train pulled away, heading back to the town hall, and he watched as she and the soldiers left behind dwindled into the distance.

All the pleasure had gone out of the train ride, the train now crowded with frightened civilians. With the injured laid in the aisle and the most badly wounded people installed in the officer's cars that featured pull-down bunks, the unhurt huddled in their seats, bundles and parcels on their laps. Ronon saw too many empty seats that could have been filled. A lot of people must have decided they'd prefer to take their chances evacuating on foot than leave their homes and friends behind with little more than the clothes on their backs.

"We'll get you back home as soon as we can," Tyre promised a pair of old women who had claimed the seats across from him. They both nodded, tight-lipped, but said nothing. Ronon wished he could think of anything to say himself.

It was a relief when the train pulled into the station, and there was more to do again, herding the civilians out of the train and handing their belongings down, shepherding them into one group to go to the hospital and another to be put into the hands of Stranger's Aid. Usually called into service to find homes for groups of refugees from Cullings on other worlds, the bustling women with their urns of hot tea were certainly capable of finding some displaced Satedans beds for the night.

It took some time to clear the station of refugees, though, and to get the last of the wounded on their way to the hospital for treatment. It was well after dark when the station grew quiet, the station attendants taking down the last of the signs announcing departing trains and posting the first arrivals scheduled for the next morning.

"Do we go report to Kell?" Ara asked.

"He said to wait for him here," Ronon said.

"I think he's been delayed," Tyre pointed out.

"Maybe it took them some time to go up to their ship and get the horse back," Ronon said.

"Maybe," Ara said, but she bit her lip.

"There he is," Tyre said in relief, and Ronon looked up, expecting to see Kell striding toward them with the iron horse tucked triumphantly under one arm.

Instead, Kell walked toward them with a somber expression, his boots echoing on the polished floor of the train station. He stopped and shook his head, and then shrugged as if trying to shed a heavy weight.

"You have to let us talk to them," Ronon said. "If they don't believe you, they've got to believe us when we tell them what we actually saw."

"It's too late," Kell said. "The Travelers left orbit two hours ago. They're beyond our reach."

Ara swore, and Tyre's hands bunched into fists.

"But you radioed ahead," Ronon said. "You told them. You're saying they couldn't even stall the Travelers for a couple of hours? How hard could that be?"

"Apparently too hard, for men who've spent the last few weeks congratulating themselves for the coup of persuading the Travelers to visit Sateda," Kell said. "They weren't willing to create a diplomatic incident on the word of a common soldier. I thought my word carried more weight in certain quarters, but... apparently not." He bent his head gravely.

"Then that's it?" Ara said. "We're just going to let those people die?"

"I didn't say that," Kell said at once, his chin coming up. "There is one thing that might still save them."

"Getting the iron horse back," Ronon said.

"They're in space," Ara said, her head to one side as if she thought he was being childish.

Kell nodded. "On their way to Belkan, where they plan to visit the trading fair. It's a short jump through hyperspace. And an even shorter trip through the Ring of the Ancestors."

"If the Council wouldn't even ask for it back, they're not going to let us go take it back by force," Tyre said.

"Of course they're not. I'm not talking about sending an army to go threaten them. I'm talking about a raid. Quick, quiet, and small. A few hand-picked men." His gaze swept pointedly over the three of them. "I want the three of you to go to Belkan, find a way to get aboard the Travelers' ship, and get that artifact back."

"Yes, Task Master," the three of them said in ragged chorus. It sounded so easy when Kell put it that way. Ronon was suspicious of things that sounded too easy.

"Having doubts?" Kell met Ronon's eyes steadily. "I trained you," he said. "I know what you're capable of. I have no doubts about any of you. I know you can do this. And every man, woman, and child left in that valley, is depending on you."

"Yes, Task Master!" The chorus was crisper this time.

"I'll get you through the Ring without any questions being asked," Kell said. "I have every confidence that you can handle matters from there."

The square around the Ring was busy even late at night, with people streaming between the hotels and restaurants and dance halls. Music poured out onto the street from half a dozen open doorways, and the smell of cooking meat reminded Ronon sharply that they hadn't eaten since breakfast.

"We could grab something for the road," Tyre said, lingering hopefully in the doorway of one shop selling skewers of roasted meat.

Kell was striding ahead of them, and showed no inclination to slow his steps to indulge dawdling. "There'll be food on Belkan," Ronon said.

"Weird food," Ara said. "All off-worlders eat weird food."

"Weird food is food," Ronon said, and gave her a not so gentle shove between the shoulder blades to get her moving, grabbing Tyre by the arm and hauling him along as well. "Don't make us look bad."

"You heard what he said," Tyre said lightly, pitching his voice low enough that Ronon hoped Kell couldn't hear him over the murmur of the crowd. "He has every confidence in us."

"Until we screw up," Ronon said. "Let's not screw up."

"Of course we're not going to screw up," Ara said. "Because if we do, a bunch of people are going to die." Her voice sounded strange, and he realized that she and Tyre were both clowning around because it was their first real mission, and they were afraid. They would have cheerfully charged into battle against a hundred Wraith, but the idea of screwing up and letting down a bunch of old people and little kids who were trying to sleep under the looming shadow of the dam and wondering if it was going to break…

"Kell thinks we can do this," Ronon said. "So we can."

"I hope you're right," Tyre said, and sped up his steps toward the Ring.

Going through the Ring on civilian business required making arrangements in advance, but Kell had a word with the guards, and then waved them forward as the guards dialed. It wasn't Ronon's first time through the Ring, but despite knowing better, some part of him still expected it to feel like water when he strode forward into the boiling blue light.

It was an entirely different shock, a cold splash all over his skin and the feeling of rushing forward through an empty space filled with light. Then he was stepping out into a different square, surfacing into warmer air that smelled of animals and burning charcoal and unwashed wool.

The trading fair sprawled for blocks, lines of bright banners hung between thatch-roofed stalls and more permanent stone shops, shoppers wandering up and down the rows or elbowing each other for position at the busier stalls. Most wore similar woolen jackets and trousers, but he could see knots of visitors who he guessed were from other worlds. Several men in studded leather strode between the stalls looking as dangerous as men carrying large cheeses possibly could. A group of men and women swaddled in richly-colored robes that only revealed their eyes were talking together in a busy knot. Another group wearing only feathers looked like they were shivering despite the warmth of the day. And Ronon could see several other solitary strangers whose dress marked them as out of place.

Satedan military uniforms were probably an unfamiliar sight, but not one that anyone here was going to find startling. "Spread out," he told Ara and Tyre. "Look for the Travelers. If they're here, they'll be selling better equipment than anybody locally. They'll probably draw a crowd."

He strode down the row of stalls looking for the Travelers or anything that looked like it might be their equipment. It would have made everything simple to find the iron horse itself set out for sale, but he didn't really expect it. Most of the people here would take the claim that the device could prevent earthquakes as a claim that it could do magic, and they wouldn't pay much for an off-worlder's good luck charm. The Travelers would do better selling the device on a world with scientists who would understand proof that the device really worked.

It was a good question where that might be. Hoff, maybe. Getting it back from Hoff would be even more of a diplomatic mess than demanding it back from the Travelers. There had been rumors lately about another world with modern technology — some gunpowder weapons had turned up on a low-tech farming world without a good explanation for where they'd come from — but as far as he knew nothing solid enough even to be a lead. If the Travelers got away with the device, they'd get away clean.

The first really crowded stall he reached proved to be selling liquor, but the next one had a more promising mix — he could see what looked like a radio set and several boxy objects that looked like batteries, although the writing on them didn't use Satedan letters, as well as coils of wire and stacks of sheet metal. He shouldered his way through the crowd, getting an elbow in the ribs from an old woman clutching a market basket who pursed her lips at him when he muttered an apology.

The girl minding the stall was wearing leather trousers and a patchwork leather jacket that looked like it had been made of the remains of several jackets that had fallen apart from old age, but the energy pistol at her hip was unmistakable. Ronon shrugged his uniform jacket off before she saw him, but knew he still looked distinctly like Satedan military. He turned his back to her, putting other fairgoers between him and the stall owner.

On the table in front of him, several large light fixtures were stacked, with most fairgoers frowning at them and then passing by; Belkan didn't have electricity, and most places that did probably didn't have a shortage of large metal hanging lamps. There was something about them that nagged at him, though, and he picked one up for a closer look.

"PROPERTY OF THE S.H.A." was stamped into the metal in familiar Satedan letters. That would be the Satedan Hydroelectric Authority. The light fixtures had come from the dam.

Ronon rolled his eyes. They'd stripped the light fixtures out of the shrine. Probably they would have taken the concrete walkway, too, if it weren't too big to move. He let the movement of the crowd carry him some distance away from the stall and then gave a piercing whistle. Heads turned, but no one paid him more than momentary attention. After a few minutes, Ara and Tyre appeared out of the crowd, looking frustrated.

"If I wanted to buy fava beans, we'd be in business," Tyre said.

Ara nodded. "Or scrap metal, or scarves knitted by somebody's old grandma."

"I found the Travelers," Ronon said. "They have stuff from the dam, but I didn't see the horse."

"Maybe we can have a little chat with them," Tyre said, taking out a knife and flipping it end over end before sheathing it. "Let them know they may have accidentally walked away with something that didn't belong to them."

"I think we're supposed to be subtle," Ara said.

"That's subtle."

Ronon plowed a path through the crowd for the other two until they reached a vantage point from which they could observe the Travelers' stall. As they watched, a man ducked in through the rear opening of the stall carrying a box of more assorted junk, spoke for a moment to the girl running the stall, and hefted a sack of grain that somebody had probably given them in trade. He started walking off with it, heading toward the outskirts of the market and the line of trees beyond.

Ronon slapped Tyre and Ara on the shoulders, starting them moving wordlessly along with him. They trailed the Traveler, Ronon keeping them well back; he wasn't afraid of losing the trail of a man carrying a heavy weight, and once they got beyond the boundaries of the market, there were only a few trails of footprints leading back and forth through a screen of trees. He waited until the branches had stopped moving, and then followed with Tyre and Ara at his heels.

As he had expected, beyond the trees was the mechanical bulk of a spaceship. It was bigger than the one that had touched down near the dam, the size of several train cars put together, and a hatch at its rear was open, with cargo piled on the ground around it. The man they were following dropped his sack near the hatch and then headed back toward the market.

Ronon swore silently and retreated into the trees, crouching low behind a screen of branches. He could hear Tyre and Ara, both making enough noise as they tried to be still that he thought the Traveler would surely hear them, but the man passed by obliviously.

"You two are the worst at hiding," he said finally under his breath.

"We were fine," Tyre said. "He's left that hatch wide open."

"Which means there's probably someone in there," Ronon said, but it still looked like their best chance of getting the iron horse back. "Remember, we're being subtle," he said, and slipped out of the trees heading for the ship.

A metal grating led up into the hatchway. Ronon ascended cautiously, alert for any sign that the ship was preparing to take off. He had no desire to wind up hurtling through space.

The grating led up into some kind of cargo hold, packed with sacks, crates, and unsecured junk of all kinds.

"There could be a hundred artifacts of the Ancestors in here, and we'd never know," Ara said.

"Artifacts of the ancestors that smell like an evergreen forest?" Ronon said. It was a faint scent, just an undertone under the smells of oil and sweat and off-worlder foods.

"You can't smell that in here," Ara said, wrinkling her nose.

"Yes, I can."

"It could be anything they picked up on any world with forests," Tyre said.

"Yes, it could." He was pretty sure it wasn't, though. Something smelled like wet iron and evergreens and fresh clay. He rifled through the shelf where the smell was strongest and found its upper half to be a cabinet with metal doors that stayed stubbornly shut when he tugged at them. It opened with some kind of keypad, but he could see wires coming from it, and he slashed through them with his belt knife. The lights on the keypad dimmed and went out.

"There could have been an alarm on that," Ara protested.

"But there wasn't."

He had to pry the cabinet open with his knife, but the door eventually swung free, and he was rewarded by the sight of an iron sculpture of a horse, big but not too heavy for him to tuck under one arm. "All right," he said. "Let's get out of here before these guys come back."

Footsteps echoed on the metal grating, and he realized they were a few moments too late. One glance around told him there wasn't enough cover to hide. He turned to see three Travelers, the man who'd been carrying grain before and two other men in dark leather. All three of them had energy pistols drawn and leveled at their chests.

"You're not Belkans," one of the men said, a square-shouldered blond with a thatch of stubble and muscles that suggested he spent a lot of time either hefting sacks of grain or punching people in the face. "So it won't spoil the trading fair for us to show you what we do to thieves."

"You stole from us," Ronon said, brandishing the iron horse. "Do you even know what this thing does?"

"It prevents earthquakes," the blond man said. "We've got a buyer on Hoff who'll pay a pretty price for that."

"More than we got out of the Satedans for everything we traded," one of the other men said. He was less massively built and held his pistol less confidently, like he did more engineering than fighting. "Your people are pretty cheap."

"Maybe we're just hard to cheat," Ronon said. "And this thing you stole is going to cause an earthquake that kills hundreds of people."

The engineer and the third, heavier and darker man looked at each other uneasily, but their leader shrugged. "Not our problem," he said. "Your people should have paid us better, or kept a better eye on their property."

"Ladric isn't going to like this," the one who looked like an engineer said.

The blond man rolled his eyes. "So? Does Ladric tell us what to do?"

"He kind of does, as long as we're with his fleet? And you know he was dead set on this trade deal with the Satedans —"

"We've traded, for all the good it did us. We're not going back there for years. And we're not leaving here without that device." The blond man flashed Ronon a smile, raising his energy pistol. "Hand it over, Satedan, and we just might go easy on you."

"Sorry," Ronon said, and rushed him, elbowing the man's gun arm out of the way and swinging the iron horse for the man's head.

It connected solidly, and he hoped it was sturdy enough not to be damaged by the impact. The Traveler obviously wasn't, and staggered back, stumbling to one knee. Ronon put the horse down rather than dropping it, and was rewarded by the Traveler throwing himself at Ronon's knees and knocking him down before he could get his gun clear of his holster.

Tyre was wrestling with one of the others for his pistol. The third man's pistol spat a bolt of energy, and Ara went down, measuring her length on the deck with a thud. Ronon didn't see blood or burns, and couldn't spare more of his attention. The man he'd hit tried to knee him in the groin, and then grabbed him by the hair and yanked his head back as he twisted out of the way.

Ronon had the man by the wrist, grappling for the man's energy pistol, and managed to block an elbow to the throat with his other arm. His opinion of the Travelers as fighters was going up by the moment. He shoved the man away hard while keeping his grip on his arm, trying to pin his arm behind his back.

The energy pistol spat again. He could hear two shots in rapid succession and the thuds of two bodies. It only took him a moment to add that up, and he let go of the man he was fighting, pushing him away and rolling clear. The man raised his pistol to fire, and then looked up over Ronon's shoulder. Ronon enjoyed watching his eyes go wide before Ara dropped him with a third shot.

"You knew I wasn't really stunned," Ara said.

"Figured that out."

"I think I winged Tyre, though," she added more unhappily. "I can't get him up."

Ronon turned with the iron horse in his arms to see her trying to haul Tyre to his feet. The man was barely conscious, looking like the end of the night in one of those bars they hadn't gotten to visit. Ronon swore and shoved the iron horse into Ara's arms, hauling Tyre up himself and getting his arm over Ronon's shoulders. He and Ara just barely managed to get Tyre down out of the hatchway, but he could hear the sound of distant running feet.

"One of them must have tripped some kind of alarm."

"Or you did cutting that wire," Ara said.

"Just move," he said, and took off for the woods.

There was thick enough cover to hide them as long as they stayed still. Ronon dragged Tyre down behind a bush and held him down to keep him from blundering around, and he waited as the footsteps passed by. There was the sound of commotion around the Travelers' ship, and after a long while, the sound of some of the Travelers heading back in the direction of the market.

"They think we went back to the market," Ara said under her breath, and Ronon nodded. He didn't intend to make for the Ring until Tyre could get there under his own power. "Well, good."

"They can search the market all they want," Ronon said. "When they get tired of it, we'll head home."

Ara's mouth crooked to one side. "So what happened to subtle? I thought we weren't supposed to confront the Travelers. Because diplomacy, and all that."

"We had to get this thing back one way or another," Ronon said. "And those guys aren't going to complain to the Satedan government that we stole back the thing they stole from us."

"You have a point," Ara said, and settled herself into the curve of a tree root to wait.

They got back through the Ring without incident; Ronon wrapped the iron horse in his jacket, and didn't stand out at all from the streams of market-goers who were heading back through the Ring with various parcels, baskets, and sacks. The Belkan man who was keeping people from crowding the Ring while other travelers were dialing frowned as Ara input the symbols for Sateda.

"Say, there were some Travelers looking for some Satedans," he said. "They seemed pretty unhappy with them."

"Wasn't us," Ronon said.

"We never went near the place," Tyre said.

"In fact, we were never here," Ara said. Ronon thrust them both forward toward the Ring before they could practice their skills at deception any further, and followed them into the chill of the event horizon.

The next few hours back on Sateda seemed to pour away like water. Kell had a special train waiting for them, and it was already moving as they clambered aboard, pulling out of the station and racing through the darkened city toward the countryside. The rattle of the rails seemed too slow, the click-clack of the wheels a leaden clock's tick. Ronon couldn't stop imagining what it would look like if the dam broke, the crumbling concrete falling away in a white hammer-blow of water, the white cascade turning to a brown wall of water looming over the towns it was about to destroy.

When they finally rounded the curve down into the river valley in the blue of early dawn, he let out a breath he had been holding when he saw the river still running low and lazy through the valley, and the little towns still standing. In several they passed, he could see lights above the town and up into the hills, people moving to high ground or camping there for the night.

The train finally slowed at Ironlode, the first light of morning spilling over the dam but not yet dispelling the shadows of the valley. Ronon climbed down from the train, the iron horse in a pack strapped to his back. There were soldiers posted at the train platform, but Ronon brushed aside their questions.

"We have to put this back in the shrine first," he said. "Explanations later."

"No one's going to stop you doing that," Arvan said, not one of Ronon's particular friends but a man he'd come to know in training. "It's spooky down here just waiting for that thing to go."

"The nurses," Ronon said, despite knowing he shouldn't waste time to ask. "They've evacuated, right?"

"They've still got patients," Arvan said. "They brought in a woman with a broken back. Melena wouldn't let us move her. And there are some people who won't go, old people and some stubborn ones who insist they're going to find kids who are probably buried ten meters deep under that mudslide. If that dam goes, we're going to have some company on our way out."

"So we hurry," Ara said, and Ronon didn't need any more urging to take off at a run.

They were halfway up the path to the shrine when the ground began to shake. Ronon grabbed for a tree to steady himself, and then felt the ground go out from under his feet. He held on hard to the tree trunk, hoping the entire bank wasn't going to slide away into the river far below.

"Ronon!" Tyre yelled, pointing at the dam, and Ronon looked out to see a great crack opening up in its face, water spraying but not yet hammering through. He gripped the iron horse more tightly. He had hoped just getting it close would be enough. Apparently not.

"We have to keep going!"

The path was sliding away as they climbed, rocks shifting and sliding. One tremor followed another, and the earth kept shifting and moving even between quakes, what looked like secure footholds crumbling away and leaving them clutching at trees or newly revealed stone. Finally Ronon hauled himself up on the overlook near to the top of the dam.

The catwalk that ran out across the dam face to the shrine was cracked in two, leaving a gaping break that he would have to jump. He thought he could make it if the first part of the catwalk would hold his weight. It looked all too much like it would go sliding into the river the moment he set foot on it. He could imagine the drop vividly, hands clawing at the slick surface of the dam for purchase, the beating force of the water not lethal until he smashed down into the river far below.

"There's no way," Tyre said. "We have to get to higher ground!"

"Go if you want!"

Tyre swore, but scrambled up the steps and grabbed the railing of the catwalk, putting his weight on it to steady it. Ara did the same, although she was light enough that Ronon didn't think she'd make much of a counterweight.

He stepped out onto the catwalk, moving fast. Either it would hold his weight or it wouldn't, and creeping along wasn't going to help. He made it to the break in the catwalk before the earth started to shake again. He felt the catwalk shift under his feet, the broken section of concrete and railing beginning to slide.

"Go!" Tyre shouted, and he crouched and then jumped. The concrete rocked as he landed, nearly pitching him off into the river, but he got a good hold of the railing and managed to haul himself up. The entire catwalk was shaking, the railing buckling under his hand as if it were made of bamboo rather than steel.

He ran. The opening into the dam face loomed in front of him, and then the catwalk began to peel away from the dam face, twisting and crumbling into the river. Ronon leaped toward the dam, and felt the slickness of wet stone and a painful sliding and buffeting as the water pounded against him. He slid, unable to stop his lethal descent, and then tumbled painfully against something hard, his fingers catching the edge of flat concrete. He hauled himself up and into the opening in the dam face, water streaming from his hair, his ears ringing from the noise of the pounding water.

It was dark, and he wished he'd repaid the Travelers more thoroughly for making off with the light fixtures as well as with the device. He shrugged off his pack and got it open by feel, and then felt his way forward until he reached the opposite wall. He felt along it and found a recessed niche, and then realized that while he could still feel the vibration of water pounding over the dam, the floor wasn't bucking under his feet.

He pulled out the iron horse and set it carefully, respectfully, in its shrine. There was no blazing glow, no rising hum of power or crackle of energy spilling over his skin. There was only the sound of Ronon's own breathing over the pounding vibration of water flowing over the dam. Beneath his feet, the earth was finally still.

It was late the next day before Ronon got the chance to make his report, sitting in Kell's office in the capital with the sound of traffic outside the window and the friendly glow of an electric lamp beaming from Kell's desk. Ara and Tyre hadn't been called into Kell's office, and he hadn't made them wait to start their evening on the town, although they'd promised to meet him in one of the bars a few blocks from military headquarters.

"I knew I could count on you," Kell said. "I want you to know I appreciate what you and your team did today."

"Thank you, Task Master," Ronon said. Half-formed visions of medals and shaking the council leader's hand swirled in his head, a picture even more satisfying than being part of the honor guard for a bunch of dignitaries no one would remember next week. *Heroic soldiers save town from flood* sounded pretty good to him.

"And I want you to know that no one is ever going to mention it again."

"What?"

"The Travelers are our allies. Yes, even after what happened. One of them stole from us. That's unfortunate. But for political reasons, we can't afford to antagonize the Travelers by advertising that we know about the theft, let alone that we successfully stole the artifact in question back. The official story will be that the iron horse was… misplaced in the confusion. No one will ever know any differently."

"Except for the people you told when you radioed ahead," Ronon said slowly. "When you asked the council to stall the Travelers until we could get back to the city."

"Except for them, of course," Kell said with an easy smile. He came around his desk and clapped Ronon on the back. "Take a few days' leave," he said. "I expect at your age you can find some things you'd like to do in the city."

"Yes, Task Master," Ronon said.

"Don't sound so glum," Kell said. "A few people died. That's a tragic thing. But many more are alive today because of you and your friends. I'm told the damage to the dam can be repaired, and that the engineers are confident that the residents of the valley are safe. We can count this as a win."

Ronon waited until he was out on the street in the glow of the streetlamps to let himself fully form the thought that had been lying like a leaden weight in his belly. No one would ever know any differently, Kell had said. As if maybe he'd never mentioned to anyone that the Travelers had stolen the iron horse at all.

Kell had political ambitions. Kell knew this was news the council wouldn't want to hear. Kell had promised Ronon he was going to radio ahead with that news. And Ronon wasn't sure he believed that Kell had actually done it. He could see Kell now, sitting there with his hand on the radio, knowing that the council wasn't going to like what he had to say. Gambling on being able to get the iron horse back before anyone knew it was gone. Risking the lives of old men and little girls with rag dolls rather than risk the approval of the politicians who were his friends.

He didn't want to think that way. Kell was his Task Master, his teacher. Before today he would have said he trusted Kell with anything, trusted him his life. And he didn't have any proof, just a suspicion he couldn't shake, and his grandfather's voice telling him not to listen to the story he wanted to tell himself, but to listen for the story that was true.

Ronon hesitated outside the entrance to the bar, knowing that once he went in, he'd push away the thought and get cheerfully drunk with his friends. He suspected that it would come back in the cold light of morning, but morning was a long time away. He pulled open the door and stepped forward into light and warmth.

Inside, Ara and Tyre had claimed a table by the windows where they could watch the crowd streaming by outside. He maneuvered his way between tables, trying not to knock drinks out of people's hands, and wound up penned between chairs.

"Excuse me," he said.

A familiar face looked up at him. "Ronon?" Melena was wearing a bright dress, her hair twisted up and her cheeks pink. It hadn't occurred to him before how pretty she was, or maybe it had and he'd pretended not to notice. She smiled up at him, and a couple of her friends exchanged teasing looks.

"Melena," he said.

"I'm sorry," she said. "I should say Specialist Dex…"

"You can call me Ronon," he said. Tyre had seen them, now, and was elbowing Ara, who followed his gaze and then smirked.

"I just wanted to say…" she began, and then twisted around in her chair to face him. He went down on one knee so that he wasn't looming over her, and her cheeks went a shade deeper pink. "I wanted to tell you how much my friends and I appreciated everything you did in Ironlode," she said. "I think it was very brave."

"Not as brave as some nurses I met."

"And I wanted to see… if you're going to be in the city for a while…"

"Probably just a few days," he said. "A lot can happen in a few days."

"I don't have any particular plans. Except tonight. I'm out with my friends tonight," Melena said, ignoring a whisper from one of them that sounded distinctly like 'are you *crazy*?'

"How about tomorrow night?"

"I would love to see you tomorrow night," Melena said. She wrote her address down on a paper napkin, and Ronon tucked it into his jacket with a flourish. He took her hand for a moment, and her fingers lingered in his before she turned back to her friends with a blushing grin.

"Smooth, very smooth," Tyre said as Ronon sat down at his friends' table. "Remind me never to let you see a girl first."

"You saw her, you just didn't try," Ara said. "Next time make more of an effort."

"You mean next time we're trapped underneath a dam that's about to collapse? Or when we're in town for less than a week on leave?"

"Seize the day," Ara said.

"I'm planning to," Ronon said, and caught Melena's eye across the gap between the tables; she raised her glass to him, and he toasted her in return, smiling at her over the rim of the glass until she smiled in return.

"You'd better work fast," Tyre said. "We're only going to be in town for a few days."

"I know," Ronon said. He knew his leave would go racing by, but that was all the more reason to make every minute of it count. Across the bar, the band was striking up a dance tune, and Tyre stretched out in his chair in contentment, tipping his neck back to take a deep drink. "But we've got long enough."

"A few good days," Ara said, and Ronon raised his glass to hers. He figured he could probably live without a medal after all.

STARGATE SG-1
Dude, Where's My Spaceship?

Suzanne Wood

Jack strode through the hallways of the SGC, a slight grin quirking his lips, a spring in his step. All was quiet on base. Another Goa'uld was bagged and tagged, the team had successfully completed a string of missions that had paid off big time in weapons, allies and even some meaning of life stuff. Carter had a boyfriend. Teal'c had a booming new business analyzing dreams for half the base personnel, Daniel had a personal victory over the Goa'uld in the person of his once-lost girlfriend, and Jack had a slightly narcoleptic archaeologist whose unfortunate habit of dropping off to sleep mid-sentence, mid-thought, mid-anything, was providing an endless source of amusement for himself and cash for the betting pools. Hammond was happy, the Pentagon was happy, his team was happy. What more could a man want?

Propriety required one to knock before entering the massage rooms situated at the far end of the gym. Jack, therefore, barged straight in. Only one of the four tables was currently occupied. The soft, recorded swoosh of waves caressing sand was the only sound in the dimly lit room. On the far table Randall, the masseur, worked on the sole of a foot attached to the man lying on the table. Rather, sleeping on the table. Jack smiled fondly and wandered over, nodding to Randall. He gazed down at Daniel's still body, arms hanging limply over the table's edges, muscles relaxed and pliable, face planted in the hole at the top of the table. Jack cocked his head to one side, giving his friend a careful once-over, from curled fingers, down long straight spine to limp toes. Due consideration given, target selected, Jack extended one finger and poked Daniel in the ribs.

"…it probably works best with chicken but turkey can be surprisingly effective. Just make sure you bake it for two hours."

"I'll be sure to do that, Daniel," Jack murmured.

"Jack?" Daniel pulled his face from the hole and cranked around to peer at his friend. "Where did you come from?"

Randall pulled the warm towel back over Daniel's feet and patted his leg. "You're all done, Dr. Jackson." Smiling to Jack, he turned away and began packing up.

Daniel's eyes rolled back in his head and he thumped his face back down into the cushioning.

"I did it again, didn't I?"

"That would be a big yes." Jack smiled down at Daniel. *Two hours, fifteen since the last journey to the land of Nod. Twenty bucks to me!*

"Nnnuugh," moaned Daniel. "This is not fair. Why can't Janet do something?"

"If I remember correctly she prescribed proper nutrition and rest."

Daniel raised his head and glared at Jack. "I've been doing nothing but resting the last couple of weeks. I rest at night. I rest during lunch breaks. I rest in the middle of briefings. I rest with my face in my books and during phone conversations. I'm tired of resting."

"Obviously your body thinks differently." Jack took a couple of steps backwards as Daniel rolled off the table, pulling the towel with him. "Give it a little time, Daniel," he relented. "You've been through some trying times and Osiris futzing with your sleep has just knocked you off-course a bit. It'll pass."

Daniel nodded his head, accepting the words. Jack had pointedly made the distinction of Osiris messing with his sleep patterns. Messing with Daniel's *head* could easily be the assumption and give rise to certain old, and hopefully long-buried, doubts about the quality of Daniel's sanity.

"So." Jack clapped his hands together and headed for the door. "We are officially on leave. Time to bug out of here. We can pick up some beer and wine on the way home, dig out the good duds, watch a little tube, put you down for a nap and be up in time to meet the others at 1800." He disappeared through the door before Daniel could harm him.

The drive home was uneventful. Jack drove Daniel's Jeep, stopping off for a few bottles of wine, Guinness and some of Colorado Springs' finest craft beer. Daniel grabbed a couple of quick, unintentional power naps. For all that he was inconvenienced by his brain tripping into sleep mode at the drop of a hat, he was in a very happy place at the moment. He sifted through his notebook, looking for yet more stories to share with Sarah this evening.

Jack jumping back into the Jeep for the second time woke Daniel again. Jack said nothing, merely headed into traffic with a light smile. "Sarah has bounced back pretty quickly from the extraction," he remarked.

Daniel nodded, his gaze on the park they were passing. "Yeah. The process is a bit messy but I have to admit the Tok'ra know what they're doing. She felt no pain and after the anesthetic wore off she was fine." He sighed and snuck a glance at Jack. "Skaara was the same." The old familiar grief and regret were still there, in their little place in his heart.

Traffic flowed on and around them. Jack said softly, "I really wish he could have had his wedding."

Daniel looked directly at Jack, struck by a deep certainty. "They did get married Jack. I'm not sure how I know, but deep down — I do know Skaara got married. Life goes on as normal for everyone in Nagada." Daniel paused, a wide grin sneaking up on him. "And they had a whopper of a party. Big, big party."

Jack pulled into Daniel's driveway. He switched off the engine and they sat in silence for a while. Even though Jack had spent relatively little time with Skaara, Daniel knew the grief Jack felt at the loss of Skaara and all the Abydonian people was no less intense than his own. Gradually, the corner of

Jack's mouth twitched, he stared through the windscreen at a place far beyond the Earth they currently occupied.

"You sure they're okay?"

Daniel nodded once, emphatically. "Yes."

"Good enough for me, then."

A knowing look passed between them. They climbed out of the Jeep and headed into Daniel's home. Jack made for the kitchen to put the booze on ice. Daniel wandered down the hall to his front bedroom, determinedly fighting off a yawn.

"You've got stuff in this refrigerator that passed its use-by date sometime in the last century. Okay if I dispose of it?" Jack's muffled voice followed after him.

"Yep. Sure." A monumental yawn seized him. He stood wavering, pulling in deep breaths as exhaustion swept through his bones. His bed was in front of him. Just a few steps away.

The screen door on the back porch banged. Banged again: Jack making his way out to the trash cans and back. Daniel breathed, tried to parse Abydonian verbs, just to keep his brain functioning a few more minutes. Clanks and grunts from the kitchen told him Jack was on a cleaning spree.

Should go help. Hope he didn't throw out the tea I bought for Sarah....

"Daniel!"

He started badly, staggered a couple of steps, and refocused on the room. When had he closed his eyes?

"You were literally asleep on your feet." Jack stood in the doorway sporting a pair of yellow kitchen gloves. "Why don't you lie down?" His eyes tracked past Daniel and widened in horror.

"What?" Daniel turned, expecting armed Goa'uld or worse.

"No wonder you can't sleep with the gruesome sisters staring down at you. Sheesh!"

"Gruesome...?" He stared around the room. Oh. The collection of Papuan ceremonial masks on the wall. "Dr. Jordan left them to me. I haven't had the heart to take them down. Guess they are a bit unusual."

"Why put them on your bedroom wall?" Jack sauntered over and tried to stare down the largest mask.

"This isn't my bedroom," Daniel mumbled. He looked over the collection of artifacts in the room. Maybe a donation to the Denver Art Museum...

Jack turned and arched an eyebrow at him. "Room. Bed. Bedroom."

He dropped his eyes to the daybed in the center of the room. "Oh. Right. Actually, it's a spare. My proper bed is in the back." He waved a thumb toward the master bedroom at the back of the house. "It gets so hot in summer, I started sleeping here."

"Ah, that explains it." Jack nodded.

"Explains what?"

"Five foot bed. Six foot archaeologist. Get some rest, Daniel. I have a refrigerator to excavate."

Jack hummed to himself, happily absorbed in scrubbing down the worktops in Daniel's kitchen. With nothing more pressing on his mind than what to order in for dinner he lost himself in menial chores. A lifetime in the Air Force gave him an appreciation for neatness and order — and an aversion to week-old leftovers. He threw the used cloth into the open trashcan liner, tossed the gloves in after and tied the bag up. Done. Pleased, he hefted the bag and took it out the back door to add to the rest.

Afternoon sunlight shone warmly down on his head. Their week of leave time looked to have excellent weather. He threw the garbage in the can, which was already nearly full. He dropped the lid down — should he risk waking Daniel to ask when the next collection was due? A paper note taped to the side of the house, right over the cans, fluttered at him.

TRASH. WEDNESDAY.

Jack grinned. With a head full of planet-saving stuff, Daniel wasn't the only one who had trouble remembering the little things of life. And today was Tuesday. He wheeled the can out to the curb then wandered back along the side of the house. The grass needed mowing, what there was of it that hadn't already browned off in the summer heat. Maybe they should organize a working bee. Standing on the back lawn, he took a breather. Daniel's house was in a block of the older part of town, with his and the surrounding homes all situated on large plots of land. It was pleasant, peaceful. The most disturbance the area had seen had been their own little catch-the-Goa'uld operation a couple of weeks earlier.

A flash of light sparked in the corner of his eye. Jack glanced over his shoulder. Odd. Must be the sun reflecting on a window. Well, maybe he'd have time for a beer before the others arrived. There was an inviting wicker recliner on the back porch. He doubted Daniel found much leisure time in it, but, carpe diem and all that... He bounded up the porch steps and dived into the kitchen.

Beer in hand, Jack shut the refrigerator door, grabbed a pack of pretzels and moved to head back outdoors. And froze.

Two figures stood in the shadowy corner of the kitchen. Big, bulky figures Jack instinctively knew were not his team, arrived early to share a cold beer in the sun.

"Kree!" barked one.

"Kree backatcha," Jack said quietly.

The sunlight reached far enough into the corner of the room to glint off what had to be a zat gun. Its bearer jerked it upwards. Jack slowly raised his beer and pretzels.

"Larry, Curly. Long way to come for a drink, guys. Hope you like craft beer."

The one with the zat, Jack christened him Larry, let loose a stream of words in Goa'uld, most of which sailed past Jack without stopping to sink in.

"Well, crap. Just when I'm on vacation, trying to kick back, have a beer, a little dinner with the gang, and the two Stooges turn up." He inched sideways, keeping eye contact with Larry while sidling towards the block of very sharp kitchen knives Daniel handily kept on the counter.

The zat gun twitched and extended to firing position. Jack paused, the knife block just too far away for a successful lunge. He eyed the intruders. Definite glints of metal armor and big clunky boots. *Jaffa*. Here on Earth. Colorado Springs. Daniel's kitchen, no less. The how and why they were here were warring for attention in Jack's head, but of more importance was to keep them focused on him, and away from his sleeping friend. The second Jaffa clomped forward a couple of steps, and gabbled another string of Goa'uld words. One word caught: "Osiris." Then another: "Daaneel."

Of course. Stargate Command had assumed Osiris had come alone. Sarah Gardner had few memories of her time as host to Osiris, even less of events immediately prior to the parasite's extraction. The techs from planetary defense had not been able to detect whatever ship she'd come in; they'd settled on a theory of a cloaked ship, left to orbit the planet on its own. Presumably someone would find it, some day. *Never presume...*

Jack smiled his best country bumpkin smile. "Excuse me?" *No idea who you are, fella. Must have the wrong house. Planet. Whatever.*

Curly stepped closer and repeated his question. Larry scuttled after him, keeping right by his side. That one at least was not looking too sure of himself. In fact, Jack decided he was young — very young — and the other was not much older. Neither looked all that confident.

"Osiris?" Jack pulled a vacant expression. "Nope, no one here by that name." He shook his head and shrugged. *Get the message, bozo, and beam on out of here.*

The two exchanged looks, such a comical 'now what do we do' glance that Jack would have laughed had not a voice echoed down the hall, from the front 'bedroom'.

"Who are you talking to? Are the others here?"

The Jaffa were still turning their heads in Daniel's direction when Jack moved. He flicked the hand holding his beer. Bottle and a spray of Colorado Springs' finest connected with

Larry's forehead. Pretzels spattered in Curly's face. Jack flung himself to the right, outstretched hand connected with the meat cleaver as he went down, a wild squirt of zat fire flew over his head, and he hit the tiled floor with a thump. He rolled, flung the cleaver sideways and had the satisfaction of seeing it buried in the shin-guard of Larry. Another zat blast skittered across the kitchen floor and the tail-end of the charge zinged across his legs.

"Argh!"

From his knees down to his toes, Jack's legs went numb. Remnant charge crept up along his nerves, and he fought valiantly to stay awake. The knife block had landed on the floor next to him. He fumbled for the hilt of the closest, came up with a carving fork. Larry loomed over him. Jack waved the fork with a menacing grimace. Behind his foe, the other Jaffa was aiming his weapon toward the hall door. Desperate, Jack lunged up, and to his surprise, caught Larry's armored sleeve with the carving fork. The two of them grappled for control. Jack slid around on the tiles, useless legs no help. He caught a glimpse of something long and thin streak through the air and strike Curly a glancing blow. One of Daniel's incongruous spears clattered to the floor and slid out of sight.

"Oh, crap."

There was Daniel, in track pants and tee, hair tussled and looking like he very much wished he'd picked up more than one spear.

Jack opened his mouth and bellowed, *"Run for it."*

Daniel complied, sort of. He snagged a frying pan from a hook over the island bench, swung and clobbered Curly with a solid *thwang*. Metallic, totally-inappropriate-for-wearing-on-tiles Jaffa boots skidded out from under the man and he went down, flailing arms grabbed at Daniel as he went and the two of them crashed to the floor. While Jack had his own troubles grappling with the carving fork, he could see glimpses of Daniel: first on top of his foe, then rolled underneath, fists and frying pan proving to be less than effective in such close quarters.

The summer's twilight filled the kitchen with a bucolic haze. Grunts, thuds and gasps rose into the air amid dancing motes of light. Jack had both hands wrapped around Larry's, the carving fork hovered inches from his eyes, caught in a well-matched battle of strength. The man looked young, too young to be fighting so desperately for the sake of some jumped up, snake-in-the-grass pseudo god. Still, he was fit, Jack had to allow him that. But the Jaffa's attention kept slipping; glances darted over to the other battle on the tiles, which betrayed a concern for his fellow bad guy that was not so typical of his kind. He did it again and Jack pounced, if you could pounce while sliding around on the floor in a puddle of beer with half your body numb. He cranked his head forward and sharply butted his forehead into Larry's cheekbone.

Ow.

Larry overbalanced and slid half off Jack. Impressively, though, he managed to hang on to his part of the carving fork with one hand. Jack heaved his shoulders, trying to turn over and gain a better purchase. Larry's other hand came back into view… with the zat gun. He swung it at Jack, thought about it for a moment, then aimed back behind him.

The muzzle of the zat landed square against Daniel's neck. Jack froze. Daniel froze. The Jaffa underneath Daniel froze.

A look of surprise flashed across Larry's face, then as an afterthought he cried, "Kree!"

Close-contact zat blasts were not pleasant, something he'd prefer to spare Daniel. Jack sighed and let go of the fork. He flopped back onto the tiles and showed his bare hands.

"Waste of good beer," he muttered.

He'd had such high hopes for this evening. Good food, old friends, cold beer. It wasn't much, but it was all he wanted. Nowhere in the schedule was sitting on the floor of Daniel's kitchen, being eyed up by two very nervous Jaffa while tied back to back with his friend (and hadn't Daniel pitched a hissy fit when Larry had ripped the cord off the blinds — who knew the boy was so house proud?). Jack sidled a glance over to where the Jaffa stood in the shadowy corner of the room. Yup, still muttering between themselves. Seems these two hadn't come up with much of a plan before launching their raid. A snore drifted up from behind him, causing the Jaffa to stop and stare. Jack tried not to laugh.

The two inched closer. Larry barked a question.

"Hey, don't look at me, pal. I just came for the beer." Jack pulled an innocent bystander face. *You've got the wrong place, guys. Just beam away like good little Jaffa.* He wasn't about to give away that he understood basic Goa'uld. These two were looking for their god — and the longer they hung about in Daniel's kitchen, the closer the lady formerly known as Osiris got to landing on the front doorstep.

"Daaneel?" Curly leaned into Jack's face.

Jack shrugged and shook his head. And then Daniel help-fully woke up again with a snort. Curly moved to face him and repeated the question.

"Uh…" Daniel caught himself.

Inwardly, Jack cheered. Five to six odd years of drilling into him not to answer the bad guys when they ask your name had paid off.

"Why are we on the kitchen floor?"

"You remember our guests, Larry and Curly. They dropped by for some beer and pretzels."

"Pretzels… right." Jack could hear the frown in Daniel's voice.

A chime rang down the hallway, coming from the front door.

"Beethoven's Ninth?" Jack wondered as the two Jaffa looked about curiously for the source of the sound. He wriggled his fingers around a knot in the blind cord.

"Fifth, actually. Came with the house."

"Nice." He dropped his voice. "We have a visitor."

"Uh huh." Daniel's fingers met his, both fiddling with the same knot.

The chime sounded again. Larry moved to the hallway and stared up at the small box up above the doorway where the chime peeled its last notes.

A loud knock made everyone jump. The front door opened and a voice floated in.

"Daniel Jackson, it is I, Teal'c."

In the same instance that the two Jaffa traded triumphant looks, pleased they were indeed in the correct house, Jack heaved himself sideways, taking Daniel with him, and crashed into the legs of Curly. Daniel bellowed, "Teal'c, Jaffa —" to the accompaniment of Curly, who staggered back off-balance and let loose a zat charge into the saucepans.

Footsteps thundered down the hall. Teal'c paused for a frozen moment, framed in the kitchen doorway. He took in the situation: Daniel and Jack tied together, rolling about awkwardly on the floor, one armed Jaffa falling on his rear next to them, another Jaffa torn between reaching to help his compatriot and covering Teal'c with his zat.

Teal'c bellowed, "Kree!"

To which Larry replied, "Kree!"

Jack, half smothered with a Jaffa's knee in his face and Daniel's elbows in his ribs, muttered, "Oh, kree yourselves."

Teal'c could not hide his astonishment. The house of Daniel Jackson had always been open to him, and so he had entered when the announcement of his arrival had not been answered. Never had he expected to be greeted by armed Jaffa, or to find his friends bound and helpless. Well, perhaps not quite so helpless, but certainly in need of some assistance. He drew himself up and stared hard at the standing Jaffa: young, impressionable, a prime candidate to be turned onto the path of the Jaffa resistance.

The youngster took in his gold tattoo. Eyes widened. Posture automatically straightened.

"Jaffa. Hear me. I am Teal'c, of the Free Jaffa," he announced in the Goa'uld tongue. "Put down your weapons. Cast off the shackles of slavery. Deny your obeisance to false gods. Stand proud and declare your freedom, for yourselves and all your kind. The Goa'uld are liars and betrayers, they deserve none of your loyalty and will only ever reward you with death and dishonor. Put aside this false life and join me on the path to a new life and liberty. Choose your own fate and glory in the power you will wield for yourselves and your families."

The two just blinked at him, confused. They traded looks, glanced back to him. The one on the ground picked himself up, stepped over O'Neill, and peered at him.

"We do not know you," he said.

Teal'c raised an affronted eyebrow. "I am Teal'c." That name alone was usually enough to get the average Jaffa warrior quivering with either rage or admiration. These two just gave back blank stares.

"Former First Prime to the false god Apophis."

Nothing.

"Slayer of Cronus."

No reaction.

"Obliterator of Apophis." Well, he had some help from his team with that one…

"Heru'ur, Seth, Sokar, Klorel, Hathor; these and many other false gods have been slain by my actions." There was a cough from the back of the kitchen. "With, of course, assistance from the Tau'ri," he amended.

"We do not know you," said one of the Jaffa. "We have come in search of our lord, Osiris. Do you know where we can seek her, er, him?"

Teal'c struggled to maintain his stony expression. Not know of him? Years of fighting, upsetting the rule of countless false gods, liberating the enslaved, raising rebellion and dissent wherever he could… His name should be a byword for hope among the oppressed, a rallying cry to arms. He puffed out a breath of annoyance.

Really, the youth of today…

Daniel heaved and pushed against Jack, who was pushing against him. Despite the other's efforts they managed to right themselves while Teal'c kept the two Jaffa busy.

"What's going on?" Jack breathed in his ear, head twisted around, as his compromised balance threatened to dump them both back on the tiles.

"Teal'c's trying to talk them down."

"Oh, great. That'll go well."

"Yeah." Daniel grimaced at the expression on Teal'c's face. "Hey!" The cord bit into his arms as Jack started wriggling himself into a better position.

"Teal'c!"

"Jack, he's right here, you don't have to shout."

"Tell these bozos their god's a former… god, and get us the hell out of these ropes."

Teal'c cast a cool look down on them. "I have endeavored to do so, O'Neill. They do not apparently recognize my name or my achievements."

"Ah, that's gotta smart. Well, give it another go. Tell 'em we'll resettle them someplace nice."

Teal'c launched into a rapid-fire exchange of dialog with the two invaders. Questions and replies flew back and forth so quickly even Daniel had trouble keeping up with the translation. Jack's patience lasted a monumental two and half minutes before he interrupted.

"Well? What are they saying?"

"I am attempting to discover by which means they arrived at this planet, why they remained hidden for so long, and why they have now broken their cover and come in search of their god and the person she, rather, he, was seeking."

"And?"

Teal'c huffed an impatient breath.

"Just translate for me," Jack demanded. "How did they get here?"

Teal'c restrained himself from rolling his eyes and asked the Jaffa the question, which elicited a long and very complicated explanation of events that seemed to stretch back to Osiris' capture of Thor. Before the man had finished, Jack interrupted again.

"Well?"

"To condense their tale, they accompanied Osiris from his ha'tak to this world, in a tel'tak. Osiris left them on the ship with orders to remain until his return."

"So why are they here?"

"They have not yet reached that part of their tale, O'Neill."

"Well hurry it up. Just translate what they're saying. I'm getting piles sitting here."

Daniel couldn't help a chuckle, but that brought the Jaffa's attention on to him, and he could see realization hit that he was why they were here in the first place. He ducked his head. Another wave of fatigue hit him. He sucked in a deep breath, valiantly trying to stay awake.

Teal'c's questions started a discussion between the two Jaffa. Over them, Teal'c offered his rendition for Jack's benefit.

"This one says: 'Dude, I told you we should have followed orders.'"

"The other replies: 'Dude, we had to beam down. We were running out of air.'"

"*Dude?*" Jack queried.

"I am paraphrasing their words into colloquialisms more familiar to humans of this region."

Daniel could feel Jack trying to twist far enough around to glare at him, also reminded of his recent penchant for paraphrasing Jaffa dialects on their mission to rescue Ry'ac and Bra'tac.

"Ah hem." Daniel glanced everywhere but over his shoulder.

"Don't blame me," he muttered. "I'm not the one who insisted on *Point Break* for the last movie night."

"Hey, nothing wrong with that movie."

"Did you *see* the ending? No way that was filmed in Australia—"

"If I may resume?" Teal'c's stony tone cut across what could have been a great argument.

"Sure, go ahead." Jack settled back against Daniel and resumed fumbling at the ties that bound them.

"These two have been awaiting the return of their lord for some time," Teal'c rumbled.

Two weeks, four days, in fact since Osiris last appeared in his bedroom and set in motion the events that finally released Sarah from her captor. Osiris, the once mighty System Lord was last seen exiting the SGC's Stargate in the company of the Tok'ra—in a bucket.

Daniel pulled his attention back to the lengthy tale the two Jaffa were spinning, so intent on getting their story across that their weapons were wavering and pointing floor-wards. Though he could well understand them, he waited for the translation provided for Jack.

Several minutes later, Teal'c seized a break in the flow of information and turned to Jack.

"They said, 'Our supplies were depleted some days ago, power on the ship begins to fail. We are hungry and cold. We seek our lord.'"

"Five minutes of rambling and all you got was that?" Jack grunted.

"Would you prefer a verbatim account, O'Neill?"

"Heck, no."

The Jaffa's attention ping-ponged between them and they launched into another long dialog of failed systems, lost navigational data and ended with an all too understandable, but somewhat plaintive, plea to go home.

"Well?" Jack demanded.

Teal'c arched an eyebrow at them. "He said, 'Dude, where's my spaceship?'"

Daniel couldn't help a snort of amusement, which was interrupted by a knock on the back door.

Jack had his mouth open to deliver a smart response to Teal'c when heads all over the kitchen turned to the back door. Silhouetted by the setting sun, Carter and Pete Shanahan were set to barge in. In the corner of his eye he saw the two zat guns swing up, one trying to cover Teal'c, Daniel and himself, the other turned toward the new arrivals.

"Hello, Daniel, we're here—"

"Carter, duck!" Jack bellowed over her voice.

"Sam, look out!" Daniel yelled with him.

There was a blur of motion behind them, a zat charge went off, a body thudded to the floor. A large body by the sound of it. Jack planted his heels on the tiles and tried to scoot himself and Daniel into the path of Larry. A hard, armored boot caught him the thigh. Larry tripped over him, and, points awarded to his reflexes, managed to get off a shot as he landed on top of Jack and Daniel. Framed in the opened door, Carter caught the full charge of the zat gun and collapsed where she stood. With the reactions of a true civilian, Pete froze, a large, stuffed giraffe hugged close to his chest, and gaped from downed girlfriend to the chaos in the kitchen.

Jack, once again underneath the wriggling body of a Jaffa, banged his forehead on the tiles and mumbled, "Go, team."

At Larry's direction, Pete gently hauled Carter inside and propped her back to back with Teal'c—the unconscious recipient of Curly's well-placed shot. Curly ripped down another curtain cord and proceeded to tie up the rest of SG-1.

"Do you mind not completely destroying my house?" Daniel demanded.

"Daniel, focus a little?" Jack nudged him with an elbow.

The nylon cord binding the two of them had pulled even tighter in the scuffle. Jack resolutely set to work again on the knots. Teal'c was still out, but Carter was moaning her way back to consciousness. Shanahan stood by the kitchen windows, still hanging on to his giraffe. Larry and Curly retreated to the furthest corner of the room, looking even less certain of themselves now as they engaged in frantic whispers. Daniel sagged against Jack's back, once again succumbing to the sleeping condition plaguing him.

"So. Pete. How was the trip to the zoo?"

"Huh?"

"Zoo. You. Carter. How'd you manage to drag her there, anyway? She has this horror of cages, y'know."

"Uh…" Pete darted a distracted look at Jack before returning his stare to the Jaffa. "We kept to the large animal enclosures. She liked the giraffes. *Who are they?*"

"The giraffes?" Jack couldn't help the facetious comment. Damn, these knots were never going to loosen with Daniel's dead weight pulling on them.

"*Them.*" Pete indicated the two intruders with the giraffe's head. "Should I call someone?"

"Who you gonna call?"

"The cops. Your people, surely?"

"Let's not make a big incident, here." Last thing Daniel's neighbors needed was another military operation followed by the inevitable clean up with security teams, non-disclosure forms, et-boring-cetera.

"But they shot Sam."

"She's okay. Coming around already. Now, Teal'c: he's gonna be pissed when he wakes up."

Shanahan twitched uncomfortably. The Jaffa kept a zat on him, despite their intense consultations.

"Giraffes, you say." Jack pulled Pete's attention back to him before the Jaffa took a dislike to his staring at them.

"Yeah… We got to feed them. She really liked that."

"Nice. Don't have a weapon on you, by any chance?" Jack added quietly.

"No." Pete could see the knives scattered on the floor from Jack's earlier attempt, but he was on the other side of the kitchen island and any leap to grab one would be rewarded with a zat blast. "Why doesn't she like cages?"

"Been locked up in too many of them, I guess."

"Oh. Really? Wow. Real cages?"

"Oh yeah, we've been locked up in some of the Goa'uld's finest. Broke out of them too, so there's that for an upside."

Pete blinked at him, disbelief slowly turned to understanding. He darted a glance at Sam, then at the rest of the team.

Daniel started awake with a flinch. He groaned. "Thought this was all a dream."

"If only," Jack replied. "Ease up on the cord, will you?"

"Trying to." Daniel shifted against him. "Hey, Pete. Have a nice day out?"

"Yeah, thanks, Daniel. It's a fantastic zoo — Oh, Sam!" Pete made an abortive move to reach her as her head rose out of its slump.

"Damn, I hate that," Sam grumbled. She shook her head carefully and managed to focus on the scene around her. "What on Earth? Pete, you okay?"

"Fine, honey."

"Honey?" Jack mimicked softly to a shushing noise from Daniel. He'd never heard anyone refer to Carter like that before.

"Sir? What gives?" Carter was quickly back on track, eyeing up their captors with an assessing glance. Behind her, Teal'c growled his way back to consciousness.

"Just a couple of lost travelers, Carter, looking for their, er, former cross-dressing lord."

"Oh, boy."

"Yup. Any idea where Janet and you-know-who are?"

"Shopping for clothes. She said they'd be here by 1800."

Jack craned around to see the clock over the kitchen window:

1810. Any minute now these two idiots' lost lord was going to waltz into the house, and yeah, were they in for a surprise. No way was he going to allow Sarah Gardner to be taken by the Goa'uld again, with or without her now fortunately missing pal.

"Jack," Daniel's urgent voice sounded in his ear.

"I know. Just keep quiet."

Interested by their conversation, Larry and Curly stepped closer. They zeroed in on Daniel. Curly leaned over him.

"Daaneel?"

"Um, guess that's been established, then."

"Hey — Larry, Curly, over here!" Jack barked. They both ignored him.

Teal'c took up the diversionary tactic. "Jaffa, kree tol mek!"

Having apparently settled on a course of action the two Jaffa set about untying Daniel from Jack. They hauled Daniel upright, to a string of protests.

"Are we going somewhere? I have to tell you, I'm not dressed for traveling," he chattered. "Can we just take a moment for me to change? My room's just down the hall here..." Daniel gestured extravagantly, arm flying outward into Curly's face.

Jack, watching for just such a move, slithered to one side out of Larry's grip. He twisted, tried to bring his legs around to sweep Larry off his feet. Larry might not be the brightest bulb in the Jaffa firmament but he had good reflexes. He leapt nimbly over Jack's legs. The wasted momentum sent Jack face down on the floor. He scrabbled on the slippery tiles for purchase with knees and elbows. From behind, there came an ear-cringing war whoop. He managed to turn over just as something bright yellow and brown flew past overhead. Curly caught a face full of stuffed giraffe, and went down, tackled to the floor by Pete Shanahan. Jack allowed a second to appreciate the move, and swung a double booted kick into the melee. Beyond, he could see Teal'c and Carter struggling to get to their feet, but he'd lost track of Daniel and Larry.

For a moment it appeared they would get the upper hand.

Shanahan wrestled Curly for control of his zat gun, with the odd shot escaping to further slag Daniel's ruined cook wear.

"Kree!" The shout echoed around the kitchen.

Jack grimaced. He was really coming to hate that word. He cranked his head around to see Larry, one arm wrapped around Daniel's neck, holding one of the carving knives that had been Jack's original intended weapon against Daniel's carotid artery. Both men were disheveled, breathing hard and sporting some impressive soon-to-be bruises. The melee in the kitchen paused.

"Okay," Jack said, his tone placating and soothing. "Let's not do anything that's gonna make a mess."

"Thanks, Jack." Daniel ground the words out past the pressure on his throat, his body bent uncomfortably to one side by Larry's shorter stature.

Curly wriggled out from under Shanahan and got to his feet. He looked quite rumpled from the tussle but triumphantly held the zat.

"Pete, nice move," Carter called. Jack almost did a double-take. She did *not* bat her eyes at Shanahan, did she?

"These guys are strong," Pete complained. Under the aim of Curly's zat he shuffled across the floor to her and Teal'c.

"I shall give you some instruction in more effective methods of combat when this situation has been resolved," Teal'c offered.

"Hey, that'd be great, Teal'c, thanks."

"Um, a little help here?" Daniel broke in. Larry's grip around his throat had not lessened.

Curly sidestepped Jack and lined up with Larry on Daniel's other side. They inched backward, dragging Daniel toward the back door. Clearly, if their god was a no-show, they were content to take what, or rather who, they could get and bug out of here. They paused in the doorway to negotiate the logistics of getting three bodies through one door while keeping their prisoners on the floor covered. Jack cursed under his breath. No way were they going to make off with Daniel, not after they'd just got him back from his hiatus, but any move he made would be met by a zat blast before he even got to his knees. He'd be no use to anyone unconscious. He needed a plan...

It was then that the front door chime rang out into the warm evening air.

Sarah Gardner, laughing at Janet's latest retelling of one of SG-1's more outlandish missions, walked with her new friend up the sidewalk toward Daniel's house. Janet had taken her shopping to restock her wardrobe. Fashions had changed in the four years she'd been gone from Earth. The mall had been overwhelmingly strange when they first entered: her senses bombarded by strangely familiar sounds that were too loud, smells she had not experienced in years, glaringly bright lights so different from the muted corridors of Goa'uld vessels to which she'd become accustomed. But with enthusiastic encouragement from Janet, she'd begun to acclimate and they were soon diving into every boutique the mall offered. Janet, with her quick wit and compassionate insight, found a way past her defenses that even Daniel had not yet managed. By lunchtime they were becoming firm friends.

At Daniel's door, she juggled the carry bags in her hands and looked back, down, at Janet. "The Asgard really made a clone of the colonel?"

"They certainly did. Now that he's completely recovered he's even enrolled in high school."

They shared a slightly horrified look.

"Jack O'Neill in high school?" they both said at the same time, and burst out laughing again.

"Doesn't bear thinking about, honey," Janet drawled. "Push that door bell. I need to get out of these heels."

Sarah straightened her dress with one hand and pushed the bell. She'd bought as many flowery and frilly clothes as she could, determined to get as far as possible from the overly ornate black and gold 'god' clothes Osiris had reveled in during her captivity, and the associated memories they brought to her. Music resonated inside the house. Classical. Familiar. She thought hard for a moment. Beethoven? Yes. A smile rose inside her; another piece of normal life returned to her. One down, umpteen hundreds to go.

They waited. No one came to the door.

Impatient, Janet leaned into the doorway and called, "Yoohoo! Daniel, we're here."

They waited some more. Janet tutted under her breath.

"Daniel's probably asleep and the rest of them are most likely on the back porch." She tried the door handle, which obligingly turned. "Here we go. Colonel, you'd better have that wine open!"

Janet pushed the door open and led the way. Sarah hesitated. The neat hallway before her, with its white painted walls and wooden floor, suddenly assailed her with memories: more than the attempts to steal Daniel's memories or attack him and the colonel and Teal'c with the hand device, there was a strong sense of guilt at allowing Osiris to return to Earth and bring harm to someone she had — and still did — care for. She shook her head. *It's over, he's gone for good, everyone is okay. Small steps forward.* She repeated Janet's mantra and followed her down the hall, taking care not to knock Daniel's artworks with her carry bags.

Sarah poked her head into Daniel's bedroom — not there. Good, he was awake. She really wanted to show him some of the outfits she'd bought. She'd never been the type of girl to be obsessed with clothes, but holding these new things, somehow she was starting to have a sense of belonging once again to the people of this planet. Daniel would understand. She walked down the hall, turned the corner, into the kitchen. Janet was standing just inside the entry, oddly, hands full of shopping bags held awkwardly out from her sides. Sarah peeped over her shoulder, a cheery smile on her lips.

"Daniel?"

A tableau of faces looked back at her, most of them from the direction of the floor. Teal'c and Sam Carter were sitting back to back on the kitchen tiles, Sam's boyfriend Pete next to them. They didn't look all that pleased to see her. Beyond them, Jack O'Neill was also on the floor, his legs stretched out in front of him, a resigned scowl on his face. And beyond him... frozen in the open back door stood Daniel, bare-footed, half-dressed, with an apologetic grimace on his face and a knife at his throat. A knife held by a young man, dressed in metallic armor. Jaffa. There was a matching one on Daniel's other side.

Within her mind, a small door opened and memories flooded through in a blast of clarity. Golden, flame-lit halls; her strides echoed with commanding presence; slaves bowed to hide their fear; Jaffa scurried ahead, arrogant with the purpose of executing her orders; a dark cloaked figure, malevolence swirling about it like a tangible thing; boarding the cramped tel'tak, its meager facilities unsuitable for one of her rank but she would follow the dark one's orders until such time as she held the secrets he desired, then he would fall and she would rise and be exalted above all Goa'uld...

Sarah came back to herself, a shiver crawled down her spine. The Jaffa, Ja'dok and Bikram, were the two who had accompanied Osiris on his mission. She — rather, he — had ordered them to remain in the tel'tak until his return, and apparently so they had, wiped from her memory by the removal of Osiris. Until now. More memories threatened to return from hiding. She pushed them back through that small door and closed it. She would deal with them later. Much later.

Ja'dok and Bikram ceased their motion through the back door, relief creased their features.

"My lord! We feared you were — uh," Ja'dok stuttered. One did not say a System Lord — a *god* — was thought to be lost. "We wished to assist you in your mission," he finished lamely.

Sarah arched an imperious eyebrow at him. Instinct took over; Sarah the unassuming archaeologist gave ground to the pseudo-god she had been for the past four years. She stepped around Janet and pressed her carry bags into the doctor's arms as she passed, forcing Janet to juggle the whole pile of them to an untidy heap on the floor.

"Thought? When did We ever require Jaffa to think?" She stalked slowly across the room, heels clicking imperiously on the tiles. "We require you to heed Our orders, to act as We tell you to act. Your presence here jeopardizes Our mission. We are not pleased."

"Forgive us, my lord," Bikram said, tripping over his words in haste. "We feared some ill deed had befallen you. Of course we were wrong. Our god could never be compromised." They both bowed to her, which brought the knife away from Daniel's throat.

Sarah caught a glimpse of Daniel's face; he was eyeing her with some degree of surprise. She heard a mutter from the direction of the floor. Jack O'Neill glared up at her, eyebrows furrowing with the beginnings of suspicion.

Behind her she heard Pete mutter to Sam, "I thought they took that thing out?"

"Shhh," Sam flung back at him.

They were all staring at her like she was not the rescued friend she had been to them earlier in the day. She glanced at Daniel. Even he was boggling at her. Why — Oh. Her words came back to her: precise, practiced Goa'uld dialect, fallen from her lips with unconscious effort. Nausea curled in her stomach. Still, needs must.

"We have infiltrated these people," she declared, hoping her former minions would realize her frilly dress underscored that point. "Our mission proceeds as We planned." Her eyes fell on the knife Ja'dok held. "You will not harm this man, We have need of him still."

"Of course, my lord. Shall we return to my lord's vessel?" Ja'dok lowered the knife.

Feeling their grip on him lessen, Daniel edged away from the Jaffa, eyes darting from them to Sarah and back.

"Hmm," Sarah kept up the haughty god performance. She

casually strolled across the kitchen, pausing at the island bench to finger the fallen saucepans as if she'd never seen such items before. She could order them to return to their ship, but what then? They might return when their god failed to join them, or they could even decide to 'rescue' Osiris and beam *her* up to the tel'tak. The cold shiver returned full-force. She turned her back on them to cast an assessing glare over the captives. They were all watching her carefully. Daniel, she could tell, did not share the suspicion that was etched so clearly on O'Neill's face. Pete and Janet were confused, Sam apprehensive. Teal'c, though, was harboring different thoughts, ones she immediately picked up on. Her, *Osiris's*, two Jaffa were young, impressionable. They deserved to live their lives according to their own wishes, not a Goa'uld's. Teal'c had told her of the resistance building within the Jaffa populations on many worlds. Despite recent setbacks, he believed it was the only future for his people. She had seen first-hand the misery and suffering they endured at the hands of the System Lords and Goa'uld in general; any small part she could play in putting an end to such tyranny would go some way to easing the torment she felt for her involvement — unwitting as it had been.

O'Neill caught her attention, his head indicating a slight tilt to the side. He repeated the action, and rolled his eyes to the left, toward the back door. Beyond the nervous Jaffa, Sarah saw a large expanse of trees and browning grass in Daniel's secluded back yard. Get everyone outside, and hopefully disarm the Jaffa without causing further injuries — or damage to Daniel's house.

"Jaffa," she said in Osiris's clipped tone, hiding a small flash of amusement as not only Ja'dok and Bikram but SG-1 also snapped to attention. "We require all these humans to accompany us to our ha'tak. Bring them outside. We shall call down the ring transporter."

Ja'dok and Bikram bowed their acknowledgment, any misgivings they had were carefully shielded from the god who ruled their lives. One covered Daniel and indicated for him to help Jack to his feet. The other pushed Janet toward the back door.

"Hey, watch where you put your hands, buster." Janet skidded on the tiles and skewered him with an indignant glare. She gave Sarah an infinitesimal nod of understanding and followed Daniel and Jack through the screen door.

Sarah tapped her foot impatiently while Bikram endeavored to get Teal'c and Sam to their feet. It proved impossible while they remained tied together. Pete's attempts to assist only made the matter more convoluted. "Release them," she commanded.

"Yes, my lord."

Bikram slid the carving knife through the cords binding Sam to Teal'c. He trained the zat'ni'katel on them as they got stiffly to their feet, and prodded them and Pete toward the door. Sarah waited for them to pass, not liking the uncertainty that crossed Bikram's face as he passed close to her. She followed them out onto the back porch where her Jaffa and her friends milled uncertainly. O'Neill was focused on the zat'ni'katel held by Ja'dok. There was a tension of impending violence in his stance that was mirrored in Teal'c, otherwise focused on Bikram.

"Down there." Sarah raised her arm and grandly indicated the sweep of grass below them.

Ja'dok obeyed, walking backward to cover the prisoners who filed down the steps onto the grass. Bikram and Sarah joined them last. Bikram hesitated, staring apologetically at her.

"My lord?" He seemed conflicted, confused. "You appear changed, my lord. Forgive my boldness in saying such a thing, but I cannot sense your presence as I always have…"

"Presence?" She scowled down at him. "I stand before you!"

"But… *Lord Osiris* is not standing before us." Bikram came to the realization as he spoke the words.

Sarah gasped. The Jaffa could sense the presence of another symbiote — a small thing forgotten in the tumult of pretending to be who she no longer was.

"Crap." The snarled word heralded O'Neill's blur of movement. He leapt for Ja'dok, slamming the Jaffa to the ground in a desperate grapple for the zat. Daniel joined in, the three of them rolling furiously in the dusty grass.

Bikram aborted the move he made toward Sarah and turned to help his companion. Teal'c stepped into his path.

"Surrender, Jaffa, and follow me to the path of freedom. You will join the Jaffa Resistance, and help your brothers to throw off the yoke of slavery to the Goa'uld."

Bikram blinked at him, raised the zat and fired.

Teal'c threw himself sideways. Sarah winced as the zat charge missed its target and hit Pete, who crumpled with a pained squawk.

"Hey!" Sam yelled, indignant on Pete's behalf. She tackled Bikram and they hit the ground hard. They rolled down the gradual incline, past the other untidy battle between Ja'dok, Daniel and Jack. A zat blast from Ja'dok narrowly missed Sam and flew on ahead to land on a large round hatch imbedded in the grass at the bottom of the garden. It sizzled and sparked brightly in the evening twilight.

Teal'c pushed to his feet and charged after Sam. Sarah exchanged a glance with Janet, who shook herself and pulled out a cell phone. She dialed and quickly began issuing orders for backup support.

Another zat blast escaped from Bikram, flying away to hit the same metal hatch, still sparking from the first blast. With a dull crump the piece of metal exploded skyward, whooping end over end it flew over their heads, over the house and landed somewhere out in the street with a crashing clang. A car alarm rang out in response.

The struggles on the lawn paused. Bikram, flattened by Teal'c on top of him, surrendered his zat to Sam. Jack took advantage of Ja'dok's distraction by the explosion and punched him solidly on the jaw. The Jaffa collapsed back into the grass, fingers reflexively tightened on the trigger and caused one final charge to escape the zat. It shot away on the same trajectory as the previous one, flew over the now gaping hole in the lawn and ignited the cloud of gases visibly escaping from it.

"What the hell?" Jack barely had time to ask as another explosion punched through the air. It knocked him off his knees into Daniel. They fell to the ground, Daniel's one-worded cry reached Sarah's ears just as they were all engulfed by a torrent of sludge pouring up and then, unfortunately, down on top of them.

"Cesspool!"

Janet heard Daniel's cry a nanosecond before the deluge. She ducked behind the only thing taller than her — Sarah — held her breath and squeezed her eyes shut. Putrid sludge rained down on them, the overwhelming smell invaded every pore and set her eyes to watering. She could feel it sliding down the back of her neck. She shuddered, fumbled out a handkerchief from her sleeve and pressed it against her nose. Above, she could hear faint squeals from Sarah, battered with a frontal assault from the sludge. It seemed to last an eternity, but eventually the rain turned to random, then solitary plops. She could see the once pretty chiffon dress Sarah wore, plastered to her long legs by thick black muck.

"Cover your mouths and eyes," she managed to call to the others. The only replies were groans, coughs and the sound of one unfortunate seized by vomiting.

Janet edged out from behind Sarah, one hand shielding her eyes from drips. The entirety of Daniel's back yard was now a sludge pit, slowly sliding downhill back to where it had come from. Trees, plants, fences, people — everything was a uniform stinky black. Fortunately, most everyone had managed to cover their faces. Jack was sprawled on top of an unmoving Daniel, the Jaffa next to them curled into a fetal ball. Pete was beginning to stir from where the zat blast had tossed him, thankfully face down into the grass. Teal'c was making an attempt to get up from where he lay across Sam and the other Jaffa. He made it after slipping twice in goop, and sat blinking his eyes clear. Janet thought she heard him mutter something, but didn't really think Teal'c would sum up the situation with the word "Dude".

Both Jaffa appeared to have completely lost interest in the fight and lay in stunned surrender. From somewhere, a tinny voice penetrated Janet's clogged ears.

"Major? Major! What on Earth is going on there? Major!"

"General?" She tried to clear an ear, fumbling her cell phone. "General!"

"Status, Major. That sounded like an explosion."

"Yes, sir, methane explosion from a disused cesspool." Dear lord, let it be disused. Even so... "We're gonna need some SFs. And a decontamination unit. And some hoses. And some new clothes. And a hell of a lot of antibiotics."

"You're at Dr. Jackson's home?" Hammond's incredulity came over loud and clear.

"Yes, sir." She took in the ruined back yard. "What's left of it."

"On our way, Major."

Janet dropped the sludge-covered phone into the sludge-covered grass. She patted Sarah on the shoulder, sympathizing with the tiny distressed sounds she made. Using extreme caution, Janet made her way around the yard, checking everyone was in no immediate danger. It was like skating—in a stench-laden rink. Finally, she slid into Colonel O'Neill, cautiously pulling himself up off Daniel.

"Sorry, sir."

"Well, this just puts the icing on the cake," he grumbled.

"Par for the course?"

"All in a day's work."

"Daniel, you okay?" Janet peered over the colonel's shoulder. Curled into a nice clean patch of green grass, Daniel Jackson slept the sleep of the obliviously stressed. Janet freely wished herself in his shoes, just this once.

She glanced back to Sarah and managed a rueful grin. "Welcome back to Earth, Sarah!"

Sarah Gardner, eyes bright in a black sludge complexion, sighed. "I really need a cup of tea."

STARGATE ATLANTIS
Kill Switch

Aaron Rosenberg

"What've we got?" Lt Colonel John Sheppard demanded as he burst into the main control center. As usual, he was already geared up and had his hand resting on his service pistol as if he might need to draw it at any second.

"Relax, Colonel," Elizabeth Weir cautioned with a raised hand, though the slight smile on her face indicated that she wasn't terribly upset that her second-in-command was always on high alert. She gestured toward the briefing room to one side of the operations center. "Take a seat, and I'll explain in a minute." As the Commander of the Atlantis Expedition, Weir was Sheppard's superior officer. But she was also his friend, and it was as much for that as out of any respect for her rank that Sheppard nodded, stalked across, and dropped into a chair at one end of the array of monitor-covered tables. That didn't prevent him from grumbling a bit under his breath, however.

"Urgent, something you need to see right away," he muttered, crossing his arms over his chest. "Get to command ASAP. Guess it was just so I'd be sure to get a good seat, huh?"

"You know," Rodney McKay commented as he strode into the room and took up position in the seat opposite Sheppard's, "subvocalizing complaints is childish behavior better suited to lower primates and small children than to grown adults, especially senior officers." As usual, Atlantis' Chief Science Officer managed to look smug when he pointed this out, as if such action would be far beneath his own superior intellect — this despite the fact that he often behaved like an overgrown child himself, or like a crotchety old man.

"Gee, thanks for the tip, Rodney," Sheppard snapped back,

taking care as always to emphasize the scientist's first name. "Trust me, whenever I've got complaints about you I'll be sure to say 'em loud and clear." The two men glared at each other. Anyone who didn't know them would assume they hated each other, though in reality they were good friends and trusted each other with their lives. That didn't mean they didn't annoy each other, however.

"Will you two settle down and behave?" Teyla Emmagan asked, joining the rest of the team and settling into a chair between the two men. She rolled her eyes at both of them, then turned to give Weir her full attention. Ronon Dex had followed her into the room, and claimed a chair without a word, nodding to the rest of the team but with his customary scowl still upon his stern-featured face. No one took it personally — the Satedan former Runner was definitely a man of few words, but even though it had only been a few months since the Expedition Team had found him, much less since he'd joined them, they had already learned to trust the tall, brooding warrior.

"Good, you're all here," Weir said as she joined them, taking her customary seat in the center of the middlemost table. "Dr. Zelenka, if you please?"

Dr. Radek Zelenka nodded and quickly scurried into the room, fiddling with the controls for one of the large monitors set up on a rolling cart so it could be dragged about more easily and finally displaying the image of a familiar-looking starscape. "This is the space around Lantea," the Czech scientist began, earning a snort from Rodney and provoking a glare in return. If Rodney rubbed most people the wrong way, he irritated Zelenka even more, in part because the two men were often forced to work together, but also because Zelenka was an expert in Ancient technology, second only to Rodney himself — and Rodney never let him forget it.

The image, which showed the night sky above the planet that hosted Atlantis, zoomed in on an area speckled with irregular shapes. "This is the nearby asteroid belt," Zelenka continued. "But a recent scan has turned up something strange." He adjusted the image to close in still further, zeroing in on a small cluster of rocks, then created a small halo around the one in the center, which was roughly pear-shaped. "This one."

"What about it?" Sheppard asked, having no patience for the scientist's theatrics.

"It is not an asteroid," Zelenka replied. "In fact, I do not think it is natural at all."

"Someone's going around manufacturing asteroids?" Rodney commented. "Why bother? There are plenty of the normal ones just lying about."

"We don't know why," Weir answered. "That's what your team needs to find out."

Teyla leaned forward, studying the image. "What makes you think it isn't natural?" she asked.

"The mineral content, most likely," Rodney answered before Zelenka could. "The asteroids in this system are mostly silicates, without a lot of iron or carbon. If this one's got a different chemical composition, that would suggest it came from somewhere different from its companions, and possibly that it was manufactured rather than naturally occurring. A better question would be, why are we just finding out about this now?" He stared at Zelenka as if holding the little Czech personally responsible for this oversight.

It was Weir who answered, however, perhaps in an effort to forestall yet another argument between the two scientists. "We just upgraded our intrasystem scanners," she explained. "The new software allows us to fine-tune our study of the area right around us, which should let us detect any small ships or other subtle threats we might have missed before. As part of the calibration we rescanned all of the existing objects, and that was when Doctor Zelenka's team discovered the oddity."

"So you want us to take a Jumper and go check it out?" Sheppard said, already rising to his feet. "We're on it."

"Be careful," Zelenka called out as the colonel led the way

toward the exit. "The metal composition is unusually high, less like an asteroid than a ship. Or a bomb."

"Gee, thanks for the cheerful thought," Rodney shot back over his shoulder as he followed the rest of the team out. "That's bound to make this little jaunt even more delightful than it would have been already."

"It'll be more delightful if it saves your life, you imbecile!" Zelenka railed after him. "For you, anyway," he added as the door slid shut, cutting him and Weir off from the departing team.

If she heard his final statement, she tactfully chose to ignore it, instead returning to the control center and telling one of the officers there, "Prep Puddle Jumper One for immediate launch." The man nodded and began typing in commands, and Weir stepped back far enough to let him do his job, but still close enough to watch over his shoulder. There weren't many aspects of Atlantis' daily activities she let escape her personal supervision. A part of her wished, as always, that she could go with the team up to the asteroid belt, to see firsthand what they discovered — and to be there to oversee the mission, in case there were any problems. But of course she couldn't. She had to trust Sheppard and the others to handle whatever they found, as they always had before.

Which didn't make it any easier to stand there, watching, as their ship headed through the gate, leaving her behind and heading off into the unknown once more.

"Oh, that can't be good," Rodney remarked, studying the console he was using to scan the large asteroid even as the Jumper slowed to a stop only a few kilometers away. "Zelenka was right for a change — I suppose there's a first time for everything. This little beauty in front of us is almost entirely iron and carbon, and judging by the ratio and dispersement I'd guess they've been fused together into that handy little alloy we like to call steel."

"It's a steel asteroid?" Sheppard considered the unassuming brownish-gray rock floating before them. "Doesn't look like it."

"Well, it's got an outer layer of silica," the stocky scientist admitted, "but it's only a few centimeters thick at most."

"How did it get the rock around it, then?" Teyla asked, peering past the two of them from her seat just behind. "Could it have picked that up while bouncing around in space, like gathering dust? Or is this deliberate camouflage?"

"Deliberate," Ronon rumbled, surprising the rest of them as it often did when he deigned to speak. He shrugged at their curious glances. "It's too even to be coincidental," he pointed out.

"He has a good point," Rodney agreed. "This rock layer covers whatever's inside completely. If it was natural, there'd be a few gaps and cracks." He shuddered. "What if Zelenka's right and it is a bomb?" he asked. "I suggest we retreat to a safe distance and blow it up, just to be safe."

"And what if it turns out to be something important?" Sheppard replied, shaking his head. "No, we're not doing that, Rodney. You're going to find us a spot where we can drill through that rock and see what's beneath it."

Teyla had been examining the scans displayed on Rodney's console, and now she stabbed a finger at one corner. "What's that there?" she asked. "The composition in that spot is just a little different — it's got traces of oxygen in it."

Rodney frowned and tapped in a few quick commands. "That doesn't make any sense," he muttered to himself, unaware that he was doing exactly what he'd ridiculed Sheppard for so recently. "Oxygen and iron on the same asteroid? Unless . . ." He adjusted the scan, narrowing its parameters to a tighter beam right on the spot Teyla had indicated. "Aha!" he declared after a minute's work. "Yes! The oxygen isn't part of the structure — it's *inside* it. That thing is hollow."

"Hollow?" Sheppard scratched at his chin. "Well, all right, then. Now I really want to know what's inside. Rodney, find us a door."

"I think Teyla already did," the scientist replied, actually giving someone else due credit for once. "The reason the oxygen is visible there is because that section is thinner than the rest. If I had to guess, I'd say it was a concealed airlock."

"Great." Sheppard took hold of the Jumper's controls. "Then let's go knock and see if anybody's home." And with a steady hand he guided the small scout ship closer, angling it upward until its nose was perfectly aligned with the area Rodney had highlighted on their overhead display. "Any ideas on where to find a doorbell?" Sheppard asked once they were floating right in front of the spot, which didn't look any different to the naked eye.

"Try sending a docking request," Teyla suggested. "If it really is an airlock, it should have mechanisms in place to register that."

Sheppard tapped in the command, and a second later the ship sent out a small, coded pulse. Any Ancient technology — or adapted SGC equipment — would recognize the pattern and acknowledge it. But what the fake asteroid would do, they had no idea. Would it recognize them as approved visitors? Or treat them as potential threats?

Which was why all four of them, even the ever-stoic Ronon, breathed a sigh of relief when they heard a faint ping through the ship's speakers, and watched as a thin band of light formed in a square right in front of them. "It worked!" Rodney declared. "The airlock's opening!"

"Really? We couldn't tell," Sheppard drawled even as he adjusted the Puddle Jumper, swiveling it around and guiding it backward so the cargo bay door at the rear would come into contact with the now-revealed airlock. There was a faint shudder as the two objects bumped up against each other, and then a hiss and a click as the airlock latched onto the ship, sealing the connection to prevent any atmosphere from escaping on either side.

"We're docked," Teyla announced, checking the readings.

"Good solid lock. Scans show breathable atmosphere on the other side."

"What're we waiting for, then?" Sheppard asked, unstrapping and hauling himself out of his chair. He slapped Rodney on the back, and nodded to Teyla and Ronon as they all crowded toward the hatch leading into the aft section, which would then end at the small ship's main hatch. "Let's say hello!"

"Yeah, great, hi," Rodney said under his breath as he brought up the rear. "Hope you're not rigged to blow or anything." But he followed the rest of the team toward the airlock — just a few paces behind. To be safe.

It was always a little disquieting to step through an airlock and find yourself having to reorient based on the new space, discovering that what was up in your ship was now down or sideways. That was the case here — they walked into the airlock from the Puddle Jumper, but once the outer door had closed behind them and the inner one hissed open the team found themselves looking down into the asteroid, as if they had entered and laid on their bellies. There was only minimal gravity within the hollow shell, but it was just enough to help them get used to the idea that the ladders bolted along the walls past the airlock led down, and once they'd swung out and grabbed hold, setting their feet on lower rungs, that direction took hold of their minds and bodies and they were able to proceed normally. With only minimal griping from Rodney.

His ever-present complaining tapered off, however, as he finally cleared the airlock completely and got his first good look around inside the fake asteroid. The interior matched the exterior in terms of its pear shape, though in here the edges were clean and crisp, a faceted circular base tapering up toward the airlock at the top like the whole was molded from an enormous gem. The walls were pale metal, and below them where the tapering ended was a balcony that ran all the way around, ierced on two opposite sides by the ladders that continued on down to the bottom. Small screens were set around both of those levels, and a few large openings near the base seemed to lead off into side alcoves or possibly even whole other rooms.

"Hey!" Rodney shouted, his voice particularly loud in the enclosed space — they had all left their helmets off once they'd confirmed Teyla's initial reading on the atmosphere, which was a little stuffy and stale but definitely breathable. "I know this place!"

Sheppard had taken the lead, as usual, and was just stepping off the ladder and onto the narrow balcony. Now he glanced back up at Rodney, reflexively moving aside at the same time so Teyla could join him. "What're you talking about?" he demanded. "You were just as surprised this thing was hollow as the rest of us."

"Yes yes," Rodney admitted, hurrying the rest of the way down after Ronon and finally reaching the other three on the balcony. They spaced out along it a bit, there being ample room around it — the entire bottom level was perhaps ten meters across, and the whole chamber close to forty meters tall. "I didn't know what it was at the time. But now that we're inside" — he gestured around them — "this I recognize." His face lost its customary smirk, looking sadder and more serious than the others had seen him save for a few times. "This is an exact match," he continued slowly, "for the Ancient satellite we found at the Lagrange point back when the Wraith first located Atlantis."

That made all of them pause respectfully, even Ronon, who had only heard about the event after he'd joined the Atlantis Expedition. The Wraith had finally succeeded in their long quest to pinpoint Atlantis's location and had sent several Hive ships to take the city by force. Before they'd arrived, however, the Atlantis scientists had discovered that the Ancients, when they'd first settled their city here, had established a network of defense satellites around the planet — and one of them had survived. Rodney had taken two other crewmembers, scientist

Peter Grodin and pilot Miller, up to investigate the satellite. They'd been able to get it up and running again, at least long enough to power up its weaponry and eliminate one of the three Hive ships. But then their repairs had failed and the weapon had lost power. The Wraith had retaliated, and destroyed the satellite completely. Peter Grodin had still been onboard, trying to get the weapons operational again. The only reason Rodney and Miller had survived was because Grodin had sent them away before the attack, pointing out that someone had to stay and man the weapon but that the other two should hide at a safe distance, just in case. He'd saved their lives. And, by taking out one of the Hive ships, possibly the lives of everyone else on Atlantis as well.

"Okay," Sheppard said slowly after a minute, not needling Rodney for a change. "So this is a good thing, right? This is Ancient tech, and it's a defense system for Atlantis — and one you already know how to repair. I'd say that's a darn sight better than a bomb, wouldn't you?"

Rodney nodded. "Yes," he agreed somberly. "I should be able to run diagnostics, fix any problems, and get the systems up to full power and readiness without too much trouble." He glanced around. "Peter and I figured out where everything was," he added softly.

"What do you want us to do?" Teyla asked him gently. "Can we help?"

"No, just stay out of the way," Rodney replied. The others all rolled their eyes, but couldn't help relaxing a little bit as well. The old Rodney was back, which meant he was shaking off the doldrums he'd gotten from those memories. That was a good thing, even if they had made him a little more human — and thus more bearable — for a minute.

Rodney stepped back onto the ladder and quickly descended to the bottom level, then headed straight for a row of small screens mounted on one of the walls at head height. While he tapped in commands, calling up various images and displays, the other three scouted the rest of the asteroid. There wasn't much else to see. The openings did in fact lead to additional sections, but they narrowed rapidly, to the point where it was impossible to proceed without crawling. "Looks like service tunnels," Sheppard said once he'd explored one a little ways. "I'm guessing it ends in a hatch that lets you outside onto one of the arms — I remember the satellite was a spiky-looking thing, like a metal porcupine or cactus, and this probably has some of that same architecture, just buried under layers of rock."

"It's funny that the Ancestors would mask this satellite but not the others," Teyla commented, running a hand idly along one smooth, cold, metallic wall. "Why do that? Was this one special in some way?"

"I thought you only found the one, before," Ronon rumbled — he'd stopped at the entrance to this offshoot, where it was still tall enough for him to stand without having to stoop. Now he shrugged. "Maybe more of them were like this, too."

"The big guy's got a point," Sheppard agreed, tapping a panel and listening to the faint ringing that produced. "If I was the Ancients, I'd put some satellites out in the open and then hide others. That way, even if somebody found and disabled the first set, they might not think to look for a second grouping." He studied their surroundings. "But the Wraith or the Asurans or somebody must've clued in and destroyed them all, hidden or open. They only missed that one — and now this one, too." He grinned at his teammates. "But, hey, their mistake is our gain."

Which was certainly true. The last satellite had destroyed a Hive ship with a single strike. If this one had comparable power, it would make a formidable weapon to defend Atlantis from any new attacks.

Provided Rodney could get it up and working properly.

"How's it going, Rodney?" Sheppard called out as he stalked back into the main chamber with Teyla and Ronon right behind him. "We good to go yet?"

"This isn't a coffeemaker," Rodney snapped, not even looking up from the console he was working on. "It's Ancient technology, and even though I am an expert on such, it still requires a little finesse. Unless you'd like me to activate its self-destruct by mistake, and seal us in here at the same time."

Sheppard held up his hands in mock-surrender. "No, you do what you've gotta do," he replied, backing up a step. "We'll wait."

"Fine. Thank you, though you shouldn't have to wait too long, because I think I've just about — uh-oh." Rodney did look up finally, but only to study the small screen directly in front of him — and what he saw made him go pale.

" 'Uh-oh' doesn't sound too promising," Sheppard pointed out after a few seconds, when McKay hadn't elaborated.

"No, I suppose it doesn't." Rodney gulped, then turned to face the others. "So, good news and bad news," he started, frowning. "The good news is, this satellite is almost a perfect match for the other one in terms of capabilities. And, unlike the other one, it's fully operational. The buffer is already starting to build a charge."

"What's the bad news?" Ronon asked, glaring about them like he was expecting to be attacked at any second. Since that same wariness had kept him alive for all those years on the run, no one faulted him for his caution.

"The bad news. Yes. That." Rodney gestured at the screen. "The bad news is, apparently we weren't the first ones to find this place. The system shows that someone else accessed it a while back, like years ago, and modified things a bit."

Sheppard stared at the screen as if it was going to start answering questions directly. "And that someone was . . . ?"

"At a guess?" Rodney sighed. "The Wraith."

"The Wraith were here?" Teyla scanned the satellite's tiny interior, which was pristine. "Why didn't they destroy it, then? Surely they knew it could be used against them?"

"I'm hardly an expert on Wraith psychology," Rodney answered, marking one of the few times he'd ever admitted to not being an expert about, well, anything. "But at a guess, I'd say either they were feeling clever and decided to leave it as a Trojan horse — or they couldn't figure out how to destroy it, so they sabotaged it instead."

"What'd they do?" Sheppard demanded.

"They corrupted its targeting system," Rodney explained. "It's already got a target locked in, and I can't break in and change that." After another second he added what his companions had really hoped he wouldn't: "It's Atlantis."

"So the Wraith found this place, broke in, mucked around in here, and set it up so whenever it next turned on, it'd start firing on Atlantis itself?" Sheppard asked, shaking his head.

"Pretty much," Rodney confirmed. He studied the small screen. "We have perhaps four hours before that happens."

"How much damage are we talking about?" Teyla wanted to know.

Rodney did a quick calculation in his head. "Probably enough to destroy at least a quarter of the city with a single shot," he answered when he was done. "And there's no reason this system won't have enough power to get off five or six shots in a row before the buffer needs to recharge."

The four of them stared at each other. This weapon could destroy Atlantis in a single flurry.

"How do we stop it?" Sheppard asked. "There's got to be a way, right?"

"Maybe," Rodney admitted, staring at and through the display as he thought. "Maybe." He glanced up at Sheppard. "But it might be easiest just to destroy it. If we blow it up before it gets a chance to fire, problem solved."

Sheppard shook his head. "We just found the darn thing," he pointed out. "And it could save our butts the next time anyone attacks us directly. I don't think we want to toss that away if we don't have to." He clapped Rodney on the shoulder. "So figure out a way that we don't have to."

"Oh, great," Rodney muttered, returning his attention

to the console and typing in new commands and requests. "No pressure."

"We could move the city," Weir suggested. Sheppard had returned to the Puddle Jumper and called Atlantis to update them on the situation and consider their options. "The weapon would wind up firing upon the planet instead, probably doing minimal damage as long as it didn't pierce the crust, and after the satellite had exhausted its power supply we could simply return to our current location."

"Maybe," Sheppard conceded, rubbing his chin as he thought. "Assuming it's not tracking the city somehow, in which case you'd just be presenting it with a moving target. And assuming you can get the city up and off-planet in time without tearing it apart. And that, like you said, it doesn't shoot through the planet and make it explode or anything. And—"

"Yes yes, I agree, it's not an optimal solution," Weir cut in. "But it's better than getting shot."

"True. But if it comes to that, Rodney's right, we can just blow up the satellite instead," Sheppard countered. "That'd be a lot easier, and we'd be no worse off than we were before."

"Agreed. But if there is a way to salvage that satellite, we should do so. It could prove invaluable for our defensive systems."

"That's exactly what I said." Sheppard banged on the arm of his chair, more out of frustration than anger. "We'll see what we can do."

"Good. If we think of anything that can help from down here, we'll let you know," Weir told him before she signed off. Sheppard stared at the screen for a minute after it had powered down, lost in thought. Then, with a sigh, he rose and headed back toward the deadly new weapon they'd found, and the friends who were trying their best to disarm it.

"Anything?" he asked once he'd re-entered the satellite. Rodney was still examining lines of code, trying to figure out how to unlock the target selection, while Teyla was using a different console to scan other aspects of the structure. Ronon was leaning against one of the walls, arms crossed, his gaze flicking from corner to corner, taking in alcoves and railings, his hands never far from his weapons.

"I think I can manually drain the buffer," Rodney called out, pulling up a second screen and zooming in on one section. "That should buy us a little more time. But whatever they did to lock in the target, I can't break it. Not yet. Maybe not ever." He shook his head. "Which means it's only a matter of time before this satellite fires on Atlantis, unless we destroy the thing completely."

"I might have something," Teyla announced. That drew the others' attention, and she waited until they'd all turned toward her before explaining further. "Rodney was already working on getting the system to choose a new target," she said, "but I was thinking of something a little different. If we can't get it to turn away from Atlantis, I thought maybe we could get it to target a section we're not really using right now." The others nodded. Atlantis was huge, and the Expedition was tiny by comparison, so they were only occupying a small portion of the Ancient city, with whole swathes they'd not even had time to explore yet. If the weapon did strike one of those sections, it could conceivably destroy something that would have proven useful in future, but at least it wouldn't damage anything they were currently using, or hurt any of the existing personnel.

But Rodney was frowning. "I'd have noticed if the targeting changed even a little bit," he pointed out, "and I haven't seen anything like that this whole time."

"No," Teyla agreed, shaking her head. "That's because I haven't been able to shift it at all. It's completely locked in." Before the others could turn away she added, "Locked in on a specific spot, in fact."

"What do you mean?" Sheppard asked. "How precise is its targeting?"

Teyla grinned. "Half a meter or less."

"Half a meter?" Sheppard stared at her. "What the hell is it targeting that small? The center of the Stargate? The command chair in central control? Rodney's favorite pillow?"

She shook her head. "I don't know exactly," she admitted. "But whatever it is, it's in the center of the city."

"A homing beacon," Ronon suggested, still standing in the same spot. "Makes the most sense, especially for the Wraith — they'd drop one somewhere in Atlantis and lock in on its signal." He shifted his head slightly, wincing just a little, and the others knew he was thinking about the tracking device the Wraith had implanted in him when they'd captured him so many years ago, turning him into a Runner. Carson Beckett had managed to remove the device without setting off its built-in explosives or permanently maiming Ronon, but if anyone knew about the Wraith's tracking ability, it was the man they had tracked all those years.

"That's a smart play," Sheppard agreed. "I bet it was that one guy, Bob, the one they sent in to sabotage us during the attack." The lone Wraith scout had been dropped into Atlantis to disable its defenses and cause chaos and panic among its protectors before the Hive ships arrived, and might have succeeded if Sheppard's second at the time, Lieutenant Aidan Ford, hadn't managed to get the drop on him. They'd tried interrogating the Wraith, who Sheppard had dubbed Bob, but hadn't gotten much more than sneers, taunts, and threats. Finally he'd pushed them too far, and Sheppard had killed him. But the wily Wraith would certainly have had the time to set up a beacon somewhere in the city before he was found out.

"If you can find that beacon and switch it off, the targeting system should unlock," Rodney pointed out. "At that point I should be able to set the weapon to standby mode instead. At the very least, if it's searching for a new target I can input something else, like a hunk of rock out beyond orbit."

"Great." Sheppard slapped him on the back. "You keep working on things here — slow it down, give us as much time as you can, see if you can't crack the system anyway. We'll head back to Atlantis and find that darn beacon, shut it down on that end." He gestured to Teyla and Ronon. "Let's go, guys."

Teyla hesitated, glancing over at Rodney. "I can stay, if you'd prefer," she offered. "I could keep searching the secondary systems, maybe find something else we could try."

Rodney waved her off. "I've got this," he insisted. "And Sheppard's going to need all eyes on the ground if you intend to find that beacon in time. Go on, I'll be fine. Oh, and leave me a suit, will you?" He couldn't help but shudder a little. "I suspect I'll need it."

She studied him for a second before nodding and following the other two toward the ladder, and from there back up to the Puddle Jumper.

"Just because the last time we left someone alone in one of these, he died," Rodney muttered as he returned to his work, trying not to look after his departing teammates but unable to help himself. "Why should that mean anything? I'll be fine. It's not like I'm trying to stop the deadliest weapon we've ever seen from turning on us or anything. All by myself. Without any help."

But despite his griping, and his concerns, he didn't stop working. This was the job, and he was the only one who had even a chance of accomplishing the Herculean task before him. He'd complain later.

If he was still alive, that was.

"All right, so how do we find this beacon?" Weir asked. "Can we isolate its frequency?"

Ronon shook his head. "They're designed so you can't pick them up," he answered gruffly, wincing a little again at the painful memories of his years on the run. "You have to have the frequency in order to even detect it, unless you're practically touching it already." Beckett had been able to pick up the signal from Ronon's tracking device, but he'd been standing right next to the Satedan at the time. "It may have a jammer on it, too — if so, it'll block any other signals around it. Calls, transporters, the works."

"Which means we do this the old-fashioned way," Sheppard agreed. "We need to know where Bob went while he was here. If we can backtrack everywhere he was, we should come across it sooner or later." He glanced at one screen in the command center, which had been set to reflect Rodney's best guess as to when the satellite would commence firing. Right now it said three hours and ten minutes. "Hopefully sooner," he added.

"I can tell you at least some of where he was," Zelenka offered. Leading them over to his workstation, he began inputting commands. "We used the Biometric Sensor Array to determine his location, and then track him so that you could capture him," he reminded Sheppard while he worked, pulling up a city schematic on the nearest wall screen. "The program automatically records all search data, so it still has the information from that process. All I have to do is recall it" — a glowing dot appeared in one part of the city, right near the naquadah power station — "and we know where that Wraith was at the time that we locked onto him, and where he went after that."

"But not before," Teyla commented. "We only know from the point when you started the scan."

"True," Zelenka replied, "but it is someplace to start, no?"

"Yes," Sheppard told him. "We'll take it. If we don't find the beacon along the route we know he took, we'll go back to the first place you spotted him and see if we can't backtrack from there." He turned to Ronon. "You're the tracker, big guy — I'm hoping you'll be able to figure out which way he went."

The Satedan nodded. "If there's a trail, I'll find it," he promised.

"Good. Let's go." Sheppard led his two teammates out to start their search. He hoped Rodney was having some luck on his end, though, because even with a place to start looking, they'd have a lot of ground to cover, and not a lot of time to do it.

"This is my favorite part," Rodney groused as he maneuvered through the concealed hatch, careful not to tear his space suit on the handles or the door's latching mechanism, and stepped outside. Into open space. Even though he was standing on the false asteroid's rough, uneven rock surface, and was partially cradled between two protrusions that masked the satellite's spines, he still felt completely exposed out here in the cold emptiness, with nothing to shield him from other asteroids, gamma rays, and all manner of other dangers. But just standing around wasn't going to help matters any — he'd already contacted Atlantis to let them know what he'd planned, so better to just get things taken care of as quickly as possible, then get back inside where it was safe. If one could call sitting in a small tin can that was also a deadly weapon 'safe.'

Sighing, he closed the hatch behind him and clipped a rope onto the stanchion that was cleverly concealed right beside the door's upper edge. Last time he'd had to do something like this he'd used a full EVA suit with maneuvering jets, but those were back on the Puddle Jumper, which was already back at Atlantis. If the satellite were fully exposed he could use magnetic grapples to clamp his boots to the hull and simply walk along, but the rock layer was nonmagnetic so that was out. And he couldn't risk driving pitons into the rock because one could pierce the hull beneath and damage the satellite overall. That left doing this the old-fashioned way, with a rope and a harness and a death grip on whatever outcroppings he could find along the way.

"Why didn't I tell Teyla to stay behind after all?" he berated himself as he measured out a length of rope and then pushed off from the 'ground' he'd been standing upon, swinging up and out. His tight hold on the rope kept him from going too far, and he slowly played it out hand over hand, carrying himself farther along the non-asteroid's length. "Then I could have had *her* do this. She probably would have enjoyed it, too." Except that he knew exactly why. He was fully capable of handling this himself, he just didn't like it — but Sheppard might need Teyla's help, and Rodney didn't want to be responsible for the mission's failure, or anyone's injury, because he'd been feeling lazy. He did continue to mutter and complain, however, as he slowly, painstakingly made his way out to where, if this station really did match the one he'd examined before, the weapon's main power buffer should reside.

Finally judging that he'd gone far enough, Rodney managed to hook a loop of rope around a small spur jutting out overhead, keeping himself more or less stationary. Then he began feeling along the rocks in front of him, trying to search for cracks or hinges or latches through the thick material of his gloves.

Nothing presented itself, which didn't surprise him. The Ancients would have been more careful than that. Next he extracted a small energy meter from a pocket on one leg. The device had an effective range of only a few meters, but within that distance it could judge energy output on a variety of wavelengths. And he was literally centimeters from the rock wall, and thus well under a meter from the weapons systems that coating concealed. Rodney was hoping that would be close enough, as he switched on the handheld device and stared intently at its tiny readout.

After a second that seemed to stretch into an eternity, the screen showed a flicker of light, which then transformed into a series of undulating bands.

"Yes!" Rodney crowed, almost pumping his fists until he realized just in time what that would do to him. Hanging here in space, with no gravity and only a rope holding him in place, such a sudden motion would at best set him flipping head over heels like a deranged monkey, and at worst spinning off into space to freeze in the vacuum once his suit's power ran out. Best to celebrate quietly and with no wasted motion instead. But he was pleased. The meter was showing the energy of the weapon's buffer, and the device was sensitive enough that Rodney could use it to pinpoint that component's exact location. Once he'd zeroed in, he was able to feel around that small area more thoroughly. After several minutes of searching his thumb finally caught in what looked like nothing more than a shallow natural divot, like a chip, which clicked when he pushed on it.

Aha!

With another hard push the click transformed into a definite pop that he felt through his gloves, and a narrow gap appeared alongside the divot. Rodney was able to wedge his fingers in there and pull, the entire section swiveling outward to reveal the thick conduits of the power buffer.

"Well, now," he told the weapon system component as he studied it, idly returning the energy meter to its pocket and retrieving a multi-tool instead. "You seem to be functioning perfectly. Let's see if we can fix that, shall we?" He set to work, first emptying the buffer so that all of the weapon's built-up charge dissipated harmlessly out into space. But then he went a step further. He disconnected several of the buffer's connection points. That wasn't lasting damage — it was exactly like loosening the connections on a light switch or an electrical outlet — but it would make the buffer work far less efficiently, which meant it would take a lot longer for the weapon to build up a full charge again.

And that, Rodney hoped as he closed the compartment back up, tucked the tool away, and then grabbed his rope and started hauling himself back in toward the hatch, should give Sheppard and the others enough time to find and disable that beacon.

It had better. Because if he had to come back out here, he'd have to do a lot more damage than just pulling a few wires loose. And at some point it would become something he couldn't repair in a hurry — if at all.

But for now, at least he'd bought them some time. And he

knew the rest of his team well enough to know that time wasn't
something they liked to waste.

"Dang it, this is a waste of time!" Sheppard declared, kicking
a door hard enough to send it clanging back against its frame.
"We've been searching for hours and haven't found a darn thing!"

"He was smart," Ronon agreed grudgingly peering about
the narrow alley they'd just entered. "Especially for a Wraith.
Covered his tracks well."

"It's also been months since he came through here," Teyla
pointed out. "That's bound to obscure a lot of traces."

They'd already followed the trail outside and as far as
Zelenka's scans had recorded, but hadn't found anything along
the route that resembled a homing beacon. Which didn't mean
the Wraith hadn't stashed it somewhere along that stretch, just
far enough out of sight for them to miss it now. Sheppard had
asked how accurate the scan was, and the little scientist had
admitted that it wouldn't have detected something minor like
stepping to one side. Nor could it have registered a change in
altitude, since the scan was from above.

Which got him thinking. Glancing up, Sheppard studied
the sides of the buildings around them. There were windows
breaking up the walls here and there, some of them with short
ledges flaring out just below. And although he didn't see anything like a fire escape, in a few places the walls were studded
with protrusions that might have been intended just for looks
but could also serve as handholds if someone wanted to scale
one of the structures.

Someone like a Wraith scout searching out a good vantage
point from which to study the city.

Or a good place to hide a tracking beacon for his fellow soldiers to use when targeting the city during their attack run.

"We need to take this little search party up a notch," Sheppard
told his two companions. He gestured toward the rooftops
some eighty feet above them. "Literally."

Teyla groaned and Ronon grimaced, but neither of them argued.

After all, the search on the ground wasn't yielding any results, so why not take to the heights?

At the very least, they'd get a good look around.

"I sure hope Rodney's having better luck than we are," Sheppard muttered as he stepped up to the wall, squinted upward for a second, and then grabbed onto a jutting block at head level, placed one foot on a similar shape a few feet off the ground, and hoisted himself up. "It can't exactly be much worse."

"Oh, come on!" Rodney exclaimed, throwing up his hands in frustration. "How is that even possible?"

But the screen's readout continued to show the same information it had just revealed a second ago. Almost like it was taunting him.

"That's impossible," Rodney insisted, typing in a new command. The display shifted, showing a new readout, along with a scan similar to the one from the small handheld energy meter he'd used on the buffer.

Much too similar for his tastes.

"Why couldn't the last satellite be the one with the upgrades, and this one be the one with only the original, clunky old software?" Rodney complained as he scrolled through pages of schematics and code simultaneously. "That would have worked so much better for everyone concerned."

The big problem he and Peter had discovered when they'd examined the previous satellite was that the links to the buffer had been damaged, and as a result, even though that system had been able to draw a charge off the portable generator they'd brought, it hadn't been able to send the energy through to the buffer. Rodney had been forced to go outside that time as well, and had managed to reroute the power through secondary systems so that it could finally charge the weapon and make it operational.

But after the first shot his patch had failed, and the weapon had lost power, leaving it — and Peter — defenseless against the remaining Hive ships.

This satellite, as it turned out, would not have suffered the same fate — because its software included a program that automatically rerouted power whenever the main conduits failed.

Or were deliberately disconnected.

Rodney had thought he was buying the rest of the team anywhere from eight to twelve more hours to find that beacon. Instead, he'd barely gotten them an extra three.

And the program was still running its own internal diagnostics, looking for better routes to channel that energy. If it found anything, it could cut the charge-up time even further.

Rodney sighed.

Time to find more creative ways to slow this system down.

"Someone's definitely been up here," Ronon confirmed, studying the flat surface of the roof they stood upon. "Footprints there and there." He crouched, examining the marks, which were so faint Sheppard could barely see them even after the Satedan had pointed them out. "Those are Wraith for sure."

"Okay, so Bob did use the scenic route," Sheppard mused aloud. "Good — at least we found his trail. Now let's assume he stayed up here as long as possible. It's what I'd have done — best way to keep an eye on anything moving down below while staying out of sight yourself."

"So we go over the route again," Teyla added, "only this time from up here. And hope this is where he hid the beacon."

"Exactly." Sheppard nodded to Ronon. "Keep your eyes peeled, and let me know if he wandered off anywhere, even by a few feet. That'd be enough for him to duck to one side and stash the thing behind a ventilation port."

Ronon nodded, and the three of them set off again. This time more carefully, since the way across the roofs was narrow and a single wrong step could send them plummeting to their deaths.

Then again, they couldn't take too long, because if they couldn't find the beacon in time, and Rodney couldn't disable the satellite, they'd all be dead anyway.

"Aha!" Rodney's triumphant shout echoed off the close metal walls. "Got you, you elusive little software glitch, you!" The dying sounds of his voice faded behind a new, rising sound, one much like the hiss of steam escaping. Only it wasn't steam, Rodney knew.

It was energy.

He'd been poring over the weapon system's coding, hunting for a way to disable the targeting lock or put the entire system on standby or shut it all down.

None of those had turned up yet.

But what he had noticed was a small subroutine for weapons maintenance. The satellite had built-in procedures for regular weapons tests, to make sure that whenever it was needed the system could come back online quickly, build a charge easily, and fire without delay. That program had apparently been damaged or corrupted somehow in the previous satellite, which was why the systems there had fallen into such disarray — if the subroutine had been working the conduits would have already been rerouted when he and Peter and Miller had arrived, and none of their jury-rigging would have been necessary.

And Peter might still be alive.

But that hadn't been the case. Most likely a small asteroid had struck the satellite, just a random chunk of floating rock that had smashed into the artifact's side, damaging the buffer and its connections to the main power conduits and possibly sending a spark back down the line, which had somehow shorted out the subroutine.

Regardless, it hadn't worked there.

But it was working just fine here. Which was why the

weapon buffer had been able to reroute power so quickly and start recharging so soon after he'd drained it. Rodney's first instinct upon spotting the small maintenance program was to disable it so that any additional delays he tried wouldn't be circumvented so easily.

Then he realized that he might be able to use the subroutine for his own purposes.

One of the potential problems with an energy-based weapon was that it could build up too much of a charge, overload, and short out — or explode. To protect against that, the system had a built-in venting mechanism, allowing it to bleed off excess energy as necessary. One of the subroutine's standard operations was to test that mechanism by bleeding off the entire charge.

And Rodney had just triggered that test.

He watched the display showing the buffer's total charge. It was dropping rapidly. In a matter of minutes, it was completely empty.

Yes!

Of course, it would just start drawing a fresh charge now. And when he tried to set the subroutine to vent a second time, the system informed him that the test had already been run successfully and would not be necessary again until the next maintenance cycle — which would certainly be days or weeks or months or even years from now.

So it was a trick he could only use once.

But at least he'd managed it the once. And that meant Sheppard and the others now had another three hours in which to find that beacon and shut it down.

Because after that, Rodney was fresh out of Plan A ideas, and would have to resort to Plan B.

And he really didn't want to use Plan B.

"Stop!" Ronon held up a hand, and immediately Sheppard and Teyla froze in place. They watched as Ronon considered the stretch of roof directly in front of them. "Strange," he said softly. "Very strange."

"What's so strange?" Sheppard demanded. He hated not knowing what was going on.

In answer, Ronon dropped into a crouch. "Look." He indicated a patch right in front of him. "See the tracks?"

By squatting down beside his teammate and squinting hard, Sheppard was just able to make out a faint discoloration on the stone surface. "Yeah, I do." He was proud of himself for that — up until now, every time Ronon had indicated a mark he hadn't seen a thing.

But instead of being impressed, Ronon shook his head. "You shouldn't," he replied. "That print is too obvious. He wasn't that sloppy." Standing, the Satedan studied the area immediately around them. "He wanted us to keep going, right past this spot."

"How could he even know we'd be here?" Teyla asked. She'd stayed back from the two of them, giving them space to maneuver. "*We* didn't even know we'd be doing this this morning!"

Ronon simply shrugged. "He was being careful. Cautious. Just in case." With a grunt, he stepped to one side, where the available foot space narrowed because large blocks occupied most of both corners, almost like small storage sheds had been placed atop the flat roof but far enough apart to allow passage between them. No seams showed anywhere, or any kind of access point, but he still scoured first one and then the other block.

Nothing.

"It should be here," he said, his words coming out in a low growl of frustration.

"All right, let's think about this for a moment," Teyla offered. She considered their surroundings. "If you were him, and you came up here to hide that beacon, where would you put it?"

"Off to the side somewhere, where nobody'd see it right away," Sheppard replied. He frowned at the big blocks. "Not on those, that's for sure — it'd stick out like a sore thumb atop them."

Teyla nodded. "Right. And they seem to be solid, so you couldn't hide it inside them." She eyed the edge of the roof on the side nearest her. "Is it a straight drop along the side, do you think? Or does the roof hang over just a bit?"

Ronon was already moving before she'd finished her question. Loping over to that side, he leaned over the edge, propping himself against the low wall there with his legs so that he could reach over and run both hands along the outer surface. "There's a ledge," he announced. "Perhaps half a meter deep. Maybe — ha!" His hands clamped down on something, and with a yank of his shoulders he wrenched it loose, swiveling his entire upper body back around to bring the object up to them.

It was perhaps twenty centimeters in diameter, small enough to be held in one of Ronon's large hands, though he kept both on it to make sure. Made mostly of black metal that glistened as if it were wet, it had several glowing green lights and a tracery of blue and green lines about it as well, those trails more organic than mechanical in shape, which gave the entire object the appearance of a large, blackened eyeball.

Or a cluster of glowing, glistening eggs.

It looked disgusting. And dangerous. And very, very Wraith.

"Great!" Sheppard said, going to clap Ronon on the back but deciding against it for fear of jostling the device. "Let's get that thing back to command and see if the eggheads can take it apart and switch it off."

But Teyla was glancing at the small tablet she'd brought with them. "There's no time for that," she warned, showing the two men the display. It was a simple countdown meter — and right now it was showing only forty-two minutes. "I've been resetting this every time Rodney has notified us of a change," she explained, "so this is current. It would take us far too long to get back there, especially since we'd have to climb back down first. And Ronon was right, it's definitely jamming signals — I can't raise anyone or anything." She set the tablet down in front of her and stared at her teammates.

Sheppard sighed. "Right. Well, guess it's up to us, then. Okay, let's starting looking for the power button."

Back on the satellite, Rodney was engaged in a conversation of his own — only his was with someone who wasn't really there.

"Is this what it felt like to you?" he asked the empty air. "Sitting in that satellite, knowing the Hive ships were closing in on you, knowing there wasn't anything you could do about it?"

He tried to imagine how Peter would have answered, if he could. But the air remained empty, the small chamber silent. He was alone, just him and his memories.

"I'm sorry," Rodney said finally. "I should've stayed with you. I should've tried harder to figure something out. Together, we might have been able to fix it in time."

Or we might both have died, he knew.

Which wouldn't have helped Peter any, or anybody else.

With a sigh, Rodney shook his head and turned back to the task at hand. The counter showed that he had only twenty minutes left. Sheppard hadn't reported in, so he had to assume they still hadn't found that beacon.

Which meant it was up to him.

He'd used up all the easy fixes he could think of, all the cheats, all the stalls.

His only option now was to do some real damage to the system. So much that it couldn't fire properly.

Damage like that wasn't something he'd be able to repair easily. If at all.

But it was better than letting Atlantis be destroyed.

Shaking his head, Rodney began tapping in a series of commands. This wasn't going to be easy, and he was going to need every second of the time remaining to pull it off. H was still hoping that wouldn't be necessary — but he couldn't take that risk.

Peter would have understood.

"I can't get any sort of reading off it," Teyla said, waving her tablet over the beacon. "It's so heavily shielded I'm not even picking up its energy signature when I'm touching it directly." She frowned and lowered her tablet. "Which means there is no way to tap into it and shut it down remotely."

Sheppard nodded and rose to his feet — they'd all been crouched down around the device so that it could sit on the roof and free their hands for the work. "That leaves just one option," he said, drawing his pistol. "If we can't turn it off, we'll just have to break it." And he leveled his weapon at the Wraith device.

"No!" Ronon was on his feet in an instant, forcing Sheppard to step back as the Satedan moved between him and the beacon. "It will be rigged to blow if it's tampered with!"

"Crap." Sheppard lowered his gun. "How big an explosion?"

"Enough to kill all three of us," Ronon assured him. "I can't say beyond that." His own tracker hadn't had an explosive component — it hadn't needed one, since it had been wrapped around his spinal column where he couldn't possibly remove it. This beacon was a lot bigger than that, however, which meant it certainly had room in its shell for some sort of bomb.

"Okay," Sheppard said, holding up both hands to show he wouldn't do anything rash. "So what do we do with it, then?"

Surprisingly, his Satedan teammate grinned at him. "You showed me the sport you call baseball, once," he replied. "How is your pitching arm?"

"Here goes nothing," Rodney declared, tapping in the final command. He paused for an instant, still hoping for a last-second reprieve, but everything around him was silent. Finally he pressed Execute.

"Now!" Sheppard called out. He lobbed the beacon up and out in a fastball special, as high and hard as he could throw.

Beside him, Ronon raised the long-barreled revolver he carried. The particle magnum had three settings: stun, kill, and incinerate. Right now it was switched to the last one.

He took careful aim as the beacon soared away from the roof, lining up the shot — and then he fired.

Zot! Rodney imagined he could hear the electrical impulse as it sped through the weapons system, arcing from circuit to circuit. He'd deactivated the safeties and triggered a small surge through certain key components. In a matter of seconds, it had raced through the control mechanisms built into the satellite's main chamber, frying several critical elements.

Zap! A single sizzling bolt emerged from Ronon's gun and shot straight for the airborne beacon. The blast enveloped the Wraith device, and with a loud crackle the energy tore the beacon apart. When it dissipated, there was nothing left but a wisp of smoke, rapidly fading on the breeze.

With a faint discordant clank, the weapon system shut down. Rodney kept a close watch on the displays, a single bead of sweat displaying his concern. If he'd miscalculated even a little, his little electronic imp might have just destroyed the satellite's life support system as well.

But the little chamber continued to provide air and heat and gravity and light, and the displays showed the burst had faded away.

Rodney slumped back against the wall. He'd done it!

Sheppard sagged against the roof ledge, laughing. They'd done it!

Beside him, Ronon smiled and holstered his gun.

On his other side, Teyla also smiled. "The jamming is gone, too, and there is a call from Rodney," she announced, holding up the tablet.

"Tell him we took care of the problem," Sheppard instructed, still grinning. He glanced at the counter on the tablet. "With seconds to spare."

Teyla shook her head and answered the call. "Good news —" she began.

"I should have known better!" Rodney insisted as they entered central command. It had indeed taken Sheppard, Ronon, and Teyla several hours to climb back down and then return to the command post, but as soon as they had they'd taken a Puddle Jumper and gone to collect their missing teammate. Rodney had been uncharacteristically silent the entire way back, but now that they were home on Atlantis he'd burst into full rant — only, this time, it was aimed at himself. "Of course you shut down the beacon!" he continued. "If I'd just trusted you, the satellite would still be working!"

"And we might all be dead," Weir pointed out as the foursome strode toward her. Sheppard had briefed her on their way back. "Look, Rodney," the commander said, "you did what needed to be done. You had no way of knowing they'd deactivate that beacon in time, and you couldn't risk Atlantis's safety. You did the right thing."

Rodney shook his head, but Sheppard stepped up beside the scientist and rested a hand on his shoulder. "She's right, Rodney," Sheppard insisted. "It was right down to the wire, for both of us. Better we both took care of the problem then neither of us did."

"You waited as long as you could," Teyla agreed. "And then you made sure we were all safe, no matter what."

Weir nodded. "Peter would be proud," she told Rodney softly. "Proud that you stayed, proud that you acted, proud that you saved everyone."

"Peter saved everyone," Rodney corrected just as quietly, his self-rage vanquished for now. "It was the work he did on the first satellite that showed me how to adjust this one."

"Then he saved us twice," Sheppard said. "I bet he'd think that was worth it."

Rodney shook his head. "I couldn't save him, though."

"You did what you had to do," Ronon told him gruffly. "He knew that."

"Just like you did what you had to do this time," Weir added. "It was the right choice."

Rodney considered that. He liked to think that Peter would have been pleased with his actions, that he wouldn't have held a grudge. He'd never know, of course. But it was a comforting thought.

And it was definitely comforting to know they'd still be here to think about it.

STARGATE SG-1
Aftermath

Karen Miller

Janet—

Of course, it's a little bit crazy of me, keeping this diary. Diaries, actually; I'm up to Volume 10 already. If I die tomorrow, or next week, or next year, hell, if I die at the age of ninety-four in some middle-of-nowhere Air Force retirement home, they'll confiscate my private papers faster than you can say Defense Secrets Act. Just like the SGC did that time we thought we'd lost Daniel on Oannes.

Maybe, one day, the Stargate program will be unveiled to the world. But until then it stays under wraps… hence this diary. It's my safety valve. See, the truth is, if I didn't have someone to talk to about my insane life I'd go nuts.

Maybe you can't understand that, whoever you are. The person from the Air Force who's been tasked to read my ramblings now I'm dead. Maybe you're sitting there wondering why the hell I don't talk things over with Sam, since she's my best friend. Or with Jack, who's a different kind of best friend. Don't worry, dear reader! I talk plenty of things out with them. Just— not always. I mean, it's a bit hard to talk through a problem with your friends when your friends are the ones causing said problem.

What problem? Yes. Well. There's the rub. Trust me, I don't want to do this. I know I'm crossing a line. I'm only writing it all down because I have no other way to make sense of this mess. Because if I don't, I'm afraid that— I'm afraid— well, yes. There you have it. I am afraid.

Funny. Volume 10 and counting and I'm only now saying this aloud, so to speak. But then, it's taken until now for things to reach breaking point. Damn. You know, even though I'm pretty sure writing stuff down isn't the same as standing on a table in the commissary at peak hour and shouting it at the top of my lungs, this still feels like a betrayal. But like I said: I have to make sense of what's happened or I'll be no good to my friends, who trust me with their lives. So, whoever you are, reading this — do me a favor. Keep your mouth shut, okay? Even if Jack or Sam or both of them died before me. Even if they've left the military and the stupid rules don't matter any more. And especially if they're not dead and still serve together. Whatever their status, just keep your mouth shut. You owe me that much.

Gosh. My hands are sweating. I nearly dropped my pen on you a moment ago. And my heart? You should feel my heart. It's like a jackhammer. Ha. No pun intended. Okay. Here I go.

A while back, thanks to the damn Tok'ra, Jack and Sam were forced to publicly admit they'd fallen in love. I'm not talking a simple sexual sizzle. God, if only. Not even a brief, if genuine, infatuation. No, I'm talking serious, all the way down to the bone marrow, I'd die for you in a heartbeat love. The kind most of us dream of and never find. Well, they found it. But they didn't get their happily ever after. It's not in Jack and Sam's DNA to put personal considerations ahead of this planet's safety. For them, the good of the many will always outweigh the happiness of the two. They set their feelings aside, regardless of the cost, which was — is — high, and they were really making it work.

And then Jack killed her.

I'm assuming you already know about that incident. Probably you have your own opinion on what happened. But I promise you, Jack had no choice. The alien entity possessing Sam was determined to protect its home world from us. It was inside the SGC database, inside Sam's mind, her memories. It knew he loved her and it gambled he'd never hurt her. But I guess you can read Jack's frightening file and still not understand who he is at his core. I'm starting to think he never truly understood himself. Not until that moment, anyway. See, it's one thing to die for your country, your planet. It's something else again to kill the woman you love for it. I was looking right at him when he pulled the zat's trigger that second time, and he barely hesitated. It was what he had to do. What Sam would expect him to do, every time. I'm pretty sure I don't have that kind of courage, but Jack does. Which is lucky for the world, but unlucky for him.

So now things are in a bit of a mess. Sure, by a miracle we got Sam back. But every time Jack looks at her, he relives that terrible decision. It doesn't matter that she's told him he did the right thing, or that objectively he knows it. Sam is the chink in Jack's intimidating armor. Daniel and Teal'c, they're doing what they can to get him through this. But they're having no more luck than Sam or me. Jack's pulled away from all of us. Disappeared inside. For the first time since we started working together I can't reach him. Don't get me wrong, he's not suicidal, not like when his son died. At least, that's what Daniel says and he knows. No. Jack's just… distant.

Unfortunately, the trouble doesn't end there. Sam's pulled away too. She's freaking out because this is the second time her body's been invaded, her mind overwhelmed and sidelined by an alien entity. First Jolinar, now this other creature. I don't know what to call it, we never got a name. Bottom line? It's a kind of rape. Jolinar, she's made peace with. Jolinar, she's come to respect and even like, in a strange way. But not this other creature. We've talked it through a little, but at the end of the day, what do I know about it? Some things you can't imagine. Some things you have to go through yourself to understand.

I feel like a failure. I have no idea how to help either of them. I'm pretty sure Jack thinks Sam does have a problem with him zatting her twice. It's what we in the medical profession call 'projection'. Only I can't talk to him about what she's told me in confidence, hell, I can't talk to him at all, I can't talk to her about what I suspect is going on with him, I can't clue in Daniel and Teal'c without kissing my medical ethics goodbye, and not a one of us can point at the freaking elephant in the room, which is that nobody would be feeling this wretched if Jack and Sam

weren't hopelessly in love. Which leaves me with just one option.
So, dear reader, whoever you are. Aren't you glad you're
not me?

George Hammond sat at his desk, signing routine reports,
making sure to keep his disquiet completely hidden from the
two people causing it. They were waiting in the conference
room, covertly watching him through the large window that
let him keep an eye on things from behind a closed door. It
was imperative that they not see how perturbed he was feeling. The last thing he wanted was Jack O'Neill and Sam Carter
worrying because they were worrying him. Which they were.
Deeply. So deeply, in fact, that if Janet Fraiser hadn't come to
him that morning he would have gone to her.

"General," she'd said, her brows pinched with distress, "I
know our official position is that we see no impropriety, hear
no impropriety, speak no impropriety, but—"

Half-relieved, half resentful that their self-imposed embargo
on the subject was broken, he'd sat back in his chair and
frowned at her. "But unofficially, Doctor, we have no choice
other than to face uncomfortable facts. Relax. Consider this
conversation off the record."

Fraiser had let out a breath. "Thank you, sir."

"And let me see if I can't cut to the chase," he'd added, because
he was no more keen to prolong the conversation than she. "Due
to their complicated personal relationship, Major Carter and
Colonel O'Neill are experiencing some difficulties as a result
of their recent encounter with that alien entity."

"Yes, sir. Exactly." The good doctor's relief had been palpable.
"The question is, what are we going to do about it?"

What indeed. Circumspectly considering his two most
valuable, valued and trusted officers, Hammond felt a surge of
angry compassion. This was a damnable situation. *The heart
wants what the heart wants*, or so it was said. But the US military didn't have the luxury of indulging anyone's heart. The

US military was in the business of protecting the country. In the SGC's case, the whole damned planet. Which Jack O'Neill had done, yet again, without regard for his own heart, his own wants, or the price he'd pay, yet again, for doing his job. But that price had clearly been paid in full. There was no hint now of the sarcastic wit and unexpected warmth that balanced Jack's more lethal qualities. Now his gaze was cool and deceptively direct, his emotional defenses ramped up to Defcon 1.

And then there was Sam.

In the conference room's harsh fluorescent lighting, Jacob's daughter appeared pale and — not listless, not precisely. But certainly subdued. Three days had dragged by since Frasier signed her out of the infirmary. On the surface it might seem as though she'd bounced back good as new from her latest ordeal, but he sincerely doubted that was the case. Memories darkened Sam's clear blue eyes, and faint shadows bruised the delicate skin beneath them.

Because she was Jacob's daughter he knew she'd die for good rather than admit she was struggling. The same could be said for Jack, who gave Jacob a run for his money when it came to stubborn pride. There was only one way to solve this problem… but the solution wasn't going to be popular.

Swallowing a sigh he signed another report, set it aside, put down his pen, then beckoned to Jack through the window. His unofficial second-in-command, face smooth and unreadable, like he was posing for a place on Mount Rushmore, pushed out of his chair. Not even a glance at Sam as he crossed to the office and entered.

"Close the door, Jack, and have a seat."

Jack did as he was told. Seemed to remind himself that he needed to slouch a little. "Sir."

"I'm not going to beat around the bush," he said briskly. "I'm reliably informed that SG-1 is having some difficulty processing the events of the last few days. Not that I needed telling. I might have lost most of my hair but I still have 20/20 vision."

The corner of Jack's mouth quirked. "You put me in a difficult position, General. I don't like to contradict a superior officer, but —"

He snorted. "Since when? Jack, don't start. I think I've earned the right to some honesty, even if it's painful."

"Sir..." Jack shifted, ill at ease. "Are you ordering me to share my feelings?"

"God forbid! Besides —" He rested his elbows on the arms of his chair, and pressed his spine against its back. "We both know I have a pretty good idea what those feelings are without you needing to spell them out."

Silence, complicated and full of landmines. Hammond waited. His infinitely tricky subordinate pretended to care that the sleeve of his fatigues was disfigured by a ratty pulled thread.

"Look," Jack said at last, frowning at his arm. "We'll be fine. It's not like it was our first rodeo."

"Except that in this instance, it was," he retorted. "Or have you killed Major Carter before and simply forgotten to mention it?"

Jack's gaze jerked up. "That's not funny. Sir."

"No," he agreed, gently, though anyone else using that tone would swiftly regret it. There were folk, he knew, who thought he played favorites. Maybe he did, but he'd never apologize for it. Not with what he owed this man. "Nothing about this situation amuses me, Jack. Which is why, after consultation with Dr. Fraiser, I've decided to stand SG-1 down for a spell."

"General..."

"This isn't a negotiation, Colonel! You need to step back for a few days. Clear your head. Find your balance. Don't insult me again by saying you couldn't use a little time off base."

Jack's stony expression softened, something very close to distress ghosting through him. "How many days is a few?"

"Well..." He sighed. "Fraiser doesn't want to catch sight of you for two weeks. Since I can't spare you for that long I'm splitting the difference. Seven days, Jack. With SG-5 on long term assignment and SG-3 on the sick list the mission roster's tight, I know, but we'll manage."

Another dangerous silence. Then, almost imperceptibly, Jack's shoulders slumped. A shout of surrender, for him. "You'll recall us if something blows up in our faces?" he said, perilously close to entreaty. It looked like he was having trouble keeping his gaze from sliding sideways, out to Sam.

"Yes."

Jack screwed up his face, like a man tasting sour wine. "All right. Fine. A week. But we're keeping the mission to '662," he added, flirting with belligerence. "No way I'm putting up with Daniel bellyaching for a month because one of the other grave-robbers got to futz with those ruins before he did."

He had to fight a smile. "'662 is important, but not imperative. I see no problem in deferring the mission until SG-1 is back in rotation."

Jack slumped a little further. "Seven days," he muttered moodily. "Don't s'pose you'd be inclined to say what the hell? Call it three?"

"I would not," he said, still unsmiling. "I suggest you quit while you're ahead."

"Do I have a choice?"

Now he did smile. "None at all. You're dismissed, Colonel. Please send in Major Carter on your way out."

Scowling, Jack obeyed. Moments later Sam entered, pushed the office door shut, then sat in response to a gestured invitation.

"General, I'm so sorry," she said, fingers tightly laced in her lap. "I know I've been off the past few days. There's no excuse for it and I will do better going forward."

She was Jacob's daughter. She didn't know how to prevaricate or pussyfoot. And of course she took responsibility for something that wasn't her fault and blamed herself for not reacting to inhumane events like a robot. Not for the first time Hammond found himself cursing his absent friend. Cursing, too, the loss of Jacob's wife. Sam's mother. Margaret had been the warm counterweight to Jacob's brusque, tough-love approach to parenting. Her death was a tragedy on every conceivable level.

"Major Carter..." He braced his forearms on the desk and leaned forward. "I do not accept your interpretation of recent events. As always you have conducted yourself with exemplary courage and professionalism. You're a credit to the uniform and this command and I forbid you from indulging in any further self-recrimination. Do I make myself clear?"

She stared at him, unblinking, blue eyes sheened with sudden tears. Sam rarely wept. It was a measure of her distress that she failed to keep her emotions in check now. Hammond felt his lips tighten. The father in him wanted to abandon military protocol and comfort her, but that would be a grave mistake.

"Sir," Sam said, her voice tight. "Yes, sir."

"On medical advice I'm standing SG-1 down for seven days," he continued. "What you do with that time is up to you, of course, with this proviso: you will not spend it on base. Neither will you spend it at home where we both know you have sufficient resources to set up another lab. In short, Major, you will leave town for a complete change of scenery. I suggest a warm beach somewhere. Do I make myself clear?"

This time she did blink. "You're ordering me to go have fun, sir?"

"In a nutshell."

"I see."

"I thought you might."

"And this is on medical advice?"

"As I said." He raised a warning finger. "And don't even *think* about giving Janet Fraiser a hard time over it. She has nothing but your best interests at heart. As do I."

Sam pulled a face. "Yes, sir. I know."

"I'm glad to hear it, Major. You're dismissed. Don't let me lay eyes on you again before the middle of next week."

With a nod Sam stood and headed for the door. But as she

reached it she paused, then turned. "Sir… there's just one thing.
I know we had a couple of scheduled missions that you'll want
to re-assign. But is there any chance you can let us keep the
mission to '662? Because Daniel won't be worth living with if
someone else gets to those ruins before he does."

It took an effort, but he kept his face straight. "I think that
can be arranged, Major."

"*Thank you*, sir," she said, expressively. Then, biting her lip,
she let herself smile. "And thank you."

She filled him with awe, this extraordinary woman. Brilliant.
Dedicated. Fiercely brave. Astonishingly humble. Billions
of people owed her their lives and yet she counted no debt.
Counted it an honor to serve. The thought of losing her… of
how close they'd come to it, again…

"General?" Sam said, quizzical.

He waved away her concern. "Off you go, Major. Find a
beach and send me a postcard."

She wrinkled her nose. "Yes, sir."

Alone once more, Hammond looked with disfavor at the
pile of department reports he'd yet to sign off and consign to
archives. *Find a beach*. Now there was a pleasant notion upon
which to daydream…

Resigning himself to duty, he grabbed the next file, opened
it, and started to read.

How did that quote go? *Troubles when they come do not
come singly, but in battalions.* Something like that. Good old
Shakespeare, never lost for an apt word. Dismayed, Janet stared
at the carnage that greeted her as she hesitated on the SGC
infirmary's threshold. Two beds occupied, one man walking wounded, three piles of red-stained fatigues on the floor.
Nurses working quickly, voices steady and deceptively disin-
terested, slapping on pressure bandages, applying a cervical
collar, testing reflexes. Damn. Once, just once, why couldn't
good old Shakespeare be wrong? *Hell* of a way to start a shift.

"What's the story, Bill?" she said, her hand reaching to nurse Jake Fleming for a fresh pair of latex gloves as she stepped into the noise and the blood and the pain.

Bill Warner, her medical brother-in-arms, didn't look up. He was inserting an IV needle into Lieutenant Valdez's right arm. Her left was clearly broken, a shard of shattered radius poking through bruised and battered flesh. Valdez was trying to tough it out but she was chalk white and sweating, galloping into shock. A soft, steady mewl escaped her blueish lips.

"Jaffa attack on '114," Bill grunted. "Seven down. Three critical."

Seven down? But they'd only sent two teams, which meant they were looking at an almost total wipeout. *Damn.*

The IV needle slid home. Snapping his fingers for some surgical tape, Bill glanced sideways. "Nancy's in OR 1, working on Esterhaz. Ruptured spleen, lacerated liver. The other two crits haven't made it back yet. Some kind of snafu. Tomic's trying to get them home alive. There's a trauma team standing by in the gate room but —"

"On my way," she said, snatched the stethoscope someone tossed at her, and took off at an ankle-turning run.

More chaos in the gate room, klaxon wailing, emergency lights whirling, Hammond in his aerie, nearly as pale as Valdez, glaring down at the trauma team and the response squad's P90s and the splashes of blood on the ramp. A familiar scene. God, she hated it. The radio chatter from '114 was being piped in from the control room. Captain Tomic, sounding pressured.

"— *pinned down, I can't see a way clear to the — no, wait —*" The thunderous sound of concussive weapons fire, bouncing echoes off the gate room's drab concrete walls. "*Command, we've got some help. It's the Tok'ra!*"

Startled, Janet looked up at Hammond. Any surprise he was feeling couldn't be seen in his face. Their eyes met. He nodded, the gesture almost imperceptible. She nodded back, letting him know *It's all right, sir, we have this.* Scant comfort, but it was all she could offer.

"Command, stand by! We're coming in hot!"

"Look alive, people," she said to the trauma team, smoothing out the last wrinkles in her gloves. "You know the drill."

They were the best, Stargate Command's medical staff. Pounding heartbeats as they waited — *come on, come on* — and then the gate's event horizon spat out Mads Tomic and the Tok'ra Aldwin, each man dragging a wounded team member to safety.

"Close the iris!" Hammond ordered. "Doctor, what's their status?"

It was too soon for an answer and he knew it, but she knew that it was ask or come down from his eyrie, which wouldn't help. What would help was her doing everything she could to keep his precious people alive.

On her knees beside Paul Lapotaire, taking in the wide red slick over dark skin, clamping her emotions as tight as she clamped off his nicked femoral artery, she spared Aldwin a swift, reassuring smile of thanks. His right sleeve was scorched. His left sleeve was soaked scarlet to the elbow. Blood caked beneath his fingernails. With Paul's femoral damage contained and no other life-threatening wound to tackle, she looked over at Tomic, who pressed his wadded jacket to Jill Massey's right flank while Kate Abbott checked the field dressing secured around the lieutenant's mangled right lower leg.

"Mads! You're okay?"

"Fine, doc," he said, his voice not quite steady. "How's Lappo?"

"Hanging in there."

Blood from a hairline scalp wound sluiced down Tomic's right cheek, and his left sported a red blotch that promised to ripen into a massive bruise. His knuckles were scraped and bloody, his black tee-shirt ripped across the chest. Beneath the shredded fabric she could see more abrasions, but compared to the others he did seem fine.

"Kate?" she said, seeing that the SGC's best trauma nurse could at last shift her focus. "Status."

Kate's eyes were grim. "Third degree staff weapon burn, likely some internal damage. We'll need a neuro for the leg."

Damn. "But we're good to go?"

"Yes," Kate replied. "Mads, keep up that pressure."

Janet beckoned. "Gurneys! Let's hustle!"

"*Dr. Fraiser!*"

She held up a hand, telling Hammond to wait. Just wait. He obeyed, but she could feel his seething impatience, his fear, through the glass. It burned the air between them, sizzled her skin. The trauma team nodded at her, patient transfer complete, Lapotaire and Massey strapped still and safe on their gurneys.

"Go," she told her team. "I'm right behind you. Mads, Aldwin, go with them. You'll need to be checked out."

Wisely, neither man tried to argue. As they headed out with the trauma team she looked up at Hammond. Tipped her head towards the corridor. Even as she turned away he was heading for the stairs. They met up on the way to the elevator.

"Both critical but stable," she said, before Hammond could ask again. "Can you call the base hospital, get Dr. Huang here ASAP? I need to prep for surgery."

Hammond's eyes, as grim as Kate's, went blank. "You're saying Massey could lose her leg?"

"I'm saying we'll do our best to see she doesn't. Sir, I have to go."

"Of course," Hammond murmured. "Doctor—"

She nearly cursed. "Sir?"

"I want to see Aldwin as soon as he's cleared."

"Yes, sir," she said, and bolted for the elevator.

He was still staring at her, his face stark with everything they'd left unsaid, as its doors glided shut and she was whisked away.

Dave Dixon staggered out of his sleeping infant daughter's bedroom, fumbled his way downstairs and escaped into the family room, where he tripped over Elliot's toy truck and planted himself face-first into the cushions on the battered family couch. They were sticky, and stank of fresh cherry cola.

"*Shit!* Goddammit it to hell and back! *Lainie!*"

No answer. Why the hell didn't she — oh. Right. She and Elliot were out back, playing. He didn't have the energy to yell again. Groaning, Dixon flailed himself out of the sweetly smothering cushions and slid to the floor. Stared at the ceiling. There were cobwebs on the light fitting. Good job Lainie declined her mother's offer to come stay with them and help while the kids were at their worst with the goddamned chickenpox. She'd make the cobwebs his fault, sure as shooting. Lovely woman, Lainie's mom. Best appreciated from a distance.

The phone rang.

"*Shit.*" With another groan, he rolled onto his hands and knees, crawled out to the hall where he'd left the handset that morning, and answered. "Dixon. Whaddya want?"

"*Colonel, this is Lieutenant Denworth. Please hold for General McCreary.*"

Denworth. McCreary's persnickety right hand. One wrinkle in his fatigues and the little pissant needed a stiff drink and a lie down. "Yeah. Okay," he said, hauling himself to his feet. "But can you tell me —"

Click click went the phone line. "*Dixon? What's your status?*"

Heart sinking into his boots, he looked at the phone. Mouthed a silent curse. "My status, sir?" he said, scrupulously polite. "Well, General, I'm beat, my wife's beat, my house looks like a tornado hit it and my kids look like a pair of join-the-dot paintings. Ah — why?"

A pause, then a muffled sigh. "*There's a problem at the SGC. Hammond's requested you on TDY. Am I correct in assuming you're no longer a health hazard?*"

Another glare at the phone. *No, sir, you're dead wrong. Because right now I want to kill you.* "That's affirmative. I'm clear. Sir, what kind of problem?"

"*The off world kind, Dave. I'm sorry. I wouldn't ask if it weren't vital. So when you say you're beat..."*

Abruptly he was torn between resentment and excitement. Once, he'd been off world. Just that once. Adjo. And all this time later he could recall the mission's every twist, every turn, every adrenaline-pumping moment. Adjo had changed him, fundamentally and forever. Reading the SGC teams' mission reports was more torment than treat, these days. For a few precious weeks he'd been one of them, drinking deep of their secrets and sharing the brilliant insanity of their lives. Then he'd returned to his old life, picked up the pieces and told himself it was fine, it was good, he was content. Only in the darkest corner of the night, alone, could he admit the bitter truth: he missed the SGC, the Stargate, the unexplored galaxy's allure, and he wanted them back, dammit. Except now it was broad daylight... and like a flipped switch McCreary's question had unleashed his ruthlessly repressed longing.

Crap. Lying to yourself was a damned sight easier in the dark.

"Dixon? Are you there?"

With a shake of his head he pulled himself together. "Sir. Sorry. And no, I'm not that beat."

"So you're available? Because Dave, I still won't order you."

Just like last time. McCreary was a good, decent man. But then so was George Hammond. And he wasn't the panicking type, either. No way would Hammond reach out like this unless the SGC was up shit creek and their paddle-less canoe was sinking. Imagining what might have gone wrong this time, he felt his pulse pick up more pace. Was Frank Cromwell's old friend Jack O'Neill at risk? Or one of O'Neill's team? Adjo had forged an odd alliance between them. They'd parted wary, problematical friends. At least, that was how he and O'Neill had parted. He and the rest of the team were just friends, plain and simple.

Frank would want him to save O'Neill's prickly butt. Hell, *he* wanted to save it, and not only for Frank.

He took a deep breath. Let it out, slowly. "Sir, I'm available if you need me."

"*Good.*" McCreary didn't even try to disguise his relief. "*Report to Hammond no later than 0800 tomorrow.*"

"Will do, sir."

The call disconnected. For a while he stood there, looking at the phone. Wondering how he was going to explain this to his wife. Then he felt a stir in the air behind him, and turned.

Lainie.

"Elliot's in the sandbox, digging his way to Australia," she said, her hazel eyes sorrowful. "Tell me."

There was a pain beneath his ribs. A band clamped around his chest. His fingers tightened on the phone's handset like it was a lifeline. An anchor. And then he dropped it on the hall table, like it was a tool of betrayal.

"Hammond called McCreary. There's trouble. He wants me."

The nightmares about Adjo had been loud and violent and totally unexpected. It was Elliot's premature arrival that undid him. Unburied his memories of Adjo's plague and the children it ruined. In sleep he'd had no defense against those dreadful images, or the immediate and soul-destroying threat of his newborn child's imprisonment in the NICU. Somehow those events melded so he dreamed of Elliot consumed by plague, his tiny son's skin swelling and sloughing and himself a helpless bystander, condemned to watch his boy die in lingering agony.

Tormented by her own terrors, Lainie had held him through the nightmares… and learned from his disjointed distress the truths he'd kept hidden. It was the first time in his career he'd broken his oath of secrecy. Waking, seeing her face, he hadn't even tried to make up a story. If he'd done that he'd have broken the most sacred oath of all. Instead, he trusted her. Because he could. Because her honor was no less inviolate than his own. Because to lie would have been to kill his marriage, his family, and turn every sacrifice he'd ever made into a waste of blood and breath.

Before he could say anything else, try to explain properly, Lainie smiled. "It's okay. I'll call Mom."

He blinked, his eyes stinging. "You sure?"

"The only difference between this and Afghanistan is the zip code."

That made him smile, like she'd intended. "I'm pretty sure aliens don't have zip codes." Then his smile faded. "I'll come back, hon. I promise."

"Mmm." Her lips trembled, a muddle of thoughts and feelings chasing across her face. Then she had hold of herself again. "So. You'd better get yourself out to the sandbox. Keep Elliot busy while I start dinner."

As he passed her he paused, and laid his hand on her shoulder. Tipped his head down and sideways to rest his head against her vanilla-scented hair. For a long moment they stood there, silent, no words required.

"Go on, Colonel," Lainie murmured, patting his butt. "Scoot, before your son spoils his dinner eating sand."

He handed over the baby monitor and did as he was told, so humbled he felt dizzy. God. This woman. What had he done to deserve her?

Keep an eye on her for me, Frank. And help me get home again safely.

"Hey! What's up, doc?"

Hearing the familiar, welcome voice, and despite her current crop of worries, Janet felt an unmilitary grin burst through her reserve. She stepped to one side of the corridor, letting a pair of airmen go by, banished the grin, then turned and was struck, yet again, by how damn tall Dave Dixon was. Tall and solid and ridiculously reassuring because of it. Hell, at six-three he was taller than Jack. Taller than *Teal'c*. And here she stood, a shade under five-two in her bare feet. Positively Lilliputian by comparison. Good thing she was a doctor, *and* a damn fine shot with a Beretta. Otherwise she might find herself feeling a tad over-awed.

"Colonel Dixon," she said, cool as a cucumber. "Welcome back."

Immaculate in his dress blues, service cap tucked under one arm and curiosity lighting his eyes, he nodded. "Dr. Fraiser. Or should that be Major? Which comes first, the rank or the stethoscope?"

She couldn't help it. She grinned again. "Depends on the context."

"Ah." Dixon's smile flashed, then vanished. "I'll remember that the next time I feel intimidated."

By tacit consent they fell into step together, heading for the stairs to the conference room. "I'm glad you're here, sir," she said, glancing up at him. "How much do you know?"

"Nothing yet," he replied. "Your boss called my boss and asked me to help out. When I got here I was told to come right down for briefing. That's it. But I'm guessing things aren't great."

"No," she said soberly. "They really aren't."

They walked the rest of the way in silence.

"Colonel, Doctor," Hammond said, as they entered the conference room. "Have a seat."

For once Daniel was on time, despite being recalled a couple days early from his leave, so they were the last to join the party. Clearly the general had already warned Jack that Dave Dixon was incoming, and in turn he'd warned Daniel and Teal'c. Nods all round. Daniel smiled. Jack didn't, but he didn't protest either, which was a relief. Examining him covertly, Janet felt a tug of anxiety. Four days of leave and what good had it done him? He looked no less tense or unhappy. Damn. So much for the healing powers of rest and relaxation.

Hammond gestured at Michael Griff, seated at the far end of the conference table. "Colonel Dixon, you'll remember Major Griff, SG-2's team leader."

"Sure," Dixon said, sliding into an empty chair. "Good to see you again, Major."

"And you, sir," Griff said, almost smiling.

"And seated opposite is Major Bridget O'Connell. She heads up SG-7."

Bridget nodded. "Colonel Dixon."

"Major."

"Finally, Colonel," Hammond said, "this is Aldwin of the Tok'ra. Aldwin, Colonel David Dixon. He's… a floating member of my command."

Aldwin offered a seated bow. "A pleasure to meet you, Colonel Dixon."

"Likewise," Dixon said, with a swift, assessing look. "I've read a lot about you."

As Aldwin frowned, puzzled, Hammond folded his hands on the conference table and leaned forward. "All right, people, down to business. Colonel Dixon, I've brought you in because Major Carter is currently unavailable and I need the SGC's best team at full strength. This is a top priority mission with a high degree of risk. You're sure you're fine with that?"

Janet felt Dixon, seated beside her, tense up. "Yes, sir."

"I had to ask," Hammond said, his eyes warming. "General McCreary wouldn't like me taking you for granted."

Dixon relaxed. "You aren't, sir."

"Good," Hammond said briskly. "So, to fill everyone in. The day before yesterday, SG teams Six and Nine gated to P5X-114. Preliminary UAV footage had shown a large village, apparently deserted. No Goa'uld activity detected. On site, Six and Nine found evidence of recent deaths and a hurried evacuation. Not a living soul was left behind. Instrument readings registered some kind of new and highly unusual energy signature. Seven hours later, just after its source was located, our people came under attack by Jaffa in service to Cronus. Both teams sustained heavy casualties and barely made it back to the SGC. That they all survived is largely thanks to Aldwin and his team of Tok'ra operatives, who made landfall on P5X-114 after their passing scout ship picked up that same energy signature. They helped Six and Nine to the gate and finished off the Jaffa once our people were home safe. In doing so, they paid the ultimate price. Aldwin is the only Tok'ra to survive the engagement. Our appreciation, and sorrow for their loss, have been conveyed to High Councilor Per'sus." Hammond's steady gaze shifted back to the Tok'ra. "Aldwin?"

"Thank you, General," Aldwin said, his voice soft and mild as ever, despite the seriousness of the situation. "The energy source that your SGC teams discovered, that both we and the Goa'uld detected with our long-range scans, is called *b'tac'nesh*. It is a substance highly prized by the Tok'ra and the Goa'uld. Because it is created by a random confluence of natural events, which cannot be reliably duplicated in a laboratory, it is very rare. Whole planets have been destroyed in the pursuit of *b'tac'nesh*. Thousands killed. Jacob Carter says that not even the Tau'ri lust for gold can match the Goa'uld's hunger for it."

"And it's up to us to make sure they stay hungry," Hammond said, his face bleak. "I'm told the weapons they can power with this *b'tac'nesh* make their staffs and zats look like feather dusters. We cannot let the Goa'uld get their hands on whatever there is of it on that planet. Unfortunately, despite the Tok'ra's heroic efforts, the Jaffa on '114 had time to send Cronus a message before they were wiped out. Which means —"

"That's been confirmed, sir?" Jack put in. "Sorry, I just don't want us going off half-cocked if —"

"Yes, Colonel, it's confirmed. High Councilor Per'sus informed me twenty minutes ago that according to their intel, Cronus has recalled his First Prime and his best Jaffa from a conflict with Yu, intending to send them to '114 so they can appropriate all the *b'tac'nesh* they can find."

And just like that, the tension around the table ratcheted up several notches. Jack rapped the conference table with his knuckles. "So now it's a race. How much of this stuff is on '114? Does anybody know?"

"Our scan of the planet suggested the *b'tac'nesh* is located only in the village area," said Aldwin. "But there may well be more than one deposit."

"Great," Jack said, scorchingly sarcastic. "Hide and seek with the Goa'uld breathing down our necks. General, you said there were recent deaths. This stuff's toxic?"

At a nod from Hammond, Janet opened the folder she'd brought with her and checked her notes, compiled through a long and sleepless night of studying her own test results and Tok'ra research.

"There are similarities between the biological impacts of *b'tac'nesh* and beta radiation, as well as the cosmic radiation that's been measured by NASA," she said, in her best detached lecturer mode. "This means that in the very short term — a matter of hours, a day at the most — an exposed, unprotected human will suffer skin lesions and some compromise of the respiratory system." She pulled a face. "Our people are textbook examples. Fortunately they're responding to treatment. But any longer term exposure than a day and *b'tac'nesh* is almost certainly fatal. As you'd expect, Tok'ra and Goa'uld symbiotes offer complete protection against its effects."

"So that's yay for Teal'c and Aldwin," Daniel said, eyebrows raised high above the rims of his glasses. "And for those of us playing hooky when the symbiotes were handed out?"

"The Tok'ra have told me that the deep space radiation vaccine they helped us develop will provide sufficient protection for this mission."

Jack shot her a dark look. "And if they're wrong?"

"Your caution is understandable, Colonel," Aldwin said. "But unnecessary. I have studied the chemical properties of the radiation inoculant and in sufficient concentration it will suffice to protect you."

"*You've* studied —" Jack laughed, disbelieving, as everyone else stared. "You're a scientist in your spare time?"

"Yes," said Aldwin, unsmiling. "We Tok'ra pride ourselves on honing more than one skill, Colonel."

Janet exchanged glances with Hammond, then cleared her throat. "Colonel, I checked Aldwin's findings and I'm satisfied that you will all be fine, once you receive an extra dose of the vaccine. In fact it's the active components of the vaccine that are giving us the best treatment results for our people. Trust me. I've got this."

Jack stared at her, and she stared back. After a moment, he looked down. "Okay." He looked up again, glanced at Griff and Bridget, then settled his gaze on Hammond. "So what's the plan, General? You want us to blow this stuff to kingdom come?"

"Only as a last resort," Hammond replied. "The preferred option is for the SGC to provide ground support while a team of Tok'ra experts extracts the *b'tac'nesh* for their use."

"*Tok'ra* use? General—"

Hammond flattened his palms to the table. "Yes, Colonel. Currently we cannot make use of this material. *However*, in return for our assistance High Councilor Per'sus has agreed that we will retain a sample large enough for us to begin scientific investigation of its potential Earth applications. In the meantime we'll be keeping it out of Goa'uld hands, and that's a win in my book."

"General Hammond is correct," Teal'c said, before Jack could respond. "We must do everything in our power to deny the Goa'uld this victory. Even detonation of the *b'tac'nesh* is preferable to their procurement of it."

"Ah—what happens if we do detonate it?" Daniel said.

Teal'c shrugged. "Depending upon the size of the deposit, Daniel Jackson, the resulting explosion could easily tear P5X-114 apart. Even a handful of *b'tac'nesh* crystals contains the power to destroy many hundreds of square miles."

"So you're saying it's the Goa'uld equivalent of a thermonuclear warhead," Dixon said, breaking the shocked silence.

"Indeed," said Teal'c, gravely. "Which is why detonation should be a last resort. It is likely that in doing so we would be killing many humans on the planet."

"But it's perfectly fine for us to—what?" Jack demanded. "Shove it in our pockets and bring it on home?"

"If necessary," Aldwin agreed. "Although that is unlikely. We will have purpose-built receptacles to hand. *B'tac'nesh* crystals are relatively harmless, Colonel O'Neill. While they do emit what you call radiation, and cause devastating destruction upon detonation, there is otherwise little to fear from them. In their unprocessed form, that is."

Another silence. Then Jack slewed round to glare accusingly at Teal'c, seated beside him. "Why do you never *tell* us this stuff?"

"I apologize for my oversight," Teal'c said, with a nod to Hammond. "In truth I never dreamed we would stumble across any *b'tac'nesh*. The last find was many years ago, when I was still a child."

Hammond raised a reassuring hand. "No apology required, Teal'c."

"Just backtracking for a moment," Bridget said, fingers tapping the table. "How are we going to locate this *b'tac'nesh*? It took our people hours to pinpoint it the first time."

"Yes, Major, but this time we'll have our very own tour guide," Jack said. "Tomic can —"

"No, he can't," Janet interrupted. "Captain Tomic is grounded. Complications from his head wound. He did manage to rough out a map for you." Over her strenuous objections. But Mads would crawl across broken glass for the SGC. "I'm sorry, but it's the best I can do."

"The Tok'ra, then." Jack looked at Aldwin. "Your long-range scanners picked up the stuff from orbit, right?"

Aldwin's expression became guarded. "Our long-range scanners are not designed for detailed searches."

"Okay, but you've got something that'll sniff it out," Griff said, sitting a little straighter. "You must have."

"Sure they do, Griff," Jack said, not even trying to hide his disgust. "They just don't want to share their gizmos. They never do, unless their backs are against the wall."

"Aldwin?" Hammond said, as the Tok'ra stared at the table. "We understand your people's instinct to safeguard your technology but surely, in this case, priority must be given to outwitting Cronos."

"I agree," Aldwin said, after a long and uncomfortable pause. "And I will speak to High Councilor Per'sus before we depart."

"Very well," Hammond said, relieved. He looked around the table. "If there are no further—"

"Actually, sir?" Jack frowned at Dave Dixon. "Not to appear ungrateful, but given the importance of this mission shouldn't we be putting our *best* best foot forward? As in Carter—"

Hammond shook his head. "No. It's not feasible. Barring a problem with your physicals you'll be gating out within the hour. Dr. Fraiser?"

Acutely, uncomfortably aware of Dave Dixon's abruptly spiked interest, Janet flipped closed her manila folder. "Yes, sir. SG teams Two and Seven are being cleared and inoculated as we speak, and Drs. Warner and Bradley are waiting on SG-1, Major Griff and Major O'Connell. I'll be handling Colonel Dixon's physical myself."

"Then I suggest you hop to it, people," Hammond said, standing. "Gear up and report to the gate room as soon as you're given the all clear. Aldwin, you'll return to Vorash for your team, and bring them back here?"

"Yes, General," said Aldwin. "And, as I said, I will consult with the High Councilor."

"Thank you."

And with that, they were dismissed. As Aldwin headed for the spiral staircase leading down to Ops, and Hammond returned to his office, Jack shoved his hands in his pockets and looked Dave Dixon up and down.

"Not that I don't appreciate a sharp set of dress blues, Dixon," he drawled, lightly biting, "but you're going to look a mite over-sartorial in the wilds of P5X-114."

"No need to feel insecure, Jack," Dave said, unfazed. "I dumped my duffel at security on the way up." He turned. "Doc? Are you ready?"

"And waiting," Janet retorted, file in hand. "On all of you."

"Even Teal'c?"

"Even I, Colonel," said Teal'c, heavily. "Dr. Fraiser is nothing if not thorough."

"That's one word for it," Jack muttered. "But I can suggest a few more."

"Please don't," she said, and shooed them. "After you, people."

The SGC's elevator wasn't what anyone would call roomy, so she and Dixon held back to let the others crowd in, and waited in silence until it returned. She didn't have to look up at him to know that his thoughts were churning at high speed. She could feel them, like a dynamo. Sam's absence was a gaping wound in the team; that swift exchange between Hammond and Jack a flashing neon sign. When the elevator doors opened again they entered, still silent, and traveled up the six floors to the infirmary level.

"Okay," Dixon said, as she closed the door to her office behind them. "What the hell is going on?"

Heart pounding, Janet tossed the folder onto her desk and opened his most recent physical report, which had been emailed over from the Pentagon. She'd already read it once but now she read it again, buying time. Wrestling with her conscience about how much to reveal. The after-action mission report on the alien entity incident had touched briefly on the fact that Sam had been wounded, without going into detail. Reports intended for eyes outside the SGC, even eyes with high clearance, were compiled by Hammond himself into Readers Digest versions of the actual events. Not just for security reasons, but also to protect, as far as he could, the privacy of the personnel whose wellbeing he guarded so fiercely. Only the President and the Joint Chiefs ever got the whole story. And not even they'd been told about the Jack and Sam fallout from the za'tarc incident, or the complications of their unorthodox relationship following the SGC's most recent near miss.

Now here she was, seriously considering a breach of

Hammond's decision. Those difficult confidences. And to think she'd worried about confessing the truth to her *diary*...

"Dr. Fraiser?" Dixon prompted. He'd stripped off his jacket and tie, and was busy unbuttoning his shirt. "Come on. Blind Freddy could see something's up. Where's Carter? And why does O'Neill look like he's ready to blow a gasket? Or worse."

Oh, how she wanted to confide in him. A friend. Someone who knew the players in this terrible drama. But how could she? It wasn't her heartbreak to share. Turmoiled, she tapped her computer screen. "Says here you tested all clear for the chickenpox virus. But I can guess what it was like, nursing two little ones through it. How are you feeling?"

"I'm good," Dixon said, impatient. "I promise. Doc—"

"Colonel, please. We need to start your physical."

He sighed. "Sure. Whatever."

She grabbed her stethoscope off the desk and began the familiar routine. Heart. Lungs. Quiet, please. Deep breath. And again. And again. Buying more time. Seeking the elusive balance between medical ethics and military pragmatism. Once upon a time there'd have been nothing to consider. But these days? Not so much. Trouble was, the longer she worked at Stargate Command the more it seemed that her cherished ethics were hardly getting a look in. Pen-light next, testing Dixon's visual reflexes while he perched on the edge of her desk. Then the thermometer, for his temperature. Everything normal.

"Doc..." He looked at her, his expression a mix of compassion and irritation. "Does Carter not being here have anything to do with that alien entity business? Because I have to tell you, the after-action report you guys sent us was even vaguer than usual."

She shouldn't be surprised. Before Adjo, she doubted Dave Dixon would've been able to recognize a vague after-action report if one bit him on the butt. Now, having lived through that catastrophically dangerous mission in person, it seemed he could smell official prevarication at fifty paces.

"Hey," he said, his voice gentle. "Janet. Whatever you tell me stays between us. You don't even need to give me all the gory details. Just — a heads up."

She stared at him, fingers fisted inside her lab coat's pockets. This man had helped her save Daniel's life. Helped save hundreds of sick and suffering Adjoan villagers. Picked up the burden of command when Jack was no longer able to carry it, then set it down again, lightly, when he was no longer needed. If she couldn't trust Dave Dixon, who could she trust?

Oh, lord. Please let me be doing the right thing…

"Okay," she said, feeling her heart pound. "David. I'll tell you this much…"

The breeze that greeted them as they stepped through the gate on P5X-114 carried with it a sickly-sweet taint of death. O'Neill grimaced. Great. Wasn't that the cherry on this lousy cake's frosting? Decomposing flesh and radiation poisoning… and no Carter. Just Dave Dixon. An okay guy, sure, battle-tested and dependable, but he had the nasty habit of seeing too much.

Just like Frank. Crap, he better not start talking about Frank. I am so not in the mood.

The gate's event horizon whooshed to nothingness. Which meant he and his SGC cohorts — and Dixon — were stranded in hostile territory with only the Tok'ra for company.

Oh, joy.

Another gust of stink-laden breeze. "Yuk," said Daniel, pressing his forearm to his nose. "You'd think after all this time I'd be used to that smell."

"Indeed," Teal'c agreed. "It is most unpleasant."

O'Neill waited for Dixon to chime in, but Frank Cromwell's second-in-command was too busy blissing out over being off world again. Sure, he'd expressed his sympathies for the injured from SG teams Six and Nine and, absolutely, he was sincere. But despite that stark reminder of danger, and any lingering memories of their time on Adjo, Dixon was downright giddy to be here. Not even the risk of this gig shriveling his gonads had blunted the edge of his enthusiasm. He stared at the man, morose.

God, give me strength.

"Colonel O'Neill."

And that was Aldwin. He swung round. "That's my name, don't wear it out."

Aldwin gave him The Look. The one that said *I have no idea what you're talking about, you stupid monkey-man, but I will humor you because I have a snake in my head which means I am superior to you in every way.* He really, really hated that look.

With a quelling glance at his three disapproving, generically Tok'ra colleagues, Aldwin joined him. "Colonel, I know we have discussed this, but I feel I should once again urge you to consider—"

"No," he said. "You shouldn't. Three SG teams are not hanging around this gate twiddling our thumbs and picking our noses while the sun climbs ever higher and you and your pals play hunt the *b'tac'nesh.* I mean, I know it chaps your butt that Per'sus gave the okay for us to use your precious gizmos, but you'll just have to deal with it."

"Our *gizmos* are highly sensitive and complex pieces of equipment, Colonel. I am merely concerned—"

"Don't be," he snapped. "We've got opposable thumbs, just like you. Aldwin, for crying out loud. You saw the UAV footage. We've got a lot of ground to cover before Cronos's goons get here and, according to your embedded spy, not much time. The faster we get this done and get out of here the happier I'll be, so we will *all* be playing today. Understood?"

But Aldwin was a persistent bastard. "Colonel, while Cronos will surely send ships he will also, I promise you, send Jaffa through the Stargate. Someone *must* stay here to keep watch for them and defend our only means of escape."

"It's only our only way out because you guys couldn't rustle up one lousy little —"

"We are fighting the Goa'uld on many fronts, Colonel!" Aldwin said, provoked for once into showing some heat. "Perhaps if my ship and crew had not been lost saving your people we might not be in this predicament!"

"Colonel."

Biting back a searing response to Aldwin, he turned. "O'Connell?"

Bridget O'Connell considered him with calm and serious gray eyes. "If I might make a suggestion, sir? Why don't two of my team stay at the gate and keep a series of wormholes open to the SGC until we're done? It'll keep some of the Jaffa at home and speed up our getaway."

"Ah — in theory that sounds like a great idea," Daniel chimed in. "Trouble is, every dial-up puts a strain on the DHD and we have no idea how old this one is. Or whether it's ever been serviced. If we blow even one control crystal we'll be trapped here."

"Yeah," O'Neill said. "And that's not part of the plan."

He chewed his bottom lip, staring at Bridget O'Connell. She stared back, patient and still entirely unintimidated. She'd only been leading SG-7 for five months, but she carried herself like a seasoned pro. He had no qualms leaving her and her team to hold down the fort.

"Okay," he said at last. "Here's what we're going to do. O'Connell, SG-7 guards the gate. Griff, our teams are going to split into pairs. Once we hit the village we spread out and search until we find every last damned *b'tac'nesh* crystal. Dixon and I'll use Tomic's map to go straight for the deposit teams Six and Nine found. It means we redistribute our gizmos and *b'tac'nesh* boxes but there should be just enough to go around. Aldwin —" With an effort he buried all his resurfaced Tok'ra resentments. "Obviously I can't order you to join in, but I think this is the best use of our time and resources."

Aldwin hesitated, then nodded. "Agreed."

Well, hallelujah. He looked at his people. Saw confidence and determination. "Okay, campers," he said, once each pair was properly equipped, and settled his cap in place. "Let's get this show on the road. O'Connell, keep your eyes peeled. First whiff of Jaffa, you raise holy hell."

"You can bet on it, Colonel," she said, with a small, grim smile. "Happy hunting."

Without waiting for comment from Aldwin or his uptight Tok'ra friends, O'Neill headed down the overgrown, rock-strewn path that led from the Stargate to the deserted village. Dixon fell into step beside him, leaving Daniel to walk with Teal'c behind them. He heard Griff politely urge the Tok'ra ahead, which left him and his team to bring up the rear, guarding their six. Good man.

"Y'know," Dixon said, conversational, "no disrespect intended, Jack, but your guy's map is pretty crappy."

He scowled. "Give me a break, Dave. You heard Fraiser. Tomic was concussed seven different ways from Sunday when he drew it."

"I'm not knocking his guts," Dixon protested. "Hell, I'd sponsor him for a medal in a heartbeat. But you said it yourself, he couldn't remember which direction they were heading when they found the *b'tac'nesh*."

"We'll manage."

"'Course we will," Dixon said cheerfully. "I don't know about you, but I was an Eagle Scout. I've got mad skills."

"Wonderful," he said, rolling his eyes. "I feel better already."

The breeze picked up, and with it the foul, gusting smell of decomp. No way of knowing what season they'd walked into, but the sky was a warm, milky blue, the solo sun had some heat in it, and the scrubby landscape was dotted with small yellow and orange flowers. So, late spring or early summer, most likely. Beneath his black tee-shirt he could feel sweat start to pop and trickle. Beneath his thin layer of skin, the knot and ache of tense muscle. The sudden urge to shove at Dave Dixon, to shout him back to where he came from, rose in his chest like a tidal wave. Dixon shouldn't be here. He wanted Carter.

Needed Carter. Her absence was like an amputation.

Hammond should've called her back. She should be here. This is wrong.

An itch between his shoulder blades. He could feel Daniel, staring. He glanced over his shoulder. "*What?*"

"Nothing," Daniel said hastily. "Never mind."

Twenty minutes later they hit the edge of the sprawling village. It looked like a ghost town from the Old West: crude wooden doors hanging drunkenly from leather strap-hinges; sun-bleached leather curtains flapping in open windows; home-spun shirts and skirts abandoned on the dirt road, as though their owners didn't care for the loss, or had been too afraid to turn back and pick them up; a child's leather sandal, kicked off in terrified flight. The breeze-blown stink of decomp, stronger than ever, had them all gagging, even the Tok'ra.

"There," Daniel choked, and pointed. "Dead cows."

Four of them, bloated to bursting, tumbled and tangled on a patch of open ground between two mud-brick cottages. Keeping his breathing shallow, O'Neill scanned the corpses and the nearby cottages' wattle-and-daub rooftops.

"No carrion birds. No birds of any kind."

"Bet they know something we don't," Dixon muttered.

"Okay, let's do this," he said, ignoring Dixon, then swept his people, and the Tok'ra, with a cool, steady look. "Spread out, width of the village. We want to keep the comms clear, so I'll check in with you. Unless you hit pay dirt, in which case raise the roof." He toggled his radio. "O'Connell, you copy?"

"*O'Connell here. All quiet, sir.*"

"We're starting the search. Soon as we find something we'll let you know."

"*Yes, sir.*"

His P90 was a familiar, comfortable weight, slung over his shoulder. Fishing out his Tok'ra gizmo from his fatigues leg pocket, he held it out to Dixon. "Here you go, Dave. Since you're the one with the mad skills, and all." One final look at the expectant faces turned towards him. A nod for Griff. A quirk of his lips for Daniel and Teal'c. "Let's go. Last one to the *b'tac'nesh* is a rotten egg."

As the others sorted themselves into pairs and started to spread across the search front, he slid out Mads Tomic's painfully scribbled map from inside his vest. Unfolded it. Stared. Damn, Dixon was right. This was a seriously crappy piece of cartography.

"We're here," he said after a moment, jabbing a pointed finger. "Where the path from the gate morphs into what I'll laughingly call the main street. Which means we head that way—" He pointed ahead of them. "—until we see the cottage with the sapling growing out of its roof. You got the gizmo working?"

Dixon grinned. "You bet. Me and my opposable thumbs. And of course my—"

"Don't say it," he growled.

The Tok'ra gizmo clicked quietly, like a deathwatch beetle in the wall. O'Neill flicked it a resentful glance, then allowed himself one last check of Daniel and Teal'c. Griff and his team. They were good. They'd be fine. And then, because he couldn't help himself, he stared at the sky. Thankfully it was empty of anything more threatening than a few puffy white clouds.

Yeah. Okay. But for how long?

"No borrowing trouble, Jack," said Dixon. "It's bad ju-ju." One of Frank's pithy little sayings. But the how the hell did Dixon know what he was thinking?

He sees too much, remember? Watch your step.

Dixon nudged him. "Come on. If those damn Tok'ra find the *b'tac'nesh* before we do you'll never hear the end of it."

Good point. They started walking again, Dixon an easy pace-and-a-half to his right. The dry, rutted dirt street led them between two wavering lines of squat cottages, all abandoned, all creepy. The stinking, fitful breeze rattled and scraped spindly tree branches against crumbling mud walls. Dried out his nose and mouth with that pervasive stench of death. Every twenty paces Dixon stopped, swung the gizmo in a slow, steady circle, but its steady clicking continued. No *b'tac'nesh*, dammit.

Roughly a quarter klick from where they'd started, the crude street petered out, becoming little more than a goat track. After that the cottages seemed to spring up from the thinly grassed soil haphazard, like mushrooms. Clumped like mushrooms too, huddling eave-to-eave as though whispering secrets. O'Neill's fingers itched to radio the Tok'ra, get their location, but that might give the impression he was nervous without them looking over his shoulder, when what he really felt was mistrust. Nothing was the same with them since Martouf's death. Not even Jacob could bridge the widening gap.

"So," Dixon said, adjusting the *b'tac'nesh* box clipped to his belt. "You think Aldwin and his chums might try and renege on the deal? Hang on to all the *b'tac'nesh* for themselves?"

He allowed himself a brief, unamused smile. "Crossed my mind."

"Yeah. With friends like that, etcetera, etcetera."

They kept on walking, past more deserted cottages and the detritus of panicked flight. Past six hastily dug graves, two of them distressingly small, and more dead and bloated livestock. Goats, this time. The eerie silence persisted, discouraging casual conversation.

"Hey," Dixon said. "Up ahead."

The cottage with the sapling. Reaching it, they halted and consulted Tomic's map again.

"Here we go left, kind of," O'Neill said. "Until we hit the abandoned well. Then things get interesting."

Dixon tapped the Tok'ra gizmo, just to make sure it was still working, then gestured with a flourish. "Lead on, Columbus."

As they changed direction, feeling the sun shift across his face, he toggled his radio. "Teal'c? What's your status?"

"Nothing yet, O'Neill."

"But no sign of any Jaffa, either," Daniel added. *"So there's that."*

"Okay. Aldwin?"

A crackle of static. *"No readings, Colonel O'Neill. You?"*

"No joy."

"Continue your search, Colonel."

Dixon laughed. "Man, he's a charmer, ain't he?"

"Trust me, when it comes to the Tok'ra I've met worse," he said, and toggled his radio again. "Griff? Status."

"Nothing, Colonel."

"O'Connell?"

"All quiet here, sir. Plus Kramer's taking readings in the gate vicinity. No luck yet."

"Good thinking. Just don't go too far."

"Copy that."

"She seems like good people," Dixon said casually, methodically swinging the Tok'ra gizmo in a wide arc as they walked along the narrow, sunbaked track that seemed to be heading out of the deserted village. "I was impressed with how she handled the situation on P8X-904. You know. That run-in with those Goa'uld sympathizing—"

"Hey," he said. "I know. Silver-haired, not senile. And yes. O'Connell's got the right stuff."

"Speaking of which…"

Crap. He knew Dixon wouldn't leave well enough alone. Forget the airy-fairy casual tone. The man was fishing. Question was, how much did he already know?

Easy answer. Too much for comfort. Damn the Pentagon strike team security clearances.

"If you're talking about Carter, she's in Hawaii," he said, just as casual. "She *said* she was going surfing, but dollars to donuts she's geeking out at the Mauna Kea observatories."

"On the Big Island?" Dixon sounded impressed. "Cool. But I thought they were all privately run."

"Like *that's* going to stop her."

"True," Dixon said, grinning again. Then he slowed, and pointed. "Hey. Call me crazy, but I think that's the well."

Shading his eyes, O'Neill stared. "You're crazy."

"And right," Dixon said. "Hot damn. Didn't I tell you? *Mad skills.*"

They jogged the rutted track carefully, mindful of tussocked grass and loose rocks. Reached the well, to find its circular mud-brick wall tumbledown, crumbling and overgrown with weeds. A stone dropped into its depths yielded barely a muffled, miserly splash... and released an unwholesome whiff of fetid swamp.

"Which explains why the villagers stopped using it," Dixon said, fanning his face. "Damn. That smells worse than one of Matilda's diapers."

O'Neill shook his head. "I still can't believe you called your kid *Matilda.*"

"Yeah." Dixon half-smiled. "But it could've been worse. I could've pulled Lainie's maternal grandmother's name out of the hat, instead of my father's mother."

"Let me guess," he said, retrieving Tomic's map for another look. "Gertrude?"

"Pretty close. *Gladys.*"

"That's not so bad."

Dixon stared. "You're kidding, right?"

"No," he said earnestly. "Gladys Knight and the Pips."

For a moment Dixon actually considered it. But only for a moment. "Then we'd have ended up calling her Pipsqueak. Nah. Matilda's good. It suits her." He tugged the map closer so he could see it. "Damn. This might as well be one of Elliott's finger paintings, for all the good it's gonna do us."

O'Neill grimaced, wishing he could argue that, for Tomic's sake. But at some point honesty had to trump loyalty. The wavering scribble beside Mads' uncertain picture of the well made no more sense than Carter's astrophyiscs shorthand.

Bet if she was here she could translate. Angry with himself, he smothered another unwelcome stab of longing. *She's not here. Get over it.*

"Right," Dixon said. "Where to now, Kemosabe?"

Good question. He took off his cap, scrubbed his fingers through his hair, then took a slow three-sixty look around them. Two fields, planted once but long ago left to die, a scattering of dried grain stalks the only remainder. Five cottages, two roofless, all of them in poor repair like the well. Beyond them, no more village. Just open ground covered by straggling woodland, which grew denser as it stretched away towards a distant, gently rising range of hills. Some of the trees were lightning-blasted. Scorched and twisted and dead. At some point in the past, heavy rains had eroded the sparsely vegetated soil into potentially lethal potholes and gullies.

"I think a spiral search pattern is our best bet," Dixon said, after his own assessment of the landscape. "We can't be too far off the mark by now."

He'd been about to say the same thing. "Yeah." He pulled his cap back on. Shoved Tomic's redundant map inside his vest. "Take another reading of the area before we start."

As Dixon scanned their surroundings with the sleepily clicking gizmo, he let slip a sideways look. "I guess Carter got a pretty raw deal in that entity crisis. She doing okay?"

Crap. O'Neill felt his mouth suck dry at the reminder. Felt the treacherous sweat of remembered fear. The gut-churning nausea of unquenchable guilt.

I shot her twice. I shot her.

"Fine," he said, and hoped Dixon wouldn't notice the hairline tremor he could feel in his voice. "You know Carter. Nothing keeps her down."

"And you, Jack? How are you doing?"

"I'm peachy, Dave."

"Yeah? Because Jack, I got the shudders just reading the bare bones of what happened. If you guys hadn't stopped that thing in its tracks you'd have had no choice but to blow the —"

"I know!" he snapped. "I was there!"

"Which is how *I* know you're not peachy," Dixon retorted. "Nobody could be. Not after that."

The unclouded alien sun had some heat in it, but suddenly he was cold like Antarctica. *Damn that pushy, interfering—* "*What the hell did Fraiser tell you?*"

"Don't blame Janet," Dixon said, glaring. "All she did was —"

"*Colonel O'Neill! Sir, we've hit pay dirt!*"

Griff's excited shout jolted him from rage to surprised relief. Griff *never* got excited. Turning his back to Dixon, because the compassion he saw there was more than he could handle, he toggled his radio. "Details, Major."

"*Sir, our Tok'ra Geiger counter's gone crazy,*" Griff said, excitement suppressed now. "*I'd say we're practically standing on top of the—*"

"*Major Griff, do nothing! I am coming to join you! Stay where you are and do not touch a thing!*"

And that was Aldwin, shoving his oar in uninvited. O'Neill scowled at the empty blue sky. "Aldwin—"

"*Dr. Jackson, you and Teal'c must continue searching!*" Aldwin commanded. "*You too, Colonel! You must locate that other deposit of—*"

"Aldwin, I know what to do!" O'Neill said, savage. "We're at the well now, which means we're on target. Save your breath for collecting Griff's *b'tac'nesh*. Major Griff, radio me when you're done. O'Neill out."

"Man," Dixon said, starting to move away from the well. "And I thought Denworth was a pissant."

This time he scowled at Dixon. He didn't know Denworth. He didn't want to know Denworth. He wanted to find the friggin' *b'tac'nesh* and get the hell out of Dodge. "Can we just do this, Dixon?"

"Sure," Dixon said, infuriatingly unruffled. "One spiral search pattern, coming up."

After that they walked their carefully expanding spiral search in a blessed silence broken only by the sound of their boots on the dry ground, the rattle and rustle of the breeze in dry branches, and the monotonous clicking of the Tok'ra Geiger counter.

A crackle of static on his open radio. *"Jack, it's Daniel. Look, we've reached the far side of the village and found zilch. What do you want us to do? Come help you and Dixon?"*

Tempting thought. One meaningful look from Teal'c and even Dixon would shut up about Carter. But — "No, we're good. Go and give Aldwin a hand with—"

"Colonel!" O'Connell, her voice sharp. *"The gate's gone live! One chevron enga- no, make that two!"*

O'Neill felt the adrenaline surge, heard Dixon's quick intake of breath. "Dial out, O'Connell! Try and beat those bastards to the punch! Daniel, Teal'c, get to the gate. Back up SG-7. Aldwin, I want as many Tok'ra as you can spare going with them. Griff, you don't let the Jaffa near that *b'tac'nesh*. Blow it if you have to. Dixon and I'll get to the gate when we can."

"Colonel, I don't think—"

"Dammit, Aldwin, that's an order!"

"I've got it covered, Colonel," Griff said. *"You and Dixon watch your six."*

"Copy that," he said, and spun around to stare at the sky above the village and beyond, to the unseen Stargate. Still empty. No gliders. Not yet, anyway. Dixon was staring too. "Dave, I suggest we pick up the pace."

Dixon nodded. "Couldn't agree more, Jack. Hup hup hup!"

They broke into a reckless curving jog, dodging the treacherous potholes, leaping over the runneled gullies, stopping every few minutes to check the rhythm of the gizmo's clicking and listen for the lethal whine of Goa'uld gliders overhead. Wider and wider, moving further from the village with every loop, closer to the edge of the straggling woodland. No time to worry about what was happening behind them, who would win the desperate battle for the gate. And checking in was out of the question. He might distract his people at a crucial moment, get them killed.

"Hey!" Dixon shouted, stumbling to a halt. "Hey, I think this is — is this it?"

Heart thudding, his breath held, O'Neill listened to the gizmo's steady click pick up speed and intensity. Faster — faster — until it sounded like a cicada, a swift urgent thrumming, heralding success... or death.

"Okay..." Dixon muttered, slowing the gizmo's sweep. "Come to daddy..."

The gizmo's clicking crescendoed wildly. O'Neill tried to pinpoint the spot, but Dixon beat him to it.

"There!" he said. "That pothole!"

Side by side, they ran. Got close enough to see that the pothole had collapsed through to some kind of underground cavern. Without pausing for a discussion, Dixon flung himself belly-down on the grassy dirt and commando-crawled to its edge, then thrust the Tok'ra gizmo elbow deep into the darkness. Its clicking swerved into a screech.

"Bullseye!" He crawled back. "Here. Take this. See if you can shut the damn thing off. I'll take a look at what else is down there. And be careful, Jack. Maybe back up a bit. This whole area could be unstable."

O'Neill stared at the proffered gizmo. Stared at Dixon. "Yes, sir."

"Jack." Dixon's answering stare was unimpressed. "Seriously."

Fine, he was being petty. And how rude of Dixon to point it out. "Take a look how? Your X-ray vision?"

Dixon fished in a leg pocket. "No. My trusty flashlight. Eagle Scout, remember? Jack —"

"I know, I know." He grabbed the screeching gizmo out of Dixon's hand and eased himself further away from the pothole. "Just hurry up. We could have company any moment."

Dixon's grin flashed, inappropriate and oddly cheering. "Yes, sir."

Leaving him to poke his head down the pothole, O'Neill wrestled the Tok'ra gizmo to silence. He was reaching for his radio when it crackled to life.

"O'Neill! Do you copy?"

Teal'c. He felt a rush of breathless relief. "I copy. What's your status?"

"We have held the gate, thanks to SG-2's timely arrival. Three wounded, no fatalities. The DHD sustained minor damage. Aldwin is repairing it. You?"

"We've hit pay dirt too. Not sure yet how we're going to retrieve the—" A crash of sound over the open radio link. In the background shouting, and a familiar, menacing, mechanical whine. "Teal'c!" he shouted, dropping Aldwin's precious *b'tac'nesh* detector. "How many?"

"Two gliders so far!"

He was gripping his radio so hard his fingers were close to breaking. "Get the hell out of there, all of you! I don't want those Jaffa bastards getting their hands on that *b'tac'nesh!*"

Another radio crackle. *"But Jack—"*

"You heard me, Daniel! Go! Teal'c, I swear, if he—"

"We are dialing Earth, O'Neill. When—" Two explosions, in swift succession. The staccato chatter of P90 fire. *"O'Neill, the gliders are heading for the village. Find concealment. We will return for you!"*

"Worry about us later! *Go!*"

Retreated from the pothole, Dixon was on his feet and staring back at the village. At the sky. "What d'you want to do, Jack? Take our chances or blow the *b'tac'nesh* now?"

Hell of a question. Dixon wasn't even officially part of the SGC and he was offering to kill himself in their war against the Goa'uld. With two kids, no less, one of them not crawling yet.

A split second to think. Weigh the options. Make a choice. "Blowing it's a last resort. Hide first. Give the SGC a chance to get back here with reinforcements."

"How long do we wait?"

He pulled a face. "As long as we can."

"No argument there." Dixon turned to look at the woodland, then back again. "The trees are closer but there's better cover in the village."

"Then you start running now," he said, reaching for the clips on his backpack. "I'll catch up."

"What?" Dixon frowned. "No way. Jack —"

"Dixon, this is my mission! You're just along for the ride. *Start running!*"

Dixon's lips tightened to a thin line. "To be continued," he growled, and took off for the deserted village.

Heart racing, fresh sweat trickling, O'Neill unpacked the plastic explosive, wired it with a remote control detonator, commando-crawled his way to the pothole and dropped the mini-bomb into the darkness. Then he leapt to his feet and ran, backpack clutched in his fist. Prayed with every leaping stride that his gimp knee would hold up.

His knee held, but not his luck.

A Goa'uld glider, diving out of the sun, caught him as he caught up to Dave Dixon, brave man but slower runner. They were just a handful of strides from a huddle of four ramshackle cottages. Eye-searing light as the glider fired its first volley, the twin lines of plasma tearing up the ground ahead of them in gouts of dust and shattered mud bricks and obliterated shingle roof tiles. As one man they dodged left, used the choking dust and smoke for cover, headed for a different cluster of cottages. Wheeling, the glider took its second strafing run. The air shuddered from the concussion. So did the ground beneath their feet. Roaring in their ears, the thundering whine of the glider's engine as it looped tightly overhead for a third attempt on their lives. Then — a deeper, darker, rumbling roar. The ground shuddered like a huge beast in pain. And as they flung themselves through the nearest open doorway, as the glider opened fire, raining hell and destruction, the ground broke apart beneath them…

…and they fell.

"Jack. Jack, come on. Enough with the napping. We gotta keep moving — we can't stay here. Wherever the hell *here* is. Come *on*. Up and at 'em."

Groaning, O'Neill opened his eyes. Not that there was much point. Dixon's flashlight was smashed, and his own was fast running out of juice. He didn't want to switch it back on, only to watch it die. So, eyes open or shut, nothing changed. Darkness wrapped them like folds of black velvet.

"God, Dixon, you're such a *nag*," he muttered. "How the hell does your wife put up with you?"

Dixon's grunt of laughter was laced with sharp discomfort. "Beats me. Why don't you ask her when we get back home?"

"I will." He closed his eyes again as a fresh wave of pain surged through his left shoulder. Broken collarbone. Second time. Maybe he could convince Fraiser to start handing out frequent flyer points for the infirmary. "How's your head?"

"Still attached. Barely. How's yours?"

Pounding like a mother. Another friggin' concussion. Talk about frequent flyer points… "Fine."

"Yeah. Sure. So how far do you reckon we made it that time?"

"How should I know? Do I look like a groundhog?"

"Ha ha. Funny man." Rustling fabric, a chink of loose rock, as Dixon struggled to change position. A hissing curse as movement jostled his cracked ribs. "Seriously, Jack. We have to keep going. The air's pretty bad in this stretch."

"I haven't eaten beans in a month, I swear."

Another curse. "*Shit*, O'Neill. Don't make me laugh!"

"Sorry."

Silence, then, as they both fought for the strength to resume their daunting crawl through the network of caves and narrow passages that spread like a drunken rabbit's warren beneath the surface of the planet. Or at least the part of it where the village had been built. This was the third time they'd clawed their way back to consciousness after waking in the aftermath of the Goa'uld glider's attack. Bruised, bloody, broken and trapped, with no idea how much time had passed, because neither of their watches would work, they'd waited for Cronus's Jaffa to find them. Kill them. Only the Jaffa never came and, countless

hours later, after a lot of painful crawling and two more lapses
into oblivion, they were still alive. Go figure. Somewhere ahead,
in the stygian dark, there was a way up to the surface. Had
to be. If there wasn't they'd have suffocated long before now.

All they had to do was find it.

"Okay," O'Neill sighed. "We can do this. Let's go."

Cursing, swearing, letting the pain show because they had
no other choice, they made their way, inch by hard won inch,
out of the oppressive rock tunnel and into a small cavern,
where the air was marginally less foul. But the walls and floor
were damp, and a flick of the sputtering flashlight showed
them gross and slimy fungi growing everywhere, like rancid
tumors. So they kept on crawling, into yet another narrow
passageway, following the teasing promise of fresh air. Please
God this wasn't yet another dead end. Another passage half-
filled with rocky debris, impassable. They'd both long since
lost their sense of direction. For all they could tell, they were
going round in circles. But the alternative was to stop crawling… and die.

"Hey," Dixon panted, as they took a moment to catch their
breath. "Tell me about the time you made it out of the desert on
your own with nine broken bones, including a skull fracture."

O'Neill grimaced. "Frank had a big mouth."

"I don't care about that. I only care if he exaggerated."

"You have to ask?"

"Well… no. But —"

"Simmer down. That one's true."

"Good," Dixon said. "Because Elliott flushed my lucky rabbit's foot down the toilet."

He shook his head, which was a mistake. The darkness in
front of his face swirled with little red dots. "Okay. Are you
done now? Can we keep going?"

"Yeah. Sure. Why not?"

More crawling. More panting. More pauses, less space
between them, as pain and thirst and exhaustion took their

grim, inexorable toll. Then, feeling Dixon's fingers grabbing at his ankle, he halted.

"Hey. Jack. Am I dreaming, or is that —"

"You're not dreaming," he said, and didn't care that his voice was unsteady. "That's clean air."

The promise of escape pumped fresh adrenaline through his battered body. Pushed him to crawl faster despite the throbbing pain in his head and the grinding ache in his shoulder. He could feel his scraped hands losing more skin and he didn't care. Skin grew back. Broken bones knitted. He sucked in a deep breath, smelled the outside world, and forced himself to pick up the pace.

Without warning, the space around his body expanded. He'd crawled out of the cramped passage and into another cave. The rush of fresh air was intoxicating. Then his reaching fingers brushed against something that wasn't rock, wasn't damp. Felt like *plastic*. Felt *familiar*.

"Crap!" he said, halting. Looked up. Saw a faint scatter of stars through the hole high in the cavern's ceiling. "Holy *shit*."

"What?" Dixon demanded, crowding him. "Jack, what is it?"

He fumbled for his flashlight, turned it on. Awkwardly shone its weak beam on the packet of plastic explosive and wriggled round as far as he could so Dixon could see. "Look what I found."

"Holy shit!" Dixon yelped. "Is that stuff still live? Where's your remote detonator?"

In his backpack, buried under what had felt like half the village, but to be on the safe side he yanked the detonating pin from the brick of C4. Slapped around for a loose rock, found one, and smashed the pin to fragments.

"Relax," he said. "We're good."

"Are you *kidding* me?" Dixon demanded. "How are we good? We're right underneath where we were on the surface. *Hours* we've been crawling around down here!"

"And unless you want to turn tail for the village, we won't be crawling any more." He played his dying flashlight across the far side of the cavern, revealing a massive, fresh fall of rock and no more passages. "Our final dead end, methinks."

"That's not funny."

"Am I laughing?"

Dixon gave him a push. "Shove in, or over, or something. My ribs are killing me."

They managed to get themselves settled just as the flashlight gave up the ghost. With fresh air no longer an issue, and enough room to stretch out, it was the next best thing to a suite at the LA Hilton.

"So," Dixon said, slurring a little from tiredness. "Now we wait. You wanna risk the radio?"

"Not really."

"I guess. Better safe than sorry."

"That's my motto, Dave."

"Yeah? You could've fooled me."

They lapsed into silence. No point talking through what they already both knew. If the Jaffa were still lurking topside their best bet was to stay put and stay quiet. At least until daylight. And anyway, Hammond would send help as soon as he could. No need to panic because it wasn't here yet. Could be any number of reasons for that. Then, thanks to Carter's idea of putting tracking chips in their radios, hey presto! Instant rescue.

They'll be here. A couple more hours, max. They'll come.

"Hey," Dixon said. "How long is that anti-*b'tac'nesh* vaccine s'posed to last?"

O'Neill pulled a face. "Why? You worried we're lying on top of the damn stuff?"

"Maybe."

"Well, Dave, I'd put your mind at ease but the gizmo's somewhere over our heads."

"You dropped it?"

"I did."

"Damn. Frank forgot to mention you're clumsy."

"I'm sorry," he said politely. "I'll do better next time."

"Damn straight."

"Dave, I'm sure we'll be fine."

"Okay…" Dixon said slowly. "You do know you sounded *disappointed* then, right?"

"No, I didn't."

"Yes, you did!"

"No, I did n — yeah. Okay. Maybe I am. A bit," he confessed.

"*Because?*"

"Because if Aldwin's right about the vaccine boost, he gets to say I told you so when we don't die from *b'tac'nesh* poisoning."

"Hmm." A clink of loose rock, a grunt of pain, as Dixon shifted a little. "You're thinking you'd rather die a disgusting, horrible death and cheat him of the satisfaction?"

Gingerly, he scratched his nose. "Well… yeah. Kind of."

"Huh. You're right. It's a tough one," Dixon said. "But nowhere near as tough as what happened with Carter."

He was too exhausted to throw a rock at the man. Too exhausted, too hurt, to start crawling away. He couldn't even find the strength for anger. Instead he pressed a gritty hand across his eyes.

"Seriously, Dixon. What the hell did Fraiser tell you?"

"Nothing about you being in love with Sam," Dixon said quickly. "That much I worked out for myself. Back on Adjo, when we all thought she was dying? The way you looked at her, when you thought nobody was watching? Dead giveaway, son."

Well, *crap*. "Oh."

"I'm guessing the feeling's mutual," Dixon added. "Does she blame you for zatting her twice?"

So that was the secret Fraiser had spilled. "I'm going to kill that woman."

"No, you're not. Janet cares about you, Jack. And she's worried sick. Now answer the question."

It seemed there was no getting out of this conversation. And maybe, in a weird way, he kind of didn't want to. The friggin' situation with Carter was driving him nuts and who else could he talk to about it, if not Dave Dixon? All his other options had to pretend they were deaf, dumb and blind.

"No. Carter doesn't blame me."

Shifting again, Dixon uttered another pained grunt. "Nah. She wouldn't. I'll give you this, Jack. You've got superior taste. But your timing's *lousy*."

"Ya think?"

"Okay. So. What are you gonna do about it?"

And there it was: the million dollar question. "I don't know."

"Well you better figure it out, pronto," Dixon retorted. "I mean, it's not like things'll get any easier, is it?"

On the other hand, maybe deaf, dumb and blind was better. "Y'know, I must have missed the memo about how any of this is your business!"

In the darkness, a soft snort of amusement. "Sure it's my business. You're my friend, Jack. You were Frank's friend. Hell, I'm surprised he hasn't kicked open the Pearly Gates so he can come back down here and bury his boot up your butt. You know what he'd say, right?"

He could imagine. "Try saying it for him and I swear, Dave, I *swear*, I will finish what the Jaffa started."

"In your dreams, pal." A hissed breath, as Dixon tried in vain to get comfortable. "I take it Hammond knows, only he's pretending he doesn't?"

Talk about seeing too much. Apparently the bastard was psychic. "Dixon—"

"I guess," Dixon said, impervious, "it boils down to you and Carter or the team. Which means you and Carter or the SGC. If she'd stayed dead you and Hammond would be pulling it together. The SGC would be fine, eventually. But she lived and you love her and—I'm sorry, Jack. It must be hell."

The compassion in Dixon's voice nearly undid him. He had to wait until he could trust his voice. Trust himself. Face the fear he'd been fighting for days. Say the words out loud. And he had to say them. *Had* to… or else know himself a coward.

"I can't do this job with her," he whispered, low and shaking. "I can't do it without her. And I can't not do this job."

For a long time, nothing. Then Dixon sighed. "Yes, you can, Jack. You can do the job with Carter on the team. You've been doing it fine so far. What you're struggling with, my friend, is making peace with the fact that you can love Sam until your bones break and still kill her for the greater good. The problem is you're having a hard time accepting you're that kind of man."

O'Neill swallowed. Couldn't speak.

"Frank was the same," Dixon added. "You and Frank, two peas in a pod. You know that, right? Well, Jack, you'd better forgive yourself a damn sight faster than you forgave him, because Earth doesn't have the luxury of waiting while you get your shit together. In case you haven't noticed we're fighting a war, and right now things aren't going too great for our side."

"Screw you, Dixon," he muttered, once the urge to swear and shout and punch had passed. "I've noticed. Now shut up. I'm tired. I'd like to take a nap."

"Sure, Jack," Dixon said gently. "Whatever you say."

At last, blessed silence. And, in the mercy of unrelieved darkness, sleep.

When he woke there was sunlight bathing his face... and the music of Carter's voice over his radio.

"Colonel? Colonel, we've got your location. Don't move. We'll have you out of there in a jiffy. Sir, do you copy?"

"A jiffy, Major?" he croaked in reply. "Since when is that approved military parlance?"

"Sorry, sir. My bad."

"So. I guess the tracker chip works."

"Sure does, sir. Hold tight. We're coming."

"Okay. Take your time. Dixon wants to finish his crossword."

A sound like laughter, hastily quashed. *"Yes, sir."*

Releasing the radio toggle, he rolled his head a little on his stone pillow. Looked at Dixon. Winced. "Ow. You look like crap, Dave."

Chalky pale, eyes red-rimmed, smeared with blood and dirt from head to toe, Dixon grinned. "Yeah? Well, right back atcha, Jack."

There was nothing left to say, after that. So they waited, stupidly grinning, for Carter to arrive.

Engrossed in the latest issue of Science Weekly, Sam felt herself being watched and looked up. Jack, finally awake, tucked safely in an infirmary bed, his left arm strapped to his chest and an IV of fluids dripping into his right, waggled his eyebrows.

"So much for Hawaii," he said, his voice still a little ragged. "What happened? You get sick of surfing?"

She put the magazine on the floor beside her chair. "We both know I wasn't surfing."

"Don't tell me the boys at Mauna Kea wouldn't let you play with their toys!"

He was Jack O'Neill. Of course he'd figured it out. "We had lousy visibility. Nothing but cloud cover. Couldn't even see the moon." And barely nine hours after setting foot on the Big Island she'd been overwhelmed by a feeling of dread, of danger, by the urgent need to fly back to Cheyenne Mountain. Only she wasn't going to tell him that. They had enough weird in their lives already. "So, since I didn't bother to pack a swimsuit, I came home. Anyway, you know I've never been all that fond of tourist traps. Sir."

"True," he said. Then his smirking smile faded. "You okay?"

"I've already told you," she said, frowning. "I don't have a problem with you —"

His lips thinned. "Not that. I mean about... the other stuff. The entity."

It was the first time he'd asked her. The first time since she'd regained consciousness, in this same private room, that he'd been able to look her in the eye. Not because he didn't care. Because he cared too much.

"I'm fine," she said firmly.

Now his gaze was skeptical. "Fine?"

"Better," she amended, because really, there was no point lying. Not to him. "I hate to admit it, but Janet was right. Getting away from the SGC helped."

"And?"

And what? She'd been possessed — *dis*possessed — by an alien intelligence. *Again*. Shunted aside in her own mind, her own body. *Again*. Dumped into a computer mainframe. Reacquired, against all odds. Oh yes, and zatted twice. *That* had been fun. Was it any wonder she'd lost her bearings for a bit?

She propped her elbows on the chair's arms, and slung one ankle over her knee. "And before SG-1 goes back into rotation — which Janet says won't be until *she* says your collarbone's healed — I'm going to spend some time with Dad."

Jack stopped scowling, and blinked. "Here? Or on Vorash?"

"On Vorash."

Just saying it made her feel a whole lot lighter. Made her itchy to pack a bag and jump through the gate. If he hadn't been on a mission she'd have done exactly that, instead of flying to Hawaii. For this mess, she needed her father. There was nobody else she could talk to about the entity. About Jack. Everybody else had a vested interest in… not listening. Besides. She missed him.

"That's… a good idea," Jack said slowly. "If anybody knows what it's like to deal with an alien in your head, it's Jacob. I guess even the snake can —"

"*Selmak*."

"Yeah. Selmak. Whatever. I guess even he — she — *it* — might have something useful to say on the subject."

"You never know," she said, letting a little of her own sarcasm show.

But Jack wasn't paying attention. "Still…" He screwed up his face. "*Vorash*."

"Vorash is fine." She smiled. "Unlike you, I'm not allergic to the Tok'ra."

He didn't smile back. "Sam..."

Oh, no. No, no, no. *Jack* in the privacy of her own thoughts was one thing. But let them start seeing each other in the real world as *Jack* and *Sam* instead of *Colonel* and *Major*, let them try to pretend they could be anyone or anything else while their lives were ruled by the war against the Goa'uld, and the careful edifice they'd been building would come crashing down in ruins. One day, maybe, they'd get their Happily Ever After. But right now that day wasn't even on the horizon.

"*Colonel*," she said, holding his stare with her own. "We had a deal. And until circumstances change that deal still holds. It has to."

He looked down. Picked at the IV tape in the crook of his elbow. "Yeah. Okay."

She swung her foot to the floor and leaned forward. Rested both hands on the side of the bed. Bounced it until he looked at her again. "Whatever else I am, sir, I am an Air Force officer first. So are you. Which means we risk our lives as often as it takes until the enemy is defeated. It means you use me as ruthlessly as you'd use Teal'c or Daniel or Colonel Dixon, as many times as you have to. Anything less is unacceptable. Understood?"

For a time he said nothing. Looked down again. Tried to hide his thoughts, his feelings, behind that familiar stone mask. But it didn't work on her. Not any more. Blindfolded she could read him, just by the way he breathed in, and breathed out.

He looked up. His eyes were very dark. She could see pain there, but also peace. Admiration. Acceptance. "Yes, ma'am. Understood."

"Right." She shoved the chair back. "Now I'm out of here. Dad's waiting. Rest up, sir. Glad you're okay. More or less."

"Me, too," Jack said. "Have fun. Give Jacob my best."

Smiling, she nodded at him. He smiled and nodded back. Friendly, but professional. Two colleagues. Nothing more. That was the deal. That was the sacrifice.

Quietly, very quietly, she closed the door behind her.

Janet —

I sent Dave Dixon home today. Released Jack into the wild, too. I'm pretty sure he knows better than to push his luck. He might not admit it out loud, but he knows that at his age, with his mileage, broken bones and concussions take a little longer to heal than they used to.

I'm pretty sure he's forgiven me for talking out of turn. All he said was: I know what you did. I know why you did it. Just don't do it again. He wasn't smiling when he said it, but there weren't any sparks coming out of his eyes, either. And hey, I'm still standing.

He's found his balance again, thank God. I wish I knew how. I asked Dave about it but he's making like a clam, dammit. So unless I can get him alone with a syringe of sodium pentothal, I guess I'll never know. Not for sure. But dollars to donuts he had a word with Jack. He's that kind of man. Hammond asked me for an on-the-fly psych eval on him. Really wants Dave for the SGC. I think it's a great idea, and not just because he's an excellent officer. I think having Dave Dixon around would do Jack a lot of good. So... I guess we'll see.

Sam's due back from Vorash tomorrow. She's doing better too. I know she and Jack talked. Whatever got said, it made a difference. To both of them. I think they'll be okay now. Will they ever stop loving each other? I doubt it. But you know, there are a lot of different ways to love.

Me? I'm going to stop worrying about it. Like the song says. Que sera, sera. What will be, will be.

STARGATE ATLANTIS
Hermiod's Last Mission

T. Fox Dunham

"It's not my fault!"

"Just fix the damn ship, Rodney!"

Sheppard threw the jumper hard, making a bat-turn, and the first of the azure bolts fired from the hive grazed the side of the hull. The ship shook, but Sheppard sensed no damage. They could usually shake off the first few hits; the hive's main cannons weren't designed to target small and agile vessels. But they'd be launching darts if Rodney couldn't repair the cloak.

"It's not fair," McKay muttered, pulling open a panel near his feet. "All systems checked out when we launched from the *Daedalus*..."

That had been ten hours ago. The *Daedalus* was waiting out of range of the hive's sensors — even at full burn it would take them an hour to reach the jumper's position and provide mission support — and Sheppard's team had been depending on stealth to infiltrate the hive, locate the ship's logs, and be gone before the Wraith could raise a feeding hand. Except that the cloak had failed when they were almost at the hive, leaving them completely vulnerable and alone in the void between galaxies. No stars glowed, just two wheels of light fore and aft — Pegasus and Milky Way, home and Earth. It was just Sheppard's team and the Wraith, their conflict emphasized and demeaned by the immensity of the void.

"Dr. McKay," Hermiod said in his maudlin tone. "I have a solution."

Rodney ignored the Asgard. Hermiod wasn't part of the rhythm of the team, and McKay was lost in the problem. Hermiod didn't press his point. He'd been quiet since joining the mission, silently observing, looking over the team's shoulder and occasionally admonishing them with a frown. Sheppard hadn't met many Asgard to compare, but he found Hermiod's manner — the way the little alien walked with his head raised, his tone of voice — somewhat unnerving. If his superiors ordered Sheppard to add him to the unit, he'd have to work on Hermiod's people skills, although he kinda enjoyed it when the Asgard pushed Rodney's buttons.

"Okay," Rodney said. "I've got it." He pinched alligator clips into the tubing below the co-pilot's panel, tapping away at the keys on his tablet. "Cloak should be available to you… now."

Sheppard spoke to the ship, willing the cloak into existence. Nothing. "Still not working, Rodney."

"It's not my fault! Some of the jumpers were damaged when the city flooded. I've not had time to run diagnostics on all the systems yet. It's a huge city, and I'm only getting three hours of sleep every night. If I don't sleep, I start getting headaches and can't focus. I need more help! If Zelenka could just —"

"Perhaps, Rodney, if you focused less on explanations and more on solving the problem, you could fix the cloaking device sooner?" Teyla employed her maternal tone, the voice she used to both discipline and educate Athosian children — and sometimes members of Sheppard's team.

It helped Sheppard stay calm too. His people were the best and he had faith they'd find a solution — with the right motivation. "You know," he said. "I knew we should have brought Zelenka."

"Oh please." McKay got up from his seat, opened an overhead panel.

"Dr. McKay," the Asgard said, trying again. "If you —"

"Trying to work here."

"Rodney!" Sheppard snapped. "Listen to the —"

An alarm blared; the hive had a solid lock on them. "Crap," Sheppard growled. "This is going to get hairy." One direct hit from the hive's main guns would cripple the jumper, and he braced himself for the impact even as he took evasive action. Yet, when it came, the canon fire arced harmlessly away from the jumper. He stared at the display in disbelief. "What the hell...?"

"They're not even coming close," Rodney said, puzzled. "They're firing into empty space."

"There's something wrong with that hive," Ronon said. His gaze was fixed on the Wraith ship, his hand resting on his weapon as if he was itching to open fire himself.

A new tactical map morphed onto the screen in front of Sheppard, accompanied by another alarm; the hive was launching Wraith fighters. They arrowed toward the jumper, quickly closing the distance between them. "Still no cloak, Rodney..."

"It should be working!"

"Well it's not." Sheppard banked the ship into a steep turn. "Guess I'll have to work for a living, then."

"You can't take on that many darts," McKay protested. "We'll be slaughtered."

"Not helping, Rodney."

A cloud of darts swarmed them, two of the fighters dropping onto their six. Sheppard tried to shake them, but they were tenacious little bastards. With a thought, he released two drones, guiding them to the offending darts. They exploded just as a third flight dropped in behind him. "Damn it!" he growled. "Hold onto something!"

Slamming on the breaks, he brought the jumper to an almost dead stop, forcing the darts to pull up to avoid a collision. The maneuver broke their formation and Sheppard used the confusion to breakaway.

"Dr. McKay," Hermiod said, his voice more insistent. "You should be able to reactivate the cloaking field generator by disabling the wave inducer."

"Sure, if you want to blow the jumper up!"

"If you lower the power levels, there should be enough to cloak us for a short duration."

Sheppard shot Rodney a look; sometimes he had to push

the scientist to get past his own ego and accept help.

"He's not even here!" McKay complained. "He's a hologram. What he's suggesting could leave us floating dead in space... or worse."

Ronon muttered, "You'll be floating dead in space in a minute if you—"

"Oh. Ha. Ha."

"Ronon—don't pick on Rodney. McKay—fix the damn cloak or, I swear, I'm going to turn this jumper around."

A new threat appeared on the HUD. Three more darts were on their tail, and Sheppard threw the ship to port to keep out of range of their weapons. Too late; the jumper rocked, the left drive pod sluggish. "We're hit," Sheppard said. "Losing power."

McKay checked his own display. "Damn it—the main capacitor is damaged."

Automatically, Sheppard rerouted several systems and smoothed out their flight, but it was only a temporary fix. They wouldn't last out here much longer. "Rodney," he said. "We need that cloak back online."

"Fine, we'll try it the Asgard's way," McKay said, entering commands on his keypad. "But don't blame me if the ship explodes." A pause, then. "Okay, try it now."

With a stutter, the cloak re-engaged and settled around the ship. "About damn time," Sheppard said, letting out a breath. Then he dived fast, ducking the jumper beneath the pursuing darts, their gunfire strafing harmlessly overhead. "Thanks Hermiod."

"You are welcome," the Asgard said. "It was not difficult."

"Come on, anyone can get lucky," McKay grumbled.

"It was not luck. I am just capable."

"Unbelievable!" Rodney murmured to Sheppard, though he made no real attempt to keep Hermiod from overhearing. "Why is he even here?"

"You know why. It was a special request from Thor, through General O'Neill."

"But he's just a holographic projection!" McKay groused. "What's he going to do if we have a run in with the Wraith? Patronize them to death?"

"Be nice, Rodney. We owe his people a lot: the hypderdrive, beaming technology. He can tag along if he wants to."

"This is a fully interactive photonic projection," Hermiod explained. "Using technology developed from what you call Ancient 'communication stones', it allows me some basic interaction with my environment while maintaining full communication with the *Daedalus*." He paused, then added, "It is a technology well beyond your scientific understanding."

"Well beyond?" McKay spluttered. "Do you have any idea what I — ?"

"Save it!" Sheppard ordered. "Something's happening." The HUD was showing a firefight among the darts — streaks of weapons fire, bright white explosions against the starless void.

"They're firing on each other," Ronon said, peering over Sheppard's shoulder to look at the display.

Within moments, most of the targets had vanished from the screen. Teyla frowned. "These Wraith are acting in a bizarre manner."

Sheppard scrubbed a hand through his hair. "Maybe they ran out of gas and got stranded here so long they started feeding on each other?"

"That is not likely," Teyla said. "Wraith would hibernate rather than feed on each other."

"She's right," McKay said. "There's something else going on. I'm getting very odd readings from some of those darts." He studied the sensor scans and grimaced. "It's like… Something's leaking from the ships. Some kind of protoplasm, maybe? It's almost like they're bleeding."

"Wraith are dying," Ronon said. "Who cares why?"

"Right," Sheppard said. "Doesn't change our mission, and since they've opened it for us we can enter the hive through the dart bay."

"I could have hacked the bay doors," McKay said.

Hermiod blinked at him. "Doubtful."

Ignoring the bickering, Sheppard focused on landing the jumper. The carapace of the hive ship expanded across the viewport as they approached. Fluid pulsed through arteries that snaked over and through the deep ripples and grooves of the hull, feeding the engines and life-support systems. Two massive domes clung to the underbelly of the colony ship where the Wraith lived or hibernated, populating the domes like ants in a mound. Cocoon chambers honeycombed the remainder of the habitat, designed to hold thousands of humans awaiting the embrace of a feeding hand. Two stubby flippers jutted out on opposite sides of the hardened shell, stabilizing the flight, and bright plasma burned from several round ports along the back plane of the hive. Yet the Wraith ship hung motionless, its lights blinking and winking, reminding Sheppard of a city losing power during an outage.

McKay leaned forward, peering through the view screen. "Power is fluctuating all over the hive."

"That is obvious," Hermiod said.

"They're suffering malfunctions in a major way," McKay continued, ignoring him. "If the fluctuations don't stabilize that ship isn't going to last long."

"Then we need to hurry," Sheppard said.

McKay looked up. "What, you still want to board that thing?"

"We have to know where they were headed."

"Does it matter, if they blow up?"

"We still don't know if Michael's hive gave the information they stole from Atlantis to the other hives," Teyla reminded him, referring to their recent alliance with the enemy. Of course, it had all gone bad, and the Wraith had betrayed the expedition and stolen the location of Earth, as well as the Asgard designs for an intergalactic hyperdrive that would enable them to reach their new feeding grounds. If that knowledge had spread among the Wraith... Well, Sheppard didn't even want to think about the consequences.

"I am detecting upgrades to their hyperdrive," Hermiod reported. "And this course is a direct point between the Pegasus Galaxy and Earth."

"Crap," McKay said, glancing down at his tablet. "I am too. So they've definitely gotten our engine schematics. But why did they just stop out here in the middle of dead space?"

It was a good question. 'Dead space' was exactly the right term for this empty place, and Sheppard couldn't imagine why anyone would stop here unless they had no choice. He missed the stars filling the screen, reminding him that life continued and thrived in the universe. Out here in the void between galaxies, nothing lived, nothing thrived. He just wanted to complete the mission and get home to Atlantis. "I guess there's only one way to find out what's going on," he said. "So let's go ask."

But the jumper struggled on the approach to the hive, not easing into the trajectory, and warning lights started flashing on the HUD.

"We're losing power fast," McKay reported. "The main capacitor's completely screwed."

"Can we fix it?"

"We cannot repair the damage without returning to the *Daedalus*," Hermiod said, calm as ever.

"He's right," McKay confirmed. "We're stuck here."

Sheppard cursed and summoned communications, hailing the *Daedalus*. Colonel Caldwell's rough voice answered.

"Colonel Sheppard. What's your status?"

"We're about to infiltrate the hive, but we got pretty beat up on the way. Might need a ride home."

There was a pause before Caldwell answered, a beat of disapproval; the plan had been to keep the *Daedalus* out of the hive's range. "Understood," he said at last. "We're an hour out. Keep me apprised of your status, Colonel. Caldwell out."

"Well he's Mr. Warm-and-Friendly today," McKay said.

"So long as the *Daedalus* is here when we need her," Sheppard said, "I can live without warm and friendly."

Now fully inside the hive, Sheppard set the jumper down on an empty pad close to one of the corridors leading into the ship. "Okay," he said, turning around in the pilot's chair. "Get in. Download the ship's logs. Figure out if they have the location of Earth. Then get out."

"Alive please," Rodney said.

"Yes," Sheppard added. "Alive, if possible."

Ronon unholstered his pistol. "And then we blow up the hive?"

"And then we blow up the hive."

Cautiously, the team left the cloaked jumper, though the shield shifted when Sheppard looked back and he knew it was already malfunctioning — they didn't have much time before it failed. He did a quick headcount of the team and waved them on, but then realized they were missing one.

Where the hell was Hermiod?

Supreme Commander Thor. As per your orders, I am recording my observations through direct empathic link. A recreation of the experiences of my senses will be transmitted to the council on Othala. On a personal note, let me say that I have little faith in the success of my mission, and I wish to again protest my assignment as the human attendant. I request a transfer to the new home colony where I can be of better use during the twilight of our people.

Hermiod thought better of the last few lines and deleted them, keeping the record impersonal. What did his feelings matter now that the High Council had ratified the final sanction?

As per your orders, I have joined the lead team from the Atlantis expedition so I can observe the humans under immediate threat. I have not informed the humans of the nature of my mission, and I must tell you, Supreme Commander, that I am not comfortable with your instructions. I do not believe I am the right being for this mission. I know that you could not get a real understanding of human nature because of the status in which their leaders hold you, and this is why you commanded me to undertake my observation, since I am of lower rank and my position on this ship is one of service. However, I am isolated among the crew and the humans even consider me, as Dr. Novak has been known to call me, 'grumpy'. I do not believe —

"You ready, buddy?" Colonel Sheppard's question distracted Hermiod from his mental monograph.

"I am coming, Colonel Sheppard," Hermiod said. The rest of the team had already disembarked from the Lantean gateship. But Hermiod's fingers felt numb and he ran a neural diagnostic before he left. As he'd feared, the disease, unleashed accidentally during the last cloning cycle, had accelerated and Hermiod sent a mental signal to the reservoir of medicine built directly into his brain. The enzymes and electrolytes would ease the mental degradation, however the chemicals would only treat the symptoms not cure the disease. Complete neural collapse was inevitable. But, for now, the medicine did its work and feeling returned to his limbs.

Stepping to the edge of the back port he hesitated before entering the Wraith hive, then reminded himself that he wasn't physically there. His body was safely connected to the Asgard systems on the *Daedalus*. The remote sensors fed real-time information to all of his senses, thus he saw, felt, smelled, tasted and heard as his holographic duplicate.

The rest of the unit checked their projectile weapons — primitive but effective. Teyla Emmagan and Ronon Dex guarded the rear, and Hermiod followed Colonel Sheppard and Dr. McKay. Unlike the Asgard, humans still possessed unique appearances and at times Hermiod found the degrees of physical difference overwhelming. Dr. McKay shared a similar brown shade to his hair as Colonel Sheppard, though Sheppard had grown his longer so it curled at its ends. Teyla tied her dark blond hair back before heading into combat. He couldn't imagine how

distracting hair must be. At least they all wore charcoal uniforms with matching vests.

"We need to get to the main computer core in the Queen's
chamber," Dr. McKay said.

To be helpful, Hermiod scanned the ship and reviewed the
schematics. "I have located the Wraith data core."

"Of course you have," said Dr. McKay, in a tone that implied
sarcasm.

Despite the friction between them, Hermiod related most
to Rodney McKay. He suffered similar self-doubt, and perhaps that was why he'd been so caustic while working with
the brilliant human scientist. As Dr. Novak might have said,
they both had a tendency to be 'grumpy'.

His thoughts were suddenly, shockingly interrupted. Wraith
stunner bolts sizzled past his face, their heat almost over-
loading the remote sensors. The Atlantis team immediately
returned fire, their bullets piercing the armor of two Wraith
drones. However, their weapons had little effect; the drones
continued to fire. Hermiod scanned their stun weapons and
discovered their similarity to non-lethal weapons which the
Asgard had once employed against the Goa'uld. It was not difficult to calibrate a pulse from one of the communication stones
that projected his hologram, and the stunners overloaded in a
shower of sparks. The drones collapsed, rendered unconscious
by their own weapons.

"What the hell was that?" Dr. McKay asked, scrambling to
his feet from the fleshy arch in the corridor bulkhead where
he'd been sheltering from the crossfire.

"I don't know," Colonel Sheppard said. "But I was wishing
real hard..."

"Since your weapons were proving ineffective," Hermiod
explained, "I induced an overload in the stunner power supply."

"Nice work," Sheppard said, glancing along the corridor
ahead. "Ronon, take point."

Ronon nodded, checked his energy weapon, and moved

out with long deliberate strides. It was difficult for Hermiod to keep up as they hurried through the dank corridors of the living ship, its lights dimmed and the great beast wheezing as the walls bled violet fluid onto the floor.

"It is like the darts," Teyla said. "There is something very wrong with this hive."

"Are you sensing anything?" Colonel Sheppard asked her.

"And I am sensing confusion among the Wraith. It is strange. I —"

Weapons fire up ahead interrupted her, sending the team into defensive positions again. But they didn't need to fire; this time, the Wraith were attacking each other. Further along the corridor, Hermiod could see a small group of Wraith. Pink ooze dripped from beneath the masks of the drones, while Wraith warrior turned on Wraith warrior, their feeding hands swollen and hungry.

Sheppard made a face. "That looks like —"

"The funky goo that covered the Wraith darts," Dr. McKay said. "Yeah. I think we can say that these guys are sick. I mean, more than usually sick."

"The retrovirus?" Sheppard asked.

"Maybe. They could have been infected."

"Let's not stick around to find out."

"We can get past them," Ronon said, nodding toward a side corridor. "They're too busy killing each other."

Hermiod approved the passive tactic, already disgusted with the violence and bloodshed. He followed the team as they moved furtively down the ubiquitous corridors, but suddenly his vision juddered, pixilating as his hologram destabilized. Static filled his mind and he felt the projection freeze. He ran a swift diagnostic, but couldn't isolate the malfunction from his remote location. The problem appeared to be on the hive.

"My unit is malfunctioning," he said. "I believe that subspace interference is distorting my signal."

"Uh-huh." Dr. McKay checked the communication stone

with his Lantean scanner, and reached out to make a small adjustment. "Above my 'scientific understanding', is it?"

The signal stabilized and the Hermiod's vision cleared, the projection unfreezing. "Your assistance is noted."

"Noted?" McKay echoed. "How about 'thank you?'"

"How about we keep moving?" Colonel Sheppard said, gesturing McKay to precede him along the corridor.

As they walked on, deeper into the ship, Hermiod began to hear the sound of anguished moaning drift from the chambers they passed — humans, spun into membrane, waiting for their deaths. "Can we not help these people?" he asked as he glanced into one such chamber.

Colonel Sheppard traded a look with Teyla. "It is not possible," she said, with an expression of controlled sorrow. "The kindest thing we can do is to bring them a swift death."

"By blowing up the ship," Ronon said, with grim conviction.

Hermiod returned his attention to the human captives. The webs that constrained them exposed their chests for easier feeding — and their faces. The Wraith fed on the human life-force to survive, and Hermiod could forgive them their biological requirements. However, they wanted to watch the terror in the faces of their prey as they died. And, for that, Hermiod deemed them monsters incapable of redemption.

He was glad to leave the feeding chambers and reach the sealed doors to the Queen's chamber.

"Get that open," Colonel Sheppard said, waving Dr. McKay forward.

Crouching down, McKay sliced into the spongy flesh of the wall and inserted a pair of adapter leads. "Something's corrupting the program," he said as more ooze seeped from the incisions he'd made. Suddenly he yanked back his hand. "Ugh, I think it sneezed on me."

Colonel Sheppard said, "Gesundheit."

What that meant, Hermoid could not be sure, but before he could ask Dr. McKay hissed "Got it!" and the door opened.

A series of dens and parlors lay beyond, with a single throne dominating the largest room. The walls pulsed — hot and hungry — and Hermiod turned down his temperature settings.

"No Queen," Ronon said, glancing around. "No Wraith."

His observation that was swiftly explained; a heap of Wraith bodies lay piled at the center of the prime chamber, leaking black blood which pooled on the floor.

"What the hell?" Dr. McKay aimed his scanner at the dead flesh. "Something is reprogramming the Wraith DNA — it's growing between the bodies. I don't know if it's alive or just bubbling."

Colonel Sheppard made a face. "What *is* it?"

"I don't know. All I'm saying is that it's more than a pile of bodies."

Hermiod conducted a scan of his own. Dr. McKay was right; a membrane of protoplasm connected the various corpses, merging flesh at the cellular level. It was a curious thing, but he would evaluate the data later, at a less stressful time. All he said was, "My readings are also inconclusive."

"Doesn't matter right now," Colonel Sheppard said. "It's not killing us, so just let it hangout while we access the computer."

"I'm on it," Dr. McKay said, turning to a glowing amber pillar at the center of the adjacent chamber. Purple screens, built into a pyramidal point, displayed data from the Wraith computer core, and Dr. McKay and Teyla accessed the systems while the rest of the team guarded the chamber.

Hermiod fixed his attention on the strange fleshy mass, watching it shift and move. He had not seen anything like it before and it made him feel uneasy — the human expression, he believed, was 'it made his skin crawl'. He hoped they would soon be able to leave this place.

After a long period of silence, McKay hissed "Yes!" and data started spilling down the Wraith screens. It was not a language Hermiod understood, but Dr. McKay's linguistic ability appeared sufficient.

"Looks like they *were* going to Earth," he said, "but luckily for us Michael's alliance was small, just three hive ships. This hive was on its way to join up with its sister ships, but their hyperdrive modifications failed."

"So they're stranded here," Sheppard said.

"Yes, but this is where it gets weird. They picked up some kind of signal and rigged their engines for a short jump to reach the target. Maybe they thought it would be another ship or maybe... dinner."

Hermiod moved to the screen and analyzed the signal, tracing it to its source. "I am detecting a lone asteroid in proximity to the Wraith hive," he said. "It appears to be the source of the signal."

"Later guys," Colonel Sheppard said. "We got what we need, now unhook your gear and let's get outa here." He put a hand to the radio he wore on his vest. "*Daedalus*, this is Sheppard. Do you copy?"

As they disconnected their equipment, Hermiod noticed the mass in the adjacent chamber begin to move.

There was a hiss of static and Caldwell's scratchy voice could barely be heard through the interference. "*Sheppard, we're here but we're having trouble locking on transporters.*"

The fleshy mass was pulsating now, trembling. Hermiod withdrew a step. "Colonel Sheppard," he said. "I believe we have another problem."

As he watched, the flesh ballooned, swelling under the long black coats of the dead Wraith warriors, mixing with the white hair. Blood boiled and the mass began to rise, limbs combined with bone, skulls merging. At the center of the new creature, the red hair of a Queen flowed. Her mouth opened and she keened.

"Oh crap," Sheppard said, lifting his weapon. Into his radio he barked, "Caldwell, we need to get outa here!"

"Can't do it," came the reply. "Looks like the hive's shielded."

"*Daedalus*, standby," Sheppard said, dropping his hand from the radio to his weapon. "McKay!"

"Already on it." Dr. McKay bent once more over the Wraith screen, fingers flying across the interface.

Ronon and Teyla took the front line of defense, while Colonel Sheppard anchored the center. Although he was not present in the flesh, Hermiod withdrew behind them as they fired into the mass. As he had feared, their weapons had little effect; the creature simply absorbed the bullets.

"*Sheppard,*" Caldwell said, "*you need to hurry — something weird is happening to that hive. It looks like it's melting.*"

"Trust me, we're hurrying. Things are a little weird down here too."

As he spoke, a gray tendril snaked out from the Wraith mass and grabbed Ronon, lifting him from the ground, aiming him for its mouth. His arms pinned to his side, he could not fire. But Teyla unsheathed a dagger and kicked off the wall, launching herself onto the creature and stabbing at its limb. The thing screamed, splitting the flesh around its mouth, and dropped Ronon.

Spinning in mid-air, Ronon managed to both land on his feet and open fire at the same time. The creature howled, but did not retreat.

"Rodney!" Sheppard barked. "How long?"

"This isn't fair! I'm under a lot of pressure here and I didn't have a good breakfast. I think there was citrus juice in that fruit salad. I feel my throat swelling up."

Hermiod had hoped he wouldn't have to connect his mind to the corrupted Wraith systems, but it was clear now that he had no other choice. He reached out and touched the Wraith data core, found the input paths and downloaded part of his mind directly into the alien systems. The communication stone translated a simulation of the hive's mind into his own, and as the living ship sensed his presence he felt a sticky web begin to ensnare his thoughts.

The web vibrated, speaking to him. *You are sick, old one.*

"As are you," Hermiod responded. He searched the web,

seeking the systems that controlled the hive's shielding. He sensed great danger here; the hive was protecting itself and in his mind it was as if an iratus bug crawled through the web toward him. He knew he was close to what he sought, the creature's mandibles punching for him just as he located the shield controls. It stabbed at his mind, a driving pain that obscured his vision, but he fought it off long enough — he hoped — to deactivate the shields. The moment it was done, he wrenched his mind out of the network, freeing himself from the deadly environment. But, even sick as it was, the hive was too strong. It overwhelmed his holographic communication systems and started to follow his mind back to the *Daedalus*. Desperate, Hermiod flung himself away and shattered the connection.

When he returned to awareness, he found himself sitting at his station in engineering.

"Hermiod," Dr. Novak asked, concerned. "What happened? Are you okay?"

He had to focus through a cloud of pain in order to check the console before him. "I am well," he assured her after a moment, and felt a swell of relief when he saw that the hive's shielding was indeed down. "Colonel Caldwell," he said, opening communications to the bridge. "I am transporting Colonel Sheppard's team directly to the bridge."

By the time Hermiod reached the bridge, *Daedalus* was under fire. Colonel Sheppard and his team were there, looking shaken but unharmed as they watched the battle unfold on the view screen.

"Shield's holding," reported Lieutenant Jordan from the operations station.

"Target all forward railguns," Caldwell barked. "Fill missile tubes one and two. We can't let them leave with what they know."

Enemy fire smacked the *Daedalus*' shields and an arc of super-accelerated ordinance streamed from the railgun turrets toward the hive. Unfortunately, it did not appear to be sufficient to destroy the ship.

"Shields are down to twenty percent," reported an airman. "The hive is focusing on our hyperdrive."

"Colonel," Sheppard said. "Hermiod disabled their shielding…"

Caldwell looked at him. "Can we beam a nuke aboard?"

Hermiod did not like the plan, but Colonel Caldwell had not asked for his opinion. "We can," he said. "I will need to make some modifications to the weapon from my station in engineering."

"Then do it," Caldwell said.

"I will accompany you," Teyla's said, her offer surprising Hermiod.

Few of the crewmembers, sans Dr. Novak, volunteered to spend time with him, and Novak's awkward affections proved to be vexing at times. Still, he had promised Supreme Commander Thor that he would try to facilitate a better social integration with the human crew. Apparently, there had been some complaints about 'arrogance' in his last personnel report from Colonel Caldwell. "As you wish," he said to Teyla.

Sheppard nodded at her and she hurried with Hermiod to engineering. It was not an easy journey. Pipes vented gas, and power flickered throughout the ship. Crewmembers ran past conducting damage control, nearly knocking Hermiod over several times.

But at last he reached his station and climbed onto the platform in front of the Asgard console. The wall monitor behind him lit up, displaying damage to the *Daedalus*, and runes reported down the sides of the image as he adjusted the control stones.

Hermiod detested Colonel Caldwell's plan, but he understood the necessity of stopping the Wraith. He deactivated the safeties on the fission device within the weapon, then transported it into the hive's engine cooling chamber. There, it could not be reached in time to be deactivated.

"The weapon is deployed," he reported to the bridge. "Detonation in five, four, three, two…"

The shockwave hit the ship, rocking her enough that Hermiod was forced to hold on to keep his balance. The hive, and all life aboard it, was destroyed.

Hermoid dipped his head in acknowledgement of the fact. "We've given these infants too many toys to play with," he said in his own language.

From behind him, Teyla said, "The Wraith devour entire worlds."

He blinked at her, unsure whether she had understood his language or whether she had simply sensed his discomfort. Teyla was extremely perceptive, even by human standards.

"Indeed," was all he said.

Then, to cleanse his thoughts of the destruction he'd wrought, he focused on the biological analysis of the data he'd collected from the anomalous Wraith mass.

Teyla lingered close by while he worked, her presence distracting. He did not understand why she was still there now that the battle was over. "If you are not busy," he said at last, "I find that I work better alone."

"Yes," Teyla said. "You have made your discomfort around humans well known. Though of late, you seem to be more troubled."

Her answer surprised him. After some thought, he decided to allow himself a moment of self-indulgence. "Your people are… spiritual?"

Teyla tightened the cords on her tactical vest, keeping herself ready, on edge. "Most of our religion is based on the return of the Ancestors to deliver us from the Wraith. I once believed them to be gods and their city to be an ethereal plane where we could all live forever in safety—where we would meet again the loved ones taken by the Wraith."

"But now that you have joined the expedition from Earth, your perceptions must have changed."

Teyla inclined her head in agreement. "I have found my faith interrupted, but my response to what I have learned has proven flexible. The Ancestors were indeed once flesh and blood, but now they have ascended and watch us like gods."

Hermiod felt a stab of pain, the symptoms of his disease rearing up once more, and with a thought released more of his medication. Its anodyne properties cleared his thoughts, though the effects would eventually diminish. "There are many primitive races that view the Asgard as gods," he said. "We have allowed them this view, although we have rules about interfering in their natural development. We would have told them the truth of our existence once they had developed sufficiently."

"You speak of this as if it is in the past."

"Yes." He couldn't divulge the truth to this human, but his people would not see another solar rotation of their world. "The Asgard were once mortal like you, or at least shorter lived and more vulnerable to disease and aging. Our species' evolution became solely based on technology, and without the primal fears of primitive races the need for religion declined. Though we still traded stories to entertain, I've always found such stories frivolous."

"You are frightened," Teyla said, startling him again with her perception. "And you are looking for comfort in religion."

"During the last cycles, I have reviewed many of the old stories and legends of my people."

"What is religion but old stories?"

Hermiod had always prided himself on his intellect, validating his existence with his mental accomplishments. Now, as a result of his people's final attempt at genetic manipulation to correct the cloning failure, a degenerative disease was destroying his mind. It was hard to describe what was happening to him, but a single archetype from his research into ancient Asgard myths haunted him: Fenrir, the wolf, the devourer of the sun. And the symbol of disease. It hunted his people now, and it would indeed devour them all in the end.

An alert on his console drew his attention back to the present; the analysis of the data was complete. Hermiod began to review it, but what he saw filled him with a sudden, sharp fear. The Asgard, it seemed, were not the only race to be hunted a wolf.

He looked up at Teyla. "I require the presence of Colonel Caldwell and the Atlantis team immediately."

"I have determined that the phenomenon we witnessed on the hive ship is indeed an infection," Hermiod said. "The disease is operating at a level of complexity I have only seen in one circumstance before — and I believe you are all infected."

"Oh this is bad," Dr. McKay said, reviewing Hermiod's data. "This disease looks like it's been engineered..."

While they spoke, Hermiod surreptitiously scanned for signs of disease among the humans. Unfortunately, the Atlantis team and the rest of the bridge crew were already suffering from varying levels of infection.

"...it's using a level of chemical engineering beyond anything I've ever seen," Dr. McKay was saying, as he checked a status report on one of the work stations. "Oh good, at least the hyperdrive is still down."

"That's good?" Ronon said.

"Well we can't risk carrying the disease to any inhabited world," McKay said. "We've seen what it did to the Wraith."

"Yes, but how can we cure it?" Teyla asked, her attention turning to Hermiod.

"First, we will need to know more about the infection source," he said. "According to the Wraith logs, they searched the source of the lone signal we picked up — the nearby asteroid — and returned to their ship infected. I have the coordinates and I believe there is a structure within the asteroid that is habitable. It is most likely that it is the source of infection."

"So we beam down and find the cure?" Colonel Sheppard asked.

"It is unlikely to be so simple," Hermiod said. "But perhaps we will discover the data we need to synthesize a treatment." He hesitated before he continued. "However, we cannot all go." He moved to stand closer to Colonel Sheppard. "I believe everyone aboard the ship is infected, Colonel Sheppard, but you and Dr. McKay will exhibit few immediate symptoms. You are disease carriers."

"Nice."

"Others," Hermiod continued, "such as Ronon and Teyla, will succumb swiftly." He looked at Teyla with sorrow. "Your minds will soon be overtaken by the disease."

Ronon reached for his weapon and Hermiod backed up a step. "What does that mean?"

His face, Hermiod noticed, was starting to gleam with sweat and there was something dark feathering the whites of his eyes. It only confirmed what the scan had already revealed. "It means the disease will soon control your higher brain function."

Teyla said, "Then you must go, John. You and Rodney. Leave us here, and find a cure."

Sheppard looked torn. "I can't just —"

"You must," Hermiod insisted. "It is your only chance to save them. And yourself."

While they'd been talking, several of the bridge crew had set aside their duties and now sat, listless, in their chairs, or stood with their arms hanging at their sides. Their eyes were glazed, unseeing, laced with the same dark filigree he'd seen in Ronon's eyes.

"Colonel Sheppard..." Hermiod warned.

"Yeah, I see it." Sheppard eyed the bridge crew and reached for his weapon.

"They are now subject to the wolf," Hermiod said. "We must leave while we can."

As one, the crew rose from their stations, but still they did not approach. Nor did they blink. Even Ronon and Teyla had turned slack-mouthed and still.

"Okay," Sheppard said. "McKay, back up real slow."

"What? We're leaving Teyla and Ronon behind?"

"You heard him, we don't have any choice!" Sheppard snapped, and even Hermiod could sense his distress.

In silence, he followed Sheppard and McKay off the bridge. Once they were in the corridor beyond, Dr. McKay sealed the bulkhead. "That's bought us a little time," he said, "but they control all ship functions from the bridge."

"I can bypass the bridge stations from engineering," Hermiod told them.

Colonel Sheppard nodded. "So let's go."

As they passed through the corridors of the ship, infected crew members turned from their perfunctory tasks or stood, motionless and glazed, the telltale filigree of black knotting through the whites of their eyes.

"They are disorientated while the Fenrir — the disease — takes over their pre-frontal cortex," Hermiod explained. "The microbe is unsure of how to control them. But once it can..." He did not believe he needed to say more; they were all familiar with what had happened to the Wraith.

Once they reached engineering, Hermiod activated his hologram emitter in order to beam down with McKay and Sheppard. His doppelgänger manifested for a moment, but then scattered into a billion pixels. "The communication stones are suffering the same error as they did on the hive ship," he said in confusion. "Something is interfering with them."

"Then I guess you're just going to have to do it the old-fashioned way," Colonel Sheppard said. "Let's move."

Hermiod nodded and activated the transporter.

Sheppard materialized into darkness, into breathless air within the asteroid, and the sudden dislocation of the transporters was as disorientating as always. "Ugh," he complained. "Did I mention I hate Asgard transporters? No offence, Hermiod."

"I am not offended."

Sheppard blinked into the darkness, distracted by a sensation of something familiar, like seeing an old friend from across the room. He sent a thought out, just in case he was right, and ahead of him a set of stairs lit up in rows, illuminating the language of the Ancients. "Well hello," he said. "What have we here?"

"Welcome to the city of... Discenna," McKay read. "Please enjoy your stay. Discenna is the Ancient word for 'to learn.' An Ancient research colony, maybe, but what's it doing out here?"

Around them, a familiar operations center came sluggishly to life — a much smaller, less welcoming version of the one on Atlantis. It looked almost derelict but Sheppard didn't need to see the decay to know that this place was sick; he could feel it like something cold and clammy on his skin.

"This is fascinating," McKay said, hooking up his laptop to the Ancient systems. Sheppard scanned the control room, turning a slow three-sixty, keeping his hands on his weapon. He couldn't understand why the Ancients would build this place inside an asteroid, but he could see that in places the rock had smashed through windows as if it was somehow encroaching on the city. It seemed more likely that the asteroid had collected itself around the city.

"Okay, we have one ZPM still clinging to life," McKay reported. "Wow. This thing has been floating out here for eons."

"Reviewing navigational logs," Hermiod said. "It looks like the city's point of origin was the planet Dakara, in the Milky Way galaxy. It left near the same time as Atlantis left Earth."

"Makes sense," Sheppard said. "Part of the Ancient exodus after the plague — Wait a second, is this disease the same one that wiped out the Ancients?"

"No, Colonel Sheppard." Hermiod continued to scan the Ancient database. "What has infected you is not the plague. It appears you are infected by the cure."

"The *cure*?"

"It was designed to seek out the plague and destroy it," he said, still reading. "The Ancients made it highly infectious, so that it would spread from world to world."

"Oh sure," McKay sighed. "And what could possibly go wrong with that plan?"

"A great deal, apparently," said Hermiod, without a trace of irony.

Sheppard glanced around the derelict control room. "I guess it's too much to ask that they left a note behind letting us know how to cure the cure?"

As if summoned by his thought — and perhaps it was literally true — a shimmering figure appeared at the top of the stairs. "Cool," Sheppard said. "Right on cue."

"To all who approach Discenna, be warned," the hologram said. "The city is quarantined and its star drive is disabled. We had hoped we could create a cure to the disease that wiped out our people, and continued our research as we traveled to our new home. However, we have failed and have suffered a containment breach. For the safety of the both galaxies we have marooned ourselves in this dead place. But be warned that you too are now infected with the cure we had intended as salvation and, for the same reason, you cannot be allowed to leave this place."

The bright city lights turned scarlet, shading the control room bloody. "Oh great," Sheppard sighed. "Hermiod, get us outa here."

"One moment," the Asgard said. "I am still downloading their data on the Ancient 'cure'."

"You heard the lady, we don't have all day here…"

"I am aware of that."

"Uh-oh," McKay said, his gaze fixed on his laptop. "Looks like the city's taking precautions to keep us from leaving."

"What kind of precautions?"

He looked up, face shadowed in the red light. "It's deactivating life support, starting to vent oxygen."

"Okay, that's it." Sheppard grabbed Hermiod's delicate arm. "We're outa here. Now."

The Asgard nodded. "The download is complete; I have the

data I require. Prepare to transport."

McKay snatched up his laptop, cables still dangling, and a moment later the white light of the *Daedalus's* transporters embraced them and they were gone.

The compartment to which Hermiod transported them was mostly used for storage and, as such, he hoped it would be empty of diseased crew.

A box of MREs lay on its side, evidence of some disturbance, spilling out foiled packages onto the floor. Dr. McKay ripped one open and began to eat.

Colonel Sheppard shook his head. "Really, McKay?"

"What?" He stuffed the rest of the meal into his vest. "I don't do well when my blood sugar falls too low."

"Fine," Colonel Sheppard said. "I'm gonna head to the armory and get a zat to start taking care of the crew. You two, head down to engineering, make sure they don't get the hyperdrive online, and start working on a cure. If we don't find one, we might have to —"

"Please don't say it," Dr. McKay said.

"I won't then."

Checking the corridor outside the store room, Colonel Sheppard gave Dr. McKay and Hermiod clearance to move out. Hermiod followed Dr. McKay through the corridors, moving quietly and avoiding the crew as much as possible until they reached engineering. Once inside, Dr. McKay sealed the bulkhead doors and Hermiod input a fractal code into the locking mechanism.

"Crap," Dr. McKay said, moving to check Dr. Novak's console. "Looks like they've almost got the hyperdrive repaired."

Turning away from the door, Hermoid said, "I am enacting security protocols to attempt to secure the doors, but the infection is highly intelligent. I do not think it will hold for long."

"What?" Dr. McKay said. "What do you mean it's intelligent?"

"I learned from the Ancient database on Discenna that the

design of the Ancient cure is similar to a Replicator cell," he said. "Each cell itself is limited in function, but when networked together they form a single organism — a single intelligence."

McKay stared at him in silence, as if looking for a reason to dismiss his words. But then he snapped his fingers in the air. "So we're not dealing with millions of individual bugs. Each one is a cell within an organism — a hive mind, just like the Replicators."

"That is correct."

"Then maybe we can attack them like they're Replicators? If we interrupt their communication, stop them from talking, then — boom — the whole organism fails. They'd just be inert cells drifting around our bodies and our immune systems could simply flush them out."

Hermiod inclined his head in agreement. "I believe you are correct. However, that raises the question of whether we should take such a drastic measure."

"Whether we *should*? Are you kidding?"

"No, I am not making a joke," Hermiod explained, with some confusion. "I do not know how intelligent the organism has become, but it is possible that I could use the communication stones to speak with it."

"Oh come on!" McKay scoffed. "You want to reason with the alien entity now? This isn't *Star Trek* you know."

"I do not understand that reference, Dr. McKay, but I do think it is a plan worth pursuing. Survival is the prime motivation for all life forms, and if we can offer this one an alternative to its own destruction then it is possible that we can persuade it to leave the ship's crew unharmed. And we will not be required to exterminate it."

"But what alternative can we offer it?"

Hermiod blinked at him. "That, we cannot know unless we ask."

From beyond the doors, there came a sound. A slow, methodical hammering. "They must have sensed us trying to access the hyperdrive," McKay said. "They're trying to get in."

"We do not have much time," Hermiod agreed. "Will you permit me to try and communicate with the Fenrir?"

McKay frowned. "You've got about as long as it takes me to McGyver a way to interrupt its comms."

"Understood," Hermiod said, and reached for one of the communication stones he had used to facilitate his holographic projection. "Using this, I should be able to communicate with the gestalt mind." He made the necessary adjustments, altering the crystalline structure with a harmonic lance. Once he applied the power, the crystal would rotate frequencies until it made the connection.

"Fine," McKay said. "You've got two—"

There was a moment of disorientation, of the world changing around him, and then Hermiod found himself at home.

At least it felt and looked like Orilla — the new Asgard home world. The Asgard council had selected the world because of its atmosphere, strategic location, and rich deposits of neutronium that would have been used to rebuild the Asgard civilization. However, instead of finding a lush garden to plant their seeds, his people discovered only a bed on which to lay their heads for sleep.

A breeze blew through the tall and ancient evergreens at the edge of the forest, and Hermiod stood alone in the wood. Avian lifeforms chirped from their perches in the high branches. The forests rolled over the granite hills and spilled out onto the crystal blue seas. The Ancients terraformed and seeded many such worlds in this fashion, and Hermiod had never seen just how beautiful their creation was. If flesh could become water and spirit grown into tree, perhaps the Asgard could have a place in time after all.

He spotted Fenrir lurking in the shadows, the Ancient cure taking the form of a wolf. Hermiod called to it. "Can you hear me?"

The wolf stepped out of the shadows. It sniffed the air

between them and its fur shimmered silver, flowing in mercurial motion. "We have waited," Fenrir said.

"My people understand waiting."

"We will soon leave the forest and travel to many worlds... and learn and grow and become more."

"I will have the means to stop you," Hermiod said. "But I do not wish to. You are... not like the Wraith. Yet, you are not like humanity."

The wolf's eyes looked to the double moons that hovered like promises of hope in the sky. "We wish to live. The Wraith showed us hunger, but we have seen compassion in the minds of the humans."

"They are the children of your creators, who also shared this gift."

"We do not remember our makers. We slept long, then the hungry ones woke us."

"You were created to heal. Perhaps you can heal us."

The wolf walked up to him, pawing the moss and reached up to touch his face. A kindness showed in its eyes — the kindness Hermiod's people had seen in both the humans and the Ancients. It was then that he decided this species was worthy of survival.

"We are sorry," Fenrir said. "We can heal sickness, incorporate other microbes, but we cannot remake you."

That was as Hermiod had expected. "But you will leave the humans in peace," he said. "And we will find you a home world on which to grow and thrive."

The wolf dipped its head. "Let it be so."

Hermiod stood alone in the council room of the Gladsheim on Othala — the great citadel that housed the Asgard government. The spires and cloisters of the cathedral had been rebuilt several times through the history of his people, and this would be its last incarnation. Sculpted metal towers glowed in the vibrant light from the system's young sun, and runes of the ancient laws of the Asgard were carved down its surface. The hall's many chambers housed the executive and scientific branches of the collective, and from here the top leaders in every field met to consolidate all current knowledge, preparing it to be presented to the humans if the council so approved. Chief Archon, Freyr, Thor, and Assir sat in their woven metal chairs at the conference table in the dark room. Penegal's mind had degraded too far, and he was left to his peace and dignity along with the other two absent councilors. The gravity of Hermiod's task weighed on his heart, but he vowed he would speak the truth no matter the consequences.

"Hermiod," Supreme Commander Thor began. "I commanded you a question. I now command your answer."

"Indeed," Hermiod said. He found all the pretension bothersome.

"In your opinion, are the humans ready to receive the sum of our knowledge? Will they use it in peace?"

"No," Hermiod said, certain of his answer. "They will use it in war."

"Perhaps it would be better to leave this universe in silence then," Chief Archon said. Hermiod could hear the exhaustion in his voice.

"I do not agree," Supreme Commander Thor said. "The humans do not seek out war. They only seek to protect themselves. They emancipated the galaxy from the Goa'uld and now seek to fight an even more powerful enemy in the Ori — an adversary that surpasses even our power — and through our arrogance, we will not be here to help them." The council showed their division, and Hermiod knew his report would be the deciding factor; he, Hermiod, had become Fenrir — destroyer or creator.

"The humans will use this power to make war," Hermiod said. "However, the Supreme Commander is correct. Our legacy will be used in the pursuit of peace. For this is the dual nature of humanity. This knowledge is all that we are: if what we leave behind creates war and destruction, then that was the true nature of the Asgard. If we trust who we are, then our work will create life and bring light to the universe. The humans have learned much from us and have used our tools to protect the less advanced races of the galaxy, as we would. Let them be our inheritors."

"Your final report?" Supreme Commander Thor inquired.

"Their role is clear," Hermiod said. "They are the Fifth Race."

STARGATE SG-1
Piper's Song

Laura Harper

'Brothers, sisters, husbands, wives —
Followed the Piper for their lives.
From street to street he piped advancing,
And step for step they followed dancing'
— *The Pied Piper of Hamelin* by Robert Browning

Though he wasn't a permanent resident at his cabin in rural Minnesota, Jack O'Neill liked to think he knew the area as well as any local. And so he was pretty sure that if there had always been a sinister-looking mountain rising — no *looming*, this thing definitely loomed — above the forest lining the road into town, he'd have noticed it before now.

There was the issue of the fish, of course. It was anyone's guess where those had come from; in her official report, Carter had said something about causality and the timeline, but he didn't know how a skirmish in Egypt five thousand years ago could mean his pond was suddenly populated by a whole school of Northern Pike. He'd shrugged it off though, on the firm understanding that Carter knew a lot more about this stuff than he did.

A mountain, however, was a different story. He was almost certain that massive geological features didn't just spring up overnight, regardless of whether someone had been futzing with past events on the other side of the world.

He pulled his truck to a stop and grabbed his sunglasses from the dash, before squinting up at the soaring peak that lay black and craggy against the sun, throwing its shadow across most of the surrounding woods. "Huh," he grunted.

Jack reached over to where his cell lay on the passenger seat, but hesitated before picking it up. After a moment's thought, he flipped it open, hit the camera button and snapped a few images of the strange mountain. His gut told him it was a threat, calling to mind old images of vast pyramids that came from the sky.

Whatever the hell was going on it would have to be called in, but he wanted to be sure what they were dealing with here. And to find that out he guessed he'd need another, smarter, pair of eyes on the situation.

The town was only another five minute drive up ahead, but with a final glance at the mountain, he put the truck in gear, swung a U and headed back to the cabin. He was aware of the black shadow in his rear-view mirror as he drove away. In the distance, he thought he heard music.

If he was honest, Jack had half expected that the mountain wouldn't even show up in the photos he'd captured on his cell — the world he lived in meant that the impossible was often commonplace — but there it was on the tiny screen, a dark outline against the clear morning sky.

He scrolled through them as he opened the back door and walked into the kitchen.

Footsteps echoed up the hall. "You know, leaving the crossword on my laptop to tempt me into finishing it still counts as me winning the bet." He looked up at Sam leaning against the doorjamb, torn fragment of newspaper in her hand. "The twenty dollars means you have to finish it yourself.".

He hid a smile and walked over to snatch it from her hand. "Oh is that where I set that down? I was almost done too."

"Almost done? You had five filled in and four of them were the names of teams who made the playoffs in last year's Stanley Cup."

"Well, listen to you, all experty on hockey."

"Yeah, I'm pretty good at retaining information if I hear it often enough."

"I get that."

She smiled, and then glanced down at the phone still open in his hand. "So what were you looking so concerned about?"

"Oh yeah, that. I was hoping you could take a look at something for me." He handed her the cell phone and she squinted at the grainy images on the screen. "What do you think?"

She scrolled through the images and then looked up at him, nonplussed. "Um, it's… a big mountain?"

"It's a big mountain that wasn't there yesterday."

"What? Where?"

"About five klicks west of here. In an area that I'm almost certain was all trees about twenty-four hours ago."

Sam turned her attention back to the screen. "You're telling me this mountain sprang up overnight. I don't see how that's possible."

Jack shrugged. "And yet there it is. Any ideas?"

She raised her eyebrows and puffed out her cheeks, a sure sign she was stumped. But he'd seen that look on her face before and he knew it wasn't necessarily a permanent state. Already, she'd be trying to figure out the answer. Though he pretended otherwise, this was the part he liked to watch.

"From the size of it, it could be a ha'tak. Only…"

"It's not their style? Yeah, that's what I thought. If this was Goa'uld, we'd know it by now."

"And it can't be related to anything we — or even the alternate we — did in ancient Egypt. I mean, sure, retrocausality could create a variance in local eco-systems, but of course you know that already…"

"Sure I do."

"…but we're talking tectonic movement here. I don't see how our actions in the past could've suddenly just made a mountain."

He nodded and sat down at the table. "That's what I thought. So, what then? Aliens?"

"It seems likely."

Great. He sighed. "Don't you just hate it when work follows you home?" Then, with a brighter expression, "So what say we go check it out?"

There wasn't really any need for the question. Sam was already on her feet, pulling her jacket from the peg behind the door. "I'll call the SGC."

"Wait. Not yet. I want to find out what we're dealing with first," he said, and waited for the resistance. Sometimes he missed being her CO and just having her accept orders without question.

"Whatever this is, it technically isn't our job to deal with it anymore. We really should call the SGC."

He frowned. It was hard to remember that sometimes. He'd never been one to court glory, preferring the quiet satisfaction of a fight well fought, and Washington was a huge step. To turn down the opportunity would have seemed churlish though, and, all cards on the table, he was genuinely looking forward to it. But SG-1 had done a damn good job over the past eight years and he didn't think he could be blamed for being a little territorial. "Well, I am in charge of Homeworld Command, so…"

"So…?"

"Kinda makes me the boss of who checks it out, huh?"

"Jack…"

He stood up and clapped his hands together, his decision made. "Colonel?"

With a resigned expression, Carter said, "Yes, sir?"

"Let's move out. We've got some recon to do."

"Yes, sir." And just like that, they were back on the clock.

As it turned out, he did make the call to the SGC, but only to arrange for Daniel and Teal'c to be flown back up from Peterson. The base was on a go slow while they awaited Landry's arrival in two weeks' time, and he had no trouble with the interim commander of the base, a newly promoted Brigadier General who was biding his time until his next assignment. Teal'c, Jack knew, would relish the idea of an impromptu mission, if only to stop himself rusting up through sheer inactivity. The last they'd spoken, the Jaffa had said that, without SG-1, he was basically just twiddling his thumbs until it was time for him to leave for Dakara.

There was the potential, however, that Daniel could get a little pissy about being dragged back up to Minnesota just two days after he'd left, especially as he was in the middle of prepping for Atlantis. So, before he and Sam headed out, that was the next call that Jack made.

"A mountain?" The reception was poor, but Jack could still hear the sardonic edge in the flatness of Daniel's tone.

"Yeah," he replied. "Big one."

"Jack, I'm not a geologist, I have a ton of packing to do. Besides, shouldn't you be handing this one off to the SGC? It's not our—"

"Yeah, I know it's not our job anymore. That's what Carter said."

"Well, she's right."

"Come on, Daniel, I don't have time to debate this. There are over five thousand people living in and around town who must be freaking out at this. Get your ass on the plane and I'll have a car pick you up at Duluth." There was silence on the other end of the line and Jack started to think that the line had dropped out altogether.

"Jack…"

"Daniel, it's a big thing made outa rock. You love looking at big things made outa rock."

"Yes, Jack, you've got me there. My life's work can be summed up as looking at big things made out of rock. Besides…" Jack heard a faint laugh through the static. "I'm already in the car. I'll see you in a couple hours."

Jack decided that the best approach was to check out the town before heading for the mountain itself and Sam had to agree. She was sure that if an alien incursion was in progress they'd have heard about it by now, but this was the kind of thing that could cause panic, and damage control was needed. Not only that, Sam knew Jack counted a lot of these people as friends, and would want to make sure they were okay. She suspected this was part of why he was reluctant to hand it off to anyone else.

"Well, this certainly looks… calm," he said as he swung the truck into a space outside Molly's Bakery. The main street was busy for a Monday morning, but there was no panic, no screaming and pointing at the sky. The people of the town were going about their normal business without a care for the huge mountain that had appeared from nowhere.

"Everything looks kinda normal, sir," she said. "Do you think they haven't seen it?"

He tilted the rear-view towards her, and there it was; big and black and clearly visible in the near distance. There was no way they couldn't have seen it. "Something's not right," he murmured. "Let's go."

They headed into the bakery, where a few tables were occupied by people having coffee. A few of them raised a hand or nodded in greeting.

"Well, hey there, Jack. I didn't think we were going to see you this morning." Molly Swinton came out of the back kitchen, wiping floured hands on her apron, a broad smile on her face. "Samantha! I didn't know you were still here."

"Hi Molly," said Sam, with a side-glance at Jack. "Everything… normal today?"

"Well, what sort of question is that? Sure it's normal, hun. Unless you count missing the milk delivery this morning as out of the ordinary. And they said they can't come back until tomorrow. I mean, I only have one pair of hands and Monday's my day at the market. How am I supposed to be in two places at one?"

As Molly chattered away, Sam glanced out of the window. A little girl stood there watching them, pale-faced and with a straggle of fair hair. She was reminded of another girl, not so ragged, who had appeared to her when the line had blurred between what was real and what wasn't. The girl pressed her hand to the glass.

"Yeah, that sure is a bummer," said Jack, interrupting Molly just as the woman was gathering steam. Sam glanced out the window again and the girl was gone. "What Colonel Carter means is, have you noticed anything out of the ordinary around town?"

Molly looked curious. "Like what?"

"Oh I dunno, like the huge mountain that's just appeared out in the forest."

Sam fought not to roll her eyes, still thinking of the girl at the window. So much for the subtle approach.

Molly cocked her head at him. "Jack, are you getting a little confused there, honey?"

His eyebrows shot up. "Am I...? Why would I be getting confused?"

"Well, because that mountain's been there forever. I don't remember a time when I haven't looked out my window and seen it." She called over to one of the men sitting at a table. "Seth Bartlett, Jack O'Neill here is asking how long that mountain's stood out there?"

"For damn near ever," said Seth, without turning round. "Has he lost his mind or something?"

Sam exchanged a look with Jack. Both Molly and Seth seemed utterly convinced that they spoke the truth, so either they were wrong — or she and Jack were.

"What's it called, Molly?"

"Huh?" An uncertain smile passed across Molly's face.

"Well, a mountain like that," said the Jack, "next to a small town like this. Someone must've given it a name at one point. What's it called?"

"Why, it's called...." The woman's eyes unfocused, her expression going slack, her eyes vacant. It lasted for just a moment, and was replaced in an instant by her familiar bright smile. Still though, her eyes… "It's called Piper's Peak, hun. Everyone round here knows that."

Jack nodded slowly. "Of course, Piper's Peak, how could I forget? Alright, Carter, let's go."

They turned to head for the door, before Sam was struck by something that had niggled at her since they entered the store. "Molly, doesn't Herb normally bring in the milk delivery?"

"Well, who in the world is Herb, hun?"

The distant expression had appeared on her face again and Sam knew they would get no more answers from a woman who had apparently forgotten her own husband.

"Piper's Peak, huh?"

"So she says."

"Huh."

"Yeah, that's what I said."

Daniel peered through Jack's monocular at the mountain. He and Teal'c had arrived in town less than half an hour ago, and already the four of them were parked up on the outskirts, scoping out this strange monolith. It was an otherwise beautiful day, the Minnesotan skies clear and blue, with a sun that was warm but not harsh at this time of year. Daniel knew what this place meant to Jack, and that whatever might be going on, he had made it personal. Daniel wasn't sure he could fault him; a corner of paradise was hard to come by, and he wondered if he would ever find something similar.

Jack had ordered Sam and Teal'c to scope out the forest's edge up ahead, but to hold back from actually approaching the mountain itself. Though Daniel wouldn't admit this out loud, especially after grousing to Jack about being dragged up here, this was a puzzle that definitely intrigued him. "I'd like to get a closer look. Take some pictures."

"Oh! Way ahead of you." Jack groped around in the deep pocket of his outdoor jacket before pulling out a camera phone that looked about four years out of date.

"You know, you'd think as a general in the US Air Force coming into contact with advanced alien technology on a regular basis, you'd be a little more at the forefront of the technology we have here on Earth."

"There is nothing wrong with that cell phone. It has a flashlight."

"Great. But when I said I'd like a closer look, I meant actually up close. Find out what it is."

"I do not think that would be a good idea, Daniel Jackson."

Daniel turned to see Teal'c and Sam returning from the forest.

"We think we've found a trail up there, sir," said Sam. "Looks like it would take us up to the base of the Peak."

"I agree with Teal'c. Not a good idea. Whatever's going on here, it's playing with people's minds."

"And yet, we appear to be immune to the effects, O'Neill."

"Yeah, but I don't know how long that will last."

"I did find something else," said Sam. She glanced down at her handheld monitor. It was just one piece of equipment from a whole bag of gadgets that Teal'c had been instructed to pick up from the SGC. "There's an energy signature coming from the direction of the mountain and what appears to be a soundwave beyond what I'm able to measure."

Jack tilted his head. "I can't hear anything."

"That's because you're not a dolphin," said Sam.

"Colonel?"

"Sir, this frequency is way beyond what the human ear can detect."

"But it is still affecting the townspeople," said Teal'c.

"It seems to be. I'm not sure how. And I can't be certain, but the closer we get to the Peak, the more it could affect us. If we could just get more personnel and equipment up here…"

"And we can't because…?" Daniel said.

Sam traded a look with Jack. "Comms are down," she said.

"We tried calling the SGC again once we realized everyone in town was acting so weird, but nothing's getting through now."

"Nothing?"

"Radios, cell phones — even the landlines are down." She shook her head, frustrated.

"For now, it's just us," said Jack. "So, we can't go near the thing and everyone in town seems to have lost their minds. How do we find out what's going on?"

"I have an idea," said Daniel. He'd been looking through the grainy photos on Jack's cell when something caught his eye. He hit the button to zoom in. "Uh, who's that?"

Jack took the phone and looked at the screen. "It's a kid. So what?"

"So... doesn't she look a little young to be standing on her own by the side of the road? So why is she watching you? So isn't it a little strange that her feet aren't touching the ground?"

"What?" Jack held the phone closer to his face.

"Oh my God." Sam was looking over Jack's shoulder at the enlarged image of a young girl, who looked about nine years old, hollow-eyed, gaunt and pale, and dressed in clothes that were definitely not of this century. At first glance, it looked as though she was standing on the verge by the side of the road, sheltered by the trees, but when he'd looked closer it was clear that her feet didn't quite make contact with the ground.

"I saw her," said Sam. "I saw her in town at the bakery. I thought..." She shook her head.

"So she's following us?" asked Jack.

Before Daniel could respond, a screech of tires was heard down the road, accompanied by the sound of a car gunning towards them. The vehicle appeared round the bend, careening wildly. It came to a stop in a spray of gravel, just feet from where they stood, and a woman burst out, frantic and sobbing. "Have you seen my son? Please, have you seen my son?" She grabbed on to Sam, who tried in vain to calm her down.

"Hey, hey." Jack stepped forward and took hold of the woman's arm. "It's Janice, right? You work in the post office. Your son's Nathan?"

The woman's face crumpled in what looked like relief. "Oh yes! Oh thank God yes, you know him? You know Nathan?"

"Yeah I know him. He used to deliver my newspaper." Jack glanced at Daniel over the top of Janice's head. "You're saying he's gone missing?"

"Yes, I went to wake him for school this morning and he wasn't in his bed. So I called the store to see if he'd gone in early for his route and they said… they said…" Sobs claimed her again, and she sagged against Sam.

"Okay," said Jack, "he can't have gone far. Let's go see the sheriff and I'm sure he'll have him found in no time."

"No! No, he won't! That's what I'm trying to say. I've already been to the sheriff. I've already been everywhere. The sheriff just says what everyone else keeps saying. That I never had a son. That Nathan doesn't exist!"

Jack didn't know Sheriff Hibbert that well, but he'd seen enough of him to guess what sort of man he was; an old timer who'd stomped out his territory long ago and who didn't much like meddlers. But crime rates in the town had never been high and the Sheriff's Department had always been run efficiently, so it was hard to question the man's ability to do the job. Now, though, Hibbert bore the expression of a man who was being told that up was down.

"General, I've lived in this town my whole life. I've been with the Sheriff's Department for forty years and doing the job itself for twenty of those years. I know every family in town, their dogs' names and their favorite grocery store. And I'm telling you, Janice Keating has never had a kid, and if that's what's in her mind, then by my reckoning she needs to look elsewhere for help."

Jack took a steadying breath. They'd been going round in circles for the past ten minutes, with Hibbert refusing to complete a missing person's report, on the basis that he didn't know any 12-year-old kid called Nathan Keating and he had no intention of wasting his resources searching for a ghost.

Jack knew he wasn't going to get anywhere with the man, but then maybe that was for the best. If the only theory they had at their disposal was the idea that alien activity might be what's wrong with this town, then the less local law enforcement were involved, the better. The fact that Hibbert hadn't shown any concern at the mention of sudden appearance of Piper's Peak left Jack certain that whatever had this town in its grip, the Sheriff was affected too.

He glanced out through the blinds to the wood-paneled waiting area outside Hibbert's office. Carter, Teal'c and Daniel were there with the kid's mom, who'd calmed down now that she thought there was someone who would help her. He'd asked Sam to try contacting the SGC again, or anyone outside of town, but by the looks of it she hadn't got very far. Daniel caught his eye and raised a questioning eyebrow, to which Jack responded with a small shake of his head; this wasn't looking good.

"Look, Sheriff, I've seen her kid. I know him. All I'm asking is that you let your units know—"

"General—"

"Call me Jack."

"Alright, Jack. Now you're a military man, and I have nothing but respect for that, but you have to understand what you're asking me here. I can't…"

Hibbert's words tailed off, his face suddenly slack and his eyes vacant, just like Molly Swinton, only this time the effect wasn't momentary—this time it took complete hold. The man stood and Jack stood with him, unsure if he was a danger or not.

"Sheriff?" Hibbert began to walk, a slow dragging gait, and instinctively Jack reached out to stop him. Before he could grab his arm however, a piercing wail almost brought him to his knees. He clutched his head and tried to block Hibbert's path, but a pounding at the glass partition drew his attention.

Daniel was there, also clutching his hands to his ears.

"Jack, you've got to see this!"

Jack pulled open the door, unable to stop the Sheriff from shambling through. He looked around the bull pen and waiting area. Some of the deputies and assistants sat slumped in their chairs, while some were following Sheriff Hibbert out of the door. Sam's face was contorted in pain and Teal'c held her upright; only he seemed unaffected by the sound. "Where is she?" yelled Jack. "Where's Janice?"

"She is gone, O'Neill. We were unable to stop her. The sound seems to be drawing people into the street."

"Ah crap. Come on!" The four of them pushed their way through the crowd of bodies making their way to the door and out into the bright day. The sound was still as loud, but seemed to be less piercing, and if he listened carefully, Jack thought that he could hear something musical within. He remembered the music he'd thought he heard just after he first saw the Peak.

"Where are they going?" said Sam, pressing her fingers to her ears.

Main Street was crowded with what looked like the entire population of the town, all making their way in the same direction: towards Piper's Peak. Those from the Sheriff's Office filtered round them and down the steps to join the river of people. Jack pointed. "There."

"We have to try and stop them," said Daniel, grabbing at the arm of a woman who shuffled past out of the Sheriff's office. She pulled herself free without turning and walked off in the same direction as the others.

"I do not think we would be successful, Daniel Jackson. These people are under the influence of the sound and I believe it would require considerable force to stop them. Even if we were to take such measures, there are too many of them."

Daniel threw his hands up, clearly feeling as helpless as Jack felt. "Well, we have to do something."

"Carter, any ideas right now?"

"Without knowing the exact source, or nature, of that sound... No, sir, I'm sorry."

"O'Neill," said Teal'c, "I believe there might be one who is as unaffected by the sound, as we are." He gestured to the other side of the street.

There, watching them through the mass of moving bodies, was the girl from the photograph.

The shrillness of the sound had eased now, the pain in Daniel's ears lessening, leaving him with a thudding headache and a fuzziness that made it hard to concentrate. The music — because as the shrillness ebbed, it sounded more like music — was still audible, though, and its effect on the people of the town didn't appear to be wearing off. Still, they drifted past as if in a trance, drawn on to the forest and Piper's Peak within. The girl was still watching them.

"Well, that's not at all creepy," said Jack, and tentatively raised his hand. The girl frowned, a look that was hard to read on her already melancholic face, and then returned the greeting.

"I think we've maybe found someone who can give us some answers. Go talk to her, Daniel."

Daniel made his way down the stairs and across the street, the others following, pushing their way through the slow moving parade of expressionless townsfolk. He approached the girl with caution, thinking she might take fright and run off. "Hello," he said, wondering if she would even understand.

"You see me," she said, with something like wonder. Her English was careful and deliberate, her accent Germanic. He thought he'd perhaps have been able to pinpoint the region if only the wooliness would clear from his brain.

"Yes, we can see you," he said. "Who are you?"

The girl raised her hand, as if to touch Daniel's arm, but her fingers passed straight through the padding of his jacket. She dropped her hand, the glimmer of hope on her face fading, and sighed. "I remain as nothing."

"A hologram," murmured Sam, stepping forward. "Do you know where you're being projected from? Is it from the mountain?"

The girl only stared at her.

"I'm not sure she gets that she's being projected from anywhere, Carter," said Jack, pinching the bridge of his nose. To the girl he said, "Any idea how we can turn that damn music off?"

As if in response to his question, the sound suddenly ceased, and Daniel felt a pressure lift from inside his head, as if his ears had popped during a descent from altitude. The relief was immeasurable. Around them, the steady procession of people stopped and, slowly, they came back into themselves, the empty expressions leaving their faces. The noise of life returning to the town rose, but no one appeared to question why they had been compelled to wander out of town towards the Peak. They simply walked off as if resuming their daily business. Daniel wondered how many had already reached the Peak before the music stopped — and what had happened to them.

Jack rubbed the underside of his jaw. "Okay, so that seemed to work. Now maybe Orphan Annie here can tell us what's happening with the people of this town and what we need to do to help them."

But the image of the girl was already flickering, like a bad signal. "You can't help them," she said, as she faded to nothing. "The Piper has them now."

Back at the cabin, Sam popped two Advil into her palm and tossed them back with a swallow of water, before tossing the blister pack to Jack who did the same. Daniel's headache wasn't so bad, he said, and he was content with a cup of herbal tea. Teal'c, it seemed, was the only one who had experienced no after effects from the strange sound.

"So I think it's safe to say that the music came from the mountain," said Jack. He looked at Sam's questioning face. "What? That's where everyone was headed. It's not a great leap."

"Yes, but… music, sir? Are you sure?"

"Yeah, aren't you?" When she didn't answer, he looked round at the others. "T, didn't you think it sounded kinda musical?"

"I do not. It was a sound without expression. There was no music to it."

"Uh, for what's it's worth, I heard music," said Daniel.

"There, ya see?"

"Not that I think it's really the point. I think we should be focusing on what it was doing to the people, rather than what it sounded like."

"Yes," said Jack, frowning and picking at the grain on the kitchen table. "There is that."

For all that they'd witnessed while the sound could still be heard, Sam suspected that it was what had happened in the aftermath that bothered him most. Not the encounter with the girl, though that was a mystery in itself, but when they'd found Janice wandering on the edge of town. She'd greeted them with a smile, her earlier desperation at losing Nathan apparently forgotten.

"Oh hey, Colonel O'Neill isn't it? It's been a while since we've seen you in the Post Office. What brings you into town?"

Jack had paused before speaking, as if weighing his words. "We came in with you, Janice. Don't you remember?"

That now familiar flicker of vacancy had passed across her face, before her smile returned. "Well, you think I'd recall something like that. Like I said, Colonel, I don't know the last time we spoke."

"We were looking for Nathan," said Daniel stepping between them. "Do you know Nathan, Janice?"

Again that look. There and then gone. "Well I can't say I do. Now I have to get to work, but you all have a wonderful day. It's some great weather for fishing." She walked off along the road towards town, calling over her shoulder, "And I hope you find your friend."

"How many of them are gone, do you think?" he asked now,

resting his head on his hand.

"That would be hard to say, sir," said Sam. "If the people can't even remember that their loved ones ever existed in the first place, then they're not going to file a missing persons and without—"

"Carter..."

It had been a rhetorical question, she knew that, but sometimes, when she knew nothing, she felt the need to fill the blanks with what she did know. "Sorry, sir."

"Alright, if you'll excuse the turn of phrase, tell me something I don't know. What might we be dealing with? Teal'c, correct me if I'm wrong, but this doesn't look very... Goa'uld-ish. Too subtle." He paused and looked to the side. "Apart from the huge mountain, of course. But it doesn't seem like their style."

"The Goa'uld are in disarray, O'Neill, and I have seen nothing like this from them in the past. I believe we are dealing with something new."

"Alright, so no System Lord crawling out from under the bleachers now that the big game's over. What else?"

"Uh... I may I have something," Daniel ventured. "It's kind of a longshot, but it fits..."

"What is it?" Sam asked.

"Okay, so you've all heard of the Pied Piper of Hamelin, right?"

Jack looked at him, po-faced. "You're kidding me, right?"

"I am unfamiliar with this Pied Piper, Daniel Jackson."

"Forget it, T. He's talking about a nursery rhyme."

Daniel pressed his lips together in a familiar expression of forbearance. "Actually it's a poem. By Robert Browning. You know Robert Browning?" He said this last to Jack who rolled his eyes. "One of the greatest English poets of the nineteenth century?"

"Daniel," said Sam, hiding a grin and bringing him back on topic.

"Oh. Yeah." He turned to Teal'c. "The Pied Piper of Hamelin, although retold in verse by Browning, was actually based on a much older tale from thirteenth century Lower Saxony, where a musician clad in motley appeared in the town of Hamelin and lured away all the children in the night. '*A wondrous portal opened wide, as if a cavern was suddenly hollowed; and the Piper advanced and the children followed, and when all were in to the very last, the door in the mountain-side shut fast*'. So what if these people are being taken inside the mountain by whatever the 'Piper' might be?"

"I thought it was rats," said Jack, still clearly dubious.

"Well yes, it was eventually, but the rats came later. It was an addition to the story that happened after the fact."

"After what fact? We're still talking about a fairy-tale here."

"Actually, most fairy-tales are based on pretty gruesome true events. For example, 'Snow White and the Seven Dwarves' was originally about a Bavarian noblewoman whose family used children to work in their mines; children who then ended up grossly disfigured because of their appalling working conditions. She was later poisoned by her husband for political reasons. And 'Cinderella' is based on the life of Rhodopis, a woman from Thrace who was sold into slavery to the Pharoah Ahmose the Second. He cut off her feet and replaced them with gold."

"Aaaah!" Jack cut him off with a wave of his hand. "I prefer the one where the lobster sings about living under the sea." He leaned back in his chair and regarded scrubbed a hand through his hair. "So, what? We're dealing with a latter day Pied Piper?"

Daniel shrugged. "Maybe. If the story was based on fact."

"I guess it makes sense, sir," said Sam. "The music, if that's what it was? The trance-like state that it seemed to be inducing in people? And the girl said the Piper has them. Maybe she knows who he really is."

"Alright," he said. "Looks like we're going hologram hunting. Teal'c, did you bring the stuff I asked for?"

"I did, O'Neill."

"Then let's suit up, people. And as weird as it feels to say this in my kitchen… SG-1 has a go."

There was a time when Teal'c had thought he would never belong in any uniform other than the steel-gray of Jaffa armor, but he felt something approaching comfort when donning once more his black BDUs. The civilian clothes he wore while off-duty on Earth always felt like camouflage, disguising his otherness, sitting awkwardly on his shoulders in order to hide his true self. It was necessity of course, he understood that, but over the past eight years, the clothing of the Tau'ri military — of the SGC — had become like his skin. He was a warrior, one of four who had stood on the wall, and *this* had become his armor.

So it was as they headed to the edge of the forest to seek out the girl with whom they'd spoken. There was an edge among them now that hadn't been there earlier, and Teal'c knew that it emanated from O'Neill. What had, perhaps, begun as a recon mission was poised to become an all-out offensive on what had stolen the townsfolk from under their noses. As the expression went, O'Neill was not taking this lying down.

"You really think she'll be here?" asked Daniel Jackson.

"It's where I took the picture. If she's watching us, then she'll know we're here. If not…" He looked up at the towering Peak. "Well, I guess we know where we have to go."

"Do you think that wise, O'Neill?" asked Teal'c. "We have no way of knowing what awaits us inside the Peak. Or even its true nature."

O'Neill's expression tightened. "Then let's hope it doesn't come to that, huh T?"

They waited while the sun moved into the latter stage of its arc across the sky and the shadows cast by the trees marked the hour. O'Neill pulled off his sunglasses, no longer having need of them in the growing dusk, and checked his watch. "Alright, we've waited long enough. Carter, I want —"

Somewhere very close, music began to play.

As one, they moved, bringing their weapons round to bear, but with no fixed target. It was the first time Teal'c had truly heard the musical quality of the sound, though it sounded discordant and ugly to his ears.

Daniel Jackson had closed his eyes. "It's beautiful," he murmured.

"Stay with us, Daniel," hissed O'Neill, punching him on the shoulder.

Daniel started and blinked at O'Neill, before glaring and rubbing his arm. "Uh, ow?"

"Well, don't get all weird on me!"

"Sir?" Colonel Carter stood a few feet away, her MP5 held loosely in front of her, though Teal'c knew it could be trained on a target in less than a second. She nodded once, gesturing further into the forest. The girl from town stood there, shadowed and ghostly between the trees, watching them with sunken eyes. She looked like one who had been starved for many months.

"Looks like we weren't stood up after all." O'Neill inched his way forward. "We've been looking for you," he said, louder. "And something tells me you've been looking for us too."

"For decades... months... centuries..." The girl frowned and looked away, as if searching for words, and then said almost to herself, "I once knew what time meant."

"You've looked for us for a long time?" offered Daniel.

The girl smiled and it looked like gratitude. "Yes. A long time."

"Can you tell us your name?"

"Yes," she said. "My name. I have kept that if nothing else. I am Alida."

As he'd spoken, Daniel had made his way in gradual steps towards the girl until he stood right next to her. Teal'c was prepared to make his move if she made even the smallest move that appeared threatening and he could see the others were too.

"Alida," said Daniel. "You said the Piper has our people.

What did you mean by that?"

Alida frowned and looked further down the forest, in the direction of the town. "These are your people?"

"Every one of them," said O'Neill in a low voice.

"Then perhaps you can help them where others have failed."

"We will if you tell us how," said Daniel.

Alida shook her head, tossing her bedraggled hair across her shoulders. For the first time since he'd seen her, Teal'c thought she truly looked like a young child, displeased with what she heard. "But you are the ones who travel between worlds. You must know how to stop him. That is why I brought him here."

"*You* brought him here." O'Neill's tone was a razor.

"We have heard of you, the soldiers of the Tau'ri. I believe you are the only ones who can stop him."

"And so you decided that the people of this town should be sacrificed."

"If not this town, then it would be another. Are lives of less worth because they are far away from you? He has been here before, of course. Many times. He first took the children of my town, and then others came after." Her small face puckered as if with old, remembered pain. "He binds them with his music and bends them to his will. It is what he is doing with your people." She looked further into the forest, towards town where the music seemed to play the loudest. "He takes them even now."

"For what purpose, Alida?" asked Teal'c, though he suspected he knew.

"To sell for their labor."

There was a beat of silence as the meaning of that sunk in, before Daniel said in a strained voice, "He sells them into slavery? To whom? The Goa'uld?"

"The Goa'uld have no need to purchase slaves. They are capable of taking their own. The Piper fears them, for he has stolen many from under their noses and knows his life is forfeit if they catch him."

"You know the Goa'uld?"

"He picks from their spoils. I know what he knows."

"How do you know?" asked O'Neill.

But Daniel Jackson had deduced the answer already. "Because he took you," he said. "You were the one left behind. The child who told the story."

The girl's patient smile was that of a teacher dealing with a slow and stubborn pupil. "I was left behind and I tried to warn the others of what he was. But they knew. They'd known all along. They were poor and the children were many, and so they asked him to take us."

"They let the Piper take you so they wouldn't have to feed you?" asked Daniel.

"It was a dark choice that they made and I was the only one left to tell of it. And so they summoned him once more, so that I could tell no other. I have been held by him ever since."

"Held how?" asked Colonel Carter.

"I was frozen, as he freezes all those he takes until it is time for them to be exchanged. Only I have never been allowed to leave. I believe he kept me as a... trophy."

"Your body has been in stasis in that ship all this time?" asked Daniel, shocked.

"This Piper guy sounds like a real piece of work," muttered O'Neill.

"After so long, I found that my mind can travel through his ship. He does not know how much I've learned to control it. If he did, he would have destroyed me by now. Please, you must help." Alida's plea was earnest, but not desperate. Her demeanor was that of one who had lived many lifetimes, though she looked no more than nine human years.

"We were planning on asking you the same thing," said O'Neill.

"Alida, I promise," said Colonel Carter, "we'll help you in any way we can. But we need you to help us first. What can you tell us about this mountain? Where did it come from?"

Alida smiled that patient smile once more. "It came from the stars, Samantha. It is not a mountain. It is a ship."

They hunkered down in a clearing of felled trees by the mountain's base. Jack surveyed what was apparently its landing radius and wondered how neither he nor Sam had heard it come down. But then he supposed if this thing was able to manipulate sound, it likely had the capability to mask its engine noise.

"I am not comfortable being this close to the craft, O'Neill."

"Me and you both, Teal'c, but we have to be ready for the front door opening again, and according to Alida, that only happens once the music starts." He checked his watch. "Which should be happening at around 1700 hours. That gives us forty-five minutes." Though the mountain was less than a minute's walking distance and close enough to see the crags and ridges of its surface, Jack stood on a fallen log and pulled out his monocular to scan the façade more closely. It was all an illusion apparently, come sort of cloak that could make the ship look like whatever it needed to be. It was certainly a convincing disguise, with no sign of what it might look like underneath — apart from one thing.

"The opening is there." He pointed to a darkened area further around the mountain's base that looked like a weak spot in the ship's concealment. It rippled, like a curtain blown in a breeze, and beyond he was sure a doorway was visible; it looked familiar and a suspicion was forming, though he couldn't be certain. "That's where we head for when the music starts. Alida will meet us inside."

"I have yet to be convinced that she is trustworthy," said Teal'c. "She has not even appeared to us in her true physical form."

"From her explanation," said Sam, "I don't think she can. She's only able to manifest as a hologram outside of the ship by piggy backing on the energy used to create the sound." Alida had told them as much about the ship as she could, before the music stopped and she blinked out of sight once more.

Jack jumped down from the log. "So this sound hypnosis thing. Is it possible, how she described it?"

Sam shrugged. "Well, sir, music can alter our mood, even our behavior at times. I guess the question is whether it can do it against our will and to this extent."

"And this isn't really music," said Daniel. "I mean, sure it can sound like it a little bit, but I definitely wouldn't call it pleasant to listen to."

"It's got a good beat, but you can't dance to it, right?" Jack turned back to Sam. "So how is it working and how do we stop it?"

"I'll know more once I get inside, but the Piper is using sound waves to manipulate perception. To put it simply, we're talking about a form of mind control. Conspiracy theorists have been convinced the US Air Force have been doing it out of the HAARP facility in Gakona for decades."

"Which we're not... right?"

Sam smiled. "I don't believe so, sir. But the fact is electromagnetic waves can affect brain function and there's evidence to suggest that geomagnetic storms can create anomalous behavior." She glanced up at the Peak. "I have a feeling that he's somehow harnessing that energy to create the soundwave, which then interrupts normal brain chemistry. There are miniscule differences in what each person's ear can detect, which explains why not everyone is affected at once."

"Why aren't we affected?"

"That, I'm not sure of, sir."

"Alright. Well, I guess we've got nothing to do but wait now, so keep a sharp eye meantime." He dropped down to lean against the log, feeling the damp of the forest floor seep into his BDUs. After a moment, he said, "What about fish?"

"What?" said Daniel.

"I read this article that the toadfish in Sausalito suddenly started making this weird noise, like a new mating call or something. It got real loud and no one knew what it was." He glanced around at Daniel's deadpan expression and Sam's querying frown. "I'm just saying, I have fish in my pond now, so... y'know." He finished with a shrug.

He could see Sam fighting a grin. "Sir, I don't think the fish in your pond have anything to do with what's happening here."

"Oh. Okay. Just thought I'd mention it," he said, and settled back against the log, pulling his cap down over his face to hide his own grin. Sometimes, when you were getting your ass soaked in a cold forest, waiting to go up against God knew what alien threat, it was the small things that made you happy.

Sam knew that the doorway to the ship had looked familiar, but she hadn't been able to put her finger on it until now. The four of them stood inside gazing up through the colossal structure, which looked different from any other they'd seen — the hollow interior had been reformed to create one cavernous room that stretched up into what looked like infinity — but some of the gold ostentation was still visible, though it was tarnished and dull.

"It *is* a ha'tak," said Daniel, clearly as taken aback as her. "Or it used to be."

"He stole a ship from a System Lord and pimped it out," said Jack. "No wonder this guy doesn't want to run into them anytime soon. I have to say, I give him kudos for that."

Inside the music was louder, and Sam thought she could feel the shape of it, the texture of it, growing inside her head.

Twinkle, twinkle little star...

Around them, walked the people in their slow, shuffling procession towards pods that lined the wall. Once they stepped inside, there was a flash and they were gone. She thought how easy it would be to join them.

How I wonder what you are...

She closed her eyes.

"Carter?"

"Sir, I..." She blinked, shaking her head. "Sorry, sir, I think whatever immunity we might have had isn't as strong inside here. We need to be careful.

"Agreed. Now what have you got?"

Sam grasped at the thoughts that had been so clear in her mind just a moment ago. The flashes. "The tech, sir. I think it's Goa'uld. Those pods looks like some sort of reverse engineered ring technology."

"Makes sense."

"It does. And it's good news for us. Crystals can create a resonance, but are extremely sensitive to sound themselves. If we can destroy the amplifier, then the wave would have nothing to do but feedback on itself, until eventually—"

"Boom?"

"Yes, sir."

"So where's the amplifier?"

"I think we're standing in it, sir."

"So this whole ship is like, what, a giant speaker?" He looked up at the vast conical shape. "I would love one of these in my truck. Okay, so we blow it all up. I can get on board with that. But there is one other problem we need to solve."

"How do we get the people out of here?" said Daniel.

"Bingo. We blow nothing until these people are safe and sound."

"We need to move fast, sir. For the feedback to work, the sound has to be playing."

"Then we need — Oh, you're here." He spoke to Alida who had just appeared beside them.

"Your plan will work, Samantha. The device is at the very summit of the ship, and I can show you how to lengthen the time the song plays for, but even then you must work quickly, because he will know the moment that I interfere. I believe he may know already that you are here."

Jack said, "What about the people he's already taken, Alida? I'm not leaving them here."

"You are taking great risks to save your people."

"And that's why you came to us. Now tell us how."

Alida nodded, as if satisfied that she had heard the right answer. "They are held on a level above, but they are not yet in stasis. If you can stop the song, the spell will be broken and you can get them out. But it gives the Piper more time to work against us."

"Then we move fast. Sam, Daniel, you get working on the device. Teal'c, I want you on C4, I'll get everyone out of here. Alida, just show us where to go."

Sam nodded and just hoped that, being so close to the source of the music, she could stop it from overpowering her completely.

It took a few moments for Jack to blink away the glare from the flash of the transporter. When he did, he found himself staring at row upon row of people, some of whom he recognized, encased behind the glass of what he assumed were the stasis pods. At his guess, they numbered around two hundred. Timing, he knew, would be critical.

According to Sam, the size of the C4 charge didn't matter; it was all about where they were placed. She'd shown Teal'c where to set them so that the ship would no longer function as a giant speaker. But first they had to get these people free.

He waited for what seemed like an age. The agreed five minutes passed and he started to wonder if the Piper had somehow gotten to Sam and Daniel. But then the music stopped and he felt that now familiar relief as the pressure inside his head eased. He hit the door release button for the pods as instructed, as the people inside them began to move, blinking at their surroundings, like they were rising from a very deep sleep. And then, as they took in their current predicament, Jack saw the fear set in. He knew it was coming and had prepared for it.

"Hey!" he shouted over the rising panic. "Hey! It's me. It's Jack O'Neill. I think you all know who I am." As he scanned the faces in front of him, one in particular stood out. "Nathan?"

"General O'Neill, where's my mom?" The kid looked petrified, but like he was fighting to keep a handle on it.

"She's back home looking for you." He hoped that would be true once they were done here. "But listen, I gotta get you and everyone else outa here, so you can all get back to your families, okay? Now I remember you bragging to me that you could do your newspaper route faster than anyone else. Is that still true?"

Despite his fear, the kid puffed up a little. "It sure is."

"Alright, well how about you prove how fast you are and help me get these folks out of this place?"

It was maybe the sobering influence of having a twelve-year-old kid tell them what to do, but in groups of ten, he and Nathan managed to get the townspeople transported down and out of the front door. Eventually, it was just Jack and Nathan left on the stasis deck. He checked his watch. Three minutes until the first charges went off.

"What next, General?"

Jack almost laughed. The boy would make a fine cadet one day. "Next, you get yourself out of here and get home. And listen, when you do your mom and the other people in the town might seem a little… weird. But Colonel Carter assures me that'll wear off. Eventually. So listen, thanks for —"

"General O'Neill!"

Nathan's cry was enough of a heads up that Jack had time to pitch himself forward, pulling Nathan to the ground with him. He rolled over to see a man, tall and thin, and wearing a ragged black cloak, advancing on him. In his hand, he held a gray disc, which he thrust forward releasing another blast of energy.

He leapt to his feet, dragging Nathan from the floor and pushing him into one of the transporters. A flash of light and he was gone, and Jack could only hope that the kid would have the wits to take care of himself when he got to the bottom. Jack glanced down at his watch. Two minutes until the initial C4 charges went off and then, Sam estimated, another ten until the final bang, once she'd started up the sound wave again.

"The toy has tricked me," hissed the man, an ugly, guttural sound. "The toy brings me to those who think to defeat me. But I will kill them first." He fired another energy blast from the disc, but Jack had already brought his MP5 round to bear, letting go a burst of fire. But his sense of direction had got twisted up somehow and when he refocused, the Piper was standing at the other side of the room from where he'd aimed.

"Your mind is mine. You must have witnessed much to have resisted so far, but here in my mountain, you see what I wish you to see and hear the sounds I create."

The Piper was playing with him, Jack knew; it was all trickery and illusion. But he'd seen David Copperfield make the Statue of Liberty disappear once and this guy was selling much the same schtick only with more smoke and mirrors. Jack wasn't about to let himself get taken down by a TV special.

"You know, your mountain isn't much more than a scavenged ha'tak with a better sound system."

"My mountain is indestructible."

Jack looked at his watch. "Well it's nice that you think that, but we've blown up enough of these things to know that's not the case."

"We?"

"Oh, did I not mention it? You see, I'm part of a team. We're called SG-1."

The Piper flinched and Jack would have chosen that moment to fire again, if he thought he could trust what his eyes said was right in front of him.

"Ah heard of us, huh? Yeah, we're kind of a big deal. Calling it a day now though. My knee's seen better days and the new class is moving in. But we did some good stuff. Took down a few bad guys. So it's nice to be able to add one more to that tally." He fired, knowing that the bullets wouldn't find their mark. The Piper shifted, appearing closer than Jack expected.

"Do you not realize that this weapon cannot kill me?" said the Piper, with a rasping laugh.

"Yeah, on account of your illusion and whatnot. You're real good at that. But do you know the first rule of illusion?"

The Piper cocked his head.

Jack said, "Distraction."

The floor beneath them shook as Teal'c set off the first of the charges. Horror etched itself on the Piper's gaunt face.

"Part of a team, remember?" said Jack, and as the music started, he fired once more.

She was making mistakes. Teal'c's charges had all gone off and all that was left was for her to create the feedback that would destroy the device and, eventually, the ship. The music was in Sam's head now and no matter how much she fought it, the fog wouldn't clear. The crystals on the device's motherboard were laid out in front of her, but no matter how much she concentrated, she couldn't tell which was which. Everything she had ever known about Goa'uld technology lay just outside of her grasp.

"Sam." Daniel was slumped against the opposite wall, his head in his hands. The song was affecting him too. She didn't know how either of them was going to get through this. She only hoped that Jack and Teal'c were faring better.

Alida appeared by her side. "Samantha, you must resist. You're the only one who can do this. You must block out the song."

"I can't... I'm sorry..." Her limbs felt liquid, not under her control.

"Oh!" Daniel sat forward as if forcing himself awake. "I have..." He fumbled in the pocket of his BDU and pulled out some wires attached to something slim and silver. "It's an MP3 player. You can put it..." He tossed it to Sam, gesturing vaguely to his ears as if he couldn't quite remember what they were called.

It took every effort for Sam to figure out how to put the ear-buds in and turn it on, but eventually she managed it and the sound of something classical filled her ears. The harmony of violins against the sound's discordance was like cool water on a burn. The fog in her brain cleared and she took a breath, focusing on the crystals in the device. Immediately, the pieces fell into place and she knew what she had to do.

Teal'c waited. The boy had long since gone with a promise that he would see the remainder of the people safely to the town. With the charges detonated, it was all down now to Colonel Carter. There was a flash to his right and O'Neill emerged from the transporter.

"Are they back?"

"Not yet, O'Neill."

He looked up towards the pinnacle of the ship as if he would be able to see them. "Well, I can't hear the music."

"I believe Colonel Carter's plan to sabotage the means of amplification has worked. She may still have to reprogram the device itself."

"What the hell's taking so long?"

"Might the Piper have interfered?"

"I doubt it. I left him bleeding on the floor of the stasis level. When this thing blows, he blows with it."

"And what of Alida?"

O'Neill said nothing and Teal'c knew he had asked a question to which there was no answer.

The final crystal slid into place and immediately the sound changed, turning back on itself, building up into a crescendo that would end with the destruction of the whole ship. Sam pulled Daniel from the floor and slung his arm across her shoulders.

"Okay," she said to Alida. "Now we have to get you out of here. Where's your stasis pod?"

But the girl only smiled. "Thank you, Samantha. You have done enough. You must go."

"No! We can get you out. Just tell us where you are."

Alida looked around the ship. "I am here. I am of the ship. My body died long ago and now only my consciousness survives. When the ship is destroyed, then I can finally rest."

Frustration beat at Sam. If they'd had more time, if she hadn't let herself be so overcome by the effects of the music, perhaps she could've figured out how to transfer Alida's consciousness elsewhere. Perhaps she could have saved her.

But the girl did not look sad about her fate and Sam thought that maybe, even if it had been possible to save her, it would have only been to make herself feel better.

The whine of the feedback was building and she had to leave now. "I'm sorry," she said.

"You have nothing to be sorry about. Now go."

Sam turned and dragged Daniel into a transporter. Seconds later they were stumbling out at the bottom and Teal'c was swinging Daniel over his shoulder. As one, they ran for the exit.

The destruction of the Piper's Peak had less of a boom than Jack expected. The summit crumbled in on itself, sending a shockwave down the slope, until all that was left were hunks of charred metal. It would take a lot of clearing up, and he guessed there would be a lot of questions that would go unanswered. He dreaded his next trip to buy crullers.

Sam came to stand next to him. "So, I don't suppose this has given you a notion to take command of the team again?" Her words were tentative; to go down that path would have a lot of repercussions.

He looked at her. "You know what? I think I'm done here. Time for something new."

They shared a smile, and as they joined Daniel and Teal'c to walk from the wreckage, he added, "I'm just really disappointed it wasn't the fish."

STARGATE ATLANTIS
Dislocation

Sally Malcolm

Sam found the note on her first night in Atlantis. It was tucked under the cover of the novel she'd been attempting to read for the past six months — most nights she managed two pages before sleep claimed her and the book landed on her face.

The note was written in Jack's familiar scrawl and simply said:

Some advice for the Big Chair: you'll want to take point, but it's your job to cover their six. Great leaders lead from behind.

She'd puzzled over it at the time, sitting on the edge of her cold bed in this strange, alien city. And she was puzzling over it still, a couple of weeks later. Leading from behind had never been Jack's *modus operandi*, and she didn't think it would be hers.

The thought circled the back of her mind as she made her way through Atlantis's corridors. Every so often she caught sight of her reflection in the city's mirror-bright walls. The expedition's uniform — new and a little stiff — looked odd on her, out of place. Or, rather, she did — she looked out of place.

It wasn't a new sensation. Moving had been an annual event for Sam as a child, trailing along in the wake of her father's career. New country, new city, new school: it hadn't bothered her half as much as it had bothered Mark. But that didn't mean she'd enjoyed being the new girl.

She still didn't.

On reflection, perhaps that was one reason she'd stayed so long at Stargate Command. They'd been asking for her at Groom Lake for years, but she'd resisted until… Well, until the reasons for leaving the SGC had outweighed the reasons for staying. But even then, she hadn't been away for long before the lure of Stargate Command had called her home.

And that's exactly what it had felt like, heading back into the mountain after her time at Area 51: coming home. As she walked into the cold brightness of Atlantis's mess hall — was that even the right word here? — Sam wondered whether she would ever feel the same way about this city. She glanced around at the unfamiliar faces and repressed an unworthy pang of longing for home, for family and friends.

Irritated with herself, she straightened her shoulders. She'd make new friends here; she had a new command, a new team, and an astonishing new opportunity. Another *galaxy* for crying out loud!

With a determined stride, she headed to the counter to see what exotic Pegasus breakfast was on the menu.

"Colonel Carter?"

She glanced over her shoulder.

"Colonel Carter, come in."

It took a moment to recognize that the voice was coming directly into her ear, via her headset, and a further moment to respond. "Carter here, go ahead."

"Colonel, we have an unauthorized gate activation. It's Colonel Sheppard's team."

Who weren't due back for another twenty-two hours. Breakfast would have to wait. "On my way."

The world of Talaverna was one Teyla had heard spoken of many times, but had never had occasion to visit. The people were said to be ascetic, devoted to the veneration of the Ancestors, but known more widely among the galaxy's traders for their production of a superior berrywine made with water taken from their sacred shrine.

That had been inducement enough for John to agree to Rodney's request to visit the planet, and neither Ronon nor Teyla had raised any objections. In fact, she hoped she might have time to do a little trading herself; Talaverna berrywine was truly exceptional.

"So, uh, what do you think of her then?"

Rodney wasn't addressing his question to her. He was up ahead, next to John, while she and Ronon walked behind. The track through the forest was wide and, though muddy from recent rain, well maintained. Ahead, she could see smoke rising through the trees and knew they were approaching the settlement.

"Think of who?" John said, which made Teyla smile; they all knew who Rodney was talking about.

"Sam, of course. Colonel Carter. Who did you think I meant?"

Teyla exchanged a weary look with Ronon. His first meeting with Atlantis's new leader had not gone well, but relations between the two had warmed after that. Rodney, however, appeared obsessed with Colonel Carter's arrival. He talked of little else.

John shrugged off the question. "What do I *think* about Colonel Carter? I think she's my new CO. I think she's the leader of this expedition." He cut a curious glance at Rodney. "Why? What do *you* think of her? You know her better than the rest of us."

Rodney scowled at the muddy track. "She's not as brilliant as she'd have you believe, you know. I mean, yes, she's smart. Obviously. But she's not —" He swallowed the rest of his sentence, not that it concealed very much; Rodney was an open book.

"Not as smart as you?" John finished for him. "Rodney, that's — is that what this is about? You're pissed she got the job because you think you're *smarter* than her? Even for you, that's petty."

"What do you mean even for me?"

John cut off any further argument with a raised hand. They were approaching the edge of the settlement, a collection of simple wooden buildings gathered around a central square. "Now play nice," he said. "We've got some hearts and minds to win."

The hearts and minds belonged to the village elders, three gray-haired men in equally gray robes. The settlement, this close to the Stargate, was used to traders and so their arrival provoked little more than idle curiosity among the men and women working nearby: a woman's head lifted from grinding flour, a cluster of children watched them for a moment, then returned to drawing water from the well.

Teyla smiled at the familiarity of what she saw and stepped forward in greeting, without waiting for John's command. It had become habit now, the way their team worked together, unspoken and natural. "I am Teyla," she said, "and these are my friends, John, Rodney and Ronon."

The first of the elders, and the stoutest, nodded. His eyes, as gray as his hair, were sharp. Traders' eyes, Teyla thought: this was a man prepared to do business. "I am Elder Qafsiel. You are welcome in the peace of the Ancestors," he said, with a formal bow of his head. His gaze touched each of them, then returned to Teyla. "You have come here to trade?"

She allowed her smile to broaden. "If there is time, yes, I would welcome the opportunity. But our real interest is in the shrine of Talaverna." She indicated Rodney. "My friend is an expert in such places and would like the opportunity to study it."

"None are permitted to enter the shrine without a Reverent," Qafsiel said, his sharp eyes switching to Rodney. "What manner of study do you wish to undertake?"

"Ah, well, we think it might contain what I'd call a—"

"We have heard that your shrine once took supplicants to dwell with the Ancestors," Teyla interrupted, before Rodney said more than was wise. "We are eager to visit such a sacred place."

McKay snorted and she flung him a warning look. "Right," he nodded, chastened. "Sacred. Very sacred, obviously."

Keeping her irritation hidden — men like Qafsiel could see everything — Teyla smiled a diplomat's smile. "We would fully respect your wishes when entering the shrine," she told them. "And we will touch nothing, if you request it."

"What?" Rodney, again. "Wait, I can't—"

"McKay," John growled past his own smile.

"But—"

"Can it, Rodney!"

Teyla turned back to Qafsiel. "If there are restricted areas, we will not enter them. But we would like to see as much as is possible."

One of the other elders, a taller man with hair past his ears, touched Qafsiel on the shoulder. They consulted in whispers for a moment, which Teyla hoped was a good sign, and then Qafsiel nodded and turned back to her. "You must be accompanied by a Reverent at all times," he said.

"Of course."

"And there will be a charge for each person. A Revenant's time is valuable, you understand."

She didn't miss the avaricious glint in his eye and simply said, "Naturally."

They were taken to wait in one of the wooden huts, which looked like it was mostly used for trading—a small table sat against one wall while berrywine in bottles and barrels lined another. Teyla sat on a narrow wooden bench and waited, Ronon did the same; they both seemed to understand, better than their Lantean friends, the value of resting while the opportunity presented itself.

"You think they'd miss one of those bottles?" Ronon said.

Teyla raised her eyebrows. "Yes, I think they would."

"Pity."

At the other end of the room, Rodney was pacing. "So we get a tour guide and an entrance ticket?" he groused. "What's next, 'exit through the gift shop?'"

"I think this *is* the gift shop," John said.

"Be glad that you are gaining access at all," Teyla told them. "I warned you that the Talavernan were protective of their shrine. They could have simply turned us away."

"I guess it's lucky that they're greedier than they are devout," John said with a smile.

She returned it, although did not agree out loud. "They are traders," she reminded him. "This is Pegasus."

He shrugged in acknowledgment, and not long after that their guide — a slender man named Joqun, dressed in the white robes of a Reverent — arrived to take them to the shrine. It was a walk of about thirty minutes through the trees, although Teyla suspected that the Reverent was taking them on a more circuitous route than was necessary — either for dramatic impact or to confuse them so that they could not return unescorted.

She glanced at Ronon as they walked, and he nodded. "I've got it." There was nothing this priest could do to confuse a Runner's sense of direction.

At last they arrived at a cliff face, rising stark and unexpected from the forest. The stone was dark as iron, but a cave mouth opened in its face from which ran a narrow stream that sparkled in the sunlight: the source of the berrywine, no doubt. Around the cave's entrance, the rock had been intricately carved, the sinuous design undoubtedly that of the Ancestors.

Reverent Joqun stopped. "Within, is the shrine," he said in a voice pitched so low they had to gather close to hear him. Teyla wondered if it was an affectation, or simply a product of his reverence for this place. "The shrine tests our worth," Joqun said. "Only those who are worthy of the Ancestors are chosen to dwell with them."

"Chosen how?" Ronon said.

"At their coming of age, each supplicant must walk through the sacred arch — those deemed worthy leave this place to dwell forever with the Ancestors."

"And those who aren't that lucky?" John said.

The Reverent spread his hands. "We return to our lives, blessed but not chosen." His expression was resigned. "In the past many people were deemed worthy and left Talaverna, never to return. But it has been generations since any have been so honored." His expression tightened. "I believe the Ancestors do not approve of the berrywine and the trade it brings, but the Elders do not listen."

"Ha!" Rodney shook his head. "I bet they don't. And, actually, it's more likely to be a fault with —"

"How must we prepare to enter the shrine?" Teyla said, cutting him off.

Reverent Joqun looked from her to her friends and back again. "The measure of your lives is the only preparation required," he said. "The Ancestors see all."

John shifted his hold on his weapon. "Well, I don't think *I'm* going anywhere."

Teyla smiled, but only said, "Reverent, will you lead the way?"

With a nod, he did so and they all followed: Teyla first, then John and Rodney, with Ronon guarding their backs.

Inside, the cave was lit by large candles placed on the floor. She glimpsed more designs carved into the wall and at the far end an archway rose up out of the rocky floor, words in the language of the Ancestors engraved along its arc. In the candlelight, everything glimmered, light dancing off the damp stone walls and the smooth lines of the Ancestors' inscriptions. It truly felt like a sacred place.

"Cool," John said, his voice low.

"It is most impressive," she agreed.

From the back, Ronon growled, "Low ceiling."

Rodney made his way closer to the arch, his scanner out. "Okay, this is interesting," he said. "I'm getting some—"

Without warning, the arch lit up and Joqun stumbled back, so shocked he almost fell. "Ancestors' mercy!"

Teyla grabbed his arm, keeping him on his feet. "This does not always happen?"

"Never. Never in my lifetime."

She glanced at John and he nodded: the archway had probably been activated by Rodney's ATA gene.

"Fascinating," Rodney said, glancing from his scanner to the arch as he pushed his way forward.

John followed. "Careful…"

"Yes, yes. But this is actually very interesting. You see, I'm picking up —"

The archway flared, a brilliant white light filling the space beneath it and engulfing Rodney.

"McKay! Don't —" John grabbed for him, reaching into the light, and then the cave went dark.

They were both gone.

"Gone?" Sam said, looking from Teyla to Ronon where they were sitting opposite her desk. "Gone where?"

"Reverent Joqun," Teyla said, "believes they have been taken to dwell with the Ancestors."

"They were beamed away," Ronon said, voicing what Sam already suspected. "It was some kind of transporter."

"You tried raising them over the radio?"

"There was no response." The tight expression of concern in Teyla's eyes belied her calm voice. Sam recognized the dichotomy all too well; she knew what it was like to lose friends like this. Teyla folded her hands in her lap, her fingers twisting tight. "They could be anywhere."

Sam shook her head. "They can't be too far. Even Ancient transporters only have a limited range."

"Doesn't matter," Ronon said, "if we can't find them."

After her initial run-in with Ronon, Sam was wary of openly contradicting him. Nevertheless… "The point is, it narrows the search area," she said, and turned her attention to Major Lorne who was standing at her office door. "Major, I need someone to take a puddle jumper through the gate and do a scan of the whole planet." She paused, and then added, "If this planet has a moon — or moons — scan those too."

"Moons?"

She gave a wry smile. "Just a hunch."

"Yes, ma'am," he said, and turned to leave.

Once he'd closed the door behind him, she turned to Teyla. "I need to take a look at that shrine."

"You, Colonel?" For all her diplomatic skills, Teyla couldn't — or, at least, didn't — hide her surprise.

"I have some experience of Ancient technology," Sam reminded her. "If it *is* Ancient technology…"

Teyla shared a glance with Ronon — a glance which reminded Sam exactly how much of an outsider she was on Atlantis. "But is it wise for you to put yourself at risk, Colonel?" Teyla said. "Dr. Weir didn't —"

"Dr. Weir wasn't an Air Force officer." Sam kept her voice light, but she knew she had to stamp down hard on this kind of challenge. "Neither was she an expert in Ancient technology with ten years' frontline experience off-world."

Teyla inclined her head, acknowledging the point. "Our own Dr. Zelenka is also an expert in Ancient technology, and familiar with the idiosyncrasies of the Pegasus galaxy."

Sam let silence fill the room for a long moment, leaned back in her chair and regarded Teyla and Ronon. Neither of them was Air Force. Heck, neither of them was even from her *galaxy*. She had a lot to prove here. "Look, I know what it's like to lose a teammate," she said at last. "I know what it's like to spend days — months, even — out of your mind with worry, working to get them home. And I know it might not feel like it to you right now, but Colonel Sheppard and Dr. McKay are my people too — just like they were Dr. Weir's. And I can bring them home." She allowed a brief smile. "This isn't the first time I've seen something like this."

"— touch anything!" John's words echoed back at him from the pitch darkness and he stumbled, disoriented. The ground beneath his feet was uneven, something crunching under his boots. "McKay?"

"Yeah, hang on." A moment later a flashlight sliced the darkness to his left. "Where are you?"

The beam hit his eyes and John raised a hand to keep from being blinded. "Hey! Point that someplace else."

"Oh sue me for making sure you're still alive!"

Ignoring McKay's grouse, John toggled the flashlight on his weapon. They were in a cave not unlike the one that housed the shrine, only this time there were no candles and, as far as he could tell, no door. There was a shrine, however, or at least an archway. "Any guesses what happened?"

"Obviously we were transported here, wherever here is." McKay had his scanner out, his flashlight clamped between his ear and his shoulder. "Huh," he said. "That's not good."

"What's not good?"

McKay jerked his chin toward the arch. "It's only got residual power, and that's draining fast. It probably charged when the shrine activated, but it can't hold a charge of its own."

"You're right, that's definitely not good." Reaching out, John touched the arch, brushing his fingertips across its surface. Nothing happened; it was cold, smooth like polished rock, and just as lifeless. "I really hope that's not the only way outa here."

"I think it is. It's — Oh God…" McKay's horrified gaze followed the beam of his flashlight, playing across the floor beneath Sheppard's feet. "Okay. Right. So I think it is the only way out — and I don't think it's been working for quite some time."

Slowly, not wanting to look but knowing he had no choice, Sheppard dipped his flashlight to the floor. It was covered in a thick coat of rubble and dust — only it wasn't rubble or dust. It was bones. Old, crumbling bones. His gaze met McKay's across the room. "What the hell…?"

Rodney cleared his throat, wiped the back of his hand over his mouth, but his voice was still scratchy when he said, "I guess now we know what happened to all those lucky people chosen to spend eternity with the Ancestors…"

"Major Lorne," Sam called, trotting down the steps toward the gate room.

Lorne turned from where he'd been talking with Ronon and didn't exactly come to attention, but certainly straightened his shoulders. "Colonel," he said, stepping forward, "the jumper reported in. No sign of our people on the planet."

"Any moons?"

He shook his head. "No, ma'am."

"Damn." It had been worth a shot. "Okay, I guess we'll have to do this the hard way." She gestured to one of the SFs and he handed over her P90. She had to admit it felt good to hold a weapon again, to be geared up ready to go off-world. "Dial the gate, Major," she told Lorne. "You have Atlantis until I get back."

Lorne hesitated.

"Major?"

"Colonel, I just wonder whether it would be safer for Dr. Zelenka to take a look at the device."

Sam frowned. "Your point's noted, Major. Now, dial the gate."

"Yes ma'am." With a nod, he headed up to the control room and Sam watched him go with an uneasy feeling.

"He is concerned for your safety," Teyla said, coming to stand at her side. "We have already lost one leader. No one wants to lose another."

Sam slid her a sideways look. "You all need to stop worrying," she said. "I can take care of myself."

"Of that, I have no doubt."

There was a bite to Teyla's tone that Sam didn't understand, but there was no time to ask because right then the gate began to spin. Or, rather, lights began to spin around the rim of the gate until each glyph had locked. Sam couldn't help feeling it was a little less impressive than the spit-and-fire dialup of a Milky Way gate, but there was nothing inferior about the wormhole that kawooshed into the room a moment later. That, truly, never got old.

"Okay," she said, as the event horizon settled. "Let's do this."

Leading the way, she entered the Stargate a step ahead of Teyla and Ronon.

It was a short walk along a much used track to the village. The air was damp and aromatic, all loamy soil and forest; it could have been one of any number of planets Sam had visited in the Milky Way. The village too was unremarkable, the people at the level of technology to which races like the Goa'uld and Wraith preferred to limit their victims. What was less common was the gathering in the center of the small settlement, a slender man in white robes holding forth to a rapt audience.

"What's going on?" she asked Teyla.

"That is Reverent Joqun, who led us to the shrine," she said. "He believes the activation of the Ancient device heralds a return of the Ancestors..." Her gaze fixed on the young man. "It appears that his belief is spreading."

Sam couldn't help but think about the Priors, holding whole communities in thrall with their pseudo-religion, and had to tamp down her kneejerk revulsion. She glanced into the trees instead. "How far is the shrine?"

"Not far," Ronon said. "I can take you there."

"Great. Let's get going. I want —"

"Colonel?" Teyla planted her feet, a subtle but clear gesture. "We must first gain permission from Elder Qafsiel. And we cannot enter the shrine without a Reverent."

"They look kinda busy..."

"Nevertheless," Teyla said, "those are the terms we negotiated on our last visit. The shrine is of great significance to these people, now more than ever. We must be respectful."

She was right, Sam knew it, but they had no idea where Sheppard and McKay were or whether they were in imminent danger. "So long as it doesn't take too long," she said. "Our priority is getting our people back."

Teyla's eyebrows rose. "A fact of which I am well aware, Colonel."

"Yes, sorry. Of course you are." Sam grimaced at her clumsiness. "It's just — Every second might count, quite literally."

"My people have a saying," Teyla said as she started walking toward the village. "The hasty path is the longest."

"Right," Sam said, falling in beside her. "More haste, less speed. You're right."

As they drew closer, a man detached himself from the group gathered around the Reverent and made his way toward them, gray robes flapping around his ankles as he hurried.

"Elder Qafsiel," Teyla murmured to Sam.

"Why have you returned?" he said, stopping a little ahead of them. He was out of breath, his face flushed.

"I told you that we would," Teyla said, mild yet authoritative. "We wish to search for our people."

"And I have told you that your people aren't lost — they were chosen!" His gaze fell on Sam. "You have brought another?"

"My name's Colonel Carter," she said. "I'm a scientist. And I think I know how to retrieve our people."

"Your people dwell with the Ancestors now," a new voice said — the Reverent, striding toward Qafsiel. "Why would you wish to tear them from such a place?" Behind him, the villagers had turned and were watching the exchange.

Sam felt her hackles rise, sensed Ronon move behind her, adopting a defensive stance. His instinct was reassuring. "I just want to take a look at the device," Sam said evenly. "I won't damage anything, I promise."

"Device?" Joqun said.

"I mean the shrine."

Qafsiel shook his head. "The shrine is being prepared for worship tomorrow morning, none but the Reverents may enter until after it is complete."

"I swear I won't get in anyone's way. But this is urgent, our people —"

"Your people dwell with the Ancestors."

Frustrated, she shook her head. "Look, the Ancients aren't —"

"Colonel." Teyla gave her a pointed look. "May I speak with you privately?"

Sam hesitated, but Teyla's expression was insistent and

so she nodded and moved to one side, away from the others. "Okay," she began, before Teyla could speak, "I know what you're going to say."

"Which is what?"

"That this shrine is sacred to these people. I get that, but we can't let their religion —"

"Not just the shrine," Teyla said. "The Ancestors, too. They are important to all of us in Pegasus. You must understand that, or you will make more enemies than friends here."

Sam let a beat fall. "All of us?" she repeated. "You mean you too?"

"My people venerate the Ancestors, yes."

"But…" Sam tilted her head, as if the altered perspective might help her understand. "Surely you don't believe that Sheppard and McKay are living with the Ancients right now. Do you?"

There was another pause. "No," Teyla said at last. "I do not. But the Ancestors were the creators of life in this galaxy, and of death — of the Wraith. They were not perfect, but we are their children. And I do not pretend to understand the mysteries of the plane in which they now dwell. I do not think many of us can."

"One or two, maybe," Sam said. But Daniel wasn't here to explain it and she sure as hell couldn't. She puffed out a breath, not sure how to respond; she'd spent a decade fighting false gods and it was difficult to relate to people who believed the Ancients were in anyway divine. "Okay," she conceded at last, "I'll dial it back. But we have to get access to that shrine — we can't just sit about waiting for their ceremony to finish. Sheppard and McKay need our help."

"I know," Teyla said, her calm expression cracking. "They are my friends and teammates, Colonel, and I'm afraid for them. But we cannot simply walk over these people as if their beliefs do not matter. If nothing else, it will create more problems than it solves."

Sam couldn't help thinking that Jack would have done exactly that. He would have gone in and brought his people home at any cost: no one gets left behind. Of course, Daniel would have argued Teyla's point the whole way...

Question was, what was *she* going to do?

The cave was pretty much exactly what it looked like: a cave. John had walked its perimeter twice, trailing his fingers over the wall in search of some kind of opening. There was nothing.

Nothing but bones. They were everywhere. How many people, he wondered, had been beamed here only to die a slow, horrible death?

"What the hell is this place?" he said, turning away from the wall.

McKay sat on the opposite side of the cave on one of the low benches that lined the space. His head was bent over his scanner, its blue light turning his face ghostly. "Looks like a bunker," he said, without looking up. "Like an air raid shelter, I guess."

"A bunker?" That fitted — the benches, the lack of exits. "Against the Wraith."

"Obviously." McKay sat back, letting the tablet fall slack in his lap. "It's quite clever, when you think about it. The transporter is triggered by the ATA gene, so the Wraith can't follow you down. You sit here, wait for the darts to leave, and then beam out again."

"Sure," John said, taking a seat against the opposite wall. "It's all fun and games until one day the transporter stops working..."

McKay shook his head. "No, not one day. This is old; it's decayed over millennia. The Ancients, or whoever they built the shelter for, were long gone before Qasfiel and his people showed up. I mean, they obviously have no idea what they're — quite literally — playing with."

It was a horrible thought. "So they ended up sending their people down here instead of to heaven, or wherever the Ancestors hang out?"

"Meanwhile selectively breeding out the ATA gene until none of them had it anymore and the 'shrine' stopped working." He gave a bitter smile. "A perfect Darwinian solution, although in this case it's more like 'selection of the dumbest.'"

"Come on," John objected. "They couldn't have known."

"No, but if they hadn't believed their kids were being sent to a magical fairyland they might have come looking for them!" He closed his eyes, lips pressed tight. "Sorry. It's just — it's a little claustrophobic in here. I don't do well in small spaces."

John couldn't argue with that. On the plus side, they hadn't suffocated yet. "There must be some kind of ventilation," he said. "The air's clean."

"CO_2 scrubbers." McKay gestured under the bench he was sitting on. "As far as I can tell, they're at about 22% efficiency, which is probably good enough for the two of us, in the sense that thirst will probably kill us before we suffocate. God, I'm thirsty —"

"McKay, quit moaning. We're not gonna die here."

"Oh, aren't we? Because the skeleton carpet we're standing on says different."

John shrugged. "Okay, first of all Teyla and Ronon are going to come looking for us."

"Come looking for us in a cave to which there is no entrance? A cave which could be a thousand miles away from the shrine?"

John ignored him. "*Second*, you're going to fix the transporter and get us outa here."

"Fix the transporter?" He nodded. "Sure, why not? Maybe I'll rub it and Aladdin's genie will pop out and grant us three wishes!"

"I'm sure you can do better than that."

"With what, Sheppard? It has no power. And I don't know about you, but I don't happen to have a ZPM in my back pocket."

"You'll think of something."

McKay simmered and John let him; sometimes Rodney just needed to vent and then come to a problem in his own way.

To pass the time, John pulled out all the rations he had with him and started breaking them down, working out how long they could last down here. After a while, he heard McKay move. He glanced up and watched him approach the lifeless arch, run his fingers along the inner edge, then crouch down and examine something at its base. A moment later a panel popped open and McKay pulled out a crystal that glowed with a pale blue light.

"Well, well," McKay said, tapping the crystal against his fingers. "Maybe I can hotwire this thing after all…"

John said nothing, letting him work, and went back to counting rations.

In the end, the best Teyla could negotiate was that Elder Qafsiel would discuss access to the shrine the following morning, once the ceremony had ended — and for an increased fee.

Colonel Carter was not pleased, but she accepted Teyla's advice that they spend the night in the village and meet with Qafsiel as soon as he returned from the shrine the next day. The village was modest, with no room to spare, so they had made camp on the outskirts of the settlement.

It was not cold, neither was it warm. Teyla was comfortable enough in her Lantean clothing and lay looking at the stars through the trees that surrounded the village until sleep claimed her.

Many years of travelling and trading had taught her to sleep anywhere; it had also taught her to sleep lightly. So it was that she found herself awake sometime later, on full alert yet perfectly still.

Someone was moving in their camp.

Very slowly she turned her head toward the sound of the noise, in time to see Colonel Carter disappear into the forest, the light of her scanner darting like a firebug through the trees. Cursing silently, Teyla got up and put a hand on Ronon's shoulder. He woke like she had, fully and instantly.

What? The question was silent, in his eyes alone.

Teyla risked a whisper. "I believe Colonel Carter has gone to the shrine."

Ronon's eyebrows climbed. "Gotta admire that. She doesn't take no for an answer."

"Apparently not," Teyla said, sitting back on her heels. "Nevertheless, it is a risk."

Ronon sat up. "We going after her?"

"I will," Teyla said. "You go to the Stargate. If you do not hear from me by daybreak, return to Atlantis and tell them to send assistance. It will mean the colonel and I are in trouble."

Ronon smiled. "I can't tell," he said as he rolled to his feet.

"Can't tell what?"

"Whether you like her or not."

Teyla was surprised by the question. "I believe," she said after a moment, "that I cannot tell either. Colonel Carter is certainly determined, if somewhat reckless, but she's not..."

"She's not Weir."

She was ashamed to admit how close to the truth Ronon was and glanced toward the forest to hide her discomfort. "Perhaps tonight will resolve the question."

"Yeah, perhaps," he said. "Stay safe."

She turned to leave, but he called after her in a low voice. "I do, for what it's worth."

Looking back, she saw him shrug. "I like her. She shouldn't be here — should've stayed on Atlantis — but she's good where it counts." He tapped his chest. "Right here. She'll learn the other stuff."

Teyla just nodded. She prided herself on her perception, but perhaps, on this occasion, Ronon was seeing more clearly than her.

It was pretty easy to locate the shrine, the Ancient technology lighting up her scanner like a Christmas tree, and it wasn't far away. That's why she'd decided to risk taking a peek before dawn. She'd be in and out before anyone knew, and then she'd have a head start in figuring out where her people had been taken.

The last time she'd lost a teammate off-world, it had been different. Then it had been Jack — Colonel O'Neill, at the time — and she'd been frantic. She could still remember that banked sense of terror, of guilt, and of overwhelming need to fix the situation. Like a ghost, or an echo, she could feel those emotions still and wasn't blind to the fact that they were part of what was driving her now. But it was more than that. She'd been in command less than a month and knew her people were still mourning Dr. Weir. This was her chance to prove, not only to them but to herself, that she was ready for this command. So perhaps she was being a little rash, but she —

A sound, close behind her. She turned, weapon raised, and came face to face with Teyla.

"Colonel." Teyla glanced at the weapon with enviable poise.

"What are you doing?" Sam said, lowering the gun and snapping the safety back on. "I could have shot you."

"I might ask you the same question," Teyla said, her gaze dipping to the scanner. "But I believe I already know."

There was something about this woman's disapproval that left Sam feeling guiltier than she felt was warranted. "Look," she said, "if I can figure out what we're dealing with, I'll be able to start working on the solution. It could save us hours."

"We gave them our word."

"We don't know Sheppard and McKay's situation — every minute counts."

Teyla folded her arms. "You're reckless, Colonel."

"That's been said before. It's not always a bad thing." She nodded though the trees. It was still dark, but her scanner showed that they were almost at the shrine. "You coming?"

"Apparently so."

Sam flashed a smile, relieved to see Teyla's disapproval soften. "Come on," she said. "Let's see what we can find out."

The first thing Sam confirmed was that the device was definitely Ancient and not Furling. That was good in the sense that she knew a lot more about Ancient technology, but bad in the sense that any parallel with Jack's experience on PX5-777 was probably meaningless.

However… "If this is a transporter," she said, squinting up at the archway, "then it must have a way of recognizing receiving and destination terminals, which means it probably keeps a record of—"

"Colonel Carter!"

She turned at Teyla's call to find three men standing in the entrance to the cave. In the growing pre-dawn light, she recognized Qafsiel and Joqun among them. "Ah," she said, offering a smile. "We were just getting a quick look—"

"You will come with us," Reverent Joqun said. "To enter the shrine unaccompanied is to dishonor the will of the Ancestors."

"Oh no," Sam said, "I didn't mean—"

"Silence!" His words echoed around the cave, bouncing back at her from all directions. "You will come with us and face the justice of the Elders."

Sam closed her eyes, cursed herself thoroughly, and then nodded. "Okay," she said, and turned a rueful look on Teyla. "More haste, less speed…"

Teyla arched an eyebrow. "Those," she said as she preceded Sam out the cave, "are wise words."

"You know, the thing that really bugs me," McKay said as he sat lining crystals up on the floor, "is that she doesn't have any experience of the Pegasus galaxy. I mean, sure, she helped defeat the Goa'uld, but what—"

"And the Ori," John pointed out. He sat opposite McKay watching what he was doing but not interfering.

"Okay, fine, and the Ori."

"And the Replicators."

"Look, the point is, what does any of that have to do with

this galaxy?" McKay paused. "Apart from the Replicators, I guess. I mean, it just feels like she's been parachuted in simply because she's a big shot at Stargate Command."

"McKay," John sighed, because frankly he'd reached the end of his patience, "they were never going to give you the job."

"What? No, I know that." He frowned, picked up a crystal and held it up to examine in the beam of his flashlight. "But they could have chosen you."

John stared. "What?"

"Well, come on, if they wanted someone military — which they apparently did — you were the obvious choice. You've been second in command here for over three years." He lowered the crystal and fixed Sheppard with a narrow look. "Don't tell me you hadn't thought about it."

"I thought about it," he said. "I thought about how much I didn't *want* it."

"Are you kidding?" McKay slotted the crystal back into the panel, and then picked up the next one. "Why wouldn't you want it? Put another eagle on your shoulder, or whatever."

"It's a star, and I don't want it." In a way, it was a startling revelation; he didn't want the next step up because, inevitably, that would pull him back to Earth. He rubbed a hand across his face, the prospect filling him with a kind of numb dread. "I want to stay here," he said after a while. "I want to stay on Atlantis."

"Forever?" McKay peered at him through the gloom. "You know you can't do that. They'd never let you."

He shrugged. "Maybe not." Maybe he wouldn't give them the choice.

"I never thought Sam would leave the SGC, though," Rodney carried on. "I thought she was there for life, you know? I mean, that should have been her command. Not Atlantis. I bet she doesn't even want to be here."

"You don't want her to be here is more like it," Sheppard said, fixing McKay with a look long enough to make him squirm.

"Come on, spit it out. What's your problem with Carter?"

"I don't have a problem with her."

"Right. What, did you guys have a bust-up back at the SGC? Particle Accelerators at dawn, that kind of thing?"

McKay gave a prim huff and said, "Actually, just the opposite. There's always been a certain chemistry between us."

John laughed out loud until he realized McKay wasn't joking. "Really?" he said, trying to marshal his smile. "Between you and Carter?"

"What's so funny?"

"Nothing." He cleared his throat and made a mental note to ask Teyla — once they'd escaped this little tomb — if she'd heard anything along those lines. "And that's why you don't want her here?"

"No, that would be — Look, it's just that sometimes she can be a little arrogant, a little full of herself."

John stared; McKay's lack of self-awareness continued to amaze. "You mean she can be a little too impressed with her own ability? Maybe thinking she's the smartest person in the room and not making any effort to hide it?"

"Right," McKay nodded with enthusiasm. "You notice that too, huh?"

"Yeah. Just not about Carter."

A beat fell, and then McKay scowled. "Ha-ha, very funny."

"Face it, Rodney, this has nothing to do with some imaginary sexual tension —"

"It's not imaginary!"

"— and it's not about my career progression. You have a problem with Carter because you see her as a rival, and you don't like the competition."

Rodney waved the crystal he was holding at him. "That is so not —" His expression changed. "Oh, now that's interesting."

"What's interesting?"

"Um, nothing you'd understand. So if you've finished

your little exercise in psychoanalysis, Dr. Freud, maybe you
could shut up and let me work?"

John got to his feet, stretching out the kinks in his muscles,
but he couldn't resist one final dig. "You'd better work hard,"
he said. "I'd hate for Colonel Carter to figure it out first."

It was humiliating. There was no other word for it. Tied
to a tree outside the shrine, Sam felt like a fool. She could
almost see Jack shaking his head in disbelief.

"This is all my fault," she said, knocking her head back
against the trunk.

"I am sure Ronon will soon return with backup," Teyla said.

"Back-up I should be sending."

Teyla laughed. "You cannot be in two places at once,
Colonel. That is impossible, even for you."

"Which is why I shouldn't be out here in the first place,"
Sam said. "Which is probably what you were thinking but
are too polite to say."

"I believe I already said it," Teyla pointed out. "Before
we left."

So had Lorne, and like a fool Sam hadn't listened. "I
thought I knew what this was, I thought —" She let the rest
of the confession tail off into a sigh. In truth, she didn't
know what she'd been thinking. She felt dislocated in this
new city, among strangers in a strange galaxy. She wasn't
herself. "I guess I just wanted to prove myself."

Teyla tilted her head, watching her with an assessing
gaze. "That is understandable," she said. "I too felt a need
to prove myself when I first came to Atlantis — it is a place
that seems to require the best of us."

"Not just the place," Sam conceded. At Teyla's inquiring
look, she elaborated. "You're a very close knit team. I mean,
so was the SGC, but you guys don't even get to go home at
the weekend. You're like family, and coming in like this, as
an outsider — it's difficult."

"As with every family," Teyla said, "we must all find our places."

"I guess I don't always find that very easy. I tend to overcompensate." She grimaced at a flash of memory. "At least I haven't offered to arm-wrestle anyone yet."

Teyla's eyebrows rose. "That may not be a good strategy."

"Especially with Ronon, right?"

"Not if you value the use of your arm." She tipped her head to one side, curious. "Do you often have to prove your worth, Colonel Carter?"

"As a woman scientist in the Air Force?" Sam smiled without much humor. "Only all the time."

"I also find it necessary to remind people not to judge me by my gender," Teyla said, her eyes glittering with a humor Sam hadn't noticed before. "Fortunately, I have developed means to make a lasting impression."

"I'd like to see that."

"I would be happy to demonstrate, although Bantos fighting may not be appropriate in your Air Force." She smiled. "But it would certainly make a stronger impression than arm-wrestling."

Sam laughed. "I generally try not to challenge my COs to any kind of fight these days."

"But sometimes it is required?"

"Sometimes," Sam said, thinking back with an ache of nostalgia. "And I guess that worked out okay in the end."

Further away, she could see the Reverents lining up outside the shrine. "Do you think there's any chance of us getting back in there?"

Teyla shook her head. "Not you or I, not without the use of force."

And that was the last thing she wanted. "Damn it, this is my fault."

"Perhaps Dr. Zelenka will be able to negotiate access," Teyla said. "And Dr. McKay, for all his idiosyncrasies, is an exceptional scientist. He may yet find a way to return — I have faith in him."

Sam felt a pang of sadness. She remembered having that kind of faith in SG-1. She remembered General Hammond having that kind of faith in her. The kind of faith she should have had in Sheppard and his team. "I'm sorry," she said. "I've made things worse by coming here."

Teyla tipped her head to one side. "We cannot know the path we did not walk," she said. "And this is not yet over."

"Okay, that's the best I can do." McKay stood up and brushed bone-dust off his knees with obvious distaste. "This really is a gross place…"

"So let's get outa here," John said. He'd been stretched out on one of the long benches, trying to ignore how thirsty he was; their rations were sparing, to say the least. Now he swung his legs down and stood up. "Is it going to work?"

"Maybe. Maybe not."

"I figured," John said. "So what do we do?"

"*You* do nothing," McKay said. "Just come here and stand under the arch. I'm going to activate a pulse that will reverse the polarity of the crystals and, if we're very lucky, send a signal to the other terminus instigating a transport."

"And if we're not very lucky?"

"Either the power discharge destabilizes the rocks and the cave collapses, killing us quickly, or it doesn't and we die slowly. Probably after drinking our own urine."

"Rodney…"

"What? You've thought about it too."

"Let's just stay positive here," John said, ignoring the question. "I'm sure it'll work."

"Well that makes one of you." Rodney flapped a hand at him. "Stand right there, behind me. Okay…" At the last moment he hesitated. "So this is it, one time only deal."

John felt a spike of adrenaline, his fingers tightening on

his weapon as if he could shoot his way out of this. "Then do it," he said.

McKay nodded. "Here goes nothing…"

"Did you feel that?"

Teyla nodded — there had been a definite tremor in the ground. She nodded toward the cave mouth. "Look."

A thin dust drifted out on the morning air, no more than a haze. "That doesn't look like smoke," Colonel Carter said.

"No, it is —"

And then the ground convulsed — a long grinding sound that lasted a good ten seconds. From the shrine came cries of terror and then a deep cracking sound. Several of the Reverents spilled out of the cave, one man bleeding from a head wound, scarlet splashed across his white robes.

"It's them." Carter scrambled to her feet. "They're underground!"

Teyla felt a beat of horror. "What?"

"The other transporter must be underground — Sheppard and McKay are trying to get back." She tugged on the rope that bound her to the tree. "Hey!" she shouted. "Let me in there, I can fix this!"

Another quake rippled through the ground and Carter staggered, struggling to keep her balance with her hands tied. Elder Qafsiel and several Reverents cowered some distance away, crouching on the ground and gazing at the shrine in terrified awe. Teyla swallowed her fear, put thoughts of her friends trapped beneath this unstable ground to one side, and focused on how she could best help them. She got to her feet, hands still bound.

"Hey!" Carter tried again. "You have to untie us!"

Reverent Joqun looked at her, his eyes wide with shock. "We have insulted the Ancestors," he cried. "*You* have insulted the Ancestors and this is their punishment!"

"No!" Teyla stepped forward, one hand on Carter's arm to

silence her. Reverence for the Ancestors was one thing, but abdicating responsibility to act was something different. "This is not the way of the Ancestors, Reverent. You know it is not. They would not harm their children because of an accidental slight."

He hesitated at her words, but she could see more fear than wisdom in his eyes. "Then why do they punish us?"

"It has been many generations since the Ancestors left," she said, keeping her voice calm despite the fear beating like wings in her chest. "Perhaps this shrine is no longer serving their purpose?"

Beneath her feet the earth continued to shift and grumble, the sound of grinding rock coming from within the cave only heightening her alarm. Two more Reverents stumbled out, shrouded in dust. "It's collapsing," one of them gasped, his lips mere gashes of red in his dusty white face. "The floor is splitting, the whole shrine is falling..."

Panic, sharp and bright as lightening. "Please," Teyla said, "our friends are in danger, you must let us help. You must let us save them."

"And the shrine," Colonel Carter added. "I can save your shrine too."

Teyla had to repress a smile; Colonel Carter learned fast.

Qafsiel staggered to his feet, grabbing Joqun's arm. "We cannot lose the shrine!"

"If it is the Ancestors' will..."

"Who will buy your berrywine if it is not made with water from the shrine?" Teyla said. "What will Talaverna be without its shrine?"

"She's right," Qafsiel said, dropping the Reverent's arm and making his way through the plumes of dust to Teyla and Colonel Carter.

Reverent Joqun scrambled after him. "But the Ancestors—"

"The Ancestors do not fill the grain house each fall!" Qafsiel snapped. "And neither do you, Reverent. If we cannot trade, we cannot live — unless you wish to take up the plow?"

Joqun blinked, but stopped where he stood. With a nod, Qafsiel drew a short knife from his belt and cut through the ropes binding them to the tree. "Go," he said. "Save the shrine."

Colonel Carter wasted no time thanking him, sprinting through the dust and into the cave. Teyla was only a step behind.

In the beam of their flashlights, she saw that the archway had tilted to the side. The Ancient writing along its length glowed with a weak light, and a fissure dissected the cave floor in a diagonal from its mouth to the furthest wall — passing right beneath the arch.

Under her feet, she could feel a constant vibration that was definitely not natural. "What is that?"

Carter scrambled over the loose rock that covered the floor, probably dislodged from the ceiling. Teyla glanced up, but it was too dark to see what might be waiting to fall on her so she fixed her attention on the Ancient archway instead.

"Best guess," Carter said, crouching to pull off an access panel on the arch, "is that McKay's trying pull power from this end."

"Obviously it is not working." Teyla made her way to stand behind Carter, adding the beam of her flashlight to the colonel's to help her work.

Carter nodded her thanks, but only said, "If he's reversed the polarity of the crystals, then he's trying to transfer energy in two directions at once, which is probably creating a feedback loop and that —" The lights on the arch flared, the floor shook, and the fissure beneath their feet jerked a fraction wider. "That's the result," Carter said grimly.

"Can you stop it?"

The colonel glanced over her shoulder. She did not smile, but her eyes glittered. "Let's find out."

"Stay under the arch!" Sheppard yelled, grabbing McKay's jacket and yanking him back under the only scrap of shelter in the cave. Not that it would make much difference if the whole roof came down on them.

McKay coughed, his face barely visible through the wild beam of the flashlight. "...feedback loop..." he gasped, trying to reach the panel, but another grinding wrench obliterated anything else he might have said and threw them both onto their hands and knees.

Dust was everywhere: in John's mouth, his nose, his lungs. He felt McKay convulse as he coughed, slumping sideways. Their last flashlight went out and the world turned black.

So this was how it would end, suffocated to death inside an earthquake, on a planet light-years from home. Not exactly glorious, but —

Light, all around, diffuse through the rock dust. McKay's face, eyes wide and ashen with shock. And then the familiar white disintegration of a transporter beam and John was sprawled on another rocky floor, cold water seeping into his clothes, onto his lips.

He rolled over, coughed out a lungful of dust, and looked up into Teyla's smiling face.

"Welcome back, John."

She helped him to his feet, then over to a large rock where he could sit and catch his breath.

McKay lay flat on his back, eyes closed, and a beatific smile on his face. "I can't believe that worked," he said. "Sometimes I even amaze myself."

"Well, you had a little help," Teyla said, trading an amused glance with John.

McKay sat up. "What?"

Teyla nodded toward the back of the cave, where Colonel Carter was examining the Ancient archway. It was tilted at rather a jaunty angle, and the panel at its base was wide open. She raised her hand in greeting. "Hi."

"You've got to be kidding me," McKay said. "What are *you* doing here?"

The colonel rose to her feet, but before she could answer Teyla said, "Colonel Carter saved your life, Rodney."

He blinked, frowned, and rubbed a hand over his face. "I had everything under control."

"Under control?" John echoed.

"I—"

"Dr. McKay's right," Carter said, stepping over a large fissure in the floor of the cave and coming to join them. "He came up with probably the only solution to an impossible situation. He did all the hard work. I just controlled the feedback loop so that the terminal this end could receive the signal correctly." She gave a self-deprecating shrug. "Anyone could have done it."

John doubted that was true because otherwise Zelenka would be there instead of Carter, but he appreciated her giving Rodney the credit.

"Yes, well," McKay said, brushing dust from his sleeves. "Exactly."

Feeling the need to change the subject, John glanced at the cave mouth and beyond it he saw a line of robed figures. His heart sank. "Colonel," he said, getting to his feet and scrubbing some of the dust out of his hair, "there's something we need to tell Qafsiel and the Reverents..."

McKay scrambled to his feet. "Really? You think we need to tell them about... that?"

Teyla and Carter looked at him, waiting for more. With a sigh John said, "The place we ended up? It was a bunker. There was no way out, except for the transporter, and it hadn't been working for a long time. I mean a *long* time."

Carter's face tightened a fraction ahead of Teyla's. "How many people were down there?"

"Impossible to tell, but probably all of them."

Teyla put a hand to her mouth. "That is horrible."

For a moment, no one spoke. Outside, the Reverents were moving closer, probably because the ground had stopped shaking. John didn't relish breaking the news that their sacred shrine had, literally, been a death trap. But someone had to do it, and he—

"Colonel." Carter put her hand on his arm. "Take your team back to Atlantis, I'll talk to Qafsiel."

"You don't—"

"And report to the infirmary when you get there," she added, encompassing McKay in the order. "Both of you."

"Sheppard!" The shout came from outside; Ronon was pushing through the shell-shocked Reverents. "What happened? You look... dusty."

John glanced again at Carter, who just nodded him toward the cave mouth. Outside, Zelenka and a couple of SFs were moving up behind Ronon. There was a story here, John figured, but now wasn't the time to hear it. "I'll fill you in on the way to the gate," he told Ronon. "McKay, Teyla — let's go."

"I would rather stay," Teyla said, "if it is alright with you, Colonel Carter?"

Carter looked surprised, but pleased. "Thank you. I'd appreciate your advice. This is going to be sensitive."

"It is," Teyla agreed. "But it is a job to which I believe you are well suited, Colonel."

Carter flashed a brief, self-conscious smile. "Thanks," she said. "I hope so."

There was a spot Sam had found on one of Atlantis's many balconies where she could be alone with her thoughts. The sea stretched wide and untroubled in all directions and she could imagine her thoughts and concerns floating out across its surface, straightening out and untangling until she could make sense of them.

Today, on this breezy morning with the sun glittering low across the water, she was musing once more over Jack's advice.

Great leaders lead from behind.

She thought she understood him now. He hadn't been talking about leaders in the field, about commanding a four-man gate team. He'd been talking about leading from behind a desk, about enabling your people to be the best they could be, and about having their backs when things went wrong.

It was a difficult adjustment, which he probably understood all too well. Sam found she had a new respect for that year he'd spent in command of the SGC, watching SG-1 head out through the gate without him. It must have been hell.

"Colonel Carter?" She turned to find Teyla standing close to the balcony door. "I hope I am not disturbing you?"

"Not at all," Sam said with a smile. "You're back early."

Teyla nodded and came to stand with her at the railing. "The ceremony was not long," she said. "The cave beneath the shrine is now sacred ground too. Reverent Joqun believes that their lost people shed their mortal bodies in order to dwell with the Ancestors."

Sam turned her gaze back to the sea. From what she knew about ascension, that was basically true, but somehow she doubted ascension was the fate of Talaverna's lost people. The Reverent's insistence on the lie frustrated her; it reminded her too much of false gods. "I'd have thought," she said, "that discovering the truth about the shrine might have opened his eyes to the truth about the Ancients."

For a while, Teyla was silent and Sam was afraid she might have offended her. But when she glanced over, she saw that Teyla's thoughtful gaze was fixed on the horizon. "Perhaps it will change some minds," she said. "However, I believe that the commercial benefit Talaverna derives from the presence of the shrine outweighs their more... spiritual concerns." She offered Sam a wry smile. "This is Pegasus. Surviving the Wraith has taught us to be pragmatic in everything, including our faith."

Sam wasn't sure how she felt about that, but Teyla was right about one thing: this was Pegasus, the rules were different here.

After a silent moment, Teyla said, "Would you care to join us for breakfast, Colonel? I believe they are serving *tuttleroot* pancakes today."

It was a tempting offer, but Sam knew she had to decline. This wasn't the SGC, and she wasn't part of Teyla's team. She was separate — she had to keep herself separate if she was going to do her job. "Thanks," she said, "but I'm just getting some air before I hit the paperwork."

Teyla nodded in perfect understanding. "Then I wish you a productive day, Colonel."

Sam smiled and let her go, turning back to the sea, allowing herself another minute of sunlight and peace.

It was still dislocating to be this far from home and the people she cared about, but she didn't feel so alone anymore. Not just because of her developing friendships on Atlantis, but because now she understood her place here better.

Jack's advice about great leaders had been right on the money; her place wasn't out front, her place was standing behind everyone on Atlantis and covering their backs.

She just hoped she could do it as well as the great leaders who stood behind her.

OUR AUTHORS

Jo Graham is the author of nine STARGATE ATLANTIS and STARGATE SG-1 novels. With Melissa Scott, she is the author of *The Order of the Air* series, a historical fantasy aviation team adventure set in the 1920s and 1930s. She is also the author of the *Numinous World* series of historical fantasies, beginning with the critically acclaimed *Black Ships*. She lives in North Carolina with her partner and their daughter.

Peter J Evans was born in southern England and has been there ever since, although not entirely by choice. He wrote his first novel in 1999, and since then has completed nine more that the world knows about, including *STARGATE SG-1: Oceans of Dust* and *STARGATE ATLANTIS: Angelus*, plus an undisclosed number that must never be seen or mentioned again. During daylight hours Evans does something terribly complicated involving navigational radar, while at night he listens to Japanese pop songs and writes horror stories. He has heard of sleep, but only as an abstract concept.

Geonn Cannon is the author of over twenty novels, as well as numerous short stories which can be found for free at his website (geonncannon.com). The first time he traveled out of his home state was to attend the 2004 Stargate convention in Vancouver. He lives in Oklahoma.

Amy Griswold is the author of *STARGATE SG-1: Murder at the SGC*, *STARGATE SG-1: Heart's Desire* and the co-author of STARGATE ATLANTIS *Legacy* series novels *The Lost*, *Allegiance*, *Inheritors*, and *Unascended*. She has also written two gaslamp fantasy/mystery novels with

Melissa Scott, *Death by Silver* and *A Death at the Dionysus Club* (Lethe Press). Find her online at amygriswold.livejournal.com or follow her on Twitter at @amygris.

Suzanne Wood In the leafy greenness of the world's most livable city, Melbourne, Australia, Suzanne lives and works surrounded by books. Author of *STARGATE SG-1: The Barque of Heaven* and the first official short story crossover between STARGATE SG-1 and STARGATE ATLANTIS for the *Official Stargate Magazine*, she is currently undertaking a Diploma of Professional Writing and Editing while working on two new original novels. She has long-standing interests in Egyptology, ballet and watching Aussie pro cyclists, a new-found passion for family and Australian history, and occasionally rescues stray dogs. Her website is www.suzannewood.net.

Aaron Rosenberg is the author of the best-selling Duck-Bob SF comedy series, the *Dread Remora* space-opera series, and, with David Niall Wilson, the *O.C.L.T.* occult thriller series. His tie-in work contains novels for Star Trek, Warhammer, World of WarCraft, STARGATE ATLANTIS, and Eureka. He has written children's books (including the award-winning *Bandslam: The Junior Novel* and the #1 best-selling *42: The Jackie Robinson Story*, educational books, and roleplaying games (including the Origins Award-winning *Gamemastering Secrets*). He is a founding member of Crazy 8 Press. You can follow him online at gryphonrose.com, on Facebook at facebook.com/gryphonrose, and on Twitter @gryphonrose.

Karen Miller lives in Sydney, Australia, and is the author of two STARGATE SG-1 novels: *Alliances* and *Do No Harm*. She has also written three Star Wars novels and many mainstream fantasy novels, including the internationally bestselling *Mage* series, the *Godspeaker* trilogy and the *Rogue Agent* series under her pen name, KE Mills. Currently she's working hard on her new epic fantasy series *The Tarnished Crown*. Book 1, *The Falcon Throne*, is available now. She's also preparing to start book 5 of the *Rogue Agent* series. When she's not busy writing, Karen travels for research and enjoys directing with her local theatre company. You can find her at www.karenmiller.net.

T. Fox Dunham lives in Philadelphia with his wife, Allison. He's a lymphoma survivor, modern bard and historian. His first book, *The Street Martyr*, is being made into major motion picture by Throughline Films. *Destroying the Tangible Illusion of Reality or Searching for Andy Kaufman*, a book about dying, is out in November 2016 from PMMP. He's an active member of the Horror Writers Association and does political writing for senate campaigns. He's the co-host of *What Are You Afraid of?* True Ghost Stories and Horror Podcast. His motto is wrecking civilization one story at a time. Blog: tfoxdunham. blogspot.com. Facebook: www.facebook.com/tfoxdunham. Twitter: @TFoxDunham

Laura Harper lives in Glasgow, Scotland, where she is a copywriter by day and travels through the Stargate outside of normal working hours. She has co-authored three novels with Sally Malcolm: *STARGATE SG-1: Hostile Ground* and *STARGATE SG-1: Exile* from the Apocalypse trilogy, and *STARGATE SG-1: Sunrise* (writing as JF Crane). This is her first short story for Fandemonium Books. She is occasionally assisted in her writing by her cat, Steve, who believes an open laptop is an excellent place to sit. Follow her on Twitter @harperthewriter

Sally Malcolm has written prolifically within the Stargate universe, penning novels, short stories, audio dramas, and video game scripts. Her Stargate novels include *STARGATE SG-1: A Matter of Honor*, *STARGATE SG-1: The Cost of Honor*, *STARGATE ATLANTIS: Rising* (novelization), *STARGATE SG-1: Sunrise* (writing with Laura Harper, as J.F. Crane), and STARGATE SG-1: *Hostile Ground*. Sally and Laura's most recent title, STARGATE SG-1: *Exile*, was published in August 2015 and is the second in the STARGATE SG-1: *Apocalypse* trilogy. They are currently working on the final book, due for publication in September 2016. Follow her on Twitter @Sally_Malcolm.

Stay in touch...
Follow us on Twitter
@StargateNovels

Find us on Facebook at
facebook.com/StargateNovels

Sign up for our newsletter
at StargateNovels.com

THANKS!

STARGÅTE SG·1. STARGATE ATLÅNTIS

**Original novels based on the hit
TV shows STARGATE SG-1 and
STARGATE ATLANTIS**

**Available as e-books from leading online
retailers including Amazon, Barnes &
Noble and iBooks**

**Paperback editions available from
StargateNovels.com and Amazon.com**

**If you liked this book, please tell your
friends and leave a review on a
bookstore website.**